The Wolf Hunt:
A Tale of the
Texas Badlands

A DERRICK MILES MYSTERY

THE WOLF HUNT: A TALE OF THE TEXAS BADLANDS

WILL BRANDON

FIVE STAR
A part of Gale, a Cengage Company

GALE
A Cengage Company

Copyright © 2021 by Barbara A. Brannon
Five Star Publishing, a part of Gale, a Cengage Company

ALL RIGHTS RESERVED.
This novel is a work of fiction. Names, characters, places, and incidents are either the product of the author's imagination, or, if real, used fictitiously.

No part of this work covered by the copyright herein may be reproduced or distributed in any form or by any means, except as permitted by U.S. copyright law, without the prior written permission of the copyright owner.

The publisher bears no responsibility for the quality of information provided through author or third-party Web sites and does not have any control over, nor assume any responsibility for, information contained in these sites. Providing these sites should not be construed as an endorsement or approval by the publisher of these organizations or of the positions they may take on various issues.

LIBRARY OF CONGRESS CATALOGING-IN-PUBLICATION DATA

Names: Brandon, Will, 1957– author.
Title: The wolf hunt : a tale of the Texas badlands / Will Brandon
Description: First edition. | Waterville : Five Star, [2021] | Series: A Derrick Miles mystery
Identifiers: LCCN 2021000432 | ISBN 9781432877590 (hardcover)
Subjects: GSAFD: Western stories. | Mystery fiction.
Classification: LCC PS3602.R36145 W65 2021 |DDC 813/.6—dc23
LC record available at https://lccn.loc.gov/202100432 First Edition. First Printing: April 2021

First Edition. First Printing: April 2021
Find us on Facebook—https://www.facebook.com/FiveStarCengage
Visit our website—http://www.gale.cengage.com/fivestar
Contact Five Star Publishing at FiveStar@cengage.com

Printed in Mexico
Print Number: 01   Print Year: 2021

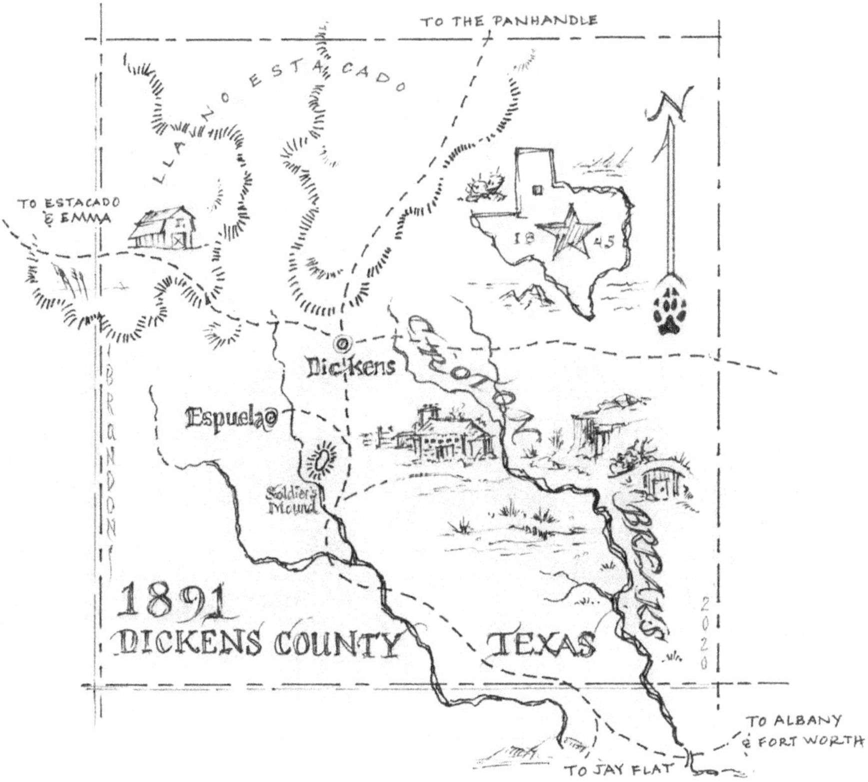
TO THE PANHANDLE
LLANO ESTACADO
TO ESTACADO & EMMA
N
18 45
Dickens
Espuela
Soldier's Mound
CROTON
BREAKS
BRANDON
1891
DICKENS COUNTY
TEXAS
2020
TO ALBANY & FORT WORTH
TO JAY FLAT

Chapter 1
The Wide-awake

{In which Capt. Derrick Miles and Dr. Frank Hooper discuss guns, hats, and boots.}

In the fifteen years during which I have been acquainted with Captain Derrick Miles, I have admitted him to be of a peculiar sort—prone to bouts of profound meditation triggered by the partaking of tea extracted from a certain cactus found in the Chihuahuan Desert, for instance, or excitable in the extreme when a moment of epiphany is visited upon him, say, in the bathtub.

But nothing prepared me for the distressing sight that greeted me late on a blustery autumn afternoon—the twelfth of October, I well recall—upon my return to our shared bachelor quarters above the bootmaker's shop.

"Good God, man, don't do it!" I shouted instinctually and almost lunged at him, before wiser caution caused me to step back. "Why don't you . . . hand me . . . the gun?" I said in a more measured tone.

Derrick Miles, seated almost in profile to me at the teak-and-brass campaign desk as I stepped through the doorway, continued to hold the weapon at arm's length with its barrel pointed toward the center of his face, which appeared so thin in the shadows as to be almost cadaverous. He made no move for several long seconds. I held my breath. He inched the muzzle closer and squinted his eye toward it in the waning light.

"Miles, please—"

"Bring that lamp over here, would you, Hooper?"

I hesitated to shift my gaze from the scene, as though by my very force of will I might hold all the parts of it frozen and forestall disaster.

"That oil lamp, yes, please. And light it."

I abandoned my vigil for long enough to fetch the lamp. I slipped a friction match from the box on the table, cranked up the wick, and struck the match, keeping Miles in my sights. I lit the wick and moved closer, shining the glow on the firearm whose business end was situated a fingerbreadth from Miles's eyeball.

"Aha, I knew it!" he exclaimed, so suddenly I almost lost my grip on the lamp.

"Knew what?" I asked in relief, as he lowered the gun.

"A hardened residue of varnish impregnated with grains of black powder."

"As one might expect to find inside the barrel of a gun?"

"As one might expect to find inside the barrel of a gun that hasn't been fired in some months—or years."

"You had some concern on that score?"

"At least we know there's no chance our visitor was a Ranger."

Miles continued to dangle my duller intellect just out of reason's reach, a not infrequent circumstance in our exchanges. "We've had an unanticipated visit. Our caller, Hooper, does not appear to have been a Texas Ranger. And that is very good indeed, since, where there is a Ranger, there also is trouble."

"Ah, certainly." I struggled to keep up. "You had a caller while I was away at the hospital, but did not see him?" Had Derrick Miles benefited from even the slightest contact with any stranger, he would surely have swiftly deduced the man's occupation, birthplace, age, nationality, and more. Such were his estimable powers of detection.

Miles rose slowly from his seat and indicated the door through which I had come. "That is correct; I was out for the day as well, attending the mayor's meeting with members of the state Railroad Commission, about which I will enlighten you later. While you and I were gone a man lingered long enough in the upstairs corridor to have dropped crumbs from his biscuit. But he also left behind two valuable possessions. The gun—a six-chambered Colt revolver commonly known as the 'Peacemaker'—and this."

Still holding the gun, Miles stepped over to the hat rack beside the door. From amid a row of pegs on which hung his favorite Boss-of-the-Plains Stetson, a plaid Scottish hunting cap he sometimes wore in adverse weather, an ancient and stained cavalry hat, and my own second-best black bowler, he lifted an old-fashioned, wide-brimmed sort seldom seen these days in Fort Worth, Texas.

I removed my preferred bowler from my head and rested it on the vacated peg, smoothing my hair back from my brow and brushing the dust from my moustache. I hung my overcoat, also dusty from the streetcar ride across town, on the hook beneath it. Miles motioned me to the velvet settee beside the hearth, where Mrs. Simpson's boy had set coals to burn in the grate. I welcomed the warmth after the shock I'd experienced at first seeing Miles with the gun.

"Take a look, Hooper," he said, turning the hat so I could inspect its inside. There I read, stamped in gold, "BOLLMAN | PHILADELPHIA | 1871."

"What do you deduce from this information?" he asked, standing with his back to me, hands clasped behind him.

"Our visitor was a gentleman and a Yankee?"

He turned to warm his other side. "Perhaps. One of sufficient age and thrift as to have held onto his hat for two decades, and to have preserved it all the way West. You might recall, as I do from an advertisement in an old issue of *Puck*, that the renowned haberdasher was established in sixty-eight. And something else."

I peered closely to examine the napless black felt of its manufacture, which appeared to me to be of superior quality but scuffed; the wide silk hatband, which was glossy but soiled; and the sweatband inside, where I noted a small paper label tucked in. "Six and seven-eighths! The owner must have a rather small head. Do you concur?"

"Indeed, my dear Hooper. You'll catch on yet. But you have failed to note one matter of some importance."

"I have?"

"Run your fingers across the crown, and lean in and use your olfactory sense as well. What do you detect?"

I did as instructed, and my fingers immediately picked up traces of dark particles, a whiff of which revealed the smell of—coal smoke. "The owner has arrived on the train—rather recently, I suppose."

"Precisely. You do my methods proud," said Miles, standing and proceeding to light the gas lamps beside the mantel as he spoke. "Have I ever told you how gratifying I find your studious attentiveness, and the faithfulness with which you record our deliberations? Some men, not necessarily radiating light of their own, possess the rare gift of reflecting it from others, and some, while not generating waves of ideas themselves, excel at bouncing back an original sound, magnified and transformed. By Jove, Hooper, I see that quality in you. I am greatly in your debt."

He had seldom come so near to a compliment, and I must admit that his words gave me keen pleasure, for I had often been piqued by the indifference of Miles—five years my junior—to my admiration and to the continual attempts which I had made to spread the fame of his practice. I was proud, too, to think that I had so far mastered his approach as to apply it in a way which earned his approval. He now took the hat from my hands and examined it for a few minutes with his naked eyes.

Then with an expression of interest he carried it to the window, where he looked over it again in the fading light with a convex lens.

"Interesting, though elementary," said he as he returned to his favorite corner of the settee. "There are certainly one or two indications upon the hat. It gives us the basis for several deductions."

"Has anything escaped me?" I asked with some self-importance. "I trust that there is nothing of consequence which I have overlooked?"

"I am afraid, my dear Hooper, that at least one of your conclusions may have been off the mark. When I said that you amplified my thinking I meant that in noting your fallacies I am often steered towards the truth. Not that you are entirely wrong in this instance. The man certainly hails, originally, from distant parts. But he may have spent more time on the frontier than is immediately evident. Do no theories suggest themselves? You know my teachings. Think!"

"I can think only of the obvious conclusion that the man must be at least somewhat absentminded."

He chuckled. "No flies on your hide, Hooper. But we can delve deeper. With what groups of wearers has such a hat customarily been associated?"

"Well, it puts me in mind of a certain country preacher I once knew, who rode the circuit in South Texas when I practiced in Galveston. A Methodist, I believe."

"Now, it's doubtful the owner of the hat is presently a minister here, don't you agree?—since you and I are aware of the clergy in all the churches of this city. What, then?" Miles strode to a tall cherry bookshelf from which he pulled a bound volume. He thumbed it until arriving at a certain page. "Eureka!—here we have it."

I cocked an eyebrow expectantly.

Miles intoned in singsong, "Of all the hats I ever see, / The wide-awake is the one for me: / 'Tis only truth when I declare, How it's the fashion everywhere!"

I waited, unenlightened, for more.

"A bit of doggerel published in *Notes and Queries*, volume 10, September 1872. Penned by one Stephen Jackson, Esquire, in 1859, as 'A New Song on an Old Hat,' to be sung to the tune of 'The Leathern Bottle.' "

Just for good measure, Miles lifted his violin from its stand and bowed a few notes. But the melody triggered no recognition on my part, and he set the instrument down again with a tone of resignation.

"The style of hat, my dear Hooper, is known as a wide-awake. It was first popularized by two groups during the era of Lincoln: one, his ideological partisans; another, members of the Society of Friends in England and elsewhere."

"The Quakers?"

Miles returned to reading the verse. "And what d'ye say to the huge broad-brim / That shades the Quaker starch'd and prim?" He snapped the book shut. "The poem goes on for some seven or eight stanzas of such. I'll spare you them. Now, Hooper, make your pick. Friend of Franklin and Penn, or adherent of Honest Abe?"

I shook my head, smiling, in amazement at his virtuoso performance. "Bravo, bravo. Your ability to connect disparate bits of information astonishes. Not to mention your recall of detail, worthy of Mr. Brady's photographic art itself."

"Which is it, then?"

"I'll have to venture . . . the latter choice, given the political discourse with which the papers are filled these days. Labor disputes. The Grange. Tariffs. Dealings with the Railroad Commission."

"Very well, then, let us test your theory." Miles picked up the hat again and handed it to me, along with the magnifying glass. The raised angle of his beaked nose and the pursed set of his lips sent the unmistakable message that I'd taken the wrong fork in the road. "What do you see?"

I peered through the glass at the black felt and ran my hand across the crown. "Mmmm . . . ouch!" Something small and sharp had pricked the tip of my right index finger.

"Mesquite thorn, no?"

I licked the blood from my fingertip. "That smarts." I continued my perusal, noting a frayed portion of the brim that appeared to have been, well, *chewed*. But before I could venture more, Miles strode abruptly to the mantel and leaned his elbow there thoughtfully.

"Now the prime question remains: why does a Philadelphia Quaker debark from a train on the Texas frontier, take pains to visit the office of a consulting detective, then depart again without leaving behind so much as a print of dirt from his shoe, but instead leaving his frayed hat on the bench, and underneath it his revolver? *That* is what we need to know."

"He was—in a hurry?"

"One might surmise."

"He was—indisposed, or distracted, or, God forbid, waylaid . . . ?"

"Those are likewise possibilities. But let us consider that first principle of forensic science, which is—"

"Occam's Razor," I finished for him, having been schooled on the thesis upon various occasions. "Among numerous possibilities, the simplest is the likeliest."

"Very good. And, our lodgings being situated above the busy shop of a certain workman, and the visitor's arrival and departure leaving no evidence on the floorboards, what explanation might spring to mind?"

"Boots!" I cried, chastising myself that this point had eluded me. "The visitor was downstairs being fitted for a pair of boots."

"And perhaps still is. If he is fortunate, he will retrace his steps and recall where he laid his hat."

About that time I heard, outside the still-open hall door and below, a tap of leather on tongue and groove. Then another, and another. The taps approached with some hesitation, continuing upward. Miles moved his lips, counting the stairs silently. *Fourteen . . . fifteen, sixteen . . . seventeen.* He raised his fist and pantomimed in perfect time to the knock that came next.

I parroted Miles's words. "He will retrace his steps and recall—"

A voice called out. "Hallo? I say, greeting, sirs."

The man who peeked through the doorway was middle-aged, blond, of average height, though slim as far as I could surmise, underneath the long cloth coat he wore. His beard was trimmed in the Donegal style, of medium length, sans moustache. Hatless he was indeed, though not bootless. And behind him followed a small dog, which quickly trotted past its master into our quarters.

"Good evening," said Miles, rising, to the caller. "We were expecting you. And your canine companion, who is likely at this very minute fetching—"

"My hat!" cried the visitor. "I feared I might never recover it this time." The dog, a medium-sized mongrel, had gone directly over to retrieve its master's hat from the table beside the settee. The man leaned down to take the hat and pet the dog, and placed the hat again on his size-six-and-seven-eighths head. He looked quite pleased with himself for a moment, before snatching it off again. "Where are my manners?"

I went over to invite him in. "Not to worry. I am Dr. Frank Hooper, and this is my esteemed colleague, Captain Derrick Miles. Please, come in and tell us your name?"

The visitor set his hat atop his pate again for long enough to dip the front of its brim deferentially, then remove it once more. His speech was stilted and formal. "Wesley Barlow, of Estacado, Crosby County, Texas, two hundred eighty miles north and west of here as the crow flies."

Miles cast a skeptical glance my way. "Damn, that's bad!" he said, shaking his head.

The befuddled man blinked through his spectacles. "How's that?"

"Only for us, in our hypotheses. Crosby County, you say?"

"Yes, sir. And late of Philadelphia, Pennsylvania, and Zionsville, Indiana."

"Aha! And do we surmise correctly that you belong to a particular religious sect of that region?"

He nodded. "Unless that circumstance renders thee unable to assist in the matter I have come to discuss."

"Most assuredly not," said Miles, before asking our guest, "What does Reverend Wesley Barlow, man of the cloth, ask of Derrick Miles, specialist in crime detection? Do be seated, and apprise us!"

"Mister, sir, Mister—a humble clerk of the Society of Friends. And an attorney-at-law in said county."

"*Mister* Barlow, then. Hooper and I place ourselves humbly at your service, as well, if we find we may be of assistance," said Miles. "Before we delve deeper into your business, however, I believe there is one other item you may have left behind."

Mr. Barlow did not register the hint at first, then burst into exclamation. "The revolver! Thee did safeguard it, I hope?"

"Have no concern on that score. It lies on the table yonder. Unloaded, I might add."

Mr. Barlow seemed to shrink to even less of a bulk beneath the coat, as he exhaled. "I would prefer not to have carried a firearm under any circumstance, but—"

"Go on?"

"As it happens I required one for defense, and that is partly why I have come to seek thee out. But before I had the opportunity to find thee here, as I was seated there in the corridor, waiting outside thy chambers in hopes of thy return, I heard footsteps approaching, starting up the stairs, and I—I hid the gun on the bench beneath my hat."

"You didn't wish, as a man of peace, to be mistaken for a desperado?"

"Something like that. The footsteps came no farther, and I retreated into the shadow of the corner."

"Heavens, man!" I cried. "Were you being pursued?"

"Not exactly . . . it's simply that I had not gone abroad in such a metropolis, nor in such a vicinity of evil, in many years, and after what has transpired in recent days I must have acted out of an overabundance of caution."

"And these—recent events gave you cause for fear?" asked Miles.

"Quite so. I traveled a full day and night by coach and then a day by train to bear witness of some extremely distressing occurrences in our region. Along the coach route our party of four—plus the driver and his guard—were beset by threat of beast and, at the very end, disembarking from the train compartment here at the very outskirts of the city only blocks from thy door, I encountered crime and vice of a most venial sort. After I alighted from the arduous journey at nearly dawn and proceeded on foot to my hotel, a blackguard leapt from the shadows and demanded money. I was able to satisfy him with a few coins from my pocket, my purse being well hidden, but as I withdrew I was accosted from another direction by a—a—"

"A grifter? A cutpurse?" I offered.

"I hesitate to say it. A woman of—eh, easy virtue."

Miles suppressed a smile. "Hell's Half-Acre," he said. "I must apologize on behalf of our adopted city. Fort Worth has become the standard-bearer for unsavory activity, I'm afraid—what with all manner of cowpunchers, carpetbaggers, and camp followers coming and going, with often questionable motives. I hope you weren't worse harmed."

"No, God be praised, except for thoroughly ruining my footwear as I ran senseless for blocks in search of a gentler quarter. I felt compelled to arm myself at the first opportunity, however. I went straightaway to Fowler's pawn shop and purchased the piece at second hand, then sought out a cobbler to repair my boots. I had no idea I'd landed literally at thy doorstep when I left them with Lewis downstairs."

"That makes two matters about which I have been correct, at least," said Miles.

"What are those?" I inquired.

"That there's truly no more useful site for a detective's office than upstairs from one of the first places any newcomer will go upon arriving in the city—the bootblack's—and that any man who leaves his gun behind on a bench isn't accustomed to shooting for a living."

Barlow let out a sigh. "Thee is most true on the latter statement. In my law practice I have specialized in land transactions, contracts, wills, that sort of thing. Nothing that would typically bring me into contact with the criminal element."

Miles went over and picked up the man's gun, and handed it butt-first to its owner. "Your next task might be to acquire a holster," he said. "And to clean your Colt thoroughly before you insert it." He then returned five bullets into the man's palm.

I stepped in to smooth over the awkward moment. "Might I offer us all some nourishment?" I took the opportunity to suggest. "You must be ravenous, Mr. Barlow, if you've had no meal or rest since morning."

"I slept away most of the day at the hotel," he admitted. "And thee is right, I would be most thankful for a morsel. I've had nothing other than the dry biscuits I brought with me from the train."

The dog, as though sensing the mention of food, perked up its ears.

Though it was nearly the dinner hour and the wind was still blowing mercilessly outside our windows, I lifted the telephone receiver on the side table and called downstairs for Mrs. Simpson, who grudgingly agreed to send her boy around to fetch a tray of sandwiches for us from the saloon. We were not at a loss for libations, as Miles and I customarily kept a goodly selection of whiskies and ports on hand. Mr. Barlow refused any, accepting only water.

Miles settled into the armchair near our guest and sipped his Jameson's, neat. "Let us learn more about the recent events you mentioned, Mr. Barlow."

"Yes, right. I came to thee, Derrick Miles, because I recognized that I am myself a simple man but now faced with a most serious and extraordinary problem. Recognizing, as I do, that thee is the second highest expert in the West—"

"Indeed, sir! May I inquire who has the honor to be the first?" asked Miles with some asperity.

"For strictly practical and business matters the work of the Pinkertons must always appeal strongly."

"Then had you not better consult them?"

"I said, sir, to the precisely practical mind. But in matters of solving great mysteries it is acknowledged that Derrick Miles stands alone. I trust, sir, that I have not inadvertently—"

"Just a little," said Miles. "I think, Mr. Barlow, you ought to just get down to business and tell me plainly the exact nature of your problem."

The wind, at that moment, whipped the downstairs door

The Wolf Hunt: A Tale of the Texas Badlands

shut as Jake the servant boy trudged up the seventeen stairs with our supper. The dog twitched its ears in interest but did not move from its spot. We fell to our repast as Mr. Barlow laid open the case.

Chapter 2
The Curse

{In which Mr. Wesley Barlow of Crosby County, Texas, reveals one clan's darkest secret.}

"I brought with me some documents that will help explain," said Barlow.

"I observed one of them as you entered the room," said Miles, pointing to the man's side pocket.

Barlow extracted a much-creased sheet and began to unfold it. "This map is fairly old, as things in Texas go."

"From 1854, unless it is a very good forgery."

"How can thee ascertain that information with such precision, sir?"

"You allowed an inch or two of it to protrude as you entered, showing a bit of the map's distinctive engrossing. You may recall that I'm quite familiar with the maps of our state, having served some months with the army at Fort Griffin during the Indian campaigns of the Red River. This one, unless I'm mistaken, is a later authorized copy of Captain Marcy's expedition survey of 1854—easy for me to remember, as it is also the year of my birth."

"I apologize for bringing none more recent; thee will soon understand why this document in particular is relevant." Mr. Barlow pushed his spectacles up on his nose, drew the map from his side pocket, pushed aside our plates, and unfolded it on the dining table. I brought over the old oil lamp to provide additional illumination.

"Observe, gentlemen," he said, "in this roughly sketched but quite accurate map, something of the nature of the country that lies between here"—he indicated just off the page to the right, where that map did not extend to embrace our present location in Fort Worth—"and here, at the western edge, in Dickens County. West of here it is primarily broken and rugged land, threaded through by tributaries of the Red, Wichita, and Brazos river systems, remote and difficult to access. Until recently it was Comanche country. Captain Marcy in the 1850s indicated springs, peaks, what few forts that existed, and the wagon road from New Mexico; the advent of the railroad would not occur until more than twenty years after."

"I well recollect that occasion," said Miles, "having arrived here in the city by rail not long after the line's opening."

I chimed in here, not wishing to interrupt our guest but eager to stake my claim as something of a pioneer as well. "As do I. It was that very train, the Texas and Pacific in July of seventy-six, that introduced me to Derrick Miles, fresh out of the army's service with the rank of captain." Miles shot me a glance. "But that, of course, is a story for another day."

"What is important to note on this copy of Marcy's map," our guest said, "is the great void west of where the Brazos forks at about the one hundredth meridian. Marcy indicated this series of rugged peaks, here, but left the country beyond empty. In that space, faintly penciled at the far edge, pray tell me what thee sees."

Miles leaned closer. "I make out . . . 'Quaker colony, est. 1879.' "

"That, sir, is where our people settled after a long journey from Indiana. And where we have remained to farm in peace, despite hardships. Know you the meaning of 'Estacado'?"

"It is Spanish for 'staked,' is it not?" Miles offered. "A descriptor applied to the plains by the soldiers under Coronado, who found the escarpment to resemble a palisade."

"Thee is correct, though some hold with alternate theories.

That Coronado's scouts marked their way across the trackless plain with sticks, for instance. But that is not our concern at present. Our situation lies just below the caprock escarpment, here in the eastern portion of which, as of seven months ago, has been legally organized as the County of Dickens." He moved his finger slightly to the right on the map, where I could see further pencil markings around the engraved hachures. "The annotator of this map has drawn in the wandering lines of two creeks. These intermittent streams traverse the vast holdings of the Spur Ranch, carving rugged canyons through a remote portion known as the Croton Breaks."

"It is a country with which I am somewhat familiar, and I certainly know of the celebrated Spurs," said Miles.

Mr. Barlow lowered his voice. "The region remains unknown to most, except the cowhands of that ranch, who even themselves report the occasional disappearance of cattle in the jagged breaks, never to be seen again. It is a land of treacherous river bottoms that seem innocuous, only to trap the unwary animal or rider fast in quicksand; and creeks that rise to raging floods after brief rainstorms upstream. The dark recesses of canyons have for centuries hidden Indians; they still harbor venomous rattlesnakes and vicious badgers and hydrophobic polecats and other wild creatures of which I will presently tell thee. The land is subject to searing heat, blistering cold, and northers—like the one we seem to be experiencing tonight—that can come on so suddenly the mercury drops sixty degrees in an hour."

At our guest's words I registered the chill that had settled over the room and went to add more coals to the grate. Mr. Barlow continued as I brought the tray over and refilled all our glasses, his with water, ours each with whiskey. The dog lay obediently at his master's feet, accepting a bread crust slipped to him from the table.

"I must beg your pardon for taking the long way round,

gentlemen, for some history is necessary if one is to make a sound judgment, I believe.

"Some years back, when American beef was at a premium and investors from across the Atlantic spied opportunity to control costs by buying up tracts of rangeland being broken up by fence, a certain member of the British nobility acquired a portion of the Spur holdings. Basil Wolverton II—styled Baronet Wolverton of Brent—migrated lock, stock, and barrel to his new ranch in America, bringing with him his young wife and his servants. It was rumored that he hoped to increase his wealth but also to reconcile with his surviving younger brother, who had left the ancestral isle some years before him. In due time the baronet renounced his British citizenship and title and pledged allegiance to his adopted country, where the locals simply took to calling him 'the Earl' despite his actual rank.

"That was a decade past. I served as the Earl's local counsel in some of these property transactions and in due time made the acquaintance of his wife and household, our neighboring counties having much in common in civic life and commerce. Estacado's small gathering of Friends are always willing to help out our fellow settlers in times of crisis, of which we have shared many.

"I became something of a confidant and even, I dare say, a spiritual adviser to the Earl. He was—I almost said *is*, although it has been some days since the mysterious tragedy that claimed his life—he was a capable and shrewd man in business matters, though prone to a periodic melancholy that may have figured into his demise."

"I am sorry to learn of your loss," I said. "And, one assumes, a loss to your community as well."

"Indeed, yes. Thee is kind to note it." The man nearly broke down in tears, and drew out a handkerchief with which to dry his eyes before resuming his saga. Miles remained intently focused as the story seemed to be approaching the crux of its problem.

"Lady Wolverton—herself an angel of beneficence to the cowboys of their ranch and the surrounding area—became ill within a year of their arrival in Texas, a factor that wore on her husband's mental state increasingly, as her health declined. Olivia Wolverton suffered from a debilitating condition of the nervous system that manifested in increased redness and sensitivity about the face, and partial loss of control in her limbs. Eventually she became confined to a wheelchair, a difficult circumstance on a working ranch, as you can imagine.

"The couple traveled to consult doctors in Austin. Observing a peculiar butterfly-shaped pattern apparent in the lesions on Mrs. Wolverton's face, the physicians quickly concurred on a diagnosis—"

I could not refrain from interrupting, medicine being my own field of professional training. "*Lupus erythematosus,* I'm sure you were about to say. The symptom is classic, and the prognosis, I fear, was not hopeful."

"Lady Wolverton did not survive that long winter, a particularly harsh one throughout Northwest Texas, as you must recall. At least there were no children to grieve. All that season cattle froze, driven en masse against fences, and four-legged predators skulked about, feeding as they might on carcasses. The Earl himself grew thin and wan, and obsessively fearful. He seemed to dwell on a long-ago story from the days of the first Baronet Wolverton, back in Devonshire, and more recently on the account of a curse placed on his Texas lands by the Comanche tribe as they had been lately driven from their ancestral hunting grounds. The fatal occurrence of lupus—'the wolf'—only fueled his obsession with the myth. He became convinced of a conspiracy of sorts."

At this I slid back in my chair once again, fearing the account was about to steer away from the empirical and scientific into the realm of the metaphysical.

"You gentlemen have heard, perhaps, of the dire wolf?"

"An enormous ancient species naturalists consider long extinct," replied Miles.

"The Indians claimed the dire wolf appears at times of impending tragedy, to stalk, to scare, perhaps to kill," said Barlow, his tone measured.

"What credence would a man of business, a man of faith, lend to a native folktale?" asked Miles.

"As I have said, Basil Wolverton was known to fall into occasional fits of choler; these seemed aggravated, understandably, by his wife's failing health and untimely death. He became very careful to lock all doors to the ranch headquarters, whether inside or out, whether his employees were present or not. He never left home unarmed, even to attend church or business in town. He turned distrustful. Eventually he dismissed all his work staff save one married couple—a woman who oversees the house itself, and a ranch manager to look after the much-diminished Wolverton herds.

"But more than that," Barlow continued, "increasing depredations of cattle *have* in truth been reported in the region below the caprock, and by numerous citizens. It has been an extremely hot, dry summer we've had, you see, and wolves and coyotes have been observed with some frequency as they have been forced to range farther in search of water—and food. The bounty for lobo scalps has been raised to five dollars a head as incentive. Ranchers have set traps and spread poison, but captures of the predators have been few."

Miles considered this last information. "I see," he said, peering out the window to the west as though trying to transport his deductive capacity to the distant landscape, "how nature may be lending credence to legend."

"Yes," said Barlow. "And now—I am getting to the heart of the matter—the tragedy of the Earl's death has incited great speculation and concern, extending throughout the county and surrounding settlements. Such news may not have reached your ears here, however—our frontier newspapers being few and sporadic compared to your own daily *Gazette*."

"You are correct, sir, that I have not been made aware of it," said Miles.

"But I bring with me, also, Captain Miles, the *Dickens Progress* from Friday last that should lay out the known facts more clearly than I could recite them."

Mr. Barlow handed the single broadsheet to Miles, who held it to the lamp and, after a moment, read the relevant article aloud.

DEATH OF DICKENS "EARL" REPORTED THIS MORNING. The sudden death last night of Basil Wolverton II, whose name had been mentioned as a possible candidate for county judge in the recent election, having given up a peerage in his native Britain and taken the oath of loyalty to this country, has cast a gloom over the region. Though the Earl, as he was familiarly known, had resided at the Wolverton ranch house for little more than a decade, his upstanding character and business acumen had won the admiration and respect of the citizens. The Earl, as is reputed, inherited his fortune from mining ventures in England, and later made large sums himself in the Texas cattle industry and in railroad investments.

It was widely understood that charitable assistance to many needy organizations and individuals, credited only as anonymous gifts, originated in actuality with Basil Wolverton. Additionally, as Wolverton and his late wife had no children, it was his openly expressed desire that the community should, within his own lifetime, profit by his good fortune, and many causes will miss the benefit of his philanthropy. Generous donations to causes such as the war widows' benevolent society and the Espuela School have been frequently chronicled in these columns.

The Earl had also recently offered up his assistance in organizing a hunt with the objective of ridding our region of the pest which preys upon livestock and threatens the traveler. Wolverton had pledged the sum to cover the services of a guide and related expenses. Plans for a fall hunt were halted when ranchers learned of Wolverton's sudden and tragic demise.

Miles folded the paper to expose the next column of type more fully to the light and read on.

SHERIFF DISPELS RUMORS. The circumstances connected with Wolverton's death cannot be said to have been entirely cleared up by this morning's investigation, but at present there is no reason to suspect foul play, or to imagine that death could be from any but natural causes.

The Earl was a widower, and a man who may be said to have been in some ways of an eccentric habit of mind. Neighbors, including Mr. Wesley Barlow, friend of the deceased from nearby Estacado, and the ranch manager and his wife, have said that of late the Earl was not in the best of health, and that frequent episodes of shortness of breath, changes in skin color, and acute attacks of nervous depression may have indicated some affliction of the heart.

According to ranch manager Antonío López and his wife, Felicia, the housekeeper, the Earl was in the habit every evening before dark of riding out to the edge of the canyon to survey the land on his ranch below the caprock. This custom was also attested to by a neighbor, Mr. Rufus Griswall, and his daughter.

Yesterday evening, October eighth, on a brisk but still night following a day of gray and drizzle, the Earl had declared his intention of starting the following day for Fort Worth, and asked López to be ready to drive him in the buggy to the train station in Albany. At twilight he went out as usual for his nocturnal ride along the fence line, in the course of which he was in the habit of dismounting and smoking a cigar. By nine-thirty p.m. his horse, a large bay, returned without its rider. López, hearing the horse outside and finding the hall door still open, became alarmed, and, lighting a lantern, went in search of his boss. López traced the horse's prints down the trail to a gate leading out onto the breaks above the canyon floor. There were indications that the Earl had dismounted and stood for some little time there. The body was discovered close by, on the other side of the open gate.

López, unable to move the body alone, said that without further delay he rode at a gallop back to the house to inform his wife, who raised an alarm by means of the large dinner bell mounted on the porch post of the house. Several ranch hands, roused from the nearby Spur, arrived, along with the aforementioned Mr. Griswall. Together the men took the wagon and retrieved the body. One of the hands was then sent posthaste to Estacado to fetch Mr. Barlow, counsel and friend to the Earl.

One Webster, a horse trader, was riding along the Mackenzie road a quarter mile away at the time, but he appears by his own confession to have been the worse for drink. He declares that he heard strange cries but is unable to identify whether they were human or animal, or to state from what direction they came.

No signs of violence were to be discovered upon the Earl's person, nor had the rifle he customarily carried been discharged, and though the sheriff's evidence noted an almost incredible facial distortion, it was explained that that is a symptom which is not unusual in cases of dyspnea and death from cardiac exhaustion. This explanation was supported by the post-mortem examination at the doctor's office in Crosbyton, which showed long-standing organic disease, and the coroner determined the death to be from natural causes.

Miles cleared his throat.

Burial to be private; a memorial service will be scheduled for some future date, following attempts to locate relatives.

It is hoped that any living heir to the Wolverton estate should settle at the ranch and continue the good work which has been so sadly interrupted.

It is understood that the next of kin is the son of Basil Wolverton's late younger brother, Nigel. The young man when last heard of was in Arizona Territory, where he has been sought to inform him of his loss.

Miles drew out a long breath and took another sip of his Jameson's.

"That," said Mr. Barlow, "is the full public account of the death of Basil Wolverton."

"I must thank you for coming so far, over such treacherous territory, to bring this case to my attention," said Miles. "And I thank you as well for your systematic approach to describing it. This article, you say, contains all the public facts known within the first hours of the event?"

" 'Tis a lucky circumstance that the weekly paper comes out on Friday afternoons. The editor happened to have been one of those summoned soonest to the scene and rushed his issue into print. I obtained a copy from him right off the press, judging it to be of use in my mission."

"Indeed. Then tell us anything you know that was *not* reported in the paper." He leaned back and templed his fingertips in a judicial mien. Most of Miles's visage was obscured in shadow, however, and I could not readily gauge his reactions.

"In doing so," said Mr. Barlow, who had begun to show signs of some strong emotion, "I am telling thee of observations I have not confided to anyone. Such reticence runs counter to my upbringing in Quaker plain speech. But my reasons for withholding such information from the coroner and the newspaper are several. One is that a man of faith shrinks from appearing to endorse a popular superstition. And further, I wanted to do nothing that might hamper the fortunes of my neighboring county or cause harm to a friend's reputation. But I will be frank in the expectation that thee will preserve my confidences."

"I assure you that your trust is well placed," said Miles. "Go on."

"Dickens County is sparsely inhabited and served by no railroad nor means of communication other than a few haphazard telegraph stations. Those who live there must rely on one another, and on services from their neighboring county. For this reason I saw a good deal of Basil Wolverton. With the exception of Judge John McQuarrie of the Bar M Ranch; Mr. Rufus Griswall, the dowser and geologist, and his daughter; and the farmer Hagins, who has recently arrived to establish a cotton gin, along with Mr. Hank Smith and his wife of the Blanco Canyon Rock House in my own county, there are few other people outside of our own settlement within a day's ride in any direction, whose interests have aligned with my own.

"I have said the Earl was a private man, but the chance of his land deal brought us together, and shared concern for civic life kept us so. He subscribed by mail to news from throughout the United States as well as from Britain, and many a stimulating evening we spent together discussing world events and local affairs alike.

"Over the course of this long, hot summer it became increasingly plain to me that the Earl's nervous system was strained to the breaking point. He had taken exceedingly to heart this fable which I have related to thee—so much so that, although he would ride over the grounds near to his ranch headquarters by day, nothing would induce him to go down into the breaks, day or night. He allowed his herds to dwindle almost to nothing, instead diverting his investments into the railroads. He often relied upon me to disburse his charitable distributions, to account for their successful transfer and also to mask their source.

"Incredible as it may appear to thee, Captain Miles, the Earl was honestly convinced that a dreadful fate overhung his land. Others in his close company can attest to this impression as well. The idea of some ghastly presence constantly haunted him, and on more than one occasion he had asked me whether I had on my journeys spied any strange creature or come upon larger-than-usual animal tracks.

"I can well remember driving up to the Wolverton headquarters one September evening in my buckboard, at the late hour when the setting sun casts long shadows over the valleys. He chanced to be at the door of his house. I had descended from my perch and was standing in front of him, when I saw his eyes fix themselves over my shoulder and stare past me with an expression of the most dreadful horror. I whisked round and had just time to catch a glimpse of something which I took to be a large calf passing at the head of the path. So excited and alarmed was he that I was compelled to go down to the spot where the animal had been and look around for it. It was gone, however, and the incident appeared to make an extreme impression upon his mind. I stayed with him all that night, and it was on that occasion, to explain the emotion which he had shown, that he confided to my keeping that narrative which I have shared with you just now. I mention this small episode because it assumes some importance in view of the tragedy which followed, but I was convinced at the time that the matter was entirely trivial and that his excitement had no justification.

"It was on my advice, afterward, that the Earl was preparing to travel to Fort Worth and thence down to Austin for his health. It grieves me to consider that my friend would have traveled in peace, perhaps, in the very train car I occupied coming here, had events not taken such a turn!" Mr. Barlow paused for a moment to regain his composure, then continued.

"His heart was, I knew, affected, and the constant anxiety in which he lived, however chimerical the cause of it might be, was evidently having a serious effect upon his state of mind. I myself had suggested that a sojourn at Barton Springs might do him enormous good, and that a few months among the distractions of the capital city would send him back a new man. Mr. Griswall, a mutual friend who was much concerned at his state of health, was of the same opinion. Then at the last instant came this terrible catastrophe."

I nodded, indicating my sympathy with the unfortunate Wolverton's plight but also the wisdom of Mr. Barlow's prescription. Miles remained impassive as Barlow continued his testimony.

"On the night of the Earl's death López the ranch manager,

who made the discovery, sent a man out to the colony at Estacado to fetch me, as I have said, and I returned that very night with him to the Wolverton ranch. The county had experienced a little rain, the first in more than three months. The Earl's body, splashed with mud, had been removed to the ranch house, where it was laid on a plank table in a spare bedroom. I was shocked to note its condition, the limbs as gruesomely splayed as they might have been in a very moment of terror, the facial features contorted in apparent fear. I grieved for the horror and pain my friend must have experienced in his final moments. The body, López said, was already stiffened when he had come upon it."

Miles interjected, "How many hours, do you surmise, elapsed between the time of the event, and the time of López's discovery?"

"I cannot say for my own account, and López could not be sure either, though he was certain that the Earl left on his ride at twilight, about five-thirty in the evening, and it was after ten when the riderless horse arrived at the house; it took López another fifteen minutes to follow the trail."

"Certainly sufficient time for *rigor mortis* to have set in," I noted. "Stiffening begins with the eyelids, neck, and jaw, as early as two hours after death. As for the appearance of the facial features you describe, Mr. Barlow, it would have taken a severe shock indeed for such an expression to have resisted the immediate relaxation of muscle tissue that typically precedes stiffening. It must have—" I registered the sobering effect of my clinical words upon Mr. Barlow, and retreated in embarrassment.

"Do continue, Mr. Barlow," urged Miles, and our guest snapped back to the difficult task he had come to fulfill.

"After saying a brief prayer for the departed I asked López if he might accompany me down to the site where the Earl had breathed his last. I felt it my duty as Wolverton's attorney and executor of his estate to witness all evidence for myself.

"We rode along the fence to the gate, carrying cedar-knot torches to light our way and taking care to disturb the damp earth no further than necessary. Once I reached the gate, however, it was obvious to me that the frenzied activity of men and horses had already obliviated prints of feet and hooves that might have lent clarity to events. The site, regrettably, had been quite compromised from an evidentiary standpoint. I berated the ill fortune that I had not been on hand sooner—or even to have accompanied the Earl that night and perhaps forestalled his death!

"I resigned myself to returning at daylight, which I did alone after remaining the evening at the Wolverton house. At that point, with the benefit of shadows cast by the early light, I made a most startling discovery."

Miles leaned forward, and I set aside my self-absorption and paid close attention.

"Signs on the ground indicated that events were quite as López and the ranch hands described: the Earl had indeed dismounted at the gate, stood for a while smoking his cigar, as indicated by traces of fallen ash and a few still-observable prints of his boots. Additionally, there were no spent bullets about, nor sign of any struggle. But the Earl's footprints, I now saw as the damp mud had hardened like ceramic molds, altered their character from the time that he passed the ranch gate, and that he appeared from thence onward to have been walking upon his toes."

"Curious," Miles added.

"Yes," said Barlow. "And in this region and just beyond, there were deep footprints."

"Footprints?"

"Footprints."

"A man's or a woman's?"

Mr. Barlow looked strangely at us for an instant, and his voice sank almost to a whisper as he answered. "Captain Miles, they appeared to have been the footprints of a gigantic . . . wolf!"

CHAPTER 3
DIRE DEEDS

{In which Miles and Hooper interrogate their visitor from Crosby County.}

The wind chose that moment to rise in intensity, causing the shutters of our quite solid and quite urban dwelling to clatter against the clapboard. Had we been attending a dramatic performance at the Opera House the effects could not have been more perfectly timed in the action, for the howling gale evoked nothing so much as the keening voice of an ethereal canine in the night. I felt a shudder pass through me.

The Quaker's own voice faltered, and he reached for his water glass and took a long gulp. Miles leaned forward, his dark eyes reflecting the lamplight.

"You saw this?"

"As clearly as I see you."

"And you said nothing?"

"I did not want to stir up speculation on the basis of a folktale—or to be thought a fool. But I have since begun to wonder."

"How was it that no one else saw it?"

"The marks were some twenty yards from the body, not easily discerned by the light of torch and lantern the night before. And further rain that afternoon erased that which I had seen, before the coroner and the sheriff arrived to investigate for themselves."

Miles leaned back and pressed his fingertips together. "Coyotes are common in that part of the country, as they are here," he mused.

"No doubt. But the size of the paw pad was a good six inches across, with the extended nail print that distinguishes it from that of dog or coyote."

"What about mountain lion—or panther, as it's known around these parts?"

Barlow leaned back in his chair, as though to indicate the ridiculousness of such a confusion. "Here in the Panther City thee knows well the distinction, Captain Miles. The print of the feline is wide rather than long, and exhibits no nail marks, as the claws are retracted when the animal is walking or running."

"Yes, precisely so." Miles appeared to calculate these data with a methodical nature that put me in mind of the difference engine which I had seen demonstrated during a visit to Boston some years back. "You say it was large?" he continued.

"Enormous, and with what might have been a scar or defect on one of the feet."

"But it had not approached the Earl?"

"The coroner swore there were no marks of any kind upon the body."

"And you've said the night was clear and chilly, after a damp and raw day—but not actually raining."

"That is right; until the following day, we'd not seen a good drenching rain for some months. I had even wondered if the Earl lingered longer than usual, to take in the fresh and humid air."

"What is the trail like?"

"It is part of an old wagon trail, about eight feet across, flat-packed caliche and red dirt but worn by shallow ruts. On one side it is closed in by mesquite and hackberry, nearly impenetrable; on the other by fence."

"Barbed wire, I assume?"

"The devil's rope, as they say. Yes."

"And the news article mentions a gate?"

"Yes, the cedar-pole gate in the fence that leads to the spring."

"Is there any other opening or side path?"

"None."

"So that to reach the trail one either has to come down it from the house or else to enter it by the ranch gate?"

"That is correct. From the gate, the trail eventually leads down the canyon to the spring and across a meadow, where an old half-dugout, likely from Captain Marcy's time, stands."

"Had the Earl reached this dugout?"

"No; he lay a good hundred yards from it."

"Now, tell me, Mr. Barlow—and this is important—the marks which you saw were on the trail and not on the surrounding ground?"

"Yes, right on the trail; no marks would have been readily discernible in the brush."

"Were they on the opposite side of the trail from the ranch gate?"

Barlow nodded. "Yes; they were on the edge of the trail beyond the ranch gate." He answered each query with conviction, with an expression equal parts conviction and puzzlement.

"You interest me exceedingly," said Miles. "Another point. Was the gate closed?"

"The padlock was unlocked; the gate stood open. We'd had some run-ins with fence cutters in the county a while back, and the Earl at the time had taken pains to defend his boundaries with armed guards and to lock all gates. Once the law came to Dickens County, they've seen little more of that kind of trouble."

"How high is it?"

"About four feet high."

"Then anyone could have climbed over it with a little effort?"

"I imagine so, yes."

"Damnation, man, did no one even examine the scene with care?" Miles burst out.

A slight rise of my eyebrows was enough to remind my colleague of our guest's sensibilities.

"Excuse my language."

"Certainly," Mr. Barlow replied. "I looked, myself."

"And found nothing?"

"It was all very confused. The Earl had evidently stood there for five or ten minutes."

"How do you know that?"

"Because the ash had twice dropped from his cigar."

Miles's expression, as mercurial as the wind, shifted yet again. "Excellent! This is a colleague, Hooper, after our own heart. But the footprints?"

"He had left his own marks all over that small patch of caliche and dust. I could discern no others."

Derrick Miles struck his hand against his knee with an impatient gesture. "If I had only been there!" he cried. "It is evidently a case of extraordinary interest, and one which presented immense opportunities to the scientific expert. That red-dirt page upon which I might have read so much has by now been smudged by cattle and erased by the boots of curious cowboys. Oh, Mr. Barlow, to think that you should not simply have telegraphed me to come out to you straightway!"

"I could not call thee in, Captain Miles, without risking the information becoming public and stirring up a hornet's nest, as I have said. Besides, besides—"

"Why do you hesitate?"

"There is a realm in which the most acute and most experienced of detectives is helpless."

"You mean that the thing is supernatural?"

"Well, I wouldn't go so far as to say so—"

"But you apparently think it."

"I hesitate to say . . . but on the day after the tragedy a visitor came to the ranch to tell me of incidents that are hard to reconcile with the settled order of Nature."

"Go on?"

"Sightings of wolves have been reported, as I mentioned to you earlier—with increased frequency, even in towns. So have killings of cattle, a few sheep. This visitor, a protection man well known on the Spurs and now sheriff of my own county, was in a position to know of these. When he received word of the Earl's passing from one of the ranch hands, he came to pay his respects, and after learning I was there, he called me aside.

"Now Bill Standifer is counted a trustworthy sort, loyal if not always even-tempered. He must have had some motivation for reporting to me what cowpunchers and railway advance men had seen, and why. And he must have felt it advisable to confide in me why there had been some consternation over the idea of mounting a hunt in the neighboring county."

Barlow paused to let this sink in, and Miles prompted him again. "What have the men reported?"

"In recent weeks, Standifer told me, several people in the vicinity of the Croton Breaks had spied a creature unlike any known to science skulking about the badlands. Word came to him whispered as though practical-minded ranchers and hardy settlers were afraid to admit their eyes might have deceived them. But all agreed it was a huge, yellow-eyed, four-legged mammal, bristling with gray fur but luminous and ghastly. All related the same story of this dreadful apparition that put them in mind of the dire wolf of the legend. And this is curious indeed: none reported tracks. Standifer thought I'd want to know."

"And you, a Quaker of straightforward faith, believe it could be supernatural?"

"I do not know what to believe."

Miles nodded sagely. "My investigations, Mr. Barlow, have been confined strictly to this world," said he. "In a modest way

The Wolf Hunt: A Tale of the Texas Badlands

I have combated the evil of men, but to take on an evil beyond this world—I'm uncertain my résumé would apply. We must admit that the footmark you saw is material, however, and in that aspect I can be of use."

"The ancient dire wolf was material enough to have left numerous fossil remains, and yet the Kiowa believed him to be of the spirit world as well. And that, Captain Miles, is precisely why I came posthaste to consult with you after my conversation with Standifer."

"You have some doubt as to whether it is possible to lay the case of the Earl's death to rest, however. So, how can I assist you?"

"By advising me as to what I should do with Trey Wolverton, who arrives here by train"—Mr. Barlow looked at his watch—"in exactly one hour."

"He being the next of kin?"

"Yes. It was well known that the Earl and his wife had no issue. Beyond that Sir Basil Wolverton generally kept details of his family quiet. I, as a confidant, was privy to some family secrets, primarily that the Earl had long been estranged from his few relations, including several nieces and nephews. To that generation belongs twenty-one-year-old nephew Basil Wolverton III, Nigel's son.

"A local attorney helped me locate Trey, as he is called, through discreet inquiries, and I wired to him in Tucson—where he had recently returned from the silver mines near Tombstone—and suggested he come to Texas at once. He is quite unaware of the extent of his uncle's holdings but is eager to pay a visit to the ranch. From the accounts which have reached me he is an ambitious young man of great energy, and as executor of Sir Basil's will I am happy to learn it."

"There is no other claimant, I presume?"

"None. Sir Basil had only the one younger brother. Nigel,

who had traveled to California with the forty-niners in search of gold and some years later died in a tubercular sanitarium in El Paso, was the father of this young Trey. A half-brother, Randall, died without issue. A half-sister, Susan, daughter of Arthur Wolverton's second wife, seems to have been a thorn in the side of the men. She appears to have been a throwback to an ancient Wolverton strain of, well, disagreeable character. She lived to a ripe old age and died an old maid in London six years ago. Trey is the last scion of the Wolvertons. At ten minutes to midnight I am to meet him at the station, and frankly, I am not myself enthusiastic at the prospect of heading back out into your infernal city. Now, Captain Miles, what would you advise me to do with him when we rendezvous?"

"Why should he not proceed straightway to his late uncle's ranch?"

"That seems the natural plan, does it not? And yet, consider the local temper—and the danger that might await him there. I feel sure that if the Earl could have spoken with me before his death he would have warned me against bringing this, the last of the clan and the heir to great wealth, to that sorrowful place. It would also be unwise, I should think, for a young and naïve newcomer to get caught up in any renewed plan to organize a wolf hunt.

"Nonetheless," Mr. Barlow continued, "it cannot be denied that, with the aggregation of ranch holdings under large syndicates like the Spur, a balance to that monopoly is greatly needed. All the good work which has been done by the Earl toward organizing a county and establishing a seat and a courthouse could be rapidly undone. I fear lest I should be swayed too much by my own obvious interest in the matter, and that is why I bring the case before you and ask for your advice."

Miles considered for a little time. "Allow me to sum up my understanding," said he. "In your opinion there is a diabolical entity at work that makes Dickens County an unsafe abode for any Wolverton—that is your opinion?"

"Thee must appreciate there is some evidence to support the possibility."

"Agreed. But surely, if your supernatural theory be correct, it could exert its malice upon the young man in Fort Worth as easily as in Dickens County. A demon with merely local powers would make a mockery of true evil, no?"

"Thee puts the matter more flippantly, Captain Miles, than thee would probably do if brought into personal contact with these events. Taking the inverse to be true, thy advice is that the young man will be as safe in Dickens County as in Fort Worth? What, I pray, would thee recommend?"

"I recommend, sir, that you take a cab, call off your dog who is scratching at my front door, and proceed to your hotel and get a bath before meeting Trey Wolverton at the depot."

At this directive Mr. Barlow rose reluctantly, and I divined in his crestfallen expression the anxiety with which he contemplated going back out into the night.

"And then?"

"And then you will say nothing to him at all about a plan until I have made up my mind about the matter."

"How long does thee anticipate requiring?"

"At one p.m. tomorrow, Mr. Barlow, I shall be much obliged to you if you will meet me and Mr. Hooper at the White Elephant Saloon on Main Street for luncheon, and it will be useful if you will bring Trey Wolverton with you."

Fearing for the man's safety, I offered, perhaps against my better judgment, to accompany him to the train station. I rose and reached for my coat and hat.

Barlow's demeanor shifted instantly to gratitude—and action. "I will do so, Captain Miles," said he. Withdrawing a pencil and leather-bound notepad from the pocket of his coat, he noted the appointment, then set his wide-brimmed hat on his head and started out the door in his strange, peering, absentminded fashion.

Miles stopped him at the head of the stair. "Only one more question, Mr. Barlow. You say that before Basil Wolverton's death several people saw this apparition down in the breaks?"

"Three people did."

"Did any see it after?"

"The sheriff did not speak of any."

"Thank you. Good evening." Miles returned to his seat with that quiet look of inward satisfaction that meant that he had a challenging mental task before him. "Hooper, hand me my fiddle while you're up, would you? And you're certain you don't mind delivering your charges to their hotel?"

"Unless I can be of more assistance here."

"No, my dear fellow, it is at the hour of action that I turn to you for aid. By morning I should be very glad to compare impressions as to this most interesting problem which has been submitted to us." I knew that seclusion and solitude were very necessary for my friend in those dark hours of intense concentration during which he weighed every particle of evidence, constructed alternative theories, balanced one against the other, and made up his mind as to which points were essential and which immaterial.

I therefore accompanied Mr. Barlow in a hansom cab to fetch his Arizona arrival, saw the pair safely to the hotel, and returned promptly to our lodgings. There I retreated to my own quarters at the opposite end of the hallway, gladly washed my face in the basin and changed into my nightgown, and slipped into a deep slumber beneath the covers, pulling the quilts up around my ears to relieve the noise of the relentless wind.

On Tuesday morning I woke, somewhat later than my usual

custom, to sunlight streaming through the east-facing window of my bedroom and only the sounds of industry and society emanating from the street. A new day had begun on Houston Street.

It was nearly nine o'clock when I found myself in the sitting room once more. My first impression as I opened the door from the hallway was that a fire had broken out, for the room was so filled with smoke that the light of the lamp upon the table was blurred by it. As I entered, however, my fears were set at rest, for it was the fragrant but strong fumes of a heady cedar-and-sage mixture which took me by the throat and set me coughing. Through the haze I had a vague vision of Miles wrapped in a heavy woolen blanket and coiled up in an armchair, hands cupping a clay vessel of tea. Several rolls of paper lay around him. The fiddle and bow had been set aside on the footstool.

"Caught cold, Hooper?" said he.

"No, it's this fuliginous atmosphere."

"I suppose it is pretty thick, now that you mention it."

"Thick! It is intolerable."

"Open the window, then! You were about to step out for the newspaper and a morsel of breakfast at the Commercial Club?"

"My dear Miles!"

"Am I right?"

"Certainly, but how?" He laughed at my bewildered expression.

"There is a delightful freshness about you, Hooper, which makes it a pleasure to exercise any small powers which I possess at your expense. A gentleman is dressed to go forth on a fine autumn day, on which the weather has turned quite agreeable. His hair is combed back, his moustache is waxed, he wears his day coat over waistcoat and pocket watch to keep track of the time, he carries his glasses in his hand for reading, and his stomach is grumbling. Where, then, could he be heading? Is it not obvious?"

"Well, it is rather obvious."

"The world is full of obvious things which nobody by any chance ever observes. Now, where do you think that I have been?"

"A fixture in this sitting room, by the look of it."

"On the contrary, I have been to Dickens County."

"In spirit?"

"Exactly. My body has remained in this armchair and has, I regret to observe, consumed in my absence an entire pot of herbal tea and neglected the necessity of sleep. Already this morning I have sent down to the survey office for the relevant railroad map of West Texas, and my psyche has hovered over it for the past hour. I flatter myself that I could find my way about."

"A large-scale map, I presume?"

"Very large." He unrolled one section and held it over his knee. "Forgo your club plans and sit with me here instead, Hooper, and I will take you on the tour."

My stomach growled once more. I went to the kitchen, took out a cold biscuit from the night before and spread a layer of butter and honey on it, then returned and pulled up the footstool beside Miles.

"Here you have the particular region that concerns us. Dickens County, nine hundred square miles, most of it on the western half consumed by the enormous Spur Ranch, and isolated within its boundaries the hamlet of Espuela. In the center portion of the county, embracing thirty-eight checkerboarded sections by my count, is the Wolverton Ranch, with its headquarters here on the marge of the Croton Breaks."

"With the broken country, canyons, and mesas all around it?"

"Exactly. I fancy the trail down to the spring, though not marked under that name, must stretch along this line, with the breaks, as you perceive, to the south and east of it. Within a radius of twenty miles there are, as you see, only a very few scattered dwellings. Here is the Bar M, which was mentioned in the narrative. There is a structure indicated nearby which may be the residence of the geologist—Griswall, if I remember right. Two other ranch camps lie farther east, those of the Pitchfork and the Browning.

"To the west, you'll note the county of Crosby, where our friend Mr. Barlow resides. Although he lives and practices law in the settlement of Estacado, in the western portion, he farms several sections out here on the caprock, on the Dickens County boundary. Then eighteen miles south"—he drew his finger downward to indicate it—"lies the infamous town of Clairemont, a frontier den of vice and violence. All are places in which the rule of law has yet to be firmly established. Protection men for the ranches are the foremost enforcers of justice. The district judge visits county seats in his circuit twice yearly; in the interim, Judge Lynch and Judge Colt generally hold sway. In none of these towns exists any true jail or prison. Between and around these scattered points extend the desolate badlands. This, then, is the stage upon which tragedy has been played, and upon which we may help to play it again."

"It must be a wild place."

"Yes, the setting is a worthy one. If the devil did desire to have a hand in the affairs of men—"

"Then you are yourself inclining to the supernatural explanation."

"The devil's agents may be of flesh and blood, may they not?" He let the map snap back into a tight scroll. "There are two questions waiting for us at the outset. The one is whether any crime has been committed at all; the second is, if so, what is the crime and how was it committed? Of course, if Mr. Barlow's surmise should be correct, and we are dealing with forces outside the ordinary laws of Nature, our investigation comes swiftly to a dead end. But we are bound to exhaust all other hypotheses before falling back upon this one. I think we'll shut that window again, if you don't mind. It is a singular thing, but I find that a concentrated atmosphere helps a concentration of thought. I have not pushed it to the length of getting into a box to think, but I may yet resort to that expediency. Have you turned the case over in your mind?"

"Why, my dreams were filled with nothing else all night. It could have been the effect of the wind, of course."

"What do you make of it?"

"It is very bewildering."

"It has certainly a character of its own. There are points of distinction about it. That change in the footprints, for example. What do you make of that?"

"Barlow said that the man had walked on tiptoe down that portion of the path."

"He only repeated what some fool had said at the inquest. Why should a man walk on tiptoe down a trail? Especially if he's left his gun holstered in his saddle and his horse grazing idly, untethered?"

"What then?"

"He was *running*, Hooper—running desperately, running for his life, running until he burst his heart—and fell dead upon his face."

"Running from what?"

"There lies our problem. There are indications that the man was crazed with fear before ever he began to run."

"How can you say that?"

"I am presuming that the cause of his fears came to him from below, in the canyon. If that were so, and it seems most probable, only a man who had lost his wits would have run *from* the house instead of towards it. Then, again, for whom was he waiting that night, and why was he waiting for him at the ranch gate instead of inside his own house?"

"You think that he was waiting for someone?"

"The man was elderly and infirm. We can understand his taking the air at dusk and riding out to check his fences, but the ground was damp and the weather inclement. Is it natural that he should stand for five or ten minutes, as Mr. Barlow, with more practical sense than I should have given him credit for, deduced from the cigar ash?"

"But it's said he went out every evening."

"I think it unlikely that he waited at the ranch gate each time. On the contrary, the evidence is that he avoided the breaks. On that occasion he waited there. It was the night before he made his departure for Fort Worth. The thing takes shape, Hooper. It becomes coherent." He settled back in his chair and closed his eyes. "Might I ask you, while you finish your breakfast, to tell me your impressions of this Trey Wolverton we are soon to encounter?"

I expelled a deep breath and began to prepare him.

CHAPTER 4
THE LAST WOLVERTON

*{In which the heir to the Wolverton estate
comes to lunch in Fort Worth.}*

After an hour's debriefing I left Miles, whose own spirits seem to have been raised by the temperate morning and bright sky, to his bow and fiddle—an instrument he'd taken up, he once told me, when he learned that David Crockett himself had played the violin. Miles tended toward melancholy tunes in minor keys, but had on occasion been known to attempt the lively Bach partitas or the romantic airs of Herr Brahms, and when the mood struck him would break out into a folk tune worthy of a square dance. I did not remain long enough to discern which was the case today.

I instead eschewed the comforts of the Commercial Club and its hearty menu and betook myself to the library of our city's newly opened university. There I read voraciously for several hours on topics ranging from the geology of the Croton Breaks to the military expeditions against the Indians, from the listings in *Burke's Peerage* to the physiology of *canis lupus*. By the time our appointed hour arrived and I stepped out of the cab in front of the White Elephant, I felt sufficiently enlightened to acquit myself without embarrassment during luncheon conversation. Our clients turned the corner on foot and I, quickly recognizing Mr. Barlow and Mr. Wolverton from the previous evening, greeted them. Barlow appeared at once relieved to have arrived safely at our appointment and yet fretful, for he glanced about anxiously.

His companion shook my hand vigorously. Trey Wolverton, I

could now see more clearly, was an alert, dark-eyed young man, sturdily built and of average height, with thick black eyebrows and a strong, pugnacious face. The lighter tone of skin on his chin testified to a clean shave after some period of wearing a beard. In contrast to the stained duster in which he'd alighted from the train the previous night, he wore a neat and stylish brown tweed suit—albeit accessoried with the same scuffed and ragged Western boots I'd noted before. He bore the weather-beaten appearance of one who spends most of his time in the open air, and struck me as a man continually on the lookout for the next opponent.

I greeted them and opened the door for both men, then guided them to the corner where Miles was already seated at his customary table, reading the *Gazette*. He folded the paper and stood to acknowledge last night's acquaintance and today's newcomer.

"Welcome to Fort Worth, Mr. Wolverton," he said to the Earl's young nephew as he extended his hand.

"I go by Trey. I'm the third to bear the name of Basil Wolverton, though I never met the old geezer." He seemed then to recall his manners. "Begging your pardon, gentlemen. My dear, departed uncle."

"Pray take a seat, then, Trey. You look fit and rested for one who's made such a long journey—though I am very sorry for the circumstances that have made it necessary."

"Out in the territory, you learn to catch sleep when you can," our client responded as we all slid our upholstered chairs up to the mahogany table. "And as for the condolences, save 'em. My pop never wanted another thing to do with his older brother after he skipped out with all the money."

This was as interesting a revelation to Mr. Barlow as it was to Miles and me, I could readily discern.

Miles deftly turned the conversation, as the waiter arrived to ladle out an aromatic beef stew. "We shall all be interested to learn more on that account, Trey. For now, tell us—you've begun to make your career in mining?"

"Silver on a good day," he said as he tucked his napkin into his collar and spooned a heaping dose of the stew between his lips. "Salt on the other three hundred sixty-four."

I found such world-weary sentiment unusual in one of his apparent youth, but I left further questioning to my partner.

"Well, welcome to Texas," said Miles, "where we've been known to go to war on occasion over such things as salt."

Mr. Barlow explained, as mineral water and menus were brought, that Trey Wolverton had in fact spent some time in El Paso, where the infamous Salt War had taken place in seventy-seven. "Trey's father, Nigel Wolverton, suffered from tuberculosis and was sent there in the eighties to recover, I understand. Sadly, his health did not improve."

I nodded my head in some sympathy with the grief this young man must already have experienced during his brief span of years.

"But we will save more of the past for the future," continued Barlow. "For the present, young Trey has experienced a more minor, yet inexplicable, loss in the few hours since his arrival in Fort Worth, of which he wants to inform you."

Miles and I looked at the young man from each side, seizing him in our gaze as though in a pair of pincers.

"An inconvenience and a sore irritation, Captain Miles."

"Do tell," said Miles.

"Well, I don't know much of Fort Worth yet, since I've spent nearly all my time farther west. But I hope that to have one of your boots go missing is not part of the ordinary routine of life up here."

Miles expelled an indulgent sigh. "You have lost one of your boots, you say? Might you have simply mislaid it, after your late-night arrival?"

"Not a chance. You see, I knew I'd need new duds before coming to meet the esteemed Derrick Miles and Frank Hooper, and as soon as the mercantile opened this morning I dashed over to buy a new suit and boots. I returned to the hotel and set the boots outside the door for the steward. Even as cheap as they were, those Texas boots took a bite out of my purse, and you can imagine how irked I was to open the door again and find only one of them there. I never even had 'em on my feet!"

"If you have never worn them, why did you put them out to be cleaned?"

"They were made of rough tan rawhide and had never been varnished. I thought a quick polish might improve their looks."

"My dear sir," cried Mr. Barlow, "it must be only misplaced. You will find it when you return to the hotel, I am sure. What is the use of troubling Captain Miles with trifles of this kind?"

"Well, I figure the famous detective might want to know about anything out of the ordinary."

"Right you are," said Miles. "Let us keep the incident in mind as we acquaint ourselves with other aspects of the situation. But it does seem a singularly useless thing to steal. I confess that I share Mr. Barlow's belief that it will not be long before the missing boot is found. In the meantime, shall we order our entrées?"

No sooner had we done so than the mercurial Wolverton descendant called our attention to another odd matter—one that proved more disturbing, however, than the former.

"I apologize if my concern over a scrap of footwear seems out of line, gentlemen," he said. "But I want to show you a letter—more of a message, I suppose you'd call it—that I found slipped under the door this morning as I left. Maybe you'll understand, now, if I seem a bit out of sorts." He laid an envelope upon the table, and we all bent over it. It was made of common, unbleached paper. The address, "Basil Wolverton III, Pickwick Hotel," was inked in rough characters; the envelope bore no stamp or postmark. The apparent surprise on Mr. Barlow's face showed that like Miles and me, he was looking upon the item for the first time.

"Who knew that you were arriving in Fort Worth? And going to the Pickwick Hotel?" asked Miles, glancing keenly across at our visitor.

"No one but Mr. Barlow, as far as I know. Of course he was already lodged there."

"Someone seems to be deeply interested in your movements." Out of the squarish envelope Wolverton took a half sheet of foolscap folded into four. This he opened and spread flat upon the table. Across the middle of it a single sentence had been formed by the expedient of pasting scraps of printed paper upon it. I leaned over to read the words, which ran "keep away from Croton Breaks, as you value your life and reason." The word "Breaks" alone had been inserted in ink.

"Now, Captain Miles," said Trey Wolverton, jabbing his finger at the page, "perhaps you can figure out what in tarnation is the meaning of this, and who's taking such pains for my welfare?"

The ominous tone of the letter, and the clandestine means of its arrival, did put the matter of the boot in a different light.

"What do *you* make of it, Mr. Barlow?" said Miles instead. "You must allow that there is nothing supernatural about this, at any rate?"

"No, sir, but it might very well come from someone who was convinced that the business is supernatural."

"What business?" asked Trey Wolverton sharply. "It seems you guys know a great deal more than I do about my own affairs."

"You shall share our knowledge before you leave this room, Trey. I promise you that," said Miles. "With your permission we will confine ourselves for the moment to this very interesting document, which must have been put together and delivered early this morning." He lifted his newspaper from the table, folded it again to the front page, and ran his eye swiftly down the columns of type.

"Intriguing article here, on free trade. Permit me to give you an extract from it. 'You may be cajoled into imagining that your own special trade or your own industry will be encouraged by a protective tariff, but it stands to reason that such legislation must in the long run keep away wealth from the country, diminish the value of our imports, and lower the general conditions of life in this nation.' What do you think of that, Hooper?" cried Miles in high glee, rubbing his hands together with satisfaction. "Don't you find that is an admirable sentiment?"

Mr. Barlow looked at Miles with an air of professional interest, and Trey Wolverton turned a pair of puzzled dark eyes upon me.

"I don't know much about the tariff and things of that kind," said Wolverton, "but it seems to me we've wandered a ways off the trail so far as that damned note is concerned."

"On the contrary, I think we are particularly hot upon the trail, Mr. Wolverton. Hooper here knows more about my methods than you do, but I fear that even he has not quite grasped the significance of this sentence."

"No," said I, "I confess that I see no connection."

"And yet, my dear Hooper, there is so very close a connection that the one is extracted out of the other. 'You,' 'your,' 'your,' 'life,' 'value,' 'reason,' 'keep away,' 'from the.' Don't you see now the source of these words?"

Wolverton snapped it up. "By damn, you're right! Well, if that isn't smart!" he cried. "If any possible doubt remained it is settled by the fact that 'keep away' and 'from the' are each found together in one piece."

"Well, now—so it is," mused Barlow. "Really, Captain Miles, this exceeds anything which I could have imagined," he said, gazing at my friend in amazement. "I could understand anyone saying that the words were from a newspaper; but that you've identified the right issue, and recognize that it came from the leading article, is really one of the most remarkable things I've ever witnessed."

"Maybe you haven't witnessed much," said Wolverton uncharitably to Barlow. "What's your secret, Miles?"

Miles responded, "I presume, sir, that you could tell iron pyrites from true gold-bearing ore?"

"Absolutely."

"And how?"

"Because that's the field in which I spend most of my days. The differences are obvious. Pyrites have hard, angular edges; gold is softer and rounder. Pyrite scratches copper, while gold—"

"So you see that detection is my special hobby, and the differences are equally obvious. There is as much difference to my eyes between the leaded bourgeois type of a *Gazette* article and the slovenly print of a tabloid as there could be between your fool's gold and the real thing. The detection of types is one of the most elementary branches of knowledge to the special expert in crime, though I confess that once when I was very young I confused the Austin *American* with the Athens *Herald*. But a lead article in the *Gazette* is entirely distinctive, and these words could have been taken from nowhere else. As it was delivered to you this morning, the strong probability was that we should find the words in either today's or yesterday's issue."

"So far as I can follow you, then, Captain Miles," said Wolverton, "someone cut out this message with scissors—"

"Penknife," said Miles. "You can see that it had a very short blade, since the cutter had to take two snips over 'keep away.'"

"That is so. Someone, then, cut out the message with a

penknife, pasted it with paste—"

"Gum," said Miles.

"With gum on to the paper. But I want to know why the word 'Breaks' was written in ink?"

"Because the sender could not find it in print. Most of the other words were all simple and might be found in any issue, but 'Breaks' would be less common."

"Why, of course, that would explain it," said Barlow, ever the peacemaker. "Have you read anything else in this message, Captain Miles?"

"A couple of other important indications leap from the page—though pains have been taken to remove all clues. Do you observe the address, printed in rough capitals rather than script? But unlike afternoon papers, the morning paper is most often found in the hands of the industrious and ambitious. We may take it, therefore, that the letter was composed by an educated man who wished to pose as an unsophisticated one, and his effort to conceal his own writing suggests that that writing might be known, or come to be known, by you. Again, you will observe that the words are not gummed on in an accurate line, but that some are much higher than others. 'Life,' for example is quite out of its proper place. All this may point to carelessness or it may point to agitation and hurry upon the part of the cutter. On the whole I incline to the latter view, since the matter was evidently important, and it is unlikely that the composer of such a letter would be careless. If he were in a hurry it opens up the interesting question *why* he should be. Did the composer fear an interruption—and from whom?"

"We are coming now rather into the region of guesswork," said Mr. Barlow.

"Say, rather, into the region where we balance probabilities and choose the most likely. It is the scientific use of the imagination, but we have always some material basis on which to start our speculation. Now, you would call it a guess, no doubt, but I am almost certain that this address has been written in a hotel."

"How in the world can you say that?"

"If you examine it carefully you will see that both the pen and the ink have given the writer trouble. The pen has spluttered twice in a single word and has run dry three times in a short address, showing that there was very little ink in the bottle. Now, a private pen or ink bottle is seldom allowed to be in such a state, and the combination of the two must be quite rare. But you know the hotel ink and the hotel pen, where it is rare to get anything else. Yes, I have very little hesitation in saying that could we examine the wastebaskets of the hotels around the courthouse square until we found the remains of the mutilated *Gazette* editorial we could lay our hands straight upon the person who sent this singular message."

"Why are we sitting around waiting for lunch, then?" said Wolverton. "Let's go around and search!"

"Not so fast. There's another important bit of evidence here—embodied not in the words themselves, but in the gaps between them." Miles allowed Wolverton to examine the letter for a few seconds before directing his attention to one particular word. "What can you discern there?" Wolverton leaned closer for a second, then jumped upon it first. "Why, the name 'Croton' is cut right in half," he cried, pleased with himself. "And the letter shapes all look different from the other words."

"Precisely. It was doubtless lifted from another document—one in which two parts of the word occur."

"And a capital letter, to boot," I added.

"Well, Captain, what do you say to that?" said Wolverton. "Where does this leave us, besides sitting here debating over details while a prankster—or even a criminal—gets away?"

"I confess that I don't immediately recognize the source of these two clippings. But it won't prevent us from scouring the trash bins of the Pickwick Hotel while we ponder on it." Miles set down his fork, snapped his fingers for the check, and stood swiftly. "Wolverton, let's see if we can't get to the bottom of the matter."

"Wait a second," said Barlow, who had picked up the letter and was holding it close to his nose and peering through his wire-framed eyeglasses. "I think I know the answer." He lowered the page slowly, and with a puzzled expression, said, "This part was taken from the name 'Crosbyton'—in our own locally printed *Crosby County News*!"

Miles slipped back into his seat again and turned to the Quaker with an expression of genuine admiration. "I believe you have supplied an essential piece of the puzzle, Mr. Barlow. Now we must discover what it all means."

"Before you all burn more daylight on your sleuthing," said Wolverton with derision, "it seems high time you kept your promise and gave me a full account of what we are all driving at."

"Your request is a very reasonable one," Miles answered. "Mr. Barlow, I think you could not do better than to tell your story as you told it to us."

Thus encouraged, the country lawyer drew his papers from his pocket and presented the whole case as he had done upon the evening before. Wolverton listened with the deepest attention and with an occasional exclamation of surprise that won out over his skepticism.

"Well, I seem to have come into an inheritance with a vengeance," said he when the long narrative was finished. "Of course, I've heard the dire wolf story ever since I was in knee britches, but I never thought of taking it seriously before. But as to my uncle's death—well, it all seems boiling up in my head, and I can't get it clear yet. You gents don't seem quite to have made up your own minds whether it's a case for a policeman or a clergyman."

"Indeed," said Miles.

"And now there's this strange affair of the letter to me at the hotel. I suppose that fits into its place."

"It seems to show that someone knows more than we do about what goes on in Dickens County," said Mr. Barlow.

"And also," said Miles, "that someone is not ill-disposed towards you, since they warn you of danger."

"Or it could be some crook's scam to scare me away. You can't fool me with that one—I've seen a few fake warning signs posted near mine sites."

"Well, of course, that is possible also. I am very much indebted to you, Mr. Barlow, for introducing me to a problem which presents several interesting alternatives. But the practical point which we now have to decide, Mr. Wolverton, is whether it is or is not advisable for you to travel to the Wolverton ranch house."

"Why should I *not* go?"

"There seems to be genuine danger."

"Do you mean from this family fiend or from human beings?"

"Well, that is what we have to find out."

"Whichever it is, my mind's made up. There's no devil in Dickens and no man on earth either one who can prevent me from going to the home of my own people, and you can take that to the bank." His dark brows knitted and his face flushed to a dusky red as he spoke. It was evident that the fiery temper of the Wolvertons was not extinct in this, their last representative.

"As you wish, of course," said Miles.

Wolverton stood and pulled a dollar from his pocket, which he laid on the table to pay his bill before Miles could even reach for his own wallet. "Time's wasting, if you ask me. It's almost three now, and if I'm going to catch a westbound train anytime soon, I'd better go see if I can find that missing boot."

With that the hotheaded young man was out the door, leaving the three of us scrambling to pay up and collect our hats and coats. By the time we stepped out of the White Elephant onto the plank sidewalk, Wolverton had more than a block's lead on us.

"Shall I flag down a cab and catch up with him?" I asked Miles. "Or run on and stop him?"

"Neither," Miles answered. "It's a fine day for a walk. Let our young heir release some of the steam he's been building up."

It took some effort to match Wolverton's determined pace, which our trio did, keeping some twenty yards behind. As our charge turned onto Main Street a block ahead of us and the streetcar momentarily blocked our view, we lost track of him for a time, and then found him again. Miles called my attention quickly to a hansom cab, carrying a man inside, which was proceeding down the street just behind Wolverton, the driver moving slowly in order to match his speed to the pedestrian's step and following only a few feet behind him.

"What do you make of this, Hooper? Come quick! Let's have a good look at the occupant—Mr. Barlow, forgive us."

The two of us broke into a run, leaving the Quaker behind, and raced to catch up with the cab. We were almost upon him, closing the distance between us and Wolverton, when the vehicle slowed to a halt. At that instant I was aware of a bushy black beard and a pair of piercing eyes turned upon us through the cab's side window. Instantly the trapdoor at the top flew up, and something was screamed to the driver, who clicked the reins and flew madly off up Main. Miles looked eagerly around for another, but no empty one was in sight. Then he dashed in wild pursuit on foot amid the stream of the traffic, but the carriage's start was too great, and already it was out of sight.

"There now!" said Miles bitterly as he returned, panting and white with vexation from the tide of buggies and buckboards, to the corner where I stood waiting for Mr. Barlow.

"Was ever such bad luck and such bad management, too? Hooper, Hooper, if you are an honest man you will record this episode also and set it against my successes!"

"Who was the man?"

"I have not an inkling."

"A spy?"

"Well, it was evident from what we have heard that Wolverton has been very closely shadowed by someone since he has been in town. How else could it be known so quickly that it was the Pickwick Hotel which he had chosen? If they had followed him the first night I argued that they would follow him also the next day. You may have observed that I twice strolled over to the window while Mr. Barlow was reading his legend."

"Yes, I remember."

"I was looking out for loiterers in the street, but I saw none. We are dealing with a clever man, Hooper. This matter cuts very deep, and though I have not finally made up my mind whether it is a benevolent or a malevolent agency which is in touch with us, I am conscious always of power and design. When our friend left I at once followed him in the hopes of spotting his invisible attendant. So wily was the man that he had not trusted himself upon foot, but availed himself of a cab so that he could loiter behind or dash past his mark and so escape his notice. His method had the additional advantage that if Wolverton had chosen to take a cab he was all ready to follow them. It has, however, one obvious disadvantage."

"It puts him in the power of the driver."

"Exactly."

"What a pity we did not get the number!"

"My dear Hooper, clumsy as I have been, you surely do not seriously imagine that I neglected to get the number? Number

304 is our man. But that is no use to us for the moment."

"I fail to see how you could have done more."

"On observing the cab I should have instantly turned and walked in the other direction. I should then at my leisure have hired a second cab and followed the first at a respectful distance, or, better still, have driven to the Pickwick Hotel and waited there. When our unknown had followed Wolverton to his lodgings we should have had the opportunity of playing his own game upon himself and seeing where he made for. As it is, by an indiscreet eagerness, which was taken advantage of with extraordinary quickness and energy by our opponent, we have betrayed ourselves and lost our man." As we waited, Mr. Barlow at last caught up with us.

"There is no object in our following them," said Miles, straightening his cravat and turning to acknowledge Barlow's presence. "The shadow has departed and will not return. We must see what further cards we have in our hands and play them with decision. Could you swear to that man's face within the cab, Hooper?"

"I could swear only to the beard."

"And I could wager it was a false one. A clever man upon so delicate an errand has no use for a beard save to conceal his features. Let's step in here, gentlemen, before we return to the Pickwick." We found ourselves in the Western Union telegraph's main office, where Miles was warmly greeted by the manager.

"Ah, Mr. Schneider, I see you have not forgotten the little case in which I had the good fortune to help you?" said Miles.

"No, sir, indeed I have not. You saved my good name, and perhaps my life."

"My dear Fritz, you exaggerate. Now, I have some recollection that you had among your errand boys a lad named Cartwright, who showed some ability during the investigation."

"Yes, sir, he is still with us."

"Could you summon him, if he happens to be on duty?—Thank you! And perhaps you'd be so kind as to change this two-dollar note for five-cent pieces." As Miles penciled in a brief telegram and handed it to Mr. Schneider, a boy looking to be in his mid-teens, dressed neatly and with a bright, keen face, arrived from somewhere in the back office. He stood now gazing with great reverence at the famous detective.

"Let me have the city directory," said Miles. He opened the booklet to a certain page and, thanking the manager, turned to the boy. "Now, Cartwright, there are the names of a dozen hotels here, all in the immediate neighborhood of the Union Depot. Do you see?"

"Yes, sir."

"You are to visit each of these in turn."

"Yes, sir."

"You will begin in each case by giving the outside porter one nickel. Here are twelve coins."

"Yes, sir."

"You will tell him that you want to see the wastepaper of this morning. You will say that an important message has been lost and that you are looking for it. You understand?"

"Yes, sir."

"But what you are really looking for is the front page of the *Gazette* with some small holes cut in it. Here is a copy of the paper; it is this page. You could easily recognize it, could you not?"

"Yes, sir."

"In each case the outside porter will send for the hall porter, to whom also you will give a nickel. Here are a dozen more. You will then learn in possibly ten cases out of the twelve that the waste of this morning has already been burned or removed. In the two other cases you will be shown a heap of paper and you will look for this page among it. The odds are enormously

The Wolf Hunt: A Tale of the Texas Badlands

against your finding it, so do not be discouraged. There are sixteen nickels left over in case of emergencies. Let me have a report by wire at Houston Street before evening." He sent the lad on his way and returned his attention to us. "And now it only remains for us to find out the identity of the cabman, No. 304, and then we will return to the Pickwick and reunite with Mr. Wolverton."

Mr. Barlow expressed relief at this plan, and our bedraggled, dusty party turned at last onto Eighteenth Street for the last few blocks' walk to the hotel.

There, before we could even ring for Wolverton, to my surprise the cabman Miles was seeking was already waiting, seated uneasily in the foyer, livery cap in hand.

"I got a message from the head office that a gent at this hotel had inquired for No. 304," said he. "I've driven my cab this seven years and never a word of complaint. I came here straight from the cab yard to ask you to your face what you had against me."

"I have nothing in the world against you, my good man," said Miles. "On the contrary, I'm impressed with your prompt response to my telegram. And I have a silver dollar for you if you will give me a clear answer to my questions."

"Well, in that case," said the cabman with a grin, "what was it you wanted to ask, sir?"

"First of all your name and address, in case I want you again."

"John Spiller, 24 Crump Street, over by the Fort Worth & Denver shops. My cab is out of Mason's Livery, near Union Station. It's just three blocks from here, which is why I came in person." Miles made a note of it.

"Now, Spiller, tell me all about the fare who came and watched the White Elephant Saloon at two o'clock this afternoon and afterwards followed a particular gentleman down

Main Street." The man looked surprised and a little embarrassed.

"Why, there's no good my telling you things, for you seem to know as much as I do already," said he. "I ain't in the custom of breaking confidences. The truth is that the man told me that he was a detective and that I was to say nothing about him to anyone."

"My good fellow, this is a very serious business, and you may find yourself in a pretty bad position if you try to hide anything from me. You say that your fare told you he was a detective?"

"That's right, sir."

"Excellent! Tell me where you picked him up and all that occurred."

"He hailed me at half past nine beside the streetcar line across from the Southern Hotel. He said that he was a detective, and he offered me two bucks if I would do exactly what he wanted all day and ask no questions. Two dollars—a week's wages for me, sir! I was glad enough to agree. First we drove down to the Pickwick Hotel and waited there until two gentlemen came out and hailed a hackney from the street. We followed their cab a little behind until it pulled up at the White Elephant and the two men got out."

"At what time?" said Miles.

"Right at one o'clock. We watched the men enter the restaurant, then my fare instructed me to wait within view of the door. An hour and a half later I was having a time of it, keeping awake in the box, when all of a sudden one of the men stepped out and started west on Main at a fast clip. The detective signaled me to keep up with him. We continued straight ahead until—"

"I know," said Miles.

"Until we got three-quarters down Main. Then my fare threw up the trap, and he shouted that I should drive right away to the Union Depot as hard as I could go. I whipped up the mare and we were there in under five minutes. Then he paid up his two bucks and a tip to boot, and away he went into the station. Only just as he was leaving he turned around and looked up at me and he said: 'It might interest you to know that you have been driving a detective of great renown.' "

"Did he say anything more?"

"He gave his name."

Miles cast a swift glance of triumph at me. "Oh, he gave his name, did he? That was imprudent. And what was the name that he mentioned?"

"He told me," said the cabman, "that I had been driving Captain Derrick Miles."

Never have I seen my friend more completely taken aback than by the cabman's reply. For an instant he sat in silent amazement, as Mr. Barlow looked on in confusion. Then he burst into a hearty laugh.

"A touch, Hooper—an undeniable touch!" said he. "I feel a foil as quick and supple as my own. He has hit home upon me very prettily! So his name was Derrick Miles, was it?"

"Yes, sir, that was the gentleman's name."

"I see. And you saw no more of him?"

"Not after he went into the station."

"And how would you describe Mr. Derrick Miles?" The cabman scratched his head.

"Well, he wasn't altogether such an easy person to describe. I'd put him at forty years of age, and he was of a middle height, two or three inches shorter than you, sir. He was dressed like a dandy, and he had a black beard, cut square at the end, and a pale face. I don't know as I could say more than that."

"Color of his eyes?"

"No, I can't say that."

"Nothing more that you can remember?"

"No, sir; not a thing."

"Well, then, here is your coin. There's another two bits waiting for you if you can deliver any more information. You'll find the listing for Derrick Miles, Consulting Detective, in the city directory."

Spiller raised his eyebrows in surprise. "You fellows work for him?"

"You might say that."

"Well, it's been quite a day, then. Good afternoon, sir, and thank you!" John Spiller departed chuckling, and Miles turned to me with a shrug of his shoulders and a rueful smile.

Chapter 5
Three Broken Threads

{In which Derrick Miles and Frank Hooper discuss mysteries of hats, boots, and guns.}

No sooner had we bid good-bye to the befuddled cab driver at the Pickwick than Trey Wolverton himself appeared, stamping down the stairs in a huff. His face was flushed with anger, and in his hands he carried an old and dusty boot. So furious was he that he was hardly articulate, and when he did speak it was in a much more rushed and agitated tone than any which we had heard from him earlier.

"Seems to me they're playing me for a sucker in this damned hotel," he cried. "They'll find they've monkeyed with the wrong man unless they're careful. By thunder, if that ignoramus can't find my missing boot there's going to be trouble. I can take a joke with the best, Captain Miles, but they've stepped over the line this time."

"Still looking for your boot?"

"Yes, sir, and I mean to find it."

"But didn't I recall you said it was a new brown boot?"

"So it was. And now it's an old black one," Wolverton said, waving it in our faces for proof.

"What! You don't mean to say—?"

"That's just what I do mean to say. I only had three pairs to my name—the new brown, my black dress boots, and the work boots which I am now wearing again. This morning they took one of my brown ones, and this afternoon they have sneaked one of the black."

An agitated bellman had appeared upon the scene, and

Wolverton practically accosted him. "Well, have you got it? Speak out, mister, and don't stand staring!"

"No, sir; I have asked all over the hotel, but I haven't heard a word about it."

"Well, either that boot comes back before sundown or I'll see the manager and tell him there are twenty other hotels in this city and it's the last he'll see of my money at this one."

"It shall be found, sir—I promise if you have a little patience it'll be found."

"See to it, for it's the last thing of mine that I'll lose in this den of thieves. Captain Miles, you'll excuse my troubling you about such a trifle—"

"I think it's well worth troubling about."

"Why, you look very serious over it."

"How do you explain it?"

"I just don't attempt to explain it. It seems the very queerest, most maddening thing that ever happened to me."

"The queerest perhaps—" said Miles thoughtfully.

"What do you make of it yourself?"

"Well, I don't profess to understand it yet. This case of yours is very complex, Mr. Wolverton. When taken in conjunction with your uncle's death I am not sure that among the scores of major cases which I have handled there is one which cuts so deep. But we hold several threads in our hands, and the odds are that one or other of them guides us to the truth. If we persist, sooner or later we must come upon the right."

It was in our client's private sitting room to which we afterwards repaired that Miles asked Wolverton of his intentions. It took little effort to observe that he had been busying himself repacking a trunk and valise that had been unpacked less than twenty-four hours before.

"You're making preparations to go?" Barlow asked him.

"You'd better believe it. If this godforsaken place is the best Texas has to offer, I might as well go ahead and get the rest over with."

"So you're determined to go to the Wolverton ranch house," Miles said, an observation rather than a question.

"As soon as I can get a train out of here."

"On the whole," said Miles, "I think your decision is a wise one. I have ample evidence that you are being dogged in Fort Worth, and amid the throngs of this city it is difficult to discover who these people are or what their object can be. If their intentions are evil they might do you a mischief, and we should be powerless to prevent it. You did not know, Mr. Wolverton, that you were followed shortly ago from the restaurant?"

"Followed! By whom?"

"That, unfortunately, is what I cannot tell you. But let's start nearest to Basil Wolverton's environs. Mr. Barlow, have you among your neighbors or acquaintances in Dickens County or thereabouts seen any man with a black, full beard?"

"No—or, let me see—why, yes. Antonío López, the Earl's ranch manager, is dark-haired, and he wears a beard."

"Ha! Where is López?"

"He is in charge of the ranch house and is there, I presume."

"We had best ascertain if he in truth is, or if by any possibility he might be in Fort Worth."

"How can you do that?"

"I don't suppose there is a telephone."

"No, I'm afraid we have no such big-city conveniences in our vicinity. But there is a telegraph strung across the fence posts to Espuela, ten miles away; that's the closest one, and they could send a rider out."

"Give me a telegraph form from that desk, then. 'Is all ready for Trey Wolverton?' That will do." Turning to Barlow, he asked for the addressee's information. "Very good. Address to Antonío

López, the Wolverton ranch house. Send to Es–*pue*–la, Texas," he pronounced aloud as he wrote. "As the locals call it," he said, turning to Barlow with a wry smile.

"I suppose it's not a bad idea to wire ahead in any case," I said.

"Now, we will send a second wire to the postmaster at Espuela: 'Telegram to Antonío López to be delivered into his own hand. If absent, please return wire to Trey Wolverton, Pickwick Hotel, Fort Worth.' That should let us know before morning whether López is at his post in Dickens County or not."

"Makes sense to me," said Wolverton.

"While we are at it, Mr. Barlow, can you tell me more about this López?"

"He is the son of the original ranch manager, who died a decade ago. They have looked after the ranch since before the Earl acquired it. So far as I know, he and his wife are as respectable a couple as any in the county, and they've always seemed quite devoted to their duties."

"At the same time," said Wolverton, "if there's no member of the owner's family around, they've got free rein to do as they choose."

"That is true, I suppose."

"Will López profit in any way by Sir Basil's will?" asked Miles.

"He and his wife stand to receive a tidy sum," Barlow responded. "It's a generous bequest. But of course the will has not been read yet."

"Ha! Did they know this bequest would come their way?"

"I do not see how they could have known; Sir Basil wanted his intentions kept private, even from family."

"That is very interesting."

"I hope," said Barlow, "that thee does not look with suspicious eyes upon everyone who received a legacy from Sir Basil, for I also had a portion of land left to me."

"Indeed! And anyone else?"

"There were many sums, some nominal, some generous, to individuals, and a few public charities. The residue all goes to Trey Wolverton."

"And how much do you calculate that to be?"

"Seven hundred and forty thousand dollars."

The heir to this considerable wealth raised his eyebrows in surprise. "I had no idea that so impressive a figure was involved," said Wolverton.

"Sir Basil had the reputation of being well off, but I did not know how very rich he was until I came to examine his securities a few weeks ago," Barlow explained. "The total value of the estate is close on to a million."

"Dear me!" exclaimed Miles. "It is a stake for which a man might well play a desperate game. And one more question, Mr. Barlow. Supposing that anything happened to our young friend here—you will forgive the unpleasant hypothesis—who would inherit the estate?"

"Since Nigel Wolverton, Sir Basil's brother, and his half-brother, Randall, died unmarried, the estate would descend to the Grahams, who are distant cousins. Hugh Graham is a cotton broker in Nacogdoches, quite advanced in age."

"Thank you. These details are all of great interest. Have you met this Hugh Graham?"

"Yes; he once came down to visit Sir Basil. He is a man of venerable appearance and of saintly life. I remember that he refused to accept any settlement from Sir Basil, though the Earl pressed it upon him."

"And this man of simple tastes would inherit Sir Basil's fortune."

"He would be the heir to the money as well as the ranch unless it were willed otherwise by the present owner, who can, of course, do what he likes with it."

"And have you made a will of your own, Trey?"

Wolverton expressed a wry laugh. "No, Captain Miles, I have never given the matter a moment's thought. A man who moves from town to town in mining camps and hasn't yet seen a boon from his efforts hardly puts that task at the top of his list."

"Quite so. Well, Trey, I am of one mind with you as to the advisability of your going down to Dickens County without delay—*after* writing out a holographic will. There is only one provision which I must make. You certainly must not go alone."

"Mr. Barlow returns with me."

"But Mr. Barlow has his farm to attend to, and his house is a good two hours' ride from yours. With all the goodwill in the world he may be unable to help you. No, Trey, you must take with you someone, a trusty man, who will be always by your side."

"Wouldn't you come yourself, Captain Miles?"

"I had hoped to, until only an hour ago," he replied. "You can understand that, with my extensive consulting practice and with the constant appeals which reach me from many quarters, it is often not practical for me to be absent from Fort Worth for an indefinite time. At the present instant one of the most revered names in Texas is being besmirched by a blackmailer, and my aid has been requested to prevent a disastrous scandal. You will see how impossible it is for me to go to Dickens County."

"Well, that's a fine kettle of fish. Looks like I've wasted a good bit of time and you've wasted mine. What do you recommend?" Wolverton said sharply.

"If my friend and associate Dr. Hooper would undertake it, there is no man who is better worth having at your side when you are in a tight place. No one can say so more confidently than I."

The proposition took me completely by surprise, but before I had time to answer, Wolverton turned his gaze on me as though he were sizing me up for the job.

"No offense, Dr. Hooper, but I wasn't looking for a babysitter. And I can't make any claim for what we'd be walking into."

"I assure you," said Miles, "that Frank Hooper is a man I'd trust with my own life. And when a crisis comes, as it inevitably will, I'll be available to advise."

Such confidence in my qualities, Miles had rarely voiced aloud. I could only follow his lead. "Captain Miles flatters me, but he does not exaggerate my dedication to duty," I said. "I'm happy to place myself at your service."

"Well, now, that is real kind of you, Dr. Hooper," said Wolverton with obvious irony. "If you're so inclined, well, I guess we'll just have a jolly old jaunt out to the breaks country."

"I do not know how I could employ my time better."

"And you will report very carefully to me," said Miles. "Now, if there's been no change in the railway timetable, tomorrow morning's 7:13 Texas & Pacific for Cisco and the spur up to Albany would be your best bet, taking the mail hack from there to Clairemont and on to Espuela. What say you, Mr. Barlow—two days' journey?"

"Yes, and happy I will be to make it. My wife and work await."

"Splendid. Then tomorrow at seven, unless you hear to the contrary, we shall meet at the Union Depot, and we shall know if there has been word from the ranch also." We had risen to depart when Wolverton gave a shout of triumph, and diving into one of the corners of the room he drew a brown boot from under the mirrored wardrobe.

"My missing boot!" he cried.

"May all our difficulties vanish as easily!" said Derrick Miles.

"But it is a very singular thing," Barlow remarked. "I searched this room carefully myself before lunch."

"And so did I," said Wolverton. "Every inch of it. That sorry porter must have put it there while we were out, hoping to dodge the blame!" The porter in question was sent for but professed to know nothing of the matter, nor could any inquiry clear it up, and we left our two clients still in consternation.

Another item had been added to that constant and apparently purposeless series of small mysteries which had succeeded each other so rapidly. The whole grim story of Sir Basil's death aside, we had had a line of inexplicable incidents all within the limits of a single day: the printed letter, the black-bearded spy in the hansom, the loss of the new brown boot, the loss of the old black boot, and now the return of the new brown boot.

Miles remained silent in the cab as we drove back to Houston Street, and I knew from his drawn brows and keen face that his mind, like my own, was busy in endeavoring to frame some scheme into which all these strange and apparently disconnected episodes could be fitted. Into the early evening he sat lost in tobacco and thought, while I busied myself in packing.

I set my satchel, valise, and large camera case by the door, ready for the morning's mission. But I could no longer hold back the question that had been burning in my mind throughout the afternoon.

"You know very well that I am amenable to any assignment with which you decide to entrust me," I said to my esteemed partner. "But this arrangement seems unprecedented, do you not agree?"

"An unprecedented stratagem may be just the thing in an unprecedented case," Miles said quixotically. "And an accessory captured alive is certainly far more useful than one captured dead. A target may fly from the trap for a kill—but a trap may also be laid to keep a target from flying."

I shook my head, certain only that I would receive no sensible insight this night.

Just before dinner the Western Union messenger rang the

doorbell, and almost at the same time the telephone rang. Miles took the call while I read the telegram: "Visited 12 hotels, sorry unable to trace Gazette sheet. CARTWRIGHT."

"That was Wolverton calling from the hotel, Hooper. He received the return telegram reporting that López is at the ranch. There go two of my threads, Hooper. There is nothing more stimulating than a case where everything goes against you. We must cast round for another scent."

"We have still the cabman who drove the spy."

"Who either made a lucky guess, or spotted me on Main Street before deciding to pull his prank. I tell you, Hooper, this time we have got a foeman who is worthy of our steel. I've been checkmated in Fort Worth. I can only wish you better luck in Dickens County. But I'm not easy in my mind about it."

"About what?"

"About sending you. It's an ugly business, Hooper, an ugly and dangerous business, and I can only hope for a speedy resolution to it. Yes, my dear fellow, you may laugh, but I give you my word that I shall be very glad to have you back safe and sound at Houston Street once more."

CHAPTER 6
TO THE WOLVERTON RANCH

{In which three men undertake a journey to the Croton Breaks of Dickens County.}

It was still dark the following morning when Mrs. Simpson's boy brought down my luggage to the waiting hansom cab, and the wind was beginning to whip up. Derrick Miles rode with me to the station and gave me his parting injunctions and advice, which struck me as not unlike the farewell of an officer dispatching his scout on a treacherous mission.

"I will not bias your mind by suggesting theories or suspicions, Hooper," said he; "I wish you simply to report facts in the fullest possible manner to me, and you can leave me to do the theorizing."

"What sort of facts?" I asked.

"Anything which may seem to have a bearing, however indirect, upon the case, and especially the relations between young Wolverton and his neighbors or any fresh particulars concerning the death of Sir Basil. I plan to make some inquiries myself as you are en route. One subject of my investigation will be Mr. Hugh Graham, the next heir, to ascertain that this persecution does not arise from him. I really think that we may eliminate him entirely from our calculations. On your end, there remain the people who surround the Wolverton ranch in the region of the Croton Breaks."

"Would it not be wise for Trey Wolverton to fire this López couple?"

"By no means. He could not make a greater mistake. If they are innocent it would be a cruel injustice, and if they are guilty we should be giving up all chance of bringing it home to them. No, no, we will preserve them upon our list of suspects. Then there are the local ranchers and farmers. There is our friend Mr. Barlow, whom I believe to be entirely honest, and there is his wife, of whom we know nothing. There are this geologist, Griswall, and the old judge, McQuarrie, who is also an unknown factor, and one or two other neighbors. These are the folk who must be your very special study."

"I will do my best."

"You are armed?"

"Yes, I thought it as well."

"Most certainly. Keep your revolver near you night and day, and never relax your precautions."

Our clients were waiting for us on the platform at the appointed hour, Mr. Wolverton in a black workman's cap and Mr. Barlow in his wide-awake, trailing his dog on a leash. The men assured us they not been shadowed during their short drive to the station.

"I beg you, Wolverton," said Miles, "do not go about alone during your journey or upon your arrival, lest great misfortune befall you. Hooper is here to keep watch and pursue the case. And by the way—did you get your other boot?"

"Nope; I grilled the hotel manager last night, but I suspect it's gone forever."

"Indeed. That is very interesting. Well, good-bye and safe travels," he added as the train began to glide down the platform. "Bear in mind, Wolverton, one of the phrases in that old story which Mr. Barlow has told us, and *avoid the breaks in those hours of darkness when the powers of evil are exalted.*"

I looked back at the platform when we had left it far behind and saw the tall, austere figure of Miles standing motionless and gazing after us. I considered for a long moment the numerous occasions on which he and I had embarked together from this very station, launching out into a new investigation and a fresh challenge, and I felt not a little unease at the responsibility that had been placed on my shoulders alone this time.

The morning grew light as we sped westward with the sun, and I spent it in finishing the breakfast sandwich and fruit I had ordered from the porter and in fending off Mr. Barlow's dog, which chose my lap for its resting place as though it, too, sensed the trepidation that lay over us all.

It was Mr. Barlow, seated next to me, who broke the tense silence that had been punctuated only by the rhythmic clack of wheel over rail. "Well, I must say that my foray into Fort Worth has resulted in more questions than answers so far. I for one will welcome a familiar country and a familiar bed—even if more investigation awaits us," he said to me.

"Yes," I said, "we have a greater mystery looming before us than the one you first brought to our door—to wit, how are recent strange events connected with any possible threat to Wolverton's well-being, and what agents or events might lie behind Sir Basil's demise? We must follow the tested methods of Derrick Miles with a keen analytical eye and logical deduction." At this, Wolverton, dozing with his head against the corner of the seat opposite us, cocked one eye partly open but promptly closed it again.

"What can thee tell me about the scope of Captain Miles's renowned abilities, and how he came to possess them?" asked Barlow.

"It is a very good question, and seeing as how we have a journey of four hours ahead of us until we reach the station at Cisco, I will endeavor to impart what I know from his accounts and my own observation." Thus as the landscape outside our window changed from towering pecan trees and rolling green meadows into sere hillocks of stunted cedar, shinnery, and buffalo grass, I related the story as I understood it.

"Derrick Miles, you must understand, is a singular character of singular intellect. This I appreciated instantly, upon my first encounter with him more than fifteen years ago. He was but twenty-two then, yet already tested by military experience in the field during the brief and bloody Red River War; already wise in the ways of the criminal mind, as an apprentice to Great Britain's finest counter-forgery team in Scotland Yard, thanks to the connections of his older half-brother in London; already an adept student in numerous academic disciplines, yet holder of a degree in none.

"I can tell you, for instance, that his knowledge of the natural and physical sciences is profound: chemistry, botany, zoology, human and animal anatomy and physiology, for instance. And geology? Why, observing dirt stains upon a man's trouser hem, he can tell by their color and consistency in what part of the world the wearer has received them. He is well acquainted with plants and poisons and their uses, though I would hardly say he has any attraction to gardening or farming. I should add in all fairness that in the humanities he is less proficient, and it is here—if I may be so immodest—that my own upbringing in a cultured Galveston household, and my baccalaureate education and medical training in New Haven and Baltimore, serve as a useful complement. In one particular strain of history he is expert, though; the field of sensational cases and literature. He appears to know every detail of every horror perpetrated in the century, and if you ever get him started—" I caught myself before I had digressed too far. "Back to Miles's learning, which as I have said was attained piecemeal: this through various coursework at the University of London, through expert mentors in this country and abroad, and through military field experience. Of partisan politics you may be interested to learn he is almost willfully ignorant, eschewing any certain position on social issues or government affairs, though a good working knowledge of American, British, and martial and maritime law serves him well, and of all nations he can name the heads of state, some of whom he has personally met and served.

"He is an expert boxer and swordsman, and adept with the cudgel, having picked up these skills abroad. He is a decent marksman with pistol and rifle. And might I add that he plays the violin well."

Mr. Barlow broke in at this point to offer me a glass of water. "That is quite a *curriculum vitae* thee has recited. In its course thee made reference to some of thy own qualifications?"

"That is right—like Miles, I am a Texan born but educated elsewhere. Our native state's institutions of higher learning are growing and gaining in reputation rapidly these days, but in my youth an Eastern boarding school, followed by college and a professional education at a long-established university, were considered *de rigueur* for families of a certain station. As an Easterner yourself, I imagine you appreciate this."

"Well, my education was home schooling in Pennsylvania among the Friends, and after migrating westward I read for the law under a Zionsville attorney who came to Texas along with our colony and helped me prepare for examinations. I sat for the bar in Austin and set up a civil practice to assist my fellow colonists. I know little of fancy boarding schools and the like."

"You have nonetheless heard of the Johns Hopkins University, I presume?"

"Oh, I read the newspapers, certainly."

"After obtaining my doctor of medicine credentials there, like you I brought my training with me to Texas—in my case back home to Galveston, where I was engaged to marry a certain young lady and expected to join my father's well-regarded medical clinic. Let us say, both of those plans were cut short. I chose a Texas city as far from Galveston's high society as I could imagine and boarded a train with only my valise and medical kit in hand. And on that northbound train I happened to cross the path of Derrick Miles."

"Thee joined his detective firm instead?"

"Something like that, although Miles was himself only recently out of the army, with a wound in need of specialized care, and not firmly set upon the inspiration of hanging out a shingle."

"He must indeed have performed some valiant service, to have earned the rank of captain at so tender an age."

"Oh, valiant service you might well call it. Espionage might be more to the point—" Here my narrative was cut short as the locomotive's brakes squealed and the cars ground gradually to a halt. Out the window I observed the large wooden water tank, and the conductor strode through the aisle announcing a brief stop at the village of Weatherford.

Trey Wolverton roused himself and made an announcement of his own. "I'm off to the necessary," he said, stretching and making his way to the rear of the car. "When I return I'd be obliged if you'd rock me back to sleep with a few more tales of the Mighty Derrick Miles."

Our party changed trains at the bustling little junction of Cisco, where the three of us, along with ten or twelve others, boarded a smaller Houston and Texas Central coach and pulled out heading northward toward Albany. There, at dusk, we would reach the end of the line, still eighty miles from our ultimate destination, and would lodge overnight at a hotel where, Mr. Barlow assured us, the rooms were quite acceptable and the price easy on the purse.

In that last stretch, Trey Wolverton gazed out the window toward the setting sun, as though by peering long and hard enough he could lay eyes on that distant estate that bore his family's name. "Texas. I never guessed *Texas*," he said, almost to himself.

I looked up from the book in which I had been absorbed during the postprandial hours of our journey. "Pardon?"

"The place where my dear departed uncle ended up. I knew the old codger came to America," he said, shaking his head, "and I guess he had to start over somewhere. But I sure as shooting wouldn't have picked him for a Texas cowpuncher."

"That is curious indeed," I responded. "You never met your uncle?"

"Nope—I knew him only by reputation. Sort of a legend, really. There were three Wolverton men of that generation: Basil; my father, Nigel; and a half-brother, Randall. Oh, and a half-sister, Susan. Pa told us kids his oldest brother, Basil, picked up and left the country for parts unknown in the 1870s. My father had already emigrated back in forty-nine with the California gold rush. One of the first Brits to go, Pa was. Took his inheritance as soon as he turned twenty-one and headed round the Horn. Same age as I am now. Then Randall went off to fight in the Crimea a few years later and never returned. Of course, I had no idea until this very week quite what they left behind, and I keep studying on it."

He eased back into his seat and breathed out heavily. "I've been asking myself ever since I learned all this . . . I can understand something about my father's decision. He didn't stand to get anything else from the Wolverton estate anyway, and in California he was able to be his own man. As for Randall, well, plenty of young idealists trooped off to war, and that was that. But Basil—coming to this rough country when he was already past middle age—" he waved his hand along the horizon, where rolling hills and thick timber had begun to give way to windswept plains—"didn't exactly jibe with the picture my pop painted."

I set the Conan Doyle novel aside with some reluctance, drawn in by my charge's sincere confidences, and encouraged him to go on. Barlow had fallen asleep in the seat, and Trey leaned forward to be heard over his snores.

"You see, my uncle—*Sir* Basil—did not simply pick up stakes and desert the nation of his birth on a whim. Back in England, as Pa told me, he enjoyed an honorable reputation as a successful financier, investing the family's wealth widely in railroads and shipping enterprises. He made millions. But in the panic of 1873 it all came crashing down. I don't know all the particulars—Pa wasn't one to let his guard down and talk much about it. But if Pa was in his cups, after a sore loss at the tables or a fruitless day in the mines, he'd admit to being bitter that Basil, the revered eldest brother, had dodged his creditors and skipped the country, bringing disgrace to the Wolverton name."

"Many lost fortunes in England's Long Depression, as I understand."

"Yes, I reckon so. There was one other thing, though."

"What was that?"

"Pa had named his only son after him. And it was too late to take that back."

"Hmm," I mumbled, striving for an empathetic tone while concentrating on committing to memory these details I must convey to Miles. Even long-ago events might well figure into the mystery.

"So here I am," Wolverton said, "one day a struggling prospector, the next the heir of a baronet. And anything else Pa could've told me about Uncle Basil, I suppose he took to his grave."

"I'm terribly sorry for your shock, and loss," said I. "Perhaps tomorrow new light will begin to shine on these murky circumstances."

Quiet fell over us both, as young Trey seemed to have delved as deeply into his family history as he cared—or dared. Mr. Barlow stirred, opened his eyes, and peered out into the gathering darkness.

"Look there," he said, watching the last rays of sunlight glint off a creek-sized watercourse meandering below us through the red soil as we crossed a long, low trestle. "It is the Clear Fork. The mighty Brazos de Dios, the arms of God, which stretches from the Staked Plain to the coast. Farther south it has been plied by Indian canoes and steamboats, and enriches the black-soil cotton country. Here it is shallow and full of alkaline minerals, its channel deceptively brief. Its quicksands can trap an unwary rider in an instant, as careless troops and freighters have discovered to their misery."

Wolverton studied the stream as we chugged across it, safe from any threat. I stared down at the infamous and innocent-looking watercourse, too. That moment the steam whistle shrieked, and I gasped despite myself.

"Al-ba-*ny*!" shouted the conductor as he strode down the aisle. "Approaching Albany station, end of the line. All passengers prepare to detrain."

As the next phase of our journey approached, I had to admit to a degree of anxiety. Would I live up to the expectations of Miles, and validate the trust he had placed in me? Would I be able, solo, to fulfill Mr. Barlow's request of us, that we determine whether any foul play had been involved in the death of the Earl? And most important of all, would we find the answers to the questions that troubled this young heir? I could only give it my best. In twenty-four hours, Trey Wolverton would lay eyes on the land that now belonged to him. We would need sleep, and our full energy, and our wits about us.

If our trio (plus the canine companion) had considered the second-class train compartment cramped and dusty, it was luxury compared to the tight quarters of the dented mule-drawn mail coach we'd boarded at dawn. We had been joined by a fourth passenger bound for Dickens County, the farmer Hagins, who was returning from a mission downstate to procure parts for constructing his cotton gin. Lucky we were, though, that the mail hack's twice-weekly run had dovetailed so neatly with our own requirements; it had saved us the necessity of eighty miles of broken territory on horseback, an expedition for which my own mediocre riding skills would have ill prepared me.

I felt rattled and saddle sore as it was, after four hours of jostling over limestone outcrops and sandy draws, around steep corners and up challenging grades. I began to understand why the mail carrier had chosen to rely on his steady mules rather than high-tempered horses over this terrain. Occasionally I would pause in my reading to lift the canvas window curtain and glimpse the landscape, which was almost completely void of settlement. At a crossroads we stopped briefly for a lunch of biscuit and ham provided by a farm wife while the driver changed out his mules, and were on our bone-shaking way again.

It took some effort to concentrate on my novel, the climax of which was approaching but the pages of which were jumping in front of my eyes like the prairie dogs popping up and back into their holes on the plains we traversed.

"What in the dickens has you so absorbed in that book, Dr. Hooper?" asked Wolverton, stretching after a short snooze and choosing a very inopportune moment for his inquiry.

"Oh, just a bit of recreational reading," said I, hoping to deflect his interest. But perversely, he was not to be dissuaded.

"A. Conan Doyle," he read aloud, peeking underneath at the spine. "*The Sign of Four.* What's it about?'

I humored him. "Well . . . a detective and his associate work to solve a crime . . ."

"Bearing any similarity to the case at hand?" he asked in a

teasing manner.

"No, not precisely; the plot is set in London, and it involves a priceless treasure brought from India, and—"

Hagins weighed in. "I read the story when it came out in *Lippincott's,* and I thought it fair-to-middling. Of course, this Doyle's no Poe, for my taste."

"Begging your indulgence, Mr. Hagins," I replied, "I feel the author is every bit as talented a detective writer as Poe or Gaboriau, and perhaps goes them one better, as he has his sleuth Holmes arrive at his conclusions through scientific reasoning rather than simply by chance."

"I seldom have the leisure for fiction myself," said Barlow, who explained that he devoted most of his reading to newspapers and the Good Book. "Colporteurs for the religious publishers do occasionally come through these days, bringing uplifting reading material out to the hinterlands."

"Give me a rollicking Mark Twain adventure any day," chuckled Hagins. "I've no patience for 'uplifting'!"

Wolverton had the final say. "Well, I'm not much of a reader a-tall myself. A tale well told by the campfire, out under the stars, is more to my liking."

At that, my fellow passengers left me to my pastime, though by that point, having reached the scene in which Dr. John Watson proposes marriage to Miss Mary Morstan, I felt rather too exposed to continue in the presence of company, and laid the volume aside.

We were, in any case, approaching our long-awaited destination. The carriage swung around up a hill, and Mr. Barlow again raised the canvas curtain on his side, as suddenly before us spread an enormous wasteland of eroded gullies and hills, thrown into dramatic shadow by the low, setting sun. Wolverton raised the curtain on his side likewise, drawing in his breath in awe at the rugged emptiness stretching north and east of us.

"We'll not cross the Croton Breaks," explained Mr. Barlow. "This is no country for any wheeled vehicle. The driver will instead follow the narrow road skirting the breaks on the north and east, the old Potter-Blocker cattle trail which will bring us soon to the Wolverton Ranch. Most of the desolate acreage of the breaks is owned by the Matador Ranch, some by the Spurs; but the Wolverton borders on it at the place where—well, at the place where poor Sir Basil breathed his last, God rest his soul."

Mr. Barlow's observation turned us all somber and reflective, and he seemed to feel obligated to carry on his travelogue. "Winding through the lowest point of this region is Croton Creek, a treacherous stream that descends a thousand feet over its sixty-five-mile length. The closest view thee will have of it is from the Wolverton Ranch overlook, though I daresay it will be nearly dark by the time we arrive."

"Let us know as we approach, if you can," said Wolverton.

"Most certainly," Barlow agreed.

"And one other thing is worth mentioning," added Hagins. "If conditions are right, in the daytime you may observe a very strange phenomenon caused by a bacterium, *Chromatiaceae*, which grows in oxygen-deprived water. Under the right conditions, Croton Creek runs ruby red, I'm told."

"What an odd thing indeed," said Wolverton. "You make it sound like—like the surface of some strange planet, not this earth!"

About that moment the carriage slowed to a stop, as a lone rider approached, rifle at the ready. I noticed Hagins's hand cautiously reach toward his own gun belt. Mr. Barlow made no move toward his Peacemaker, however, and instead shouted heartily out the window to the horseman. "A good evening to you, Pink. What concern brings thee out along the road tonight?"

"Ah, Wesley Barlow! López has been expecting you back at the Wolverton place. I'm out on a safety check. Got word a few days ago about a jailbreak down in Albany—a bad hombre on the loose and likely heading west for New Mexico. You mind telling me who else is aboard, sir?"

Barlow unlatched the door of the carriage and stepped down, but the rider did not dismount. "My fellow travelers," Barlow said, "meet the renowned John Calhoun Pinkney Higgins, in charge of security for the Spur Ranch. Pink, I'm returning from Fort Worth with the Earl's nephew, Basil Wolverton III, and our friend Dr. Hooper, and I think thee knows the new settler in these parts, Mr. Hagins."

I thought I caught a derisive snort as Higgins said, "Ah, yes, the nester. Well, you'd all best be on your way before nightfall."

Wolverton climbed over me to exit the carriage too. He strode over to the protection man and reached up to shake his hand. "Trey Wolverton," he said. "Glad to meet a neighbor. I'd be obliged if you'd accompany us along to the ranch, and give this hardworking driver some extra protection."

"Not a bad idea," I heard the driver say from up in the box. "We've encountered not another soul on the route from out east, and I'd as soon keep it that way."

"Let's go, then. Lead on, driver, and I'll bring up the rear." Wolverton and Barlow resumed their places and we were on our way again, wary now as we kept a lookout into the gloom. We slowed again for Higgins to ride ahead and open the wide wooden gate, and soon pulled up in front of a looming two-story, L-shaped structure of sandstone flanked by enormous rock chimneys and featuring a deep front porch running the length of the building. A second wing looked to be unfinished and in disrepair, left to the elements. Lamps were aflame beside the imposing front door.

"The Wolverton ranch house," said Mr. Barlow. Its new master had alighted before the rest of us and stood staring with flushed cheeks and shining eyes. We gave him a moment to take it all in—the dual prospects of wealth and responsibility likely registering in his young mind, and the mysterious circumstances of his uncle's death yet to be uncovered.

As the others of us climbed out and stretched our legs, we could see that part of the structure was in shambles and covered in a thorny vine, while finished construction was evident in the main portion of the house. The moon had risen and shone right through the open, dry-rotted rafters of the uncompleted ell, casting a pattern like prison bars onto the hard-packed dirt of the drive. From the second floor of the main portion, weak yellow light spilled from front windows that were little more than narrow vertical slits. At the far side of the house stood a stable, also constructed of sandstone block, and numerous smaller outbuildings. The yard sloped gradually downward over outcrops of hard stone toward a winding trail and a pasture fence—and beyond that, the creek, snakelike and shimmering far below and distant.

Wolverton shuddered as his eye followed the path. "Was it—there?" he asked in a low voice.

"Yes, though farther down and out of sight," replied Barlow softly.

The young heir glanced round with a gloomy face. "It's no wonder my uncle feared trouble was coming on him in a place like this," said he.

"I assure you, it's a much less daunting prospect by day, and if you'll come on inside, it looks like there's a warm fire awaiting, and likely some dinner."

"You must be Trey Wolverton? Welcome to the ranch house!" A tall, thin, dark-complexioned man in dungarees, duster, and worn work boots had stepped from the shadow of the porch. The figure of a woman, heavier-set than he, was silhouetted against the yellow light of the doorway. "Antonío López, sir, ranch manager. My wife, Felicia, and I hope you had a comfortable trip, and yes, there's stew waiting on the cookstove. There's plenty for extra mouths."

Higgins, who was helping the driver as he handed down our bags from the top of the coach, said, "Barlow and Hagins are sayin' they'd rather drive on to town while I'm here to ride along with 'em," he said.

"Thee doesn't mind if I leave and return home straightaway, Mr. Wolverton?" said Mr. Barlow. "My horse and buggy are waiting at the livery in Espuela, and my wife will be looking for me in Estacado this evening."

"And mine," added Hagins. "With this news of a criminal at large, I'm keen to get on back. My place is only a short ride from here, and if you have any need of anything, López knows the way."

"Surely you will stay long enough to have some supper?" said Wolverton, the reality of the lonely place appearing to settle over him.

Barlow tipped his wide-brimmed hat. "No, I really must go—I shall surely find a backlog of work awaiting me, and clients clamoring for my attentions after my extended absence. I would stay to show thee over the house, but López will be a better guide than I. Good-bye, and never hesitate night or day to send for me if I can be of service. And I shall ride over on Sunday after church for the reading of the will, in any case." Barlow and his dog, and farmer Hagins, promptly returned to the carriage and were gone in an instant. The sound of wheels and the hooves of Higgins's mount faded away down the ranch road, leaving us to the calls of coyotes across the hills and the cry of the wind in the night.

Trey Wolverton and I turned into the house, and the front door, bearing the rocking W brand in wrought iron, shut heavily behind us. It was a fine room in which we found ourselves, well proportioned, lofty, and heavily raftered with log vigas in the

Southwestern style. In the great stone hearth a log fire crackled and snapped; I had to wonder where, in such a treeless country, sufficient firewood could possibly have been gathered to make such a blaze. Wolverton and I held out our hands to it, for we were numb from our long drive. Then we gazed around at the high window of thick glass, the mounted heads of bucks and boars, the gun case in the corner, all phantomlike in the subdued light of a ceiling-hung oil lamp.

"It's impressive—this section, at least," said the young Wolverton. The encounter with the place seemed to have blunted his sarcastic edge somewhat.

"We must learn the background of this homestead," I said. "It shows signs of certain age and dereliction, and yet this part of Texas cannot have been open to Anglo settlers for long. Ah, here is López—maybe he can tell us?"

López and his wife entered from what must have been the kitchen, bearing trays laden with steaming pots. They set them on the long trestle table, at the end near a breakfront stacked buffet-style with china, cutlery, and napery of fine quality.

"Supper is ready," said Mrs. López. "It's just us anymore, since the Earl let the rest of the hands go after the last roundup. Mind if we join you?"

"Not at all, not at all," Wolverton rushed to reply. "We're glad for the meal and the company." López, whose lanky build, Spanish coloring and hangdog expression, and square black beard put me in mind of Don Quixote, indicated for Wolverton to take a bowl. Mrs. López ladled out the aromatic stew accompanied by hot flour tortillas, which set my mouth to watering. "Chili con carne," she said. "My abuela's recipe, made with plenty of red chiles that we grow and dry here on the place, and cilantro from the kitchen garden. It's as much as we can cultivate, with water we haul from the spring."

"Although you heard about that nester Hagins, who claims

he can make a dryland cotton crop here," said López gloomily. "More power to him, I say. Land's overgrazed as it is, and we'll need something besides cattle to rely on, if beef prices go south again."

The four of us took our places at the table closest to the fire, and Wolverton eagerly engaged his new employee in a discussion of ranch affairs as though he had been groomed for the role. It was clear to me in that moment that his acumen in the mining business could translate easily to a different endeavor, and that Dickens County ought to reckon itself fortunate if it could keep this young man who could prove such an asset to local enterprise. Señora López and I said little, but quietly consumed our stew, leaving ranch owner and manager to their necessary conversation.

As our bowls were emptied and our bellies filled, she collected the plates and returned to the kitchen. López changed the topic. "In a very few minutes, sir, you will find hot water in your rooms," he said to Wolverton. "I'll show you up there. But there's something you ought to know before you turn in, Mr. Wolverton." He paused briefly and cleared his throat before continuing. "My wife and I will be happy to stay on at the ranch until you have made arrangements, but under the new conditions, you're going to need a considerably larger outfit."

"What new conditions do you mean?"

"If you plan to take up ranching for a livelihood, as you appear inclined."

"But you and Mrs. López—"

"I only meant, sir, that in recent months Sir Basil had shifted his interests away from the ranch and sold off most of his livestock, and in that situation my wife and I, even though we're getting up past middle age ourselves, were able to look after his needs and take care of the horses and cattle with just the help of a borrowed hand. You, sir, are going to need lots more help—

and a younger, stronger manager."

"Do you mean that you and your wife wish to leave?"

"Only when it is convenient to you, sir."

"But your family has been with the ranch for years, haven't you? I'd be sorry to start off here by breaking an old family connection."

I discerned some signs of emotion upon the ranch manager's brown face, as he continued with the sensitive topic. "I feel that way, too, sir, and so does my wife. But to tell the truth, we were both very much attached to Sir Basil, and his death gave us a shock and made these surroundings very painful to us. I'm not sure we'll ever again be easy in our minds at the Wolverton Ranch."

"But what do you intend to do, instead?"

"We had in mind establishing ourselves in some business in town, or even heading farther west. Sir Basil's generosity has given us the means to do so," he said, revealing that he did know something about a gift. At that, Wolverton and I, a new wrinkle in our increasingly complex problem, took the sign to retire.

A square balustraded gallery ran around the entire top portion of the main hall, approached by a central stair. From this, doors to a parlor and a library opened on the front of the house, situated over the porch; and on the back side, opposite the deteriorated arcade, were located all the bedrooms. My own room was in a corner next to Wolverton's. It appeared to be much more modern than the central part of the house, and its clean, lime-washed walls and numerous candles did something to remove the somber impression which our arrival had left upon my mind. But with the chandelier's lamps extinguished, the hall was a place of shadow and gloom. With rows of flaring lamps to light it up, and the color and rude hilarity of an old-time square dance, it might have softened; but now, when only a man and wife went about their evening household duties wordlessly below us, it seemed spectral indeed.

Along the walls of the gallery a shadowed line of British ancestors, I presumed, in every variety of dress from the Elizabethan knight to the buck of the Regency, stared down upon us and daunted us by their silent company. Wolverton and I talked little, and I for one was glad when López mentioned that the Earl often retired to the library after supper to smoke a cigar, and suggested we might wish to do the same.

"My word, it isn't a very cheerful place," said Wolverton, easing into an upholstered chair.

I chose a Cuban from the Earl's humidor and lit it, saying nothing as I walked the perimeter of the room and examined the volumes on Sir Basil's shelves. His elegantly bound tomes ranged from the Bard to Oscar Wilde—a collector of some breadth, he'd apparently had his sources here on the prairie. A set of immense cattle horns—twisted and evilly sharp—hung on the wall above a heavy, carved desk: the sign of a Texas rancher. A portrait of a woman in white graced an ornate silver frame on the desk. A widower was Wolverton, as well, I recalled.

"I suppose one can tone down to it, but I feel a bit out of the picture at present," young Wolverton said from behind a cloud of smoke. "I don't wonder that my uncle got a little jumpy if he lived all alone in a tomb like this. However, if it suits you, we can retire early tonight, and maybe things will seem more cheerful in the morning."

"And might I suggest that we get started on our discreet inquiries right away then, too, perhaps in the town of Espuela, where I should send a telegram to Miles without delay?"

"A capital idea, Hooper. And of course, I'd like to ride out to the site of the—of my uncle's demise—while it's full daylight and we can assess Barlow's account for ourselves. We'll see what condition the stables are in, and what horses are best suited for us."

I cringed at this last, almost feeling the ache in my backside already. There was nothing for it, however, but to follow Wolverton's lead and stick close to him, carrying out the task Miles had given me to the fullest of my ability.

Before turning in I pulled out the chair of a small desk near the side window, to write a detailed report for Miles. I drew aside the curtains so I could look out. The window, larger than those on the front of the house, opened upon the yard in front of the stable. Beyond, two copses of thorny trees moaned and swung in a rising wind. A nearly full moon broke through rifts of racing clouds. In its cold light I saw, beyond the trees, a broken fringe of rocks in eerie configurations and the long, low curve of the melancholy Croton Breaks. I closed the curtain, feeling that my last impression was in keeping with the rest.

And yet it was not quite the last. After finishing my notes and crawling beneath the quilts I found myself weary and yet wakeful, tossing restlessly from side to side, seeking for the sleep which would not come. Far away a chiming clock struck out the quarters of the hours, but otherwise a deathly silence lay upon the old house.

And then suddenly, in the very dead of the night, there came a sound to my ears, brief but clear and unmistakable. It was the sob of a woman, the muffled, strangling gasp of one torn by an uncontrollable sorrow. I sat straight up in bed and listened intently. The noise could not have been far away and had surely come from inside the house. But I had to wonder whether it had been the product of my dreams after all, for it did not recur. For half an hour I waited with every nerve on the alert, but there came no other sound save the chiming clock and the rustle of the vines against the stone wall.

Chapter 7
Strangers Along the Trail

{In which the newcomers explore the Wolverton Ranch and environs.}

On the morn I rose refreshed, then dressed quickly for the day's activities, taking care to bring neckerchief and gloves for what I expected to be a dusty journey, as Trey Wolverton and I planned to ride up to the county seat after breakfast. I donned my brown bowler, the only hat I'd brought that was sufficient to shield my pate from the sun.

The dark paneling of the main hall glowed like bronze in the golden rays, and it was hard to realize that this was indeed the chamber which had struck such a gloom into our souls upon the evening before. Hot biscuits and sliced beef awaited on the sideboard downstairs, and I tucked two into the pocket of my corduroy jacket. López and his wife were nowhere to be seen.

Wolverton was already waiting at the stables when I stepped out into the sunshine. He was saddling a roan stallion; for myself, López had thoughtfully brought around a sorrel mare that looked to have a gentler disposition. The freshness of the daybreak did something to efface from our minds the unfavorable impression which had been left upon both of us by our first experience of the Wolverton ranch house, and I said as much to my companion. "I guess it is ourselves and not the house that we have to blame!" I ventured.

"We were tired with our journey and chilled by our drive, so I suppose we took a grim view of the place. Now we are fresh and well, it doesn't look half bad."

"And yet it was not entirely a question of imagination," said

I. "Did you, for example, happen to hear someone, a woman I presume, sobbing in the night?"

"That is curious, for I did when I was half asleep fancy that I heard something of the sort. I waited quite a time, but there was no more of it, so I concluded that it was all a dream. Or the coyotes."

"I heard it distinctly, and I am sure that it was really the crying of a woman."

"We must ask about this right away." The new boss of the place hollered around for López, who reappeared with a saddle for my mare. Wolverton took him aside to question him discreetly, but it seemed to me that the tan features of the ranch manager turned sallow as he registered the inquiry.

"There are only four people in the house, Mr. Wolverton," he replied, his words amplified perfectly for my hearing across the vaulted ceiling of the stable. "You and Mr. Wolverton, and myself; the only woman in the house is my wife, and I can tell you for sure the sound could not have come from her."

And yet he lied as he said it, for it chanced that after breakfast I had met Señora López in the long corridor with the sun full upon her face. She was a large, impassive, heavy-featured woman with a stern-set expression of mouth. But her telltale eyes were red and glanced at me from between swollen lids. It was she, I was certain, who had wept in the night—and if she did so her husband must know it. Yet he had taken the obvious risk of discovery in declaring that it was not so. Why had he done this? And why did she weep so bitterly? Already round this dark-skinned, black-bearded man there was gathering an atmosphere of phantasmagorical mystery, as with a figure out of an El Greco painting. It was he who had been the first to discover the body of Sir Basil, and we had only his word for all the circumstances which led up to the old man's death. Was it possible that it was López, after all, whom we had seen in the cab in Fort Worth? The beard might well have been the same. The cabman had described a somewhat shorter man, but such an impression might easily have been erroneous. How could I settle the point forever?

Obviously the first thing to do was to see the Espuela postmaster and find whether the test telegram had really been placed in López's own hands. Be the answer what it might, I should at least have something to report to Derrick Miles.

López gave me a hand cinching my saddle, while Wolverton expertly checked his mount. In our saddlebags we each secured a canteen of water and a couple of biscuits wrapped in paper. Each of us carried a pistol, and I brought along the extra accessory of the new Kodak Daylight camera I had recently acquired for documenting my travels, and which Miles's practice had already begun to find useful in forensic work. We folded our oilskins and strapped them behind us, though there seemed no risk of foul weather this day.

Following a map López had provided, we soon found the main road to Espuela. It led across rugged country for four or five miles, then flattened out on the plain for as many more—the distance was not easy to judge, given the jagged course up and down rolling hills toward the edge of the caprock. At last, visible on the plain along a small creek and set against a golden-layered cliffside a mile or so to the west, came into view a small assemblage of buildings which we took to be the frontier hamlet of Espuela. The spur, in Spanish the symbol of *caballeros*, conjured up in my mind an image of nobility and great equestrian skill. From this distance the village radiated something of a romantic air, suggested, no doubt, by its poetic-sounding name. One could almost envision the castles of Granada, the arches of an Iberian arcade, a Mexican hacienda. We paused briefly, and without dismounting I reached into my bag for the camera, already loaded with film, and snapped a frame capturing the vista.

As we rode closer to the group of rude wooden structures, however, we saw no evidence of occupation or activity, even at midmorning on a Saturday. Surely the farmers and ranchers for miles around would have business to conduct and trading to do; surely their wives would be carting their market baskets from storefront to storefront, selling eggs and buying yard goods; surely their children would be rolling hoops or chasing dogs in the street. I wondered aloud to Wolverton if I had not misremembered the day, having mistaken it for the Sabbath before the church hour.

We reined in our horses and rode slowly down the dirt lane past the hotel, the newspaper office, the school, the blacksmith shop, the Odd Fellows hall, the grocer's, the bootmaker's, and the dry goods store, whose doors were all shut and lanterns unlit. The wind, which had begun to pick up, propelled a lonely tumbleweed down the unpaved street. No sign of a courthouse or jail was apparent. At the far end of the block we dismounted beside the cotton gin, the only establishment from which we could detect any sound emanating; Mr. Hagins apparently had his parts in working order and was preparing to try out his contraption.

"Howdy," shouted Wolverton as we picked our way through the piled bales of cotton beside the shed. "Anyone around?"

The proprietor shut down his machinery and came out to greet us. "Welcome to greater Espuela," he quipped.

"Are you its only tenant?" I asked. "We hadn't expected a ghost town."

"Well, you've about put your finger on it, since a ghost town it will be in short order if the county seat election doesn't go our way," Hagins said. "Land lots went on sale this morning in Dickens City, and folks have gone up there to stake their claims in case the new settlement wins out." He went on to explain the disputation regarding proximity to the county center, which in actuality had more to do with the extent to which the county's present seat was surrounded by, and thus controlled by, the region's largest ranching interest. "Might be hard to get a fair trial under those circumstances, I'd have to admit. For now, well, court meets in the social hall and prisoners have to be kept down at Albany, since we have neither courthouse nor jail. Justice has a long way to go here in the hinterlands."

I inquired how one was supposed to send a telegram or post a letter if the office was shut down.

Hagins shrugged and suggested, "Better plan to come back on Monday—unless you want to ride on to Dickens and take your chances on fetching the postmaster out of the line at the land office. I wouldn't bank on it."

Wolverton and I thanked Hagins for the information and resigned ourselves to wait it out. We had no desire to call more notice to our mission than we already had done, and another pressing errand required our attention in the opposite direction, besides.

We led our horses to the trough of silty water beside the stables and refreshed ourselves from our canteens. Well water, it would seem, was another of life's necessities the town lacked. As we rested, several printed notices on the front door of the livery caught my eye, chief among them one on stiff, thick stock proclaiming WANTED for JAILBREAKING.

"Look here," I said. "The escaped convict the protection man told us about." A Pinkertons' mug shot of a clean-shaven man with dark brow and deep-set eyes, a prisoner placard around his neck, accompanied the text, which I read aloud softly in the eerie silence of the street.

JOSÉ MORA, the KILLER "EL PUÑO," convicted of
   murder and cattle rustling, ESCAPED from jail in Albany,

Tex., 10th Oct. Considered ARMED and DANGEROUS. REWARD of ONE HUNDRED DOLLARS for information leading to capture. Contact any U.S. Marshal or Texas officer of the law.

"As if we didn't have enough trouble on our hands," Wolverton said. "But it's a right reminder to be on our guard along the road. Keep your pistol handy." He clicked his reins and we were off again, along the road we'd just traveled.

When we reached the ranch again, in time for a brief repast, I made sure that López knew about the escapee. He had heard the alarm already from Pink Higgins, he said, but had detected no sign of any stranger about the ranch. I could have sworn the shadow of untruth flickered across his countenance once more, as it had that morning. Or perhaps the man was one whose nature tended toward paranoia, his fear and unease disguising a basic honesty.

"We should like to conduct some reconnaissance—to the site of Sir Basil's death, to start with," I said, "and then, perhaps, along the canyon edge. Do you judge it safe?"

"I'll come along," López offered. "I want to check the herds down in that pasture anyway. My wife will stay here while the hired boy is working in the stable."

We rode behind López down that fateful path until we were just out of sight of the house around a bend. There he indicated for us to dismount and walk so that we might observe the ground closely. I took out the Kodak, which he eyed with some anxiety, as though the small box contained poison or a bomb. I explained the camera's novel technology as we walked.

A week after the event, any trace of the deceased's prints had been erased by wind and later traffic, and I could discern nothing of significance. But it was useful to observe the angles and vistas, and the very gate itself. López opened it for us, and we led our horses through. By daylight I could readily perceive the forbidding landscape of the breaks. Eons of mineral-laden rivulets had bitten into the edge of the white, calcified layer, eroding away the softer red and yellow soils below and strewing rocks and boulders down the sides of steep arroyos. In some places flat-topped mesas or conical haystack peaks rose hundreds of feet above the surrounding rolling hills. Far away to the south we could make out a formation that López informed us was known as the Double Mountain, an ancient landmark for native peoples.

It struck me that this panorama, with its sweeping horizon unimpeded by tall trees or mountain ranges, could under certain conditions be considered beautiful. Awe-inspiring it certainly was, though the midday sun drained color and flattened shadows that would have made it more interesting, and the unrelenting wind obscured the valley in a haze of dust. Still, birds occasionally dove from the heights to seize on grain or prey, the prairie grasses bent and danced, and the stiff breeze provided a droning music as background.

Wolverton interrupted my contemplation with an observation of his own. "It's a desolate scene to be the last one my unfortunate uncle laid eyes on." He cut his eyes toward López. "Nice of you to bring us down here—it must bring back a fresh and painful memory. I am very sorry." López nodded silently.

"I'm sorry I never got to know the old man, too. Wish I knew more about what was in his mind," Wolverton added.

"I am no help there, sir. I wasn't privy to the Earl's personal matters. But I will tell you that he appeared genuinely fond of this ranch, and concerned for the people of this county. It's a shame he met his end alone out here."

"Yes," said Wolverton guardedly. "Well, I suppose there will be a funeral of some kind to plan, and folks can pay their respects. Say, I didn't even ask who handled the burial?"

"The undertaker from Crosbyton, sir, under the direction of Mr. Barlow," López replied. "I'm sure he could speak to the preacher on your behalf. We can hold a service whenever it's convenient for you."

"Thank you, López. Now, before you have to get on to seeing about the cattle, would you mind showing me the exact spot where you found my uncle?"

López tied his horse to the fence post and signaled for us to do the same. He opened the gate and led the way a few yards down the trail, to a slight curve obscured by hackberry and tall grasses. He pointed at the path of dust and rubble to a place undistinguishable by us from any other.

"I found Sir Basil here, lying flat on his stomach like he'd tripped and fallen forward, or like he'd be if he was stalking game, except that his face . . . his face was frozen in some awful fright."

Wolverton nodded. "And heading away from the ranch, Mr. Barlow told us?"

"Yes, that is right. I cannot imagine what would have driven him to go that direction, especially at night, knowing his fear of the land beyond the fence."

"Was his gun drawn?"

"He—he was unarmed. His gun is still in the drawer where he kept it."

"Doesn't that seem strange to you?"

López agreed. "I thought so at the time. But I cannot explain it."

I interjected a question of my own. "I'm curious—did Sir Basil know of the escaped criminal at the time?"

"No . . . no, we hadn't heard of it then," said López. "I would have advised him to forgo his regular ride, under those circumstances."

Wolverton remained silent, turning his gaze out to the horizon once more. López shifted his weight and reached for a handkerchief to wipe the dust from his brow.

"I've kept you too long," Wolverton said to the man. "Hooper and I might want to explore a bit farther, but I know you have work to return to."

López nodded and asked, "My wife and I will look for you by the dinner hour?" before shuffling back up the path to his horse. We listened for hoofprints, and watched as he spurred his horse toward the far pasture, before we spoke again in low tones.

"Now, I'm no professional tracker," said Wolverton, "but I doubt there's much chance this path will tell us anything of use."

"I suspect you're right," said I, as we combed through the grass in search of any clue that might remain. Prickly grass spurs clung to our pants legs and jacket cuffs as we parted clumps of vegetation, taking care where we stepped. But nothing seemed amiss. That was, until we came, some half a mile on and downward beneath the caprock, to a trickle of water originating deep in a cleft of the canyon wall, where the path reduced to nothing more than a steep scramble of rocks. From the hidden seep sprouted an unexpected burst of green: vivid ferns and mosses canopied by thriving shrubs. We veered off the narrow cattle track to seek the spring's source and battled our way past thorns sharp as sewing needles to a puddle that must have been known to animals, for in the thickly caked mud were many prints of paw and hoof.

Even I, with my limited backcountry experience, could make out the cloven forms of deer and hog feet. Of cattle and horse there were none; the opening in the rock would not have been wide enough to easily accommodate the entry of livestock.

"There!" whispered Wolverton suddenly. "What do you make out, Hooper?"

The mark of a padded paw, wide as a saucer and tipped with

four acute triangular indentions, was preserved there, close to the water and fresh. I drew in a breath sharply at the recognition, and in that moment the spectral and theoretical became material. Just as material, too, was the imprint alongside it of a man's boot.

Oh, that Miles were here—he would be able to read information from these clues that seem to me as indecipherable as hieroglyphics, I thought to myself. But aloud I asked Wolverton if he would locate a rock to help us mark the spot. As he did so, I again lifted the Kodak from its case. I carefully focused and shot from multiple angles, taking up most of the new film roll with close-ups and landscape documentation. Photographic film of this clue would be an invaluable record.

That we could spot no other like the wolf's lone print, we attributed to the deep cushion of grass and fern, and the obscuring effect of other wildlife. The human bootprint, we tracked as far as the main path, but there it disappeared. If there had been a route beaten down through the grass, it had been well covered, for neither Wolverton nor I could make out any flattened track or broken brush. We returned up the hill for our horses uneasily, knowing we were not alone.

On horseback we followed the trail in the opposite direction, which widened and flattened as it gave onto a wide, grassy meadow crisscrossed by numerous pathways. Wolverton took advantage of the open terrain to spur his horse, leaving me and my mare, which turned out to have a bit of a stubborn streak, struggling to catch up. I tried to manage the reins while holding onto my hat, but that effort lasted only a few seconds before my bowler went sailing. I dared not look back, lest I fail to note any number of hazards that might lie ahead, from prairie dog hole to thorn scrub to rattlesnake.

In the event, it was none of these that brought Wolverton up short as we topped a rise and rounded a corner, but instead the sudden appearance above the tall grass of a straw hat nearly the same color as the dry stalks around it, and beneath it an even more curious sight: a man, short of stature and slight of build, eyes closed meditatively and extending out in front of him in both palms a Y-shaped wooden branch.

Wolverton, riding faster than I, was almost on top of the strange figure before he managed to rein his horse to a halt. He was going for the pistol in his holster when the man shouted out, "For Pete's sake, Mr. Wolverton, watch where you're going!"

I reined in my horse beside Wolverton and smoothed the hair out of my eyes. I do not know which factor caught him more by surprise, the older man's appearance as though out of nowhere, or the limb which might have been mistaken for a weapon, or the fact that he had called him by name. It was the first time in my brief acquaintance with Wolverton that I'd seen him at a loss for words.

"I—I—what the devil—"

I slid off my horse, grateful to stand on solid ground once more, and stepped around patches of spiky yucca to extend my hand. "I believe you must be Griswall, the dowser," I said, "and I am—"

"Frank Hooper, the medical doctor, I presume," said the man, who pushed back his hat to reveal a tan, lean-jawed face. "Out here we see newcomers seldom enough that word gets around. Barlow told me. Rufus Griswall, at your service."

Wolverton was still recovering his composure. "What the hell are you doing out here, man," he called out as he jumped from the saddle, "popping up like a damned gopher and spooking my horse?"

"Why, divining for water, of course. I believe if you'll check your map you'll find we're on lands belonging to the Spur Ranch. I do occasional work for 'em."

"Seems like everybody around here does," Wolverton said petulantly, as he reached for his canteen and took a long swig.

"True enough. They're the biggest outfit in four counties. About the only steady employer." Griswall lowered the stick and leaned on it. "I lease their acreage from here to the creek."

"You graze cattle out here?"

Griswall chuckled. "I study Lepidoptera, among other natural wonders."

"Butterflies?" asked Wolverton. "Of all the bizarre things—"

"You will find, Mr. Wolverton, that the emptiest lands are the habitats best suited to observe the interrelations among all species, from insect to bird to mammal. The monarch migrates right across these lands in late summer, and its mass flight is an orange miracle to behold. Why, beneath our very feet lies the margin of an ancient sea that once fostered flying reptiles, giant lizards, and later the woolly mammoth, the pampas beast, the *bison antiquus* . . ."

As it appeared Wolverton and Griswall might have gotten onto a lengthy topic, I took the opportunity to escape and retrieve my hat, whatever chance there might be for its rescue. I hauled myself back into the saddle and, once I had managed to persuade my mare that I really did intend for her to go back the way she'd come, she grew quite willing to retrace her steps. We had gone quite a ways back, well out of sight of Wolverton and Griswall, and I was on the verge of abandoning my mission, when at last I spied my bowler in the brush.

"Eureka!" I shouted. Delighted, I jumped off to grab the hat. But before I could fetch it out of the grass, a gust of wind snatched it out of my reach. I stumbled around patches of scrub, determined not to lose it now. The impish wind led me on several more paces before I managed, at last, to lay a hand on it. The infernal horse, in the meantime, had left me in the lurch. I caught sight of her tail swishing down the path and around the bend. Now I would have to catch back up with the others on foot.

I picked the thorns from my hat and was brushing the dust from my coat when I heard the sound of steps and, turning round, found a woman near me upon the path. Where she had come from, I could not tell; the dip of the breaks had hid her until she was quite close. I could not doubt that this was the daughter of whom I had heard passing mention, since ladies of any sort were proving to be few in the breaks country. But she was an extraordinary beauty, of a most uncommon type. There could not have been a greater contrast between father and daughter, for the man I had met only half an hour before was tanned and sinewy, with light hair and gray eyes, while this woman was brown-haired and fair, and a few inches taller than he. She had a proud, finely cut face, so regular that it might have seemed impassive were it not for the sensitive mouth and the eager green eyes. With her perfect figure and elegant dress she was, indeed, a strange apparition upon a lonely canyon path. She quickened her pace and caught up with me. I had doffed my hat and was about to make some explanatory remark when her own words turned all my thoughts into a new channel.

"Go back!" she said, in a voice barely audible above the wind. "Go straight back to Fort Worth, instantly." I could only stare at her in stupid surprise. Her eyes blazed at me, and she tapped the ground impatiently with her foot.

"Why should I go back?" I asked.

"I cannot explain." She spoke in a low, urgent tone, with a curious lisp in her utterance. "But for God's sake do what I ask you. Go back and never set foot in this place again."

"But I have only just come."

"Can you not tell when a warning is for your own good, man? Go back to Fort Worth! Start tonight! Get away from this ranch at all costs!" she cried. "Hush, my father is coming! Not a word of what I have said."

She straightened and waved at the figure topping the rise, coming at a brisk run with the dowsing stick in one hand and a butterfly net in the other. "Yes, as I was just saying, we have an unexpected abundance of flora and fauna here in the breaks," she said to me, pointedly louder but calmer than before. "It's too bad you're not here in springtime, when the bluebonnets spread color across the hills."

Griswall came up short and wiped his brow with a bandana from his pocket. "Hello, Maria," said he to his daughter, and it seemed to me that the tone of his greeting was not altogether a cordial one. "I thought you were at the house finishing the report for the Entomological Society."

"Well, Papa, I got worried when you didn't come back for lunch. Oh, you are very hot! Here, I've brought water." She offered him a wire-handled tin vessel, and he took a deep draught from it.

"Yes," he said, "I was right in the middle of describing the Ogallala Aquifer for our newcomer, when I spied a ruddy daggerwing, rare in these parts and seldom found in the late autumn at all. What a pity I missed him!" He spoke animatedly, and his small light eyes glanced incessantly from the woman to me. "You have introduced yourselves, I can see."

"I was telling Mr. Wolverton that it was rather late for him to see the true beauties of this rugged country," she said.

"Well, that's curious, daughter, since *that* is Trey Wolverton coming down the trail right now." Indeed, Wolverton had just ridden around the rise, leading my wayward horse behind him.

"Oh, I—" She looked toward me, struggling to hide a glimmer of alarm on her face. "I imagined that you must be Trey Wolverton, nephew of the late baronet."

"No, no, only a humble commoner, madam," I joked, "but his friend. My name is Franklin Hooper."

A flush of vexation passed over her expressive face, and she stammered an apology. "Then we have been talking at cross purposes," said she. But as she caught sight of the real Wolverton, the sun's afternoon rays playing off his rugged good looks, she went dumb.

"Why don't you gentlemen come with us to the camp?" said Rufus Griswall in the awkward silence. "Your horses will need water and feed before you head back to the ranch, and I can show you the shortcut." Miles *had* expressly said that we should study the neighbors. I looked at Wolverton, who nodded his assent.

Griswall continued his natural-history lecture as we followed behind him and his daughter, who kept silent. "It is a wonderful place, the Croton Breaks," said he. "You never tire of the changing vistas. You cannot imagine the wonderful secrets it contains. It is so vast, and so rugged, and so mysterious."

"You know it well, then?" I asked.

"I have been here only two years. Maria and I came to Dickens County a good long while after Sir Basil settled. The residents would call me a newcomer. But my tastes and inclinations led me to explore every part of the county, and I imagine there are few men who know it better than I."

"Is it hard to know?"

"Very hard. You see, for example, this great plain to the east here with the conical peak breaking out of it—a continuation of the pasture where we met. Do you observe anything remarkable about that?"

"It would be a rare place for a gallop," said Wolverton.

"You would naturally think so, and the thought has cost several tenderfoots their lives before now. Can you make out the channel of the creek along the flat?"

"Yes, I see some patches of blue through the grass."

Griswall laughed. "That is the valley of Croton Creek," said he. "Fed by springs well hidden up in the crevices and box canyons. A false step can mean death to man or animal. I saw a yearling calf wander into it just yesterday. He never came out. I saw his head for quite a long time craning out of the quicksand, but it sucked him down at last. After rains like last week's it is quite impassable, but even in dry seasons it is dangerous to cross. And yet," he boasted, "I can find my way to the other side and return alive."

"Why would you want to?" asked Wolverton. A sensible question, to my mind.

"Well, you see deep indentations in the hills beyond? They harbor springs and seeps of pure, sweet water, places the Indians have known for years. Follow them down, and you eventually reach the creek; follow them up, and you know where to drill your water well, if you have the wit to detect the place properly."

"Perhaps you'll show me some day."

Griswall looked at Wolverton with a mix of skepticism and admiration, as though trying to size up the new arrival. "For God's sake put such an idea out of your mind," said he. "Your blood would be on my head if you didn't make it back alive."

He was an odd duck, this one, a combination of profound intelligence and loose tongue. Wolverton and I shared a look that seemed to communicate our shared understanding that he could be useful. We held back from inquiring about the particular spring where we'd seen the paw print, giving Griswall latitude to bring up the topic himself, but of this singular site he made no mention.

We rode on down the trail past a three-strand fence on which the rotting carcasses of coyotes hung.

"McQuarrie's doing," said Griswall. "Rancher won't suffer a coyote to live, though they're hardly a threat to his livestock. It's just another upset to the natural order of things once mankind begins encroaching on the domain of animals."

At that moment an unearthly utterance echoed over the breaks, impossible to my ear to tell whether bird or beast or human, or some other phenomenon. Wolverton turned toward it, trying to place its source.

It came once again, a rising, rhythmic, scratching sound, yielding to a deep-throated moan of anguish that died away in a matter of seconds.

"Good God!" I cried. "What is *that*?"

A long, low moan, indescribably sad, swept over the breaks. It filled the whole air, and yet it was impossible to say whence it came. From a dull murmur it swelled into a deep roar, and then sank back into a melancholy moan once again.

Griswall looked at us with a curious expression in his face. "Queer place, the Croton Breaks!" said he.

"But what is it?"

He leaned toward us and said melodramatically, "The cowboys say it is the dire wolf stalking its prey. I've heard it only once before." I looked round, with a chill in my heart, the sun's warmth notwithstanding. Nothing stirred over the vast expanse save a pair of turkey buzzards in a mesquite below us.

"You are an educated man, Dr. Hooper," he continued. "Surely you don't believe such nonsense as that?"

If this stranger was having us on, I didn't appreciate it. "Well, then, what *do* you think that was?"

"You gentlemen have apparently never heard the sound of the greater prairie chicken booming."

"Can't say as I have," I replied, though I had read of the species.

"It's a very rare bird—practically extinct in the West now—but all things are possible down in the breaks. Yes, I should not be surprised to learn that what we have heard is the cry of the last of the prairie chickens."

"It's the weirdest thing that ever I heard in my life."

"Yes, it's rather an uncanny place altogether. Look at the hillside yonder. What do you make of that?" On a flattened, grassy area below a cliff, a low, crumbling wall of stone formed an indistinct rectangle that stood out, on account of its regularity, among the hoodoos and strewn boulders.

"Sheep pens," replied Wolverton. "Mexican herdsmen still use stone pens in the territories. But I didn't realize they came as far as Texas."

"Comanchero herders and traders once tried to raise sheep here. They were peaceable enough that the Comanches left them alone. Cattle ranchers eventually drove 'em out. People have found a way to live on this land for centuries before white men, though. Indians occupied natural rock shelters, and you'll sometimes come upon—" Griswall interrupted his own lecture, dropping the pony's reins and grabbing for his net. "Oh, excuse me for a second! It's one of those elusive ruddy daggerwings."

In an instant Griswall was rushing with extraordinary energy and speed in pursuit of it. He dodged thorny shrubs with the agility of a rabbit, his green net waving in the air like a flag on the field of battle.

Maria took over as guide in his stead. Soon, from over another rise there floated a gray plume of smoke. A short walk brought us to the Griswall dugout, a bleak lodging to be sure; once the outpost of some adventuresome pioneer, I imagined, cut into a red-clay hillside with an opening framed by stripped cedar timbers and a roof reinforced with chunks of sod. An orchard of wild plums surrounded the dwelling, but the trees, as I had come to expect everywhere down in the breaks, were stunted and nipped, and the effect of the whole place was mean and melancholy.

Griswall was waiting for us at the door, and we ducked under the lintel as he ushered us in. "Strange spot to choose, I know," said he as if in answer to my thought. "And yet we manage to make ourselves quite comfortable here."

A solitary window set into the front wall admitted light into the cavelike space and also provided a picture-perfect view of the canyon wall in the far distance. A telescope stood mounted in front of it on a tall wooden tripod. As my eyes adjusted to the half-darkness, I was astonished to note a refinement of décor in which I presumed the taste of the young lady, and I could not but marvel at what might have brought this apparently educated man and this cultivated woman to live in such a place.

Maria made her way to a corner of the parlor that served as the kitchen and returned with an enameled coffeepot which she set on the woodstove, while her father stoked the firebox with cedar logs. She then retreated to the opposite corner, behind a curtained-off area that appeared to lead to personal quarters at the back of the dugout.

Griswall motioned for us to take seats in chairs that barely accommodated my weight or Wolverton's height. I edged into the seat nearest the window, between a floor-to-ceiling cabinet and a table stacked with books and papers; Wolverton pulled out his tobacco pouch and papers, and Griswall indicated his permission though he declined, himself, to smoke. The three of us pretty well filled the room, but even as I sat barely two feet from the master of the house, I could scarcely make out his expression in the shadowed and hazy space.

I asked our host, in what I hoped was a tactful foray into discovering something of his background that might be useful to Miles, how long he and his daughter had inhabited these parts, for the dugout impressed one with its settled elegance.

"Oh, that," said he, with an air of dismissiveness as though the genteel ménage were nothing out of the ordinary in its rough setting. "Maria brings miraculous talents for organization and taste to every project to which she lays her hand. It is the same artfulness that she applies as an editor of my journal contributions."

"And it is your journal work that brought you here to the Croton Breaks?"

If he thought me prying, he gave no indication. "That undertaking could be accomplished from any number of locales, though the biological richness of this region, to which I earlier referred, makes it particularly advantageous to be situated in the heart of it rather than to mount temporary expeditions, as I once did."

Wolverton offered a challenge of his own. "Well, men like you and me might get our schooling out in the wild, but *she* didn't learn these talents in a dugout!" He cocked his head in the direction of the area to which the daughter had repaired.

"Oh, that's for certain," said Griswall. "But Maria and I have not been so long removed from urban life as all that. She completed her studies in languages, elocution, and the natural and physical sciences before we emigrated to the frontier."

"And you do not find it dull, or lonely at times, in comparison to—" I asked, but the pot chose that moment to rattle and hiss on the stove, and I abandoned the last part of my question.

Maria quickly returned to the parlor dressed in a smock over her regular clothing, and carrying a tray with three china cups and saucers. She handed one set to Wolverton and another to her father, then placed the last on the table beside me. As she turned to retrieve the steaming pot from the stove, momentarily blocking her father's view, my eye fell on the corner of a document on the table nearest my hand, mostly obscured beneath a large ledger. The paper folder caught my curiosity only on account of the official-looking identification imprinted on it, which read "NAL LAND OFFICE, AUSTIN" and upon which had been made several lines of penciled notes. I dared not be caught snooping, and so lifted my cup in its saucer and held it out to be filled as Maria deftly made the rounds with the coffee.

"You'll forgive our lack of cream out here," said Griswall, "and granulated sugar, for that matter. In the fall we brew chicory coffee and sweeten it with raw honey. Good for whatever ails you."

Maria filled our cups with the aromatic brew, moving around the cramped room with a dancelike grace.

"No," Griswall said with some force, startling me out of my thoughts until I remembered my own question. "I find an unlimited field of work here, where I am also able to support us on the funds generated from dowsing, and my daughter is as devoted to Nature as I am; is that not so, Maria?"

"No, no, I never find the place boring," said she quickly, almost automatically. "We have books and journals, we have our studies, and we have interesting neighbors. Mr. Barlow is a most learned man in his own line. Poor Sir Basil was also an admirable companion. We knew him well and miss him more than I can tell."

"We were all rather afraid that after the sad death of Sir Basil the new rancher might refuse to live here," said Griswall in a confidential tone, as he dismissed his daughter once again with a wave of his hand, though I was sure I caught a brief and pleading look in her eye. "It is asking much of a wealthy man to come down and get to know a place of this kind, but you should know that your arrival means a great deal to the county." He pressed on into deeper matters, though with a casual air. "I suppose you have no superstitious fears in the matter, yourself?"

Wolverton harrumphed. "Not bloody likely."

"Of course you know the legend of the fiend wolf which haunts the family?"

"I've heard it."

"It is extraordinary how credulous the rubes are about here! I've heard cowhands swear that they've seen such a malevolent

The Wolf Hunt: A Tale of the Texas Badlands

creature down in the breaks." Griswall spoke with a smile, but I seemed to read in his eyes that he took the matter more seriously. "The story took a great hold upon the imagination of Sir Basil, and I have no doubt that it led to his tragic end."

"How do you suppose?" Wolverton asked, leading his host on while I made careful mental notes of his responses.

"His nerves were so worked up that the appearance of any dog or coyote might have had a fatal effect upon his diseased heart," Griswall continued. "I can imagine that he really did see something of the kind upon that last night along the canyon path. I feared that some disaster might occur, for I was very fond of the old man, and I knew that his heart was weak."

"How did you know that?"

"Wesley Barlow heard him talk of a floating-heart condition," Griswall explained. "Fatty tissue surrounding the coronary muscle. It makes the heart susceptible to shock."

"You think, then, Mr. Griswall, that some dog pursued my uncle, and that he died of fright in consequence?"

"Do you have any better explanation?" This question, he directed at me.

"I have not come to any conclusion," I replied, taken aback.

"Has Mr. Derrick Miles?" The words took away my breath for an instant. "It is useless for us to pretend that we do not know you, Dr. Hooper," he continued. "The exploits of your renowned Texas detective have reached us here, and you could not publish such colorful accounts of him without being known yourself. When Barlow told me your name he could not shield your identity. If you are here, then it follows that Derrick Miles is interesting himself in the matter, and I am naturally curious to know what view he may take."

"I am afraid that I . . . cannot answer that question."

"May I ask if he is going to honor us with a visit himself?"

"He cannot leave the city at present. He has other cases which engage his attention."

"What a pity!" said Griswall, with an air of sincere regret. "He might throw some light on the events that are so dark to us. But as to your own researches, if there is any possible way in which I can be of service to you I trust that you will just say the word. If I had any indication of the nature of your suspicions or how you propose to investigate the case, I might perhaps even now give you some aid or advice."

"I assure you that I am simply here to visit my friend Trey Wolverton, and that I need no help of any kind."

"Excellent, then!" said Griswall, slapping his knee and nearly striking my own. "You are perfectly right to be wary and discreet. Well, I apologize for making an unjustifiable intrusion, and I promise you I will not mention the matter again."

Maria returned as if on silent cue, to take up our empty cups.

Wolverton held onto his saucer for a lingering moment as she reached for it. Suddenly he said, as if the notion had just that second occurred to him, "Maybe, Miss Griswall, you would do us the honor of coming to the ranch house for dinner tomorrow? I have the unwelcome but necessary chore of planning a memorial service for my uncle, and I think your ideas might make the task considerably less burdensome."

"I'd be delighted to accept," said her father. "Maria prefers the comforts of her own home, I should let you know. But I'm sure she can share her thoughts with me, and I will be more than happy to convey them."

Wolverton appeared less than happy to have been so blatantly sidestepped. There was nothing for it but to assent, if we were to continue plying the voluble Griswall for more useful information. We learned nothing more of substance, however, and, our horses sufficiently rested, headed out on the side path that our host assured us would soon intersect with the main road to the ranch. The sun was setting over the breaks, and we certainly wished to be back at headquarters before full dark.

Wolverton said not a word as he glanced back down the hill to the faraway plume of smoke indicating the site of the dugout. We each kept a sharp eye and ear out for any sign of the escapee—or for any animal predator that might cross our path.

As we rode up out of the meadow and rounded the corner, however, there occurred a most strange and unexpected thing. The full moon had risen a ways above the horizon upon our right, shining large as the disappeared sun but reddish-orange in hue, throwing the features of the broken land into sculptural relief. We halted our horses to take in the view.

I gasped involuntarily in awe, and said quietly to my companion, "Comanche moon." He nodded to indicate he'd heard the phrase too. That season in the not too distant past, it conveyed, when settlers isolated on the frontier most feared their utter vulnerability to parties of raiding natives. I would not, in that moonlit moment, have been surprised had Quanah Parker and his band of Quahada warriors appeared over the rise, spears raised, their surefooted ponies moving at a gallop—notwithstanding that I knew quite well the chief was happily settled, with his wives and family, into the new house Mr. Burk Burnett had recently helped him build in Indian Territory, for Miles and I had visited him ourselves in the spring just past.

All of that flashed through my mind in the instant that I *did* register a human figure standing, starkly alone and silhouetted against the orange-red orb, upon the mesa a half mile or so east of us. The man was tall, thin, and dressed in what looked to be buckskins, but I could make out no feature other than his flat, ebony-black outline. I froze; could the man spy us, as identifiable in the flood of light as he was indistinguishable against it? My brain abandoned the throwback image of Indian depredations as swiftly as it latched upon the more present danger—that of the escaped outlaw.

The man exhibited no sign of stealth. He stood, manifest to any observer, with his legs a little separated, his arms folded, his head bowed, as if he were surveying some vast kingdom of scattered stones strewn before him. I turned to Wolverton and motioned slowly for him to wait while I again retrieved my camera. As delicately as I could manage, I slid from my mount and reached to unfasten the corner of my saddlebag. There was no time for setting up a tripod, so I simply propped the camera box on the saddle's cantle and directed its lens toward the moon and the mystery man. When I gauged the distance to be in focus, I pulled the shutter wire. The unavoidable *kodak* click seemed to reverberate across the silent canyon as sharply as a gunshot.

When I looked up again, the figure had vanished. I glanced toward Wolverton, who seemed ready to spur his horse straight down into the alien jumble of rocks and thorns in pursuit.

But before I could utter any plea to stop his impulse, a second eerie event caused my blood to go cold. From somewhere deep below us, as though from an unknown pit of hell hidden in the shadowed wilderness, came the cry of a lone wolf. The howl, harrowing and tormented, echoed off the rocky walls for a long minute, then ceased. It found no answer, and it did not come again.

Wordlessly my companion directed his horse back onto the path and motioned me to follow. There would be no hunt—for man or beast—until we were better prepared and in stronger numbers.

I wondered, as I picked my way along behind my client on the bright trail, what matters he might be pondering in view of the day's extraordinary events. What mysteries was his intellect struggling to untangle, as was my own? Would young Wolverton ever find his uncle's ranch a hospitable location to set down roots—or would the dangers of this raw and desolate country dissuade him? Was the flicker of attraction to the woman we had so unexpectedly encountered sufficient to pique his interest? I kept my counsel, judging this to be the wrong time to reveal to him Miss Griswall's peculiar and misdirected warning—maybe only a woman's flight of fancy in any case, though perhaps, considering the glimpses we had witnessed this night, the prophecy of a backcountry Cassandra. Tomorrow, in daylight, I would find the moment.

I wondered, as well, what activity my detective colleague might be pursuing among the bright gaslights of Fort Worth. It was not without a tinge of envy that I prayed Miles would soon be freed from his preoccupations and able to come take this heavy burden of responsibility from my shoulders.

Chapter 8
A Supper at the Ranch

{In which a will is read and a strange light is observed.}

Sunday dawned with a low hum of activity on the ranch. I opened my eyes at daybreak to the sounds of water: outside at the pump, a bucket being filled; in the animals' troughs, another emptied; downstairs in the kitchen, a ladle dipped, a kettle boiling. I pulled on my dressing gown and boots for warmth and slipped down the back stairs and out to the privy. The air was refreshing but not cold, with not a hint of wished-for moisture.

Horses nibbled at the hay set out for them in the stockade, as the shadowed figure of the hired boy moved about his morning chores. I paused a moment to listen to the yips of coyotes along the canyon rim, so different from the unmistakable howl that had continued to haunt my uneasy dreams.

Returning to the house, I passed Mrs. López, who was setting plates for breakfast. I spoke to her, to ask that my place be removed, as I had numerous matters to attend to in solitude before young Wolverton's guests arrived in the afternoon. She nodded, averting her eyes from mine, but I could tell by the set of her grim lips that this was a most unhappy woman. Something troubled her still.

Wolverton himself was up and dressed in sturdy dungarees, but carrying his suit jacket over his arm. I passed him in the corridor, and he informed me that he had asked López to show him the workings of the ranch.

"You're welcome to come along," he said, likely already knowing my response. I considered my pledge to Miles, to never leave my client unaccompanied, but decided López's company would suffice, especially in broad daylight.

"Any activity that involves a horse today, I'm afraid I'd be wise to decline," I replied. "My backside could use a day of rest."

He snickered. "I'll ask Mrs. López to bring you some liniment, old man. After she sees what she can do with this." He held up the suit he'd been wearing yesterday to show the considerable extent of the rips it had suffered as a result of his gallop through the brush. I could only shake my head—at his impetuous nature but also the likelihood that such sadly damaged garments could be salvaged.

I lowered my voice to a whisper and conveyed to him the substance of Maria Griswall's peculiar warning from the day before. "I suggest you make careful observations, and note anything out of the ordinary," I advised. "And do exercise caution. You'll want to be back here hale and whole for the reading of the will."

"Not to worry, Granny. You go mind your knitting, and let the men tend to the fences."

Wolverton's teasing galvanized my will to compose a letter to Miles, though I had slim hope that my words would reach him in time to help set our minds at peace. Not only did I feel I had made no progress whatsoever toward solving the case with which Miles had entrusted me, since arriving I had encountered even more levels of enigma. I laid a pillow across the seat of the straight-backed chair and sat down to pen and ink.

My dear Miles,

I trust this missive finds you—whenever it finds you—in good health and spirits. It is my sincerest hope that you will have brought to a close the business that required you to remain in Fort Worth, for your investigative skill is sorely needed here.

The ranch manager, López, and his wife, Felicia, have made us comfortable, though they are of a reticent turn and seem to be experiencing some personal vexation unrelated to our arrival. They have notified Wolverton of their wish to leave the ranch's employ when he is more fully settled here.

Of that eventuality I am not certain; the place is rather run down and livestock have suffered of late for want of sufficient water and good pasture. I am enclosing my quickly sketched portraits of the Lópezes and a rough drawing of the ranch house, in hopes these will help you better envision the situation. Wolverton has not yet voiced an observable interest in the ranching life in so remote a site, though this is somewhat understandable; he will not be able to fully evaluate his prospects until hearing the terms of his late uncle's will, about which Mr. Barlow is scheduled to enlighten us later today.

He has, however, shown keen interest in the female neighbor whom we met on yesterday's ride across the canyon on horseback. (I can picture the incredulity on your face as you read this. Do not laugh, Miles; I have sacrificed much in the line of duty.) You recall Mr. Barlow's mentioning Mr. Griswall and his daughter. He is an eccentric of diverse interests; she is a rare flower in this rough country. Her polished beauty caught the eye of our young client in an instant, but not before she had delivered to me a most impassioned warning—mistaking me for the Wolverton heir. She urged that he leave at once, as the place is one of extreme danger. We have not seen any but incidental mysteries as to why this should be so. I am most anxious for you to come and judge for yourself.

In the interest of providing you any clue, however tangential, that might reveal more about the citizens of Dickens County, I need to describe the Griswall residence for you. I believe I can do better justice through the enclosed drawing of their dugout than through words alone. But I will say that this household struck me as a most peculiar juxtaposition of frontier ingenuity and imported sophistication. I have sketched for you from brief memory the faces of Griswall father and daughter, and have also reproduced for you the snippet of a document which I happened to spy upon their table yesterday. My training in anatomical drawing and labeling do come in handy at times, n'est-çe pas?

I will enclose a photographic print indicating another of these mysteries, presuming that I shall have the opportunity to set up processing chemicals on the premises to-night. This wolf of legend has shown himself in the evidence of a paw print, and a most disturbing howl last night. I can fully understand how rumor of a monster has spread. But there is nothing, so far, to link it with Sir Basil Wolverton's death.

It is my intention to post this to-morrow, the 19th Oct., in Espuela, and hope for its speedy delivery. I remain,

Your friend and humble servant,
Franklin C. Hooper, M.D., A.F.&A.M.

I slipped the sheet into an envelope but left it unsealed. As for the problem of developing my films from yesterday, I would have to search out a closet suitable for a darkroom and secure permission to set up chemicals tonight if I were to include them in the next post.

For the rest of the morning I propped my back on pillows in bed, the engrossing pages of the Holmes novel diverting my attentions from my aches and pains. I do not recall falling asleep, nor remember a moment when my lids ever became heavy, but when I woke it was to Mrs. López shaking my shoulder, bringing strong coffee and horse liniment on a tray, and reminding me that it was two o'clock and guests would soon be arriving.

Mr. Barlow was first. As I washed my face and buttoned my shirt I heard the wheels of his buggy crunch across the dirt yard and slow to a halt, then heard him call out a greeting to Wolverton and López. By the time I finished dressing and went downstairs, Barlow was seated with Wolverton in the parlor, brandishing a roughly printed broadsheet of the *Crosby County News* and deep in talk of developments in his county.

"—how fortunate, yea, prescient, I believe, to have staked claim to arable land farther east in Crosby County, as the entire community is making plans to move in that direction, lock, stock, and barrel!"

"You didn't feel remorse about abandoning the Quaker colony?" asked Wolverton.

"Frankly," said Barlow, "it was ill situated to start with, out of the way for freighters, scant of water, and, as it turned out, partly situated over the boundary of the county to the west. The new survey even shows our cemetery to be across the line in Lubbock County. We will start anew at Emma."

"We are hearing more and more about these county seat wars," I said, entering and shaking Mr. Barlow's hand. "May I join you?"

"Ha! Get your beauty rest, Doc?" said Wolverton, raising his teacup and crooking his pinkie finger.

"Good afternoon, Dr. Hooper," said his more gracious guest. "I trust thee has indeed rested on this autumn Sabbath?"

"Yes, thank you, and I *sorely* needed it." I gave Barlow an abbreviated account of the previous day's adventures, omitting its ending. Before any of the others arrived, however, I leaned in to confide one matter with Barlow. "Trey and I did come upon one enticing clue, and I hope to share the photographic evidence of it with you as soon as I can set up a temporary darkroom."

"We saw it for ourselves, Mr. Barlow," Wolverton said, *sotto voce*. "A paw print like—the one you described. Dr. Hooper, if you are able to process your own films, by all means, we must locate a spot for you this very evening. And it will be especially useful that I've invited Mr. Barlow to stay over. He can drive us into Espuela in the morning to conduct our business, and you and I can return by the mail hack."

"That is the best news I've heard all day, I'll admit," I said—thinking of transportation that did not involve the back of a horse.

Our talk turned once again to the unfinished topic of county seat elections, since our neighbor had advice for Wolverton on that score.

"Thee is also fortunate in how thy property is situated, Trey. Should thee decide to occupy or keep it, of course," said Barlow.

"And why is that?"

"Thee may judge that there is little value in what may appear at first an unpromising landscape. Thee has pasturage that will support larger herds in the wetter years that we all hope will return. Only a small portion of the land is good for farming, that is true. But thee has ample water from a flowing well, and springs in the vicinity. Thee is not far from the center of the county, in a district that might well attract the eye of the railroad in due time; thee will want to keep a close eye on court filings, and in that task, proximity to whichever town wins your upcoming contest will prove handy. Thy holdings are but ten miles from either."

Wolverton folded his hands and contemplated this advice.

"One other thing, though, is worth watching." Barlow slid to the edge of his seat and lowered his voice. "Thy neighbor Mr. Griswall has a keen nose for the land and its elements. He understands geology, especially the formations bounding this ancient inland sea. He may be searching for more than water."

"What do you—" young Wolverton started to ask, and I recognized the gleam that had leapt into the eye of one with experience in mining operations himself. But Barlow put a finger to his lips.

"I believe others are approaching. Let us talk later on this subject."

Indeed, López was showing Wolverton's other guests into the parlor. Barlow introduced the first man as Judge McQuarrie, the rancher whose pastures shared fence with the Wolverton spread on the north. He seemed an imperious sort, ordering López to take his coat and ten-gallon hat as though he were a manservant and not the manager in charge of a large ranch himself.

"How fares thy lively daughter, Judge?" asked Barlow quietly.

"Bah! Not—not of a temper to accompany an old man across the breaks on a Sunday." He turned, muttering something under his breath about a serpent's tooth, and wandered over, scowling, to examine a large framed oil of a West Texas landscape on the wall.

"Hm," he said. "This was done by that itinerant painter who came around these parts, I think the Earl once mentioned?"

"Thee remembers right," said Barlow. "LaBorde was his name."

"I hope to hell Sir Basil didn't leave that to me," the Judge grumbled. I could have sworn I saw out of the corner of my eye, when he thought we'd all turned to greet the next guests, the man spit upon the canvas.

Rufus Griswall was right behind him, going straight for the decanter on the sideboard as though long accustomed to helping himself. Trailing him was an unexpected guest, however: Maria followed, in a light blue frock and with a shy smile that instantly caught Trey Wolverton's glance.

"What a pleasure to have your daughter among our company!" he cried, standing and shedding the sardonic mien I had come to recognize as his usual characteristic. "I'm so happy you changed your mind, Miss Griswall."

"She didn't," growled Griswall. "I need to be in Espuela

when offices open tomorrow, and I didn't like the idea of leaving her home alone, with all this talk of a criminal about."

"Then it will be a busy morning along the road at daybreak," said Barlow pleasantly. "A bit like a procession to Canterbury, perhaps?"

Griswall ignored the allusion. "We'll head on after dinner," he said. "We can lodge at the livery and be fresh for handling business."

"What kind of business?" demanded the judge.

"None of yours," snapped Griswall.

"Gentlemen," offered Wolverton, "I'd say we've had enough of pleasantries. Why don't we allow Mr. Barlow to guide us in the matter we've all gathered to hear, and then we'll have some supper?"

Judge McQuarrie strode over to the room's most accommodating chair, a large leather-upholstered affair that I guessed to have been the Earl's, and claimed it with his bulk. Griswall pulled up a side chair, Wolverton leaned against the desk, and I kept my seat in the rocker. Maria slipped away, as Barlow moved around behind the desk, adjusted his glasses, and removed a folded legal document from his coat pocket.

"I am here to read the last will and testament of Sir Basil Wolverton II, Baronet Wolverton of Brent, lately domiciled in this county until his unfortunate death the eighth of October hence," he began. "So let us get on with it." He smoothed the paper flat and read, " 'I, Basil Wolverton II, of Wolverton Ranch, in the county of Dickens, and State of Texas, rancher, being of sound mind, memory, and understanding, do make and publish this, my last will and testament, hereby revoking and making void all former wills by me at any time heretofore made. First, I direct that my body be decently interred in a suitable burying ground in the county of Dickens in the state of Texas'—we have, of course, already complied promptly with this wish—

'and that my funeral be conducted with the custom of the neighborhood in which I now reside.' "

Barlow looked up momentarily over his glasses. "We shall determine, following the reading, how best to carry out a fitting memorial." He then continued with the Earl's specific bequests, as all present listened intently. I noted, glancing sideways, that López was lingering just outside the doorway.

The Quaker lawyer read through the short list with a solemnity he might've accorded the gospel. Sir Basil had directed particular remembrances to several acquaintances: to Judge McQuarrie, his Winchester rifle and a quarter horse of his choosing from the remuda; to Mr. Griswall, his collection of Indian art and artifacts; to the county judge, his desk, contents excepted. He also left a considerable sum to endow a widows' and orphans' benevolent fund for the county, and bequeathed his books—an impressive collection, I had already observed for myself—plus five thousand dollars to establish a public library, or expand one should it already exist at the time of his death. To the county relief pantry he left his wardrobe, to be distributed according to need.

To Mr. Barlow himself, he left a portion of fenced rangeland in the northwest quadrant of Dickens County. As Barlow commenced this paragraph he cleared his throat and remarked, "You all may imagine both my embarrassment and gratitude as my friend and client dictated the following: '. . . in hopes that he will come down from his high perch atop the caprock and experience for himself the superior merits of the ranching life.' " The decedent had had a sense of humor, I deduced.

The final two bequests caused the most commotion, however. Mr. Barlow continued reading: "I direct that my loyal ranch manager Antonío López, and his wife Felicia López, receive ten thousand dollars in cash and half of any cattle herds that should be in my possession at the time of my death." A gasp came from the doorway, where Mrs. López had apparently been listening in the shadow of her husband. Out of the corner of my eye I saw him reach to support her waist, as though to prevent her from fainting. Barlow paused—he alone, as attorney, had known this news was coming, but he seemed uncertain whether or not it would register as a surprise to the beneficiaries. "Mr. López, thee and thy wife should come, and be seated," he said rather formally. "You were a friend and aid to the Earl, and not, most assuredly, merely employees."

Barlow completed the reading with the Earl's final wish. " 'The rest and residue of my estate at the time of my death,' " he said, " 'including any property real or intangible, including ranches; registered brands; livestock; homes and other buildings, wherever located; stocks, bonds, other negotiable instruments, and cash; and I give and bequeath to my sole known nephew and heir, Basil Wolverton III, wherever he may reside; and direct that efforts be made to locate him promptly and to deliver to him a full accounting of said estate. Should such efforts prove futile, or should said Basil Wolverton III predecease me, the same property and assets described in this section shall be placed in trust for the benefit of Wolverton Hall, Brent, England, for the use and enjoyment of its owners.' "

Young Wolverton nodded silently, taking all of this in. No one else uttered a word until he at last spoke. "What happens next, Mr. Barlow?"

"As presumptive executor, I shall file this document with the clerk of court, publish a notice in the paper, allow a period for any debt claims against the estate to be presented, and then deduct my executor's fee and oversee such distributions of property as are called for. I would have already filed the will for probate, had the Dickens County clerk been available sooner. But I shall seek to handle the matter promptly tomorrow in Espuela. I had already worked with Sir Basil to maintain an up-to-date inventory of his assets, which are considerable, so this aspect of the task poses no additional burden."

"How long do you expect the process to require?" asked the judge.

"A month or two should suffice. I see no reason why these matters should not be concluded by year's end—unless, of course, complications such as unanticipated debt claims, or the production of a more recent will, or—"

He seemed hesitant to continue, as though he had misspoken, until Wolverton prompted him, "What?"

"Well, in rare cases it is not unheard of for other heirs to come forward, to challenge the probated will or even the identity of beneficiaries." He cleared his throat. "In *extremely* rare cases, I should say."

"So, you'd say, not a snowball's chance in hell, right?" said Wolverton. "Looks like pretty much everyone my uncle named is right here in this room—counting you, López—and *I'm* here, thanks to your quick detective work. Not to rush things, but a few of us will have some big decisions to make."

"Thee is correct. I will carry out my tasks with all speed."

"Well, good. So let's have some dinner, and over our meal we can talk about a fitting memorial for my dear, departed uncle."

The ranch's new master beckoned everyone to table, Mr. Barlow said a prayer for the deceased and gave thanks for the food, and then all fell to discussing the future—advice for Wolverton in managing the ranch; how to control the croton weed, which was used medicinally in tea for people but which sickened cattle; debate over the county seat election; the possibility that Dickens County would at last be able to build a bona fide courthouse.

Stories of the past were also shared, as friends of the Earl discussed how best to honor his memory. It was determined, ultimately, that a brief gathering at the schoolhouse in Espuela on the coming All Saints' Day, November first, would be appropriate, there being no dedicated house of worship in the county either. The Sunday date would avoid any conflict with the school's primary purpose. Eulogies could be spoken, people could pay their respects, and an announcement could be made concerning the unfortunate Earl's intended philanthropies.

Though Mr. Barlow pronounced the idea "Splendid!," and toasts were raised to Sir Basil's memory, I knew concern over the unsolved mystery surrounding his client's death continued to weigh heavily on him, as it did on those of us charged with investigating it.

No one around the table seemed eager to tackle that topic head-on, however. It arose through sideways mentions of cattle killings, casual queries regarding the number of pelts brought in for bounty at the last meeting of the commissioners' court, widely spread and spectacularized rumors of distant howls in the night. No further sightings of the outsized wolf had been reported in the ten days since the Earl's death, however, and the dearth of news raised the possibility that the beast had perished as well.

"Coyotes have been thick as jackrabbits on my place," said Judge McQuarrie. "And speakin' of, rabbit scalps are bringing a dollar a dozen. Might not be worth your buckshot, but for my money, layin' snares is a good way to collect some extra cash come court time."

"Thee'll have to save 'em up, Mac. Court won't meet again now till December," said Barlow.

"Got nothing better to do with my days. Say, whatever happened to our plan to get up an honest-to-God wolf hunt? Seems like as good a time as any."

Barlow ventured an answer to that question too. "Well, methinks everyone was caught up with harvest time—"

"Everyone up on the flat, you mean. We ranchers are ready anytime."

"And cattle roundup, as I was saying. And then the tent revival back in September. And now we have had the passing of our mutual friend to occupy our thoughts, as is only meet."

López weighed in. "We could put out the call any time, I think. Men would come."

"Count me in, lads," said McQuarrie. "I'm spoilin' for a chance at 'em before the weather turns off too cold."

Midway through the steak and beans, as the volume of conversation rose in inverse proportion to that of the wine remaining in the opened bottles, I saw Maria Griswall rise quietly and exit out the side door. I assumed she was headed for the privy, in that direction. But I had not been the only one to notice. Her father kept a watchful eye through the window. And it was not long before our host excused himself and left via the hallway.

When Wolverton did not return in time for dessert—a steaming apple cobbler set in the middle of the long table by Mrs. López—I myself rose, promising to be right back, and went in search of him.

The moon was already coming up, highlighting mare's-tail clouds in the west. The wind, considerably more forceful than it had been only hours earlier, bore the barest hint of moisture. Were we in for a rainstorm that evening? If so, guests would need to be on their way.

I spied our host, not alone, in the shadow of the barn. His words to Maria were low and urgent: *What did you mean by what you said to Dr. Hooper? Now he's watching me like a nursemaid.* I could not make out the words she whispered, only their tone of anguish and incalcitrance. *If there's a real danger, you have to tell me what it is,* he pleaded. She only shook her head.

Wolverton leaned in closer to her face, and I could see that his features, limned in light, had softened. *I have thought of nothing but you the past day and night, Maria. I was ready to take the money and head back to Tucson . . . but now . . .*

I tiptoed closer so I could hear her response. "You must put those thoughts aside. My papa—" The expression on her face suddenly went rigid, losing the moonstruck beauty it had exhibited a second earlier. "Papa! I didn't hear you coming."

"Apparently not," said Griswall, whose bootsteps echoed across the path.

"Mr. Griswall," said Wolverton, "I came out to make sure your daughter was all right. I'm concerned for the welfare of each of my guests, you understand. I believe she just needed some air."

"Oh, I'm certain she did. Maria, I think we must be going, if we are to make Espuela before old Cook shuts his doors for the night." He took her by the arm and guided her to the buggy, then called out for the hired boy to bring his horses. He then turned his visage to Wolverton. As he spoke, he pulled his gun from his holster and checked its chamber. "If we are to be neighbors, we will need to guard our fences, will we not? Against *any* intrusion." He replaced the pistol, armed now for their journey, and stepped into the driver's seat. "Good night, Dr. Hooper," he said. "Perhaps you and your detective colleague will both pay me a visit in the future—after I have taken possession of the legacy the Earl has left me?"

The Judge approached us, leaning into the wind and pulling on his long duster. "Strange duck, that one," he muttered, shaking his head as Griswall's buggy pulled away.

"You're leaving us, too?" said Wolverton, a statement more than a question.

"Yessirree," said the Judge as he retrieved his mount from the corral. "Thanks for the grub and the company, but it won't do to be caught out when this weather comes in."

Although Wolverton offered to ride with him to his own ranch headquarters, the Judge waved it off. "It's only a mile by the back trail, and Higgins's men will be out patrolling."

We bade him good-bye and turned to our next task: to find a place sufficiently dark for use in developing photographic film. Even the moon's dissipated light would be too great to avoid fogging the sensitive film during the delicate tasks of removing it from the camera and transferring it to the developing tank.

The house had no windowless rooms, Wolverton had discovered, nor even closets that could be shut off completely. It lacked indoor sanitation facilities, and the kitchen, besides admitting light and air through several gaps in the stone walls, was in constant use for meal preparation. We were on the verge of resorting to the privy when Mr. Barlow suggested the smokehouse. "I do recall that López has dried excellent cuts of beef in there," he said. "It should be sealed tight."

"That sounds like a capital idea," I said, and went to retrieve my camera, box of equipment, and supplies. "And one other thing: we shall need water, a gallon or so, clean and free of minerals. Can such be procured?"

Wolverton left to find López, and quickly returned carrying a crock with a beeswax-sealed lid. "López says the cistern's been almost dry for a couple months, but he has saved up jars of rainwater against an emergency."

If López was puzzled, as he surely must be at this request, and still more profoundly so when considering the barrel and plank we hauled into the outbuilding for a work surface, he made no comment and retired to his quarters.

Though the tiny house offered hardly enough room for three grown men to stand, we managed to set up a makeshift countertop on which I prepared my equipment. It seemed not so different a discipline in some ways as that of laying medical instruments with precision into sterilized trays in preparation for surgery, and I could do it even by the dim light of a single ruby-shaded candle lantern. It was well that the Eastman roll films, representing the very latest in photographic innovations and still unavailable to the public at large, would be much more convenient to develop under these primitive conditions than typical stripping films or unwieldy glass plates.

"Gentlemen," I asked at last, "are you ready to witness one of the scientific and artistic miracles of our century?"

Wolverton nodded.

"Truly, thee offers a wholly different way to experience the Inner Light," said Barlow.

I said quietly, "What you are about to experience is a preview of the future, for Mr. Eastman has loaned us, for testing, a prototype of his film-cartridge camera that can be loaded and unloaded in daylight, anywhere in the field, and a tank for developing negatives affixed to a flexible, completely transparent film. I have been privileged to use it and report on its results for some months while his patent lawyers have been refining their case. You must say nothing of our experiment, for competitors would be rabid to obtain this intelligence."

"Well, let's get on with it," said Wolverton. "What do we do?"

I shut the door behind us and opened my case. By the light of the candle lantern I donned my rubber apron and gloves. I set the camera, tongs, and timer on the plank just so, in order that I could locate each item in total darkness when necessary.

I retrieved from my case three jars of chemical tablets, along with three small graduated glass beakers and a stirring rod. I had calculated in advance the proportion of water for each. "Rodinal is a lately introduced compound for developing images," I explained as I worked. "It interacts with the silver nitrate emulsion that coats the film and—if we have been careful in our exposure and development times—reveals the latent gradations of the captured image. Let us hope!"

I mixed, stirred, and poured, then set the ruby glass atop the candle lamp and blew out the light. Once the film had finished its developing phase, I explained to my companions, I would light it again, to provide safe illumination for the next tasks. But for now, the film must be handled in total darkness while transferring it from the preloaded cartridge onto the wire roll that I would then insert into a tank about the size of a cocktail shaker.

Gingerly I handled the celluloid by its edges. The room was so close I could feel the breath of its other occupants only inches from my neck. When I completed the operation and lowered the roll into the tank, I screwed on the cover and shook the whole mechanism gently. A metaphor crept to my mind of absinthe over cracked ice.

"What do we do now?" asked Barlow.

"We can step outside and leave this for fifteen minutes or so; I shall set the timer, then we shall return to check on the developing, and wash and fix the negatives. They must then dry before we can cut them apart."

"And making prints?"

"Ah—that step must wait for the morning, for, lacking proper lighting and a laboratory, we shall use the sun itself."

My watch confirmed that it was already after nine o'clock, but we passed the interval in the parlor, enjoying the Earl's cigars once more and talking quietly of the day's events.

Wolverton poured himself a whiskey and said to us, "Gentlemen, I'm willing to chase this so-called case a little further . . . but frankly, I don't see where it's all headed."

"In my experience under Derrick Miles's direction," I responded, as gently as I could manage to avoid my words floating up to the quarters of the ranch manager and his wife, "matters often take some time to develop—much like film. It is of utmost importance that I post these photographs, and my report, to Miles at the earliest opportunity tomorrow, and we shall see what he makes of them even as we continue our charge here."

Mr. Barlow reminded us that a series of mysterious events still begged explanation. "I remain most uneasy about that strange warning thee received in Fort Worth," he said to Wolverton, "for we are still in the dark about its source, and I fear for thy safety should we leave off without some sensible explanation."

Wolverton snorted. "Still afraid there might be diabolical forces at work?"

"Listen!" I said, standing almost as an automaton—as if dragged bodily to my feet—at the occurrence of a sudden and distant sound, unearthly and cruel. "Do you make out that cry?"

The three of us sped for the door at once, Wolverton grabbing a rifle from a rack on the wall. He flung open the door and we stood still, expectant. But it did not come again, and Wolverton voiced the concern that haunted all our minds. "Surely," said he grimly, "the Judge had ample time to reach home safe from the threat of wild animals. And the Griswalls to reach Espuela as well."

We could only hope. As I checked my watch I steeled my nerve to return to our ad hoc darkroom and complete the night's work. Sealed up in the tomblike shed once again with my companions, by the eerie light of the ruby lantern I fixed the negatives, hung them across a wire to dry, and strained to make sense of the images.

In sequence, past the scenic landscape views and character studies I had taken during our journey and arrival at the Wolverton Ranch, there came a series of close-ups in which a giant paw print darkened the dark sand; and from our encounter with Griswall and his daughter, faces like black, shrunken heads of the Amazonian Jivaro, their ghoulish features painted as though with a phosphorescent tint. This was true, as well, of the candid portrait I had captured of Wolverton and the Lópezes.

My companions, neither having previously viewed a photographic negative, remarked at the strangeness of the representation.

"And what is this one?" asked Barlow, noting the image of a distant humanlike apparition, standing white as chalk against a gaping hole in the cosmos. *The man on the mesa,* I thought to myself.

"I do not know, to be quite honest," I admitted. "But we shall ask Miles's opinion on this figure as well. For now, I propose that we get some rest—and allow our deeper levels of mental capacity to tease out answers that are eluding us in waking hours."

Chapter 9
Sojourn at Soldier's Mound

{In which Hooper and Wolverton encounter the vagaries of West Texas weather and history.}

The early morning brought no particular illumination to any of us, nor to the task of producing prints, for the sun hid its rays behind a haze of gray for some hours. I would need Old Sol's full cooperation in order to expose the negative images onto the card-sized sheets of Arches printing-out paper which I had brought with me.

When at last the breeze freshened and the skies cleared, the effect was most dramatic. To the west a bank of clouds rose like a range of bruised-blue mountains, reflecting the sunlight back on the nearer landscape and gilding the earth in a fierce orange hue. I moved quickly, setting up the prints for their brief exposures to light before the wind could kick up with more force. Developing and fixing them was a simpler matter than the film had been, and soon I emerged from the smokehouse with a quite serviceable, one might even say artistic, set of photographic prints to accompany my report to Miles. I tucked them, still damp, into the breast pocket of my jacket.

"We'd best make haste," said the Quaker, who already had his buggy at the ready and was dressed in anticipation of a drop in temperature, "or we shall not beat that norther."

Wolverton agreed, and he swiftly brought the ranch wagon around as I gathered my satchel and overcoat and climbed up beside him.

We raced west toward Espuela, on the identical route we had covered the previous Saturday past rugged side canyons and over a small arroyo. But as we came up out of the creek bed and topped the rise, the wind buffeted the buggy so hard it nearly sent Barlow tumbling back in. The force of the blast was almost immediately followed by a peppering of rain—or could it have been *sleet?*—on the buggy's hood. Wolverton and I, exposed on the seat of the buckboard, reached for the slickers we had stowed beneath the seat.

No sooner had the spray of ice pellets subsided than there came a steady wind bearing a thick flurry of snow. *Snow*, incredibly! Thunder crashed. The animals, startled, whinnied and bucked, and Barlow's pair made as though to shake off their traces.

"Get the horses back down below the hill!" shouted Wolverton, hardly audible above the clatter of tack and the increasing din of the wind. He pulled the brake on our wagon and jumped from his perch, then ran to snatch the buggy's reins from Barlow's grip, turning us all about-face and forcing the whole outfit pell-mell off the exposed plain and into the lee of the canyon below. Barlow gritted his teeth and reached for the hood, to keep it from ripping away. Wolverton returned to our wagon and drove it down as I held to the dashboard for dear life.

Wolverton expertly guided men and animals underneath the relative shelter of a rock ledge, and we caught our breath as the storm swept above us like a tremendous ocean wave, obliterating the view on all sides.

"Well done, boy," said Barlow, catching his breath and drawing his cloak closer about him. "Thee'll make a plainsman yet."

"No damage, I hope?" I inquired.

"None as I can see," he replied. "Good God, I've never witnessed such an event." Barlow bowed for a moment in silent prayer, and presently raised his eyes to the white swarm. "He hath loosed the fateful lightning," said he reverently, and even an old skeptic like myself could not resist agreeing with the man.

"Have we the makings of a fire?" Barlow asked after his moment of grace. "I have been in Texas long enough to guess we may find ourselves stuck for a while."

Wolverton glanced about and remarked a goodly assortment of dry branches within easy reach. For my part, I produced from my pocket a box of strike-on matches I kept handy for the lighting of cigars and pipes. Within minutes we had a blaze going under the rock shelter, and were glad of it, for the snow and wind gave no sign of abating.

" 'Twas on just such an October afternoon up at Cañon Blanco back in seventy-one that an entire Comanche camp eluded the full might of Colonel Ranald Mackenzie and a company of the U.S. Army," said Barlow.

"I can readily imagine it," I said.

"One minute, Mackenzie has Chief Quanah in his sights—he's practically composing his victory report to Grant in his head—and the next, a norther blows in and obscures the entire band of Quahadas, tipis and horses and all," Barlow explained. "It is said they simply dissolved like ghosts into the cover of blowing snow. It would be another three years before Mackenzie once again maneuvered the Indians within reach. And when he did at last achieve victory over the red man, this very spot—upon the hill yonder—is where he repaired to while recovering from the battle at the Palo Duro. 'Tis why the place is to this day called Soldier's Mound, and why the road upon which we have been traveling is still known as the Mackenzie Trail."

Wolverton rubbed his hands over the crackling fire and withdrew a flask from his pocket. He took a sip and passed it to me. I did not refuse.

"How," he began above the howling wind, "did such a sorry

bunch of natives manage to elude the best and brightest of the American military? I've known a few Apaches and Yaquis out west. They're a pretty sad bunch," said Wolverton.

"Ah," replied Barlow sagely. "Not for nothing were the Comanche known as the Lords of the Plains, my boy. Their mastery of the horse, learned and practiced over centuries, made them ruler over this vast domain of grass, and as long as the bison provided for all their needs, well, their skill in mounted battle, and their knowledge of the trackless Llano Estacado, made them well-nigh invincible."

"That was," I interjected, "until Mackenzie figured out that the strategy to defeat the Comanche was the capture of their horse herd and the wholesale destruction of their food source, the bison. But had you known such warriors as Chief Quanah, or Chief Lone Wolf of the Kiowa, or Iron Shirt of the Cheyenne, you would readily understand."

"You knew them?" asked Wolverton, in sudden, genuine admiration.

"Well . . . I must admit to having met Quanah but once, though that single occasion was sufficient."

"Derrick Miles spent time among the Indians, did he not?" asked Barlow.

"True," I said, struggling to shout above the storm without appearing boastful. As my two companions leaned in closer to the fire, I look another swig from Wolverton's flask and launched into the story—as it was once told to me—of Miles's years on the Texas frontier.

"You see, Derrick Miles is one of those rare figures of our century who has both distinguished himself in the service of our nation, and yet remained a steadfast friend and ally of those who inhabited this continent long before us."

Wolverton, by now exhibiting the full effects of the whiskey's warmth, shook his head. "Pardon me, but that sounds like a load of horse dung. 'Sbeen fifteen years since the Injuns all went to the reservation. How can that be?"

As there appeared to be no letup to the storm, and the ledge provided as secure a shelter as it must have done for peoples throughout millennia, I found myself waxing eloquent in the spirit of times gone by. "Indulge me, if you will," said I.

"In the raucous years following the admittance of Texas to the Union," I began, "white settlers of all nationalities saw in this new state the renewal of their agricultural and industrial fortunes, not to mention—for those unlanded in the Old World—the hope of property ownership in the New. I saw this fervor in my own father, a British physician who had emigrated to Galveston, a city much in need of medical professionals. In the southern and eastern portions of Texas, populations grew and trade flourished. But it was a different story north and west of the empresarios' colonies and the coastal cities. Horrific accounts of Indian depredations reached our ears; only the most daring of traders, or the most dedicated of missionaries, or the most desperate of families, ventured into the natives' territory.

"Still, Europeans pushed west. Into that dangerous climate arrived one Woodrow Miles, an Englishman recruited by critics of the Peters empresarios to resurvey land disputed in the so-called Hedgcoxe War."

Barlow settled onto one elbow; Wolverton yawned. A couple of feet away, one of the horses snorted.

"Yes, as I was saying. Surveyor and mapmaker Woodrow Miles traveled to Tarrant County, Texas, in 1852, leaving his wife and seven-year-old son, Percival, behind in England. The elder Miles, it must be said here, greatly admired Sam Houston, hero of the Texians.

"I shall cut to the point, gentlemen, and say only that Woodrow Miles identified with his idol to the extent that he—how shall I put it—went the same way of adopting a semi-native way of life and, during his days working out of Fort Griffin, took up with a part-Indian woman, who in due time presented him with a son before returning to her Comanche kin. Woodrow named the boy for Eudora Derrick, his own mother back in Lancashire, and for the onetime president of the Republic.

"Derrick Houston Miles spent the first seven years of his life among the army men and camp followers, the traders and sutlers and officers and wives and children of the frontier fort. At the outbreak of the War between the States, however, the senior Miles, ever the adventurer, left his son in the care of a comrade at the fort who styled himself a 'Texas Ranger,' and went off to spy for the army, though I won't say which. That much is both true to Derrick Miles's memory—and tantalizingly uncertain."

Wolverton rolled his slicker into a pillow and stretched out his frame on the ground to take advantage of it. Though I could not determine whether he was still listening, I moved on toward my story's conclusion.

"Young Derrick's father pledged to return and take him to England, to meet his legitimate family. This he never did; what became of the elder Miles is unknown. The boy passed time in the company of the Rangers at Fort Griffin for the duration of the war—for few men remained to guard the frontier at all, when soldiers were so desperately required by both the Confederacy and the Union—and afterward, when the army once more turned its attentions to the so-called 'Indian problem.' Derrick Miles cultivated a portfolio of useful skills that doubtless included pickpocketing, counterfeiting, and card-sharping along with marksmanship, scouting, hunting, and other necessities of survival."

Derrick Miles's current, straitlaced client Barlow, glancing askance at me, seemed to take this new information under consideration. Wolverton cocked one eye open and appeared to be enjoying the story tremendously. *In for a dime, in for a dollar,* I judged, and pressed forward.

"In the spring of 1870, at age sixteen, Derrick Miles finagled funds and a letter of recommendation from none other than President Grant himself, to travel to England in search of his father and half-brother. There, he had no difficulty locating Percival, a student and prefect at the University of London. Under Percy's tutelage, Derrick enrolled in university coursework on an occasional basis. He excelled in science, law, and medicine but never took a degree.

"He did, however, learn of his elder brother's *sub rosa* role as an agent for Scotland Yard, helping solve the 1873 Bank of England forgeries. You may recall that notorious series of crimes?"

"Indeed," said Barlow, who could be counted upon to have read the papers. "I had not yet come west, and I do remember that the Philadelphia banks were quite nervous about it."

"Well, during that same period, Derrick's own American citizenship proved quite useful. As early as 1874, he was recruited to work with the Wells Fargo Company in developing anti-counterfeiting measures."

"Ah," said Wolverton from his prone position, "that much makes sense, if he's really that good. Wells Fargo needed all the ingenuity it could get, to secure all the gold moving from coast to coast. My pa said back then you could bite down on a coin to test it, and it'd be soft as chocolate."

"Miles helped develop measures to distinguish authentic printed currency that he to this day will not reveal," said I without disguising my pride.

"And thus his work brought him back to Texas?" prodded Barlow, who was in the process of prying open with his knife a tin of biscuits he had spirited from his pocket.

"Yes, yes . . . returning west during the Indian wars that year,

Miles was recruited as an army spy. To this day he theorizes that the surname he shared with one of the campaign's generals, Nelson Miles, was a factor gaining the attention of the U.S. military, though he is certain he bears no kin to the man. Furthermore, it is still not widely recognized that Miles's sympathies turned to the Indians' side, and most citizens have no clue that it was Miles who, with his precise understanding of the Comanche tongue, persuaded Quanah Parker to absent himself in advance of the decisive Battle of Palo Duro Canyon in September of seventy-four." I felt a twinge here, as though I might have, under the influence of drink, revealed a bit too much.

"Still but a tyro, he was assigned to accompany captives to Fort Marion, in Florida, the following year. Foiling an attempted escape of his charges—in which the exact events remain cloudy—he was promoted to the rank of captain.

"Miles soon returned to Texas having privately determined to cut ties with the army, however, and in 1876, weary and injured, he resigned his commission and hung out his shingle as a consulting detective. He took the inaugural Texas and Pacific train into Forth Worth . . . as did I, making his acquaintance aboard." I skirted mention of the scandal that had caused my own westward flight, not to mention the sensational crime that had occurred in our adopted city on the very day we had arrived there.

I concluded my tale with mention of a few cases Miles had famously accepted and even more famously solved since, dropping the names of Charles Goodnight and William F. Cody and Jay Gould, in addition to that of Chief Quanah, whose admirable foresight in bridging two worlds I praised profusely.

I had hardly taken note of the dying light, until Wolverton pointed out how the driving snow had transmogrified into a dense curtain of fog. "We'll not make Espuela this night," he said, and Barlow sagely agreed.

We drew straws for a watch and resigned ourselves to a cold, hungry sojourn out of doors. If lobo had howled once more above the blanket of white I could not have said, in those darkling hours, for the whiskey and exertion took their toll, and I wrapped myself in the shroud of my overcoat and slept as one dead.

Chapter 10
Mysterious Signals

*{In which Frank Hooper and Trey Wolverton
each disposes of errands, encounters a woman,
and seeks to apprehend a lawbreaker.}*

The next morning, after the adverse weather passed, we brushed ourselves off, hauled ourselves up out of the canyon, and made fast progress into Espuela. The road exhibited almost no effect of the storm in the way of mud: what precipitation had fallen, the wind seemed to just as swiftly have swept away.

In town we tied up, and each man alighted to tend to his separate tasks. Barlow's concerned the schoolhouse that served as temporary quarters for the county clerk, with an aim to filing the Earl's will for probate. Wolverton's took him to the bank, where he hoped to cash a draft to replenish his funds. Mine involved the post office, where I sealed up one set of the thoroughly dry prints, my letter, and my drawings in an express envelope and addressed it to Derrick Miles.

"How long do you estimate delivery to require?" I asked the postal clerk, who appeared considerably less concerned with speed than I. There was nothing for it, however, but to hand over the parcel and my handful of coins and hope for the best.

The post office was but a rude shack, and as I turned to go I perused the wall on which were posted bills and bulletins of various sorts. A notice of the upcoming county-seat election was secured by rusty thumbtacks, as were an announcement of a property auction to be held two weeks hence and an advertisement, in screaming capital letters of various sizes, from a land-lot sales firm. A handwritten note on a sheet of foolscap offered a reward for wolf hides. I remarked there, as well, the likeness of the escaped criminal, whose blurry features stared back from the poster. It conjured a similarity I could not place, and it was unsettling in its hardened scowl. I took note of the thousand-dollar reward and attempted to fix the image in my memory.

As I stepped out onto the street, I passed Griswall going in. I tipped my hat. I was about to offer a more civil greeting and an appreciation for his recent company, but he brushed past, and I shrugged. The man was a conundrum.

I ambled down the packed dirt thoroughfare, if thoroughfare it could be called. I passed the grocer, the dry goods store, and the land office, into which I peered, to discover a duo engaged in heated discussion. Moving an entire town, it would seem, was a complicated business.

As I crossed a narrow alley between wooden structures, I nearly ran right into a female figure almost completely shrouded in a brown burnous. Her face was covered as well, wrapped Bedouin-style so that I almost did not recognize the lady as our Sunday supper guest. As I turned in abrupt recognition, she glanced back at me simultaneously, and the veil slid from her visage. For a mere second I registered, as if through the momentary opening of the camera's shutter curtain, the bloom on her cheek, the tumescence of her moist lips, the aqueous brightness of her eye; and my memory just as fleetingly sprang to a long-ago scene along the South Texas strand, to a mouth *I* had once kissed. She whom I now encountered, I knew without corroborating attestation, was a woman in love.

The veil was just as swiftly replaced, and the figure disappeared through the door of what passed for Espuela's only lodging establishment. I snapped to my senses. I had to find my client, before he further enmeshed himself in a romance that held unknown risk for compromising his safety.

The bank? No, Wolverton had left a good half hour earlier. The bootmaker's? No, and truth be told, he'd probably given up by now on the likelihood of replacing his footwear. The saloon? Perhaps. I was about to cross the street in search of it when a woman of a certain age, dressed plainly in dun cotton shift, approached me and laid a solicitous hand on my arm.

"Excusing my manners, sir, but thee is the esteemed Doctor Hooper?"

I reached to straighten the lapels of my jacket. "The same, madam," I replied. "Are you in need of a physician?"

"Not just yet," she said, leaning toward me as one vouchsafing a confidence, "though surely in due time."

If this matronly stranger expected a spark of understanding from me, she was destined for disappointment. "Pardon me?"

"Thee has come to see to Sir Basil's concerns, is it not so?"

"Why, yes, madam, but I am regrettably too late to help him," I said, partly in jest.

"Yes, God rest his soul. What I mean is, I wish to convey my most sincere thanks to his executor for the girl Sir Basil commended to our humble household," said she. "My husband and I would have been hard put to handle our fall chores without her help, and it's to the Earl's generosity we owe our very survival this harvest season."

Her speech provided the sliver of a clue. "You and your husband live in the Quaker community, I take it?"

"Mr. Larkin teaches at the academy and raises wheat on the farm. Our sons have families of their own nowadays, and I myself am unable to be the helpmeet I once was." Her voice dipped to a whisper. "We are most grateful for the young woman the Earl sent us to assist with clerical and household duties. Thee should know she is settling in well in our spare room."

I suspected I should not pry further, but accepted her thanks with equanimity. If Mr. Barlow knew of any such arrangement, he had strangely omitted it from his earlier disclosure of facts. I would quiz him at the first opportunity. Until then, I bid Mrs.

Larkin farewell, with appreciation for her kind words.

"I shall call for thee soon," she said to me, and was on her way, a brown figure as sturdy as a donkey in her plodding pace, and as inscrutable.

I stood pondering how much I should say of the matter to Barlow or Wolverton, when the latter sauntered to my side.

"What the devil was that about?" he inquired.

"I am not quite certain—though I have about determined that any circumstance, however complex, is further complicated by the involvement of a woman."

He glanced at me quizzically. I straightened my coat buttons and put him off for now. "I must say, I am glad you've returned in fine fettle. Is your business concluded?"

He patted his vest pocket. "Ready when you are, Hooper. Let's get back to the ranch."

Wolverton and I arrived in sight of the ranch just after dusk, following an uneventful wagon ride back along the Mackenzie Trail. Had I encountered Mr. Barlow again before our departure, I would have sought a way to ask about the odd Quaker woman, Mrs. Larkin, who surely was known to him. But that question must remain unasked and unanswered for now.

The gales of the previous day had dissipated, and the night was still. From a way off came the hoot of an owl, and the coyotes took up their customary call-and-response. I was near to nodding off in my passenger's seat when I heard Wolverton's voice, low but urgent, next to me.

"What's that light yonder?" he asked, and I snapped to alertness again.

"Where?"

"Out across the breaks, there—" he indicated with his free hand. I spied what he meant—a pinpoint emanating from somewhere in the valley, far below the purple shadow of a ridge.

Only from our particular position could we see it, for in another instant, as we rounded a curve in the track and an intervening hill blocked the spot, it was eclipsed.

But by now the ranch headquarters was in view, and from it emanated a much more distinct source of light. A lantern threw its beams outward from the second-floor veranda toward the canyon's edge.

"Fine homecoming López has arranged for us," Wolverton said with irony, "if he expects to welcome us from the opposite side of the house."

With a glimmer of comprehension I saw precisely what he meant. "That lamp," I whispered, "is not intended for you and me."

Wolverton slowed the team to a walk, then stopped several yards from the stable path. He motioned for us to step down, and we did so with as much stealth as we could muster as he tied the reins to the outer gate post. He waved me behind him, and we gained the house on foot, avoiding the scrape of boot on stone in the twilight. Had we been burglars on the make we would hardly have conducted our mission with more success, for we were able to enter the kitchen door noiselessly and were nearly to the top of the back stairs when Wolverton drew his pistol and shouted in the direction of the lantern's glow.

"López!" he called out as we rounded the corner. "The master of the house has returned! What goes here?"

In rapid succession came a sudden crash and clatter; the light danced and disappeared, and a woman screamed.

"*Dios mio!* . . . Mr. Trey?" replied López in the darkness as we raced toward the surprised figures. "You—you have given us a fright!"

"What goes, I say?" Wolverton insisted, his demand backed by the enticement of his drawn weapon. I could scarcely make out the expression on López's face in the shadow, but I was sure he had no difficulty imagining the sternness on Wolverton's.

López replied weakly as he struggled to relight the candle in the lantern. "We have been keeping a watch . . . for you. It is so good to have you back safely. I would—would have sent the boy for you last night, but the weather was too raw," he finished. The flame took hold once more, and his trembling hands latched the glass and lifted the light. His dark eyes, magnified through the lantern, were full of horror and astonishment as they darted from Trey Wolverton to me.

"Keeping a watch for someone, but not us," Wolverton said. "We saw the light across the breaks. And it's not the first time. What is the meaning of it?"

"I don't know what you mean, sir." His agitation was so great that he could hardly speak, and the shadows sprang up and down from the shaking of his candle. "I . . . ah . . . was making sure all the windows were fastened, after the storm."

"You didn't think it better to do that chore by daylight?"

"It's my, ah, habit to check all the windows at night."

"And your wife? Has she nothing better to occupy her time than to accompany you on such rounds?" I added. It was plain to see that the ranch manager was hiding something, and Wolverton appeared determined to get to the bottom of it.

"Look here, López," said Wolverton rigidly, "you may have been the boss around here when my uncle was alive, and you assuredly have the benefit of age and experience over me, but I want the truth out of you—right now. *Qué diablos está pasando aquí*, man?!"

The ranch manager quivered as a captive about to be taken prisoner. "*No me preguntes, se lo imploro—por favor*, do not ask me! The matter is not my secret to tell, I swear. If it concerned no one but myself I would not try to keep it from you."

A sudden idea occurred to me, and I took the lantern from

López's trembling hand. "He must have been displaying it as a signal," said I. "Let us see if there is any answer."

I held it out over the porch rail as we had observed, and stared out into the darkness of the night as I swung it slowly back and forth like a brakeman's light. Vaguely I could discern the black bank of the cottonwoods and the lighter veins of sedimentary rock, for the moon was behind the clouds. And then I gave a cry of exultation, for a tiny pinpoint of yellow light had suddenly transfixed the dark veil, and it glowed steadily across the void. "There it is!"

"No, no, sir, it is nothing—nothing at all!" López broke in. "I assure you, sir—"

"Move your light to the side, Hooper!" cried Wolverton. "Look there, how the other one is a mirror image! That's no coincidence. What is this conspiracy, López, and who are you signaling?"

The man's face became openly defiant. "It is my business, and not yours. I will not tell."

"Then you and I will wait right here while Dr. Hooper rides for the sheriff."

"Do what you have to, Mr. Trey. I can't betray a trust."

"By damn, I'll do what I must," he swore. "Hardly a full week on my own family's property, where you have lived under this roof for longer than I've been on this earth, and here I find you deep in some dark plot against me."

"No, no, sir; no, not against you!" cried Señora López, the deep sob that escaped her throat reminding us of her presence. It was the same heartbroken voice that had disturbed my dreams on my first night in this place. "Oh, Antonío, have I brought you to this? It is my doing, Señor Wolverton—all mine. My husband has done nothing except for my sake, and because I asked him."

I raised the lantern high; Wolverton kept the pistol level.

She continued, "My unfortunate brother is starving down in the breaks. We cannot let him perish at our very door. Our light is a signal to him that food is ready for him, and his light is to show where my husband is to deliver it."

"Your brother?" I asked.

"You tell him, Antonío," she said to her husband. *"Vamos."* She emerged from the shadows, her face wet with tears and more horror-struck than her husband's.

López cleared his throat. "My wife's brother," he said wearily, "is the escaped criminal, José Mora."

At this admission Mrs. López broke down. "We have been aiding him—with food and warmth, nothing more," she said between gulps. Trey Wolverton and I both stared at the woman in amazement. Was it possible that this woman was of the same blood as one of the most notorious criminals in the country? I now recognized the resemblance I had detected in the poster, the solid, grim, round face, the deep-set eyes.

"So he is down there tonight, madam?" I interjected. "It is our duty to inform the authorities."

"Please, please hear me first—then I would not blame you for doing as you think right."

Wolverton kept the pistol trained on the couple but nodded his assent.

"I am the eldest of eleven children of *la familia* Mora from old Coahuila. Pepe—Josepe—is the youngest. We spoiled him, as I think you say, when he was small, and gave in to his every wish. My mother laughed when Pepe learned to lift the key from her apron pocket and my father spared the rod too much when Pepe brought home stolen candy from the neighborhood store. Then as Pepe grew older he met wicked companions, and the devil entered into him until he broke my mother's heart and dragged our name in the dirt. From crime to crime he sank lower and lower until it is only the mercy of God which has saved him from hanging; but to me, sir, he was always the little barefoot boy I had nursed and played with.

"That was why José broke out of prison, sir. When they locked him up in Albany for cattle rustling, he knew that I was not far away and that we could not refuse to help him. He guessed it would not be long till a posse from Laredo arrived to seek justice for murder. When he appeared here one night, weary and broken, with the white men hard at his heels, what could we do? We took him in and fed him and cared for him. Then you returned, sir, and my brother thought he would be safer in the breaks than anywhere else until the danger was over, so we advised him to hide there until he could run. But at night we make sure if he is still there by putting a light in the window, and if there was an answer my husband took out some bread and food to him. It was robbing none but *los perros,* nothing but table scraps for the dogs.

"Every day we hoped that he was gone, but as long as he was there we could not leave him to the wolves. There is no conspiracy against you, I promise you. That is the whole truth, I swear it on my mother's grave, and if there is blame in the matter it does not lie with my husband but with me, for whose sake he has done all that he has." The woman's words rushed forth like a river, with an intense earnestness and sore regret.

"Is this true, López?"

"Yes, Mr. Trey. Every word of it."

Wolverton's tone softened, but he did not lower the gun. "Well, I cannot blame you for standing by your own wife. But how can you be certain Mora had nothing to do with Sir Basil's demise, or any other crime in this vicinity?"

"He arrived here two days after Sir Basil's death," said López flatly, though the shift of his eyes away from Wolverton's belied his confidence. The manager, it seemed, could not be certain himself what part his brother-in-law might have played in recent events.

"Go to your quarters and stay there," Wolverton ordered, "and we shall talk tomorrow about your future here." When the couple were gone he held the lantern and peered again over the rail into the evening chill. Far away in the black distance there yet glowed that one tiny point of yellow light, now stationary.

"I wonder he dares show the light," said Trey Wolverton.

"It may be so placed as to be visible only from here."

"Very likely. How far do you think it is, a mile, maybe?"

"Not more than that. It cannot be far if López has had to carry out the food."

"And there he is waiting, a villain and a felon, in my own backyard. I have no choice but to apprehend him if I can!"

If my client felt inclined to take justice in his hands, then it was my duty to accompany him, however unprepared I might be to grapple with a murderer among the rocks at night. I was not unfamiliar with the type, of course, having assisted Miles on numerous cases, but this was different. We had not the benefit of Derrick Miles's military skill and keen acumen regarding the criminal mind. Moreover, I knew not enough of my companion's craft to trust him—and just enough of his temperament not to.

As for the Lópezes, we owed them no allegiance: it was not as though they had taken us into their confidence. Their secret had been forced from them. Mora was a threat to the community, a brazen scoundrel for whom there was neither pity nor excuse. We were only doing what any citizen must, in taking this chance of putting him back where he could do no further harm. With his brutal and violent nature, others might have to pay the price if we held back. Any night, for example, our neighbors the Griswalls, or the old Judge, might be attacked by him, and I knew, when he voiced my very thoughts, that I had rightly discerned the prime motive that made Trey Wolverton so keen upon the operation.

"Maria may be in grave danger this moment," he said almost to himself.

"I will come with you," said I.

"Then grab your boots and get your pistol." He hung the lantern on a hook, then turned and sped down the stairs. "Let's see if we can put out this villain's lights for him."

A faint breeze had risen. We hurried through the shinnery and soapberry, trusting the rustle of the wind to cover our approach. The night air was heavy with the smell of sage released by yesterday's storm as it wafted in our direction, and a veil of clouds soon dropped over the moon. Both natural events I took for good signs, as they would shield us somewhat from discovery. The pinprick of light still burned steadily in front of us, guiding our way.

"We must close in on him rapidly, using surprise to our advantage," Wolverton said so quietly I could scarce hear him over the pounding of my pulse in my ears.

He stopped for a minute to gauge our distance. "What do you imagine Miles would say to this?" he asked, teasing. "How about that hour of darkness in which the power of evil is exalted?" As if in answer to his words there rose suddenly out of the vast gloom of the breaks that strange cry which I had already heard upon the borders of the labyrinthine Croton Breaks. It came with the wind through the silence of the night, a long, deep, guttural growl, then a rising howl, and then the falling moan in which it died away. Again and again it sounded, the whole air throbbing with it, strident, wild, and menacing.

Wolverton caught my sleeve, his bravado suddenly less in evidence. "My God, what's that?"

But we both knew the answer. "Hooper," said my companion answering his own question, "*that* was the cry of a wolf." My blood ran cold in my veins, for there was a crack in his voice which told of the sudden horror which had seized him. This young man, however bold, was not immune to terror.

"What's that the folks around here call it?" he asked.

"What?"

"The ranchers. What was the name of the animal?" His mind, which I had come to regard as customarily sharp, seemed blunted by real fear.

"Oh, they are just yokels. Why should you mind?"

"Tell me, Hooper. *What do they say of it?*"

I hesitated but could not escape the question. I spoke softly, hoping not to betray the anxiety I myself felt. "They say it is the cry of the dire wolf."

He groaned and was silent for a few moments. "A wolf it was," he said at last, "but it seemed to come from miles away, over yonder, I think."

"It's hard to say out here, once it dies away."

"It rose and fell with the wind. Isn't that the direction of the Croton Breaks?"

"Yes, it is."

"Well, it was down there. Come now, Hooper, didn't you think yourself that it was the howl of a wolf? I am not a child. You need not fear to speak the truth."

"Griswall was with me when I heard it last. He said that it might be the calling of a strange bird."

"No, no, it was a wolf. My God, can there be some truth in all these wild stories? Is it possible that I am really in danger from so lurid a cause? You don't believe it, do you, Hooper?"

"No, goodness, no."

"It was one thing to joke about it in Fort Worth, I'll admit, and another to stand out here in the remote breaks at night and to hear such a sound. And my uncle! Barlow's description of the paw print beside him as he lay dead. Then the prints we saw, undeniable from your photographs. It all fits together. I've never considered myself a coward, Hooper, but that sound clean froze my blood. Feel my hand!" I did; it was as cold as a block of marble. "What do you advise we do now?"

I hadn't expected our brash young client to consider any suggestion of mine, much less yield to it. "Shall we turn back?"

He thought about it for only an instant. "No, by thunder—we have come out to get our man, and we'll see it through. We are after the criminal, and a—a dire wolf may be after us. Come on! We'll do what men must, even if all the hounds of hell are loose in the wilds of West Texas."

We stumbled along through the hoodoos and hills, fixing upon the speck of light at each turn. There is nothing so deceptive as the distance of a light at night, and while at times the glimmer seemed to be far away upon the horizon, at other times it might have been within a few yards of us. But at last we could see whence it came, and we knew that we were indeed very close. A guttering candle had been cleverly stuck in a crevice of the rocks, flanking it on each side so as to keep the wind from it and also to prevent it from being visible save in the direction of the Wolverton ranch house. A great sandstone boulder concealed our approach, and crouching behind it we gazed over it at the signal light. It was strange to see this lone candle burning there in the middle of the badlands, with no sign of life near it—just the one straight yellow flame and the gleam of the rock on either side of it.

"What shall we do now?" whispered Wolverton.

"Wait here. He wouldn't venture far from his light." The words were hardly out of my mouth when we caught sight of the man. Over the rocks, in the crevice where the candle burned, thrust forth a leather-brown face, framed with tangled beard and wild hair, a face seamed with use too hard for his years. It might well have belonged to one of the grizzled herdsmen who had once kept sheep in the hillside pens, or to a weatherworn Comanchero trader, or to an even more ancient tribe that once peopled the breaks. Like a crafty and savage animal that has heard the steps of hunters, he turned his ear our way. Something had aroused his suspicions. Did López show some code unknown to us, I wondered, that had warned him? Or had we given our position away by some faint noise? I was close enough to read the anxiety upon the man's wicked face. Any instant he might run for it.

Wolverton and I sprang forward at the same moment but were startled by a rock hurled in our direction, which shattered against the boulder that had been our hiding place. The criminal turned to fling a curse at us, and I caught one glimpse of his stocky figure as he sprang to his feet and took off running. The moon broke through the clouds for an instant and lighted our way over the brow of the hill. From its vantage we spied our man running down the other side with the alacrity and precision of an antelope. He danced over the outcrops like some Hopi Kokopelli or stolid leprechaun, handily outpacing us.

Had I the luck of a Billy Dixon, a long shot of my revolver might have crippled him, but I had brought the weapon only to defend myself if attacked and not to shoot an unarmed man who was running away. Though Wolverton looked to be a capable runner and in fairly good training, my inexperience surely held him back, and we soon found that we had no chance of overtaking our man. Winded, I watched the criminal for a long time in the moonlight until he was only a small speck scrambling up the side of a distant cliff. Wolverton gamely pursued him until outdone, but the space between him and his prey grew ever wider. He hiked back to where I sat panting upon a rock, from which we watched El Puño disappearing in the distance.

★ ★ ★ ★ ★

We agreed to alert the law upon the next opportunity, and to convey to the Albany authorities where they should look for their missing man. But we rued bitterly the missed chance of bringing in José Mora as our own prisoner. What Wolverton intended to do with the Lópezes upon the morrow remained to be seen; we had not the energy to speak of it as we trod wearily homeward, cheated of victory.

Chapter 11
A Ride to Estacado

{In which a letter spurs Frank Hooper to action.}

I slept hardly a wink as we waited for dawn. Though I had not the stamina to stand watch, I found my rest disturbed by wakeful worries of what daylight would bring. We must convey our knowledge to the attention of the authorities somehow, I knew. But whom could we really trust here?

More troubling still, now that the criminal knew we were onto him, what desperate measures might he try? I speculated that the Lópezes might not hesitate to open the house doors to him. Wolverton and I might be murdered in our sleep. In a less lethal turn of events, we nonetheless might find ourselves humiliated for allowing the fugitive to slip from our grasp. I rolled beneath the thin cotton quilt as a seaman in a storm-tossed berth. Questions unanswered since the outset pricked at the edges of my deeper nightmares. We'd made no headway whatsoever regarding the missing boots, nor the pasted-up warning message, nor the mystery man in the hack back in Fort Worth. We had reached no certain indication that any of these even bore on the case at hand. Perhaps all were simply unrelated oddments, rather than loose beads from a related strand wanting only to be properly restrung. I tried to force myself to *think*, as Miles would have advised.

And where the devil was Derrick Miles in all this? I had done my utmost, though sorely tested, to faithfully discharge my duty. Yet this was all too much. I deserved to be brought into his full confidence and not to be kept in the dark as a schoolchild. If, that is, I could *find* the man.

Day broke with weak sunlight peeking through small patches in the frayed curtains. The air was chilly. I tucked my feet wearily into my slippers, drew on my dressing gown, and went down the hall to knock on my client's bedroom door.

No answer was forthcoming. I tried the knob and found it unlocked. Pushing the door inward with a tinge of fear—*what if?!*—I saw no sign of violence. The bed was made, and Wolverton's soiled jacket from the previous night hung on a peg beside the wardrobe. I stepped into the room. Shaving implements bore signs of recent use, and the towel lying over the side of the basin was damp. His boots were gone.

I hurried downstairs. López and his wife had started a fire in the iron stove and were tending to kitchen matters as on any ordinary day.

"Have you seen Mr. Wolverton?" I blurted out.

"*Sí*, he saddled up and rode away an hour ago. I could not say where," replied López flatly.

"Have you no care for his safety?" I cried.

"I cannot control his actions. I advised him to be wary of snakes, for they are still about even this late in the year."

As if *that* were our prime worry, I wanted to shout. But I turned on my heel instead and ordered him, over my shoulder, to get my mare ready. "And you—*you* are to remain here until I return with the sheriff," I scolded. "You and your wife have aided a wanted man, and if you are smart you'll increase your chances of leniency by sticking to your post."

"There is . . . there is something you might wish to show the sheriff when you see him, sir," López said, in a tone that might have signaled contrition, except for its hint of smugness.

"What?" I turned back and barked at him. "Have you been

withholding evidence?"

"No, no, certainly not," he said. "My wife found a note yesterday when gathering up Sir Basil's clothing for donation. We set it aside for you."

López picked up an unsealed envelope from the sideboard and handed it to me. I withdrew a folded piece of plain writing paper and took it over to the window to study it carefully.

Its wording was most extraordinary, but what was even more remarkable was the method of its creation. The letter had been produced on a typewriter, which I assumed to be, even in the year of our Lord eighteen-ninety-one, not commonplace on the frontier.

Dear Baz,

I am in a bit of a fix. I need a loan of 100 $, which I promise with all my heart to repay as soon as I am able. Just name the terms. I have nowhere else to turn.

I realize this request is quite forward of me, and I would not ask were it not as important as life itself. Will you meet me at the back gate of your ranch tomorrow night at 8? I will explain everything. No one must know, especially Himself.

Yours with sincerity, and trust,
L. L.

P.S. Burn this after you have read it.

I looked up at the Lópezes, who stood mute, their faces as impassive as those of the Easter Island stone figures. "Who wrote this, and what does it mean?"

"I am sure," Señor López began evenly, "any of us eager to understand Sir Basil's death would like to know that."

"If this is your way of holding out for some deal, López—"

"No! But maybe we can be more help to you in freedom rather than captivity."

I considered that as I perused the letter more carefully. "You say you found this among Sir Basil's effects?"

Señora López replied, "It was in the pocket of his green corduroy coat. It was not the one he wore the night he was— *that* night—" She faltered. "I seem to recall that Sir Basil was wearing the green coat on Thursday, when he had gone to Espuela on business."

"And you were sorting through his clothing yesterday to prepare it for donation to charity, you say?"

"Sí. I have already passed along some items as Mr. Barlow instructed. But there are more. I have gone through pockets with care."

"And you have found nothing else?"

"Nothing important . . . a button here, a handkerchief there. A dime. A pencil. I have left all these things on his desk."

"And who is this L.L., who's familiar enough to call him 'Baz'?"

After shaking his head and appearing to reach deep into his memory, Senor López answered me. "I know of no man with those initials. But I expect if we could lay our hands upon the one who wrote it, we would learn more about Sir Basil's death."

"Had Sir Basil ever received any other letters like this?"

"Well, sir, I didn't ever see anything of his once it was out of the envelope. Wouldn't have been any of my business."

I sighed and slipped the paper back into its envelope. Now I had two tasks before me: finding my missing client, and finding the writer of this note. In the scheme of things it seemed less necessary to worry about the Lópezes, for now. For what hold had I over them in any case, if they chose to flee? Or to enact some sort of revenge?

As I strode back upstairs, with every tread I enumerated the deficiencies of this benighted place. Back in Fort Worth I would have only to lift the mouthpiece of the telephone to summon the sheriff. I could hail a cab to whisk me to my destination. I would not have to watch for snakes at every step.

By George, though, I had had my fill of unsolved mysteries. I was not going to play the role of patient bystander while I had strength in my bones to act.

In my best suit coat and second-best bowler—for I had left the best one behind in Fort Worth—I returned downstairs, mounted the mare, and made all speed for Estacado. Mr. Barlow should prove a useful ally in raising a posse, I reasoned. He might also be useful in deciphering the mysterious note, surely one of the most critical pieces of evidence yet to turn up, if it proved genuine. And there was one further task I pledged to handle before the matter grew cold. I would question Mrs. Larkin about the unnamed girl.

I stopped into the telegraph office in Espuela for long enough to check about the previous day's mail. Although my letter had gone out, the slothful clerk assured me, there had been no incoming telegram.

At the office down the street, where the sign tacked to the door read "Jeff Harkey, Sheriff," I found the deputy, Crabtree, on duty and advised that he rouse himself and get some men out to the Wolverton place.

"I heard rumor of a run-in with the fugitive Joe Mora," I said, not wholly dishonestly. "López, the manager, should be helpful in tracking him, but you'll surely need to act with caution. I shall be back from Estacado soon and will rejoin you there at first opportunity."

The deputy seemed not greatly moved by my urging, but as Sheriff Harkey was not about, there was nothing further I could do. I quit the county seat and rode on as fast as I could manage across the canyonlands, then ascended the steep path to the top of the caprock.

Once on the flatlands, I whipped the mare into a gallop. Such was my determination that I made the distance to the settlement of Estacado in just over an hour—without slowing my pace I arrived at the courthouse square before lunchtime. The town was in a flurry of movement as men prepared buildings to be moved on large rollers. Vaunting myself a regular Paul Revere of the Plains, I checked my mare beneath a large elm tree, took the reins lightly in my left hand and gripped the pommel, and swung down athletically over the horse's back end, very nearly snagging my boot in the stirrup in the process. Once I'd managed to free my leg without completely losing my balance, I looked around for witnesses and was relieved to see everyone apparently too busy to care. I tied up the horse, brushed the dust from my coat, and walked, bowlegged and sore, to the main street.

Inquiring after Mr. Barlow, I quickly located his law office. It stood on the corner opposite a handsome, two-story, wooden courthouse—to Crosby County's credit, much grander than any structure I had so far seen in all of neighboring Dickens. Though Barlow's single-story box-and-strip building was no palace, it was tidy, with lace half-curtains in the windows and an expertly lettered shingle hung over the door.

I knocked and turned the knob. "Halloo?" I called out, hardly recognizing the cracked utterance as my voice.

The lawyer himself appeared from down a short hallway, and I judged from the surprise and concern on his face that I must have looked a fright. "Dr. Hooper! Is all well?"

I made to answer him but the only sound from my throat was a papery croak.

"Thee must be parched! Come, sit, I'll fetch a glass of water."

I removed my bowler and wiped from my brow a river of

perspiration, which immediately turned to mud on my white handkerchief. Once installed in Mr. Barlow's upholstered wingback chair, the moisture-starved tissues of my vocal cords refreshed, I tried to set his mind at rest.

"I have come from the Wolverton Ranch with urgent news of unexpected developments, and a further mystery about which I seek your help. But all is as well as can be under the circumstances, I suppose."

"Trey Wolverton is not with you?"

"Struck out on his own this morning. I can only presume him safe, as I would hardly have been useful as a search party of one and had no other direction to turn but here. I've sent the sheriff's deputy back that way."

"What—what about the Lópezes? Has something happened to them?"

I launched into an abbreviated account of the past two days' events, ending with the pursuit of the criminal.

"A dangerous situation indeed! And unfortunate for Señora López. But a posse must be gathered at once. The fugitive could have fled anywhere by now."

"Yes, I suspect it was Wolverton's objective to raise the alarm. The men of Dickens County may have already apprehended the man by now. But in the meantime, another matter has arisen, concerning Sir Basil's fate."

I reached into my breast pocket for the envelope, which was only slightly bent from my exertions, and handed it to him. I allowed him time to absorb its contents.

Mr. Barlow frowned. " 'Tis a new mystery indeed. I am sorry to learn that another member of our population is in some unexplained trouble, but greatly concerned as to how it may have affected Sir Basil—if the time indeed lines up with the night of his passing."

"Yes, it would appear so. You recognize this 'L.L.'?"

"I have a theory."

"Do you consider it material to the case for which you brought in Miles and me?"

He rubbed his chin. "I would not have, but the proximity of events is both suspicious and strange. I believe I know the writer of the letter well, in fact, as there is only one person I ever witnessed use that familiar nickname with Sir Basil."

"And he is available for questioning?"

"She . . . might not be."

"A woman! Was Sir Basil—"

"If I am correct in my guess, it is not what thee must think." Barlow sighed. "I had no idea there might be a connection with a recent spate of gossip around these parts, or I would have told you. But it is a long story, and perhaps we should talk as we ride."

I was delighted that he had read my mind. "You'll come back to the ranch to help, then?"

He nodded and rose. "We'll need some sustenance for the road first. Let us procure some meat and bread from Stringfellow's store, and we shall stop by my farm on our way."

I stood, too, on my aching feet. "I have one other matter to look into here in Estacado first," I said. "A Mrs. Larkin, whom I encountered in Espuela, made it a point of expressing her thanks to the late Earl for commending a certain girl as household help. I had hoped to pay a visit."

"Let us go there on our way as well, then," said Barlow with the slightest raise of an eyebrow as he lifted his wide-brimmed hat from a hook and set it atop his head. "She and her husband, and their large family, operate a weekly newspaper from a sod dwelling just outside of town. Come—thee is hungry, and should gird up for the return journey."

We let our horses drink to their content while we purchased aliments for ourselves. Barlow paid for beef jerky and ham, along with two fresh biscuits and a tin of crackers, and a paper bag of shelled pecans. I'd noticed that Barlow had retrieved the Colt pistol from his desk drawer and slipped it into his belt. He purchased ammunition and asked if I was sufficiently supplied as well. I bought a box of bullets, plus a cleaning kit and oil, remembering the sad condition of Barlow's gun the last time I'd seen it. I added a canteen to the bill, too—I had been foolish in the extreme to ride out without one and wouldn't make the same mistake again.

The ride to the Larkin place was a short one, and we had no opportunity to talk of the letter. At a large sod half-dugout surrounded by a belt of tall cedars and a grove of leafless fruit trees, a sunbonneted woman paused in her washday tasks as we rode up, and I recognized her as she who'd stopped me the other day.

"Sister Larkin!" Barlow greeted her warmly. "Thee is well, I hope?"

"Yes, Brother Barlow, we are all healthy and happy. Thyself too?"

He dismounted and tipped his hat, but did not remove it. "Fine, just fine. I have little time for a social visit, but I wanted to bring my friend Dr. Hooper by, as he told me he has recently made your acquaintance."

"Why yes! Welcome, Doctor—I did not recognize thee."

I walked over to shake her hand, which was damp from the washing. "I apologize for my appearance, madam—it is a dusty ride from Dickens County."

She laid the washboard across the tub and started to beckon us inside, when a fresh visage peered from behind the sheets that hung on a line in the side yard. It was a pert, freckled face harboring large green eyes, a face belonging to a lass in her teens, perhaps, and it was surrounded by a rococo frame of red-gold curls that gave the effect of a portrait hanging on a gallery wall.

"Finish your chores first, Lili," said Mrs. Larkin, "then come on inside and make us some tea, please."

I caught the girl's expression as it shifted from bright-eyed interest to shock. But before she could duck back behind the sheets, Barlow called out to her, "Elizabeth?"

The young woman's cheeks reddened and she turned away swiftly.

"Is she the girl you mentioned to me, Mrs. Larkin?" I asked. "The girl you said Sir Basil sent to you?"

"The very one," she answered. "She has been a blessing already. A wonder with the children, and you wouldn't believe how she has learned to set type for the newspaper!"

Barlow seemed caught up in cogitation, but finally said, "Dr. Hooper, I think you may have an answer to both your questions in one. Sister Larkin, would it be possible for us to talk with Elizabeth—Lili—for a few minutes in private?"

"Oh, yes, surely, why—I'll fetch her and take the children outside while you visit. I'm sure she'll be wanting the doctor's advice."

Mrs. Larkin went to the door and called out, twice, before Lili emerged from behind the wash she had been pinning to the line. The girl carried a folded bedsheet in front of her, almost as a disguise, it seemed, for her full form was now apparent to me. I had no trouble recognizing from the slight swelling beneath her skirt why she would soon need a physician's services.

Barlow rose and ushered her through the doorway with an avuncular arm around her shoulder. "Elizabeth McQuarrie, I'd like you to meet Dr. Frank Hooper, a guest at the Wolverton Ranch, where he has already made the acquaintance of your father."

"Thank you, Barley, but I have no father," she said, turning smartly in my direction. In the shaft of light from the doorway, her eyes met mine. There was no mistaking the steel determination, more like outright insolence, in them. "Perhaps you mean Himself, the Judge."

"It was you who wrote the note, then," I said, attempting to meet her stare for stare as my vision adjusted to the murky interior. I drew the folded paper partway from my vest pocket but did not open it.

She blanched and put the cloth sheet down on a small desk, not quite covering the typewriter that sat on it. Barlow stood speechless, still taking in the evidence of the girl's advancing pregnancy.

I broke the silence with a suggestion that we rest a spell in Mrs. Larkin's parlor and put everyone's questions to rest.

"Miss McQuarrie, I assure you—" I began, but got no further before she broke in.

"Mrs., you mean. I am a married woman. Mrs. LaBorde, thank you very much." She slid a stool from beside the kitchen partition and perched on it, smoothing her skirt with her hands so that the thin band of gold on her finger now glinted in the ray of light. Mr. Barlow edged down into an upholstered chair, an expression of dismay on his face. I sat at the desk.

"LaBorde? Like the painter whose work we saw at the ranch?"

The girl brightened. "That's him, yes! Raphael LaBorde. We were married in April down at Jay Flat." She glanced down at her waistline. "What's done is done, though I've seen nothing of Rafe since my fa—the Judge sent him away. He does not know about the baby."

"Your husband, or your father?"

"Both. Either. That's why I had to turn to Baz. There was no one else who could help."

Barlow cut in. "Elizabeth's nicknames for us, since we first came to know her family. Basil and Barley. She thought it amusing." He glanced at her, the wistfulness in his eyes quickly hardening.

"Why don't you let me tell my side of things, Barley?" she asked, in an acid voice. "For once."

Barlow sighed and indicated she should proceed. I crossed my hands over my midsection, sat back, and waited. A clock on the wall ticked away the moments, as I checked my anxiety over Trey Wolverton's whereabouts. I supposed this was the long story Barlow had been saving for our ride, but we might as well have it out now.

"At the McQuarrie homestead there are not many opportunities for any kind of social life, as you can imagine," began Elizabeth/Lili. "Especially since my mother died, which has been nearly four years now. I was twelve, and heartbroken. I longed for companions, but there were only the servants' children and the occasional visitor.

"That changed for the better when Mr. Griswall and Maria came on the scene. Imagine my excitement—a young woman not too much older than myself, only an hour's ride from our place! Our fathers became acquainted, and Maria and I became friends, sort of. And we all enjoyed invitations to the Wolverton Ranch on occasion—the ranch lay between our place and the Griswalls' dugout, convenient for us both. We could sit and visit out under the trees while the men talked politics and business and such. Baz became like a grandfather to me, and his compatriot Barley here like a wise uncle.

"Well, we were all thrilled when word got around that Baz was bringing the famous artist who was staying down at Putoff Canyon to come paint portraits of the Wolvertons. Baz had miniatures he'd brought from England, you see, but he wanted large canvases for his great hall. Mr. LaBorde had studied with a French master and had come to Texas to paint landscapes, but he agreed to accept the commission. He stayed for a week at a time last spring, and I met him at one of Baz's dinner parties. I was very—taken with his work."

Barlow could hold his tongue no longer. "I knew the man had taken a—a fancy to thee, Elizabeth," he burst out. "But this, *this*—"

"Calm down, Barley. It's all perfectly aboveboard. Like I said, Mr. Wolverton, we knew the Judge would never give his blessing, and so we rode out to the preacher at Jay Flat."

"You know full well he challenges the legality of the union. Thee is only fifteen, lass!"

"I can't help what the Judge thinks. If my mother and those W.C.T.U. biddies had had their way, the age of consent would've been raised to—*thirty*! I'd *never* have had a chance at marriage, or a chance to get away from all this. Just look at poor Maria!"

I stepped in before the conversation could swerve further from its main focus. "You were saying, Elizabeth—"

"Lili. *If* you please."

"Lili, how does this all tie to the note?" I urged.

"Show it to me first," she demanded. "You might be bluffing."

I did, and after examining it she continued, a bit less glib in tone. "Well, when the Judge discovered our elopement, he sent Mr. LaBorde packing. Told him never to set foot in Dickens County again. I'm pretty sure there was a shotgun involved.

"As for my part, the Judge practically locked me away and forbade me to leave the premises while deciding what to do with me. I had no way to send word to my friend Maria, no way to communicate with my husband, no way to escape. I was without independent means other than what coins I had saved from taking in typewriting jobs.

"This could not go on; I was miserable and so was my—the Judge. He threatened to send me to his sister in Georgia, which sounded even worse to me than my imprisonment in Texas. I feared I would never find my dear Rafe again, and I'm sure that's exactly as Himself intended.

"That's when Basil and Barley stepped in. They proposed that I instead come work for the Larkins, who needed help with their household and the newspaper. Barley made the arrangement with the family, but I'm pretty certain Baz paid for my board—wasn't that right, Barley?"

The man nodded in unhappy admission, and the girl continued.

"The post would also allow me to continue typewriting work for pay. There would be sufficient business in Estacado to make it worthwhile. I accepted the arrangement with the private expectation that I could soon save up enough to leave. But then, I found out about *this*." She indicated her abdomen, with its unmistakable roundness. "Mrs. Larkin figured it out, too. I begged her to keep my confidence, and she did."

"Then why the need for the urgent letter?" I asked.

"It wouldn't have been long till my situation would be evident to all. I wanted more than ever to escape and find my husband. An opportunity arose one day in Espuela, when I had ridden there with the Larkins to work on some legal documents for Mr. Barlow. I spied Maria Griswall alone in her father's wagon and came up with a desperate plan. If she would deliver a note for me, I had an idea for us both to get away."

"She took the note to the Earl for you?"

"I ran back into the clerk's room and typed it on the spot. Gave it to Maria in a sealed envelope."

"And she delivered it as planned?"

"As things transpired, I have no way of knowing," she said. "The letter was supposed to have been destroyed. How did it come into *your* possession?"

"I shall hold that information in confidence for the moment,"

I said, glancing in Barlow's direction. "For now, we may need you to come to Espuela with us. For your safety."

Barlow cut in. "You should be careful, Elizabeth. The note ties you—and Maria Griswall—to the time of Sir Basil's death."

The genuine shock that came over the girl's face at the realization she may have not only played a role in that tragic event but perhaps be considered a suspect in his murder told me that she was almost certainly not the guilty party. But we had surely stumbled upon a matter of material significance, our first real breakthrough in the case. We could not afford to let her out of our sight.

When she opened her mouth again, all of the bravado had melted from her tone, and she spoke with precise formality. "Mr. Barlow, if I may retain you as my attorney in the matter, I will gladly tell you both everything I know."

"Go ahead, then. Thee must understand that Dr. Hooper is aiding in the investigation of Sir Basil's death, and any information you wish to share will be vitally important to us both. He works for me and will keep your revelations in confidence just as I will."

She nodded gravely. "As I was saying, an occasion arose when I saw Maria with—Mr. Griswall in Espuela. I crafted the note and gave it to her. I whispered my plan to her. The Larkins would be lodging for two nights at the Espuela Inn while they visited relatives and conducted business, and I would be there with them, keeping to my lodgings. They would not be watching. I would hire a horse and slip away with my belongings after supper, and meet Baz by the ranch gate. From there, once he had departed, Maria would ride out to join me, and we could be across the breaks and on our way to Fort Worth by morning."

"I must say," remarked Barlow, "this sounds like a most foolhardy project."

"Perhaps. But we were each desperate in our own way."

"Then I must know . . . what prevented you from carrying it out?" I asked. "Something must have thwarted your plan, or you would not be here, and she still there."

She sighed deeply. "I never kept the appointment. The Larkins were invited to join friends at the brush arbor revival in Roaring Springs, and they cut their Dickens County visit short. While we camped for three days at the springs, I had no opportunity to send another message. And by the time we returned to Estacado, the news was abroad of the Earl's death. I have not known what to make of matters for these two weeks."

Mr. Barlow looked somewhat relieved. "But you have a strong alibi."

"Why . . . of course. I cooked and cleaned and herded the Larkin children for three days straight, no mistaking."

"And of Miss Griswall?"

"Maria—Maria had her own reasons, as I said, and I have not spoken with her since."

I turned to Barlow. "I think it best I make all haste back to Espuela. We shall need the sheriff now for more cases than one."

"I agree," said Barlow. "God go with thee, and send word back as soon as you have a rider to spare. I shall keep Miss— *Mrs.* LaBorde in custody as a witness for the time being. And I shall put out a telegram to the Rangers. Heaven alone knows what you shall return to."

"One more thing, gentlemen," said the girl, fidgeting. "I wouldn't break a friend's confidence under normal circumstances, but it might be important. For her own safety."

"Whose?" I asked.

"Maria's. You ought to know—Mr. Griswall may not be who he says he is."

"What do you mean? Who *is* he, then?"

"I saw something once. Something secret." She hesitated, as though searching to bring some vaguely understood reality into focus. "I was riding out to the Griswall dugout one day last spring when I heard riders coming behind me. Now, I'm not fool enough not to be on my guard when I'm out alone. I dismounted and led my pony down the hill a ways into the breaks and just hoped he'd stay quiet.

"Two men rode by. Mr. Griswall was one of them. They slowed down and turned off the trail a little ways, coming so close to where I was concealed in the cedars that I was afraid they would hear my breathing. I peeked out to see them lift up a rock and slide a metal box underneath it, then put the rock back. I listened more than looked. The stranger mentioned land, or sections, or something—*more land is coming,* he said. 'Not ready to drill yet.' "

"That is interesting indeed."

"But the most interesting thing of all was that the stranger called him a different name. Not Griswall, or Rufus, but *Graham.*"

"Did they say more?"

"That's all I heard. It was short, and I was scared. I stayed where I was for half an hour after the men went their separate ways, before I got back on my pony and went to their house."

"Thee has been most helpful, lass," said Barlow. "Does thee believe thee could find the spot again?"

She shook her head. "I've tried to recognize it, but I haven't been that way often since. I think Maria has politely tried to keep me away, until we hatched our plan, of course. She could tell I was a bit shook up that afternoon, and she said to me—in that fashion when people want you to think they're joking, but they're really deadly serious—that I looked as though I'd encountered a wild animal."

Chapter 12
The Man on the Mesa

{In which both an identity and a hiding place are revealed.}

I made painful haste eastward again, stopping in at the sheriff's office in Espuela by early afternoon to see if he had yet arrived. Word was, Harkey was already on his way to the Wolverton Ranch. The alarm had been raised.

I opened the map of the Croton Breaks that Mr. Barlow had sketched for me during our journey here, to ascertain landmarks unfamiliar to me. Upon departing the central hub of Espuela, I chose not the well-worn path to the ranch but a slightly different course just south of it. I set my aim to the Griswall homestead.

Upon arriving there, however, I found the place deserted. No doubt Griswall had gone exploring, Maria in tow, just as on the first day we had met them in the meadow. I seethed with fury at the man's craven deception, that might leave our own unwitting client to fall headlong into an unknown trap. I struggled to apply my keenest power of deduction, as Miles would have expected of me, to account for Griswall's action and his motive. What was he hiding? His connection to the wolf story seemed stronger. Was his daughter complicit in whatever scheme drove him? Were either of them—or both—involved somehow in Sir Basil's death?

I knocked again on the door, then, hearing no response, pushed it open. It was not locked; that part was easy. It was harder to practice stealth in someone else's quarters; this part of the work I knew I was not well suited for. It quite went against my principles to pry, much less to do so with intent to pocket evidence of criminal wrongdoing if such taking were required of me. Yet I persisted.

Now that it was uninhabited and I had leisure to look about, I could see that the small parlor was crammed to the brim with artifacts and documents of all sorts. If there were some prevailing system of organization, it was not obvious to me. How, I wondered, could any man of science lay his hand on information in such a way as to be of value in his explorations?

Monographs were stacked on a shelf, intermingled with pamphlets and loose leaves like layers of a sandwich. Maps were now spread on the table, weighed flat on the corners by curiosities of rock and bone.

I opened the tall cabinet with as much calm as I could manage. Zinc-lidded Mason jars, each labeled with a string of numbers that I discerned to be notations of latitude and longitude, lined its interior shelves; these appeared to contain fluids of varying shades and viscosities. Flasks were filled with soils. Smaller phials held other liquids, some with particulate matter settled at the bottom, some of differing colors and clarities.

A particularly odd relic caught my eye as I glanced into the shadowed depths of the tallest shelf. A human skull, brown with age and misshapen, leered down empty-eyed from the corner, where it sported a black beaver top hat. I stepped back, unnerved, and almost tripped over the chair leg before regaining my composure.

I searched about for answers, taking care to lift papers, or the covers of books, only with the edge of the penknife I had slid from my pocket.

As I examined the jumble of documents atop the desk, there, mostly obscured by a stack of several newspapers, lay an issue of the *Crosby County News,* crumpled slightly as though it had been hastily inserted into the pile. The paper did not amount to much—only a single broadsheet of local items—but oddly, from a bold headline that started off "Harkey Announces" and ended "County Sheriff," a rectangle had been sliced, as had a portion of the "Crosbyton County News" banner.

I gasped in recognition of the technique, and the situation in which I had previously seen it put to use. I slid the paper from the stack, refolded it, and slipped it into my jacket pocket, thinking it might prove useful.

In the front corner of the room, pointed toward the one window which gave onto the immense, jagged breaks, was the telescope Trey Wolverton and I had observed on our first visit here. The window was open, and I walked over to the large scope on its tripod. Drawing out my handkerchief, I held the instrument steady and set my eye to the glass.

There, in the distance, I was astonished to see that the lens had been trained on a series of stone walls and crude huts that had not revealed themselves to my unaided vision during explorations with Wolverton. The dry-stacked walls appeared to have served as confinement for livestock, though they seemed too low to have impeded cattle. The huts, a grouping of three, were constructed with long gray sticks of dried vegetation lashed together with vine, the same material that provided flat, slanted roofs. From one rose a thin column of smoke as though from a cooking hearth—or signal fire. Suddenly a flash of light bounced upon the part of the canyon wall that remained in shadow. It came again, and again quickly, in an unmistakable series of three. Just below the hill, the figure of a boy came into view, scrambling like a goat up the rocks.

If this were the outpost from which the criminal Joe Mora had so successfully eluded the law, I had it in my sights now. Best I could tell, from the scrambled arrangement of the broken canyons and ridges, it was not far from the site of our encounter the previous night. I checked my gun and steeled myself to pursue the fugitive alone if that was what must be done. *Mano à mano*, if need be, I would do my duty.

I pocketed my handkerchief, closed Griswall's door silently behind me, and struck off across the breaks and made for the stony hill over which the boy had disappeared. Off to my southeast the twin mesas of the Double Mountain served for reference until I had progressed far enough down that I lost sight of the landmarks. I soon came to the mouth of the canyon, where I hobbled my horse in the shade of the rocks and proceeded on foot. I kept within my mind's eye the picture of a Tonkawa scout, moving silently on moccasined feet to within yards of the enemy, undetected.

Determined to seize the opportunity fortune had flung my way, I made deliberate progress while fixing my gaze on that particular formation that was my objective. It would have been easy, in the maze of cattle tracks, to lose the profile of rocks that served as point of reference and become completely disoriented. Behind me the sun was already dipping low above the edge of the caprock, casting side canyons into rust-red shadow while gilding every detail of their opposite ridges in sharp relief. Above, a clutch of turkey buzzards circled; they and I seemed to be the only creatures moving. Under other circumstances I would have found the landscape oddly beautiful, but at this moment I could concentrate only on again locating one small figure within it.

Amid the tangle of rock hoodoos and brush I had lost him. As the setting sun lowered by another degree, however, I recognized in clear detail the stone wall that had first captured my attention through the telescope, and as I climbed the next row of rocks I could see, set upon a relatively flat expanse partly hidden by the natural curve of the hill, the hut that retained sufficient roof to act as a screen against the weather. The site provided as natural a shelter for man and beast as anywhere in this landscape.

I paused to catch my breath from the scramble up. This must be the den where the fugitive had been holed up. At last my foot was on the threshold of his hiding place, and his secret was within my grasp. As I approached the hut, walking as warily as Griswall would do when stalking a poised butterfly with his net, I satisfied myself that the place had indeed been used as a habitation. An overgrown pathway among strewn boulders led to the dilapidated opening which served as a door. All was silent within. The criminal might be lurking there, I realized, or he might be about, prowling the breaks. My nerves tingled in fear and anticipation, but also with the unfamiliar sense of risky adventure. This was not a position in which I was used to finding myself.

I closed my hand upon the butt of my revolver and, bending low as I tiptoed up to the door, I looked in. The hut was empty. But there were ample signs that I had not come upon a false scent. Someone lived here, that much was certain, and had quit the place very recently. A packet of oilcloth, neatly rolled, lay on a stone slab upon which a Comanchero sheepherder must have once slumbered. On the wall hung the drying pelt of a large animal, larger than a coyote but smaller than a buffalo. Warm ashes had been heaped toward the center of a stone fire ring. Beside it lay a frying pan of cheap manufacture, a tin plate, and a bucket half full of water. As my eyes became accustomed to the mottled light, I spied a cast-iron Dutch oven, a tin cup, and a half-full bottle of spirits standing in the corner. Jameson's, I marveled. What criminal possessed such refined taste or the means to quench it?

To one side of the hut a split cedar log lay upon two long stones to serve as a low table, and upon this stood a small cloth bundle—the same package, no doubt, which I had seen through the telescope upon the shoulder of the boy. I opened it with less guilt than I had felt when invading Griswall's dugout, for now that I had taken one step down the road of larceny it was much easier to take a second. It contained a loaf of sourdough bread, several twists of beef jerky, and a tin of preserved peaches. As I made to set the can down again, my heart leapt to see that beneath there lay a sheet of paper with writing upon it. I raised it to the dwindling light and read the sentence, roughly scrawled in pencil, "Dr. Hooper has gone to Estacado."

I looked about me, holding the strange note in my hands, expecting at any minute to spy the occupant of this hut looking over my shoulder. My face burned with the unlooked-for attention. Was it *I*, then, and not Trey Wolverton, who was being pursued, both in Fort Worth and here in Dickens County? What could have been the purpose? And how did the boy figure into it?

It dawned on me that not since arriving here a week ago had Wolverton or I taken a single step that had not been observed and reported. We had quite possibly been unaware of a fine net being drawn round us with infinite skill and delicacy, holding us so lightly that we might be drawn tightly within its meshes at any moment. I surveyed slowly around the hut in search of any other sign of such surveillance. What other clue might reveal the character or intentions of the man who lived in this singular place? I discovered no other clue save that he must be of Spartan habits, caring little for the comforts of life. *Think, man!* I forced my mind to obey Miles's dictum.

Outside the sun dropped to just above the rim of the caprock. Its rays illuminated in gold-lined blue the string of distant pools where the creek threaded the Croton Breaks. I could make out the rough, bowed roofline of the Wolverton ranch house, obscured by the tall cedars, and beyond it a line of red haze that marked the dusty road to Espuela. A little to the south, across the creek from me, lay the house of the Griswalls. A slight breeze freshened, obscuring other sounds. I might well have been tempted to set my camera upon its tripod and prepare to take a long exposure, had the dire business for which I had come not been so all-consuming.

Instead I returned to the dark recess of the hut and crouched upon the blanket roll, willing my anxious heartbeat and labored breath to quiet as I listened for the coming of its tenant.

It could not have been ten minutes before I heard the scuff of a boot on stone. As I listened even more intently I froze—for I was certain the sound was not that of a single pair of feet alone. Two different footfalls, two different but equally measured gaits. I willed myself smaller in the space, shrinking back into the dark corner, where I wrapped my pistol in the folds of my pocket and there cocked it. I determined not to reveal myself until I had an opportunity of seeing something of the strangers. There was a long pause indicating that they had stopped. Then once more the footsteps approached, and a shadow fell across the opening of the hut.

"Lovely evening, my dear Hooper," came a well-known voice. "I really think that you will be more comfortable outside than in."

Chapter 13
Death in the Canyon

{In which one man meets a gruesome and untimely end.}

For a moment or two I sat breathless, hardly able to believe my ears. Then my senses and my voice came back to me, while in an instant a crushing weight of responsibility seemed to be lifted from my soul. That cold, incisive, ironical voice could belong to but one man in all the world.

"Miles!" I cried—"Miles!"

"Come out," said he, "and please be careful with the revolver."

I stooped under the rough lintel, and there stood Derrick Miles on the other side of the door, his gray eyes dancing with amusement as they registered my astonished features. He was thin and worn, but clear and alert, his keen face bronzed by the sun and roughened by the wind. In his denim jeans, leather vest, work boots, and faded Stetson he looked like any other cowboy of the plains, though he had contrived, with that catlike love of personal cleanliness which was one of his characteristics, that his chin should be as smooth and his neckerchief as perfect as if he were back home at Houston Street.

He had not come alone. A companion, a wiry youth possessed of a ruggedness that suggested a life on the range, stood and removed his rawhide work glove to shake my hand. "Jack Abernathy, at your service," he said, grinning. "Cap'n Miles fetched me from the JA outfit to help in your hunt."

"Your family spread?"

"No, *the* JA Ranch up in the Panhandle. Colonel Goodnight himself gave me leave."

"Whatever the case, I've never been more glad to see anyone in my life," said I as I wrung young Abernathy's hand, and then that of Miles.

"Or more astounded, I'll wager," said Miles.

"Well, I must confess to it."

"The surprise was not yours alone, I assure you," said Miles. "I had no idea that you had found our blind, still less that you were inside it, until we were within twenty paces of the door."

"My footprint, I presume?"

"No, Hooper, I fear that I could not undertake to recognize your footprint amid all the footprints of the world. No, this is what gave you away."

He reached into his pocket and handed me the dirt-stained handkerchief I had so recently employed at the Griswall cottage.

"Oh! I have been careless," said I.

"And unaware it had worked loose from your pocket, perhaps as you made that last steep climb," said Miles. "Jack spied it caught on a branch and at first thought it a signal. So we had a warning."

The observation reminded me of the urgent errand that had brought me here, and with the great encouragement of such unlooked-for reinforcements, I undertook a swift account of recent events.

When I closed with the story Mrs. LaBorde had so freshly related to me and Mr. Barlow, Miles became visibly agitated. "We grow ever closer to the wolf's lair, Hooper. I fear now for any who should cross the breaks at night, and I especially chastise myself for employing the services of a mere messenger boy from Espuela to relay information here. Under the control of a madman, this four-legged monster poses danger to all."

Miles registered the urgency of my mission, which had already suffered undue delay, to apprehend the criminal and assure the welfare of our client Wolverton. "Thus we must surely make all speed for the ranch," he cried, reaching down his saddlebag off a peg made from a broken branch wedged between stones. "Let us not tarry a moment longer."

"Are you on foot?" I asked, for I worried that the trek would lose us yet more time.

"We have mounts suitable for this country," replied Abernathy as he ducked through the entryway of the hut. He was a tall lad, perhaps a shade under six feet, of solid musculature that bespoke hard work, but with a nimble step. He ably led the way down a side path to a jumble of large boulders behind which stood a pair of gray burros in a small cedar-enclosed corral almost completely hidden from view, though it must have been no farther than twenty paces from where I had tied my own horse.

Miles explained, "Young Abernathy here has quite a way with animals. He rightly discerned that we would be better served by these nimble-footed creatures during our days in the breaks, and he made a profitable trade for our horses with Burnett when we passed through King County."

"How came you here?"

"By way of the eastern Palo Duro, where I hurried to visit with Colonel Goodnight after you and your party left Fort Worth," said Miles as he led his burro out of the enclosure. "Jack has been cowboying the past year on the Adair ranch. His reputation had preceded him."

"Reputation?"

"For tracking, he means," the boy answered. "I've been trapping with my pa since I was a kid. Told Ma I was striking out on my own, finally, and I went up the trail to Kansas. After that I hired on with the Colonel's outfit when he came through Sweetwater one time, while we were camped there."

Miles added, "We came in search of beast before man. The

escaped criminal was, frankly, a factor we had not reckoned on."

"Did you not know the fellow may still be at large, then? I was certain I had happened on his hideout."

"Let us hope that, his source of succor now unmasked, he has fled for safer parts—or else has fallen once more into the hands of the law."

"Yes, let us hope," I agreed, none too confidently. "Shall I show you the trail to the Wolverton place, or have you already figured that out too?"

We talked low as we rode—and we rode as swiftly as we dared along the path now illumined by the rising moon. I could not restrain myself from blurting out the first matter that had been pressing on my mind. Why, I asked Miles as he trotted alongside me on his burro, had he gone to such lengths to withhold his plans from our client—and me?

"A question most worthy of a thorough answer when we have settled down to our evening sherry, Hooper," said Miles. "For the time being, trust that by keeping you in the dark I was able to pursue important inquiries unhindered by local meddling. And you have been able to gain the trust of those same locals without having to feign ignorance of my behind-the-scenes activities. A regrettably necessary expedient that I am hopeful you will forgive."

"You have read my full report of Griswall and his daughter by now?"

He nodded, the set of his jaw barely perceptible in the deepening shadows.

"Yes, and more. From the General Land Office folder you so keenly observed I deduced that the man had been recently in Austin, perhaps his domicile before coming west. A map or file might make its way into the hands of an inquirer, but an enclosing folder and its irreplaceable record of transactions, kept under strict scrutiny and control, should never leave the vault. In the clerical portions of this vitally important state department no more faithful, competent and efficient force of men exists, but there is a class of land speculators commonly called land sharks, unscrupulous and greedy, who have left their trail in every department of it in the shape of titles destroyed, patents cancelled, homes demolished and torn away, forged transfers and lying affidavits.

"I found your shrewdly discovered tidbit to be of great utility in discerning something of Griswall's methods and his motives. Furthermore, his true credentials, if my hunch proves correct, divulge an interest in yet another field: that of petroleum exploration."

"Petroleum?!" I snorted. "Here?"

"That," said Miles, "is the real bonanza. And Rufus Griswall is the only one who seems to have figured it out. He is racing time, I tell you, for the first to strike oil hereabouts stands to make a tidy fortune."

I pondered the weight of that statement for a moment. "It is he, then, who is our enemy—and he who dogged us in Fort Worth?"

"So I hypothesize, as he appears to have much to gain by scaring us off the job—"

"—perhaps with rumors of a giant wolf . . ." I interjected.

"—though this supposition is only circumstantial, still, and requires more solid evidence to connect the threads."

"And the warning note—perhaps it came from the man himself?"

"Here again, it could certainly make sense, but we have no proof."

I fumbled for the inside pocket of my jacket, transferring the reins of my horse to one hand with some difficulty. "What about this?"

As Abernathy signaled for us to slow our mounts before descending to the creek, I produced the clipped newspaper I had retrieved from the Griswall place and handed it over to Miles.

"Capital, Hooper, capital!" he cried as he held up the void in the sheet to the shape of the waning moon, then turning it around to read in the dim light. Miles read the headline and supplied the missing words. " 'Run For'—help? The hills? One's life? The possibilities are numerous."

"Perhaps whoever did this was interrupted in the process."

"Or perhaps—"

Miles never got to finish his thought. Across the background night-noises of the valley just below us came that most terrible scream that was neither fully animal nor fully human, but that blended the worst anguish of both. It pierced the air and bounced off the canyon walls until we could hardly tell from which direction it came.

We all halted immediately and searched the dark for its source.

"Dear God," I gasped. "It has come again."

Miles thrust a hand out for silence. Abernathy slid a knife quietly from his boot. The cry must have risen up from the shadows of the creek and been carried up on the freshening wind, for just as Miles gestured for us to ease forward it sounded a second time, more horrible even than before, and farther up the slope. It burst out as a snarl and metamorphosed into a low growl and then a full-throated scream.

"Where is it?" Miles whispered to Abernathy. And to me, "Are you armed, Hooper?"

I drew my pistol and intended to reply in the affirmative, but no sound issued from my throat, which had gone as dry as the

West Texas desert.

"There, I think!" Abernathy pointed into the darkness as we spurred our terrified beasts farther down the slope.

"No, there!" cried Miles. Again the awful cry punctuated the night, as though for aid, or mercy. It was followed swiftly by another sound, wild and menacing, almost hypnotic in its intensity.

"It is—it has to be the wolf!" said Abernathy with sudden conviction.

"Come, both of you, on foot! Great heavens, if we are too late!" Miles leapt from the back of his beast and ran straight toward the danger, leaping over heaps of stones and dodging the twisted forms of cactus. I followed at his heels. Abernathy surged ahead, knife in hand. From somewhere just ahead of us there came a desperate gasp, and then, from what sounded like only a few feet away, a dull, heavy thud.

Single-file we broke through the brush onto the salt flat bordering the stream. Miles darted from side to side along the bank, slapping his hand to his forehead like a madman. He kicked a stump with the toe of his boot and declared, "By damn, our enemy has beaten us. We are too late."

"No, no, surely not!" I said.

"You see what becomes of holding my cards, young Jack. What a fool I have been! And you, Hooper"—he wheeled on me in rage—"you see what happens when you fail to keep your pledge, and abandon your client!" He continued his insane rant, declaring, "If the worst has happened I swear we will avenge him!"

As Miles charged uphill through the brush, seeking the source of the dreadful noise, now silenced, Abernathy proceeded more deliberately. Taking a faintly visible wildlife track a few feet below the renowned detective, the youth crouched with an Indian-like stealth, parting the vicious cactus and vines with the long knife held in front. I followed the path he blazed, keeping Miles within my sights as best I could. Our animals, we had left many yards behind us by now. I noticed that my labored breath had begun to turn to mist in front of me, and I realized I was quite chilled. The wind had picked up, obscuring our sense of sound.

Every few feet Miles looked around and swore vehemently at the fates, but the shadows revealed nothing, until he stopped cold and turned toward a cluster of boulders. By now Miles stood a full height above Abernathy on a rocky ledge.

"Can you see anything?" Miles called down to him.

"There," whispered the lad, gesturing for me to look just beyond the largest boulder, where the faint moonlight shone upon a dark object.

A low moan emanated from its direction. Miles found a toehold and lowered himself down below the ledge. All three of us stepped gingerly toward the shape splayed on the shadowed ground like some giant, tangled spider.

As we came closer the jumbled form took human shape. It was a man, lying facedown but with limbs contorted into such unimaginable angles one could hardly admit that living breath had occupied the body but moments before. His head lay twisted upon the rock it must have struck. Not a breath now emanated from the victim as we crowded around him.

Miles drew a match from his pocket and leaned down to strike it on his bootheel. As he held its sulfurous flame just above the fallen figure and shielded it from the wind, my heart rose into my throat. I recognized the victim by the unmistakable tweed suit he wore.

"Trey—Wolverton!" I managed to gasp before crumpling to my knees and laying a hand aside the bruised flesh of his head. It was a mechanical and instinctual gesture, to examine the depth of the injury, whose fatal nature swiftly became obvious to me. I let my fingers move down to the carotid artery; I could detect no pulse there. "I believe he has broken his neck in a fall from the ledge," I concluded.

The match flickered out, and we were left in the darkness with our heavy consciences.

"This is—the man we're workin' for?" asked Abernathy.

Miles pounded his fist into his palm. "*Was* the man. I should never have let him out of my sight."

"I shall never forgive *myself* for that failure," said I.

"I am more to blame than you, Hooper," said Miles sourly. "In the interest of an airtight case I have jeopardized the safety of my client, who has now paid for my obsession with his very life." He paced again, his long fingers gripping his own forehead as though to wring from it an alternate outcome. "It is the greatest blow which has befallen me in my career. But how could I know—how *could* I know—that he would risk his life alone down in the breaks in the face of all my warnings?"

"We were so close," said I, "and yet unable to save him!"

Miles whirled around and demanded, "Where is this brute of a wolf which drove him to his death? It may be lurking among these rocks at this instant. And Griswall, where is that scoundrel? We shall not wait to understand the full details of his involvement. We will avenge this needless death!"

Abernathy, whose absence neither of us had noted, returned, panting, from a brief reconnaissance, leading our mounts in a string. " 'S a wolf all right. But none like I've ever seen. Print six inches across, and a gimpy leg. Tracks lead across the creek. Should we go after 'im?" he asked in boyish eagerness.

"Much as it pains me to hold off," said an uncharacteristically chastened Miles, "I imagine we'd be wiser to fetch reinforcements."

"You're the boss."

Miles spoke soberly and deliberately, all trace of hubris gone.

"We have not yet proven Griswall's role in all this—we have evidence of his lies, but no ironclad connection between him and the beast. Both are still at large. If we move precipitously, we may lose our only chance to put the man behind bars for his sins. Furthermore," he continued, "we cannot be one hundred percent certain the wolf actually attacked Wolverton this night, as it appears our friend perished instead from the fall."

We stood with bitter hearts on either side of the mangled body, overwhelmed by this sudden and irrevocable disaster which had brought all our long labors to so awful an end. Turning his face in the direction of the north wind, Miles seemed to draw renewed strength from it. "Cunning as he is, I swear the blackguard shall be in my power before another day is past!"

"It is but a short distance to the Griswall homestead," I reminded him. "Why should we not ride there and seize him at once?"

"Our case is not complete. The fellow is wary and cunning to the last degree. It is not what we know, but what we can prove, Hooper. I am calculating a method to do just that. For now, we cannot leave Wolverton to the coyotes. Together we should be able to lift the body onto one of the burros. We must return it to a semblance of its right form before *rigor mortis* sets in, and deliver him up to the ranch."

Abernathy and I had scarcely taken a step in the direction of assisting Miles when he bent over the body and uttered a shout. He stood with an expression of joy and danced a mad jig, laughing and grasping for my hand. Had St. Vitus gotten hold of my stern, self-contained friend? Had he turned lunatic beneath the half-moon?

"A beard! A beard! The man has a *beard*!" exclaimed Miles.

"A beard?" was all I could manage.

"This man is not Trey Wolverton at all—and I wager it is my neighbor out here in the breaks, the criminal José Mora!" With feverish haste we turned the body over until its blood-soaked beard was fully revealed in the moonlight. There could be no doubt about the visage that had been pasted in every public place in the region these past weeks. And I recognized it, even in its expression of extremity, as the same that had glared upon me in the light of the candle from over the rock the night before.

Coming closer, I also confirmed the suit the dead man was wearing. "Wolverton's jacket and trousers—that's it! López must have brought the damaged garments out to his brother-in-law to aid in his escape."

"Then the clothes have been the poor devil's death," said Miles. "Reprehensible as El Puño's crimes were, still he deserved justice according to the laws of this nation, and not by some sinister plot to set a predator after another's scent."

"The boot from the hotel!" I said, putting another piece of the past together with the present.

Abernathy spoke, at last. The expression on his young face had grown as hardened and set as that of the most determined vigilante. "Why does the keeper of this wolf want your man dead?"

"Ah, Jack," sighed Miles. "That is precisely what we'd like to know. He has gone to great lengths to train the animal for pursuit of one particular clan as target. Whether with intent to frighten or intent to kill, we cannot yet tell."

Abernathy had more questions. "I wonder how Mora discovered the wolf was after him? And why didn't he fight back?"

"He heard him approaching and ran for it, I suspect," I offered.

"If you'll pardon me butting in—my ma says I oughta watch my manners about that—I don't see how just hearing a wolf would scare a tough guy all that bad."

I proffered a theory. "A greater mystery to me is why this

wolf, presuming that all our conjectures are correct—"

"I presume nothing," said Miles.

"Well, then, why this wolf should be loose *tonight* in particular. Surely, if it is held in captivity for a dastardly purpose, it does not always run free down in the breaks, or Wolverton and I, or Barlow, or McQuarrie, might well have already met an end like this in one of our own outings. If it is indeed Griswall who controls the animal, surely he would not let it go unless he had reason to think that Trey Wolverton would be there."

"My difficulty is the more formidable of the two," said Miles, "for I think that we shall very shortly get an explanation of yours, while mine may remain forever a mystery. The question now is, what shall we do with this poor wretch's body? We cannot leave it here to the carrion pickers."

"I suggest we proceed with your original plan and deliver it uphill to the ranch. Lawmen will be about and can deal with the victim."

"Right you are," he replied.

We had progressed forward only a short way from the creek when Miles stopped me with an urgent whisper. "Hooper, what's this? It's the man himself, by all that's wonderful and audacious! Not a word to show your suspicions—not a word, or my plans crumble to the ground. Jack, you hang back. Look down and say nothing." A figure was approaching us over the breaks, carrying a lighted knot of wood aloft in one hand. The moon shone upon him, and I could distinguish the erratic stride of the water witcher. Rufus Griswall halted when he saw us, and then came on again.

"Why, Dr. Hooper, that's not you, is it? You are the last man that I should have expected to see out in the wilds at this time of night. But, dear me, what's this? Somebody hurt? Not—don't tell me that it is our friend Trey Wolverton!" He hurried past the three of us and examined the dead man splayed across the back of the burro. I heard a sharp intake of his breath, and the torch nearly fell from his fingers.

"Who—who's this?" he stammered.

"It is Mora, the escaped criminal from Albany Jail."

Griswall turned a ghastly face upon us, and the supreme effort he had effected to overcome his amazement and disappointment was not lost on us. He looked sharply from Miles to me, ignoring our young companion. "Dear me! What a very shocking affair!"

"He appears to have fallen over the rocks back there. Our group was scouting in the breaks when we heard a cry."

"I heard something also. That was what brought me out. I was uneasy about Trey Wolverton."

"Why about Wolverton in particular?" I could not help asking.

"Because I . . . had suggested that he should come visit. When he did not I was surprised, and I naturally became alarmed for his safety when I heard the commotion down here. By the way"—his eyes darted again from my face to Miles's—"did you hear anything else besides the man's cry?"

"No," said Miles; "did you?"

"No."

"What do you mean, then?"

"Oh, you know the stories that the cowpokes tell about a phantom wolf, and so on. They say it roams the breaks and can be heard howling at the moon. I was wondering if there were any evidence of such a sound tonight."

"We heard nothing of the kind," said I.

"And what is your theory of this poor fellow's death, Doctor?" asked Griswall.

"I have no doubt that anxiety and exposure have driven him off his head. He has rushed about the wilderness in a crazy state and eventually fallen over here and broken his neck."

"That seems the most reasonable theory," said Griswall, and he gave a sigh which I took to indicate his relief. "But what do *you* think about it, Captain Miles?"

Miles, not previously known to his secret adversary, bowed his compliments. "You are quick at identification," said he.

"We have been expecting you in these parts since Dr. Hooper came out. You are in time to witness a tragedy."

"Yes, indeed. I have no doubt that my friend's explanation will cover the facts. It is an unpleasant remembrance I shall take back to Fort Worth with me on Sunday."

"Oh, you return so soon?"

"That is my intention."

"I hope your visit has cast some light upon those occurrences which have puzzled us?"

Miles shrugged his shoulders. "One cannot always have the success for which one hopes. An investigator needs facts, and not legends or rumors. It has not been a satisfactory case." Miles spoke in his frankest and most unconcerned manner.

Griswall still looked hard at him, then turned to me in the shadows. "I would suggest carrying this poor fellow to my own house, but it would give my daughter such a fright that I do not feel I could make that offer. I shall be on my way, gentlemen, to reassure myself of her safety, if you'll excuse me."

Looking back we saw the figure clamber up over the path through the breaks as he had come, and the three of us resumed our solemn trek up the opposite hill toward the Wolverton Ranch, hoping desperately to discover its owner whole, hale, and unaware of the events we had experienced this night.

Chapter 14
To Catch a Wolf

{In which young Jack Abernathy meets his match.}

Another half hour's steady ride brought our party and our gruesome burden within sight of Wolverton Ranch headquarters. Lanterns blazed in the upper windows, and the distant commotion of horses and men could be heard.

We rode in silence, each man occupied by his own thoughts. Thus in deep contemplation of our circumstances was I when, in the lead and about to make the final switchback on the trail leading up out of the canyon, I heard a mechanized click that brought me up with a start.

"Who goes there?" challenged an unfamiliar voice.

Before I could reply, Miles shot back from behind me, "Who is inquiring?"

The click promptly revealed its source as the barrel of a rifle pointed at my temple, as the man in a dark vest and gray hat holding it stepped into my path. The moonlight glinted off the cinco peso badge pinned to his vest. The gun never wavered.

"Well, I'll be damned," said Miles. "Sergeant William McDonald. How are you, Billy?"

"Captain it is, now. Fine, just fine," he said.

Miles moved closer and put out his hand to the man in warm greeting. Though I knew full well Miles's scant regard for the Texas Rangers in general, McDonald was a fine lawman and an old and trusted friend. "What brings you here?"

"Jeff Harkey put out the call. Desperado on the lam from Albany, you might've heard. Several of us hightailed it here from Fort Griffin to help search." He scratched his head and lowered the rifle. "I hate to admit it, but we've come up empty so far. The man's a genius when it comes to eluding the law."

"Ah, no longer, my friend," said Miles, moving aside to reveal the corpse lashed to the burro. "Mora has paid the ultimate price for his sins, I am afraid."

McDonald peered over at the dead man. "A bully job you've pulled off, Miles!" He shouted to his cohort, who, by now alerted by the commotion, were heading down the hill from the house.

"Not I," Miles objected. "But by the ingenuity of my colleague Dr. Hooper here. It was he who deduced the connection to the Wolverton household, and fearlessly traced Mora to his wilderness hideout."

Ranger McDonald clapped me on the shoulder with a cuff that nearly sent me reeling, caught off guard as I was by Miles's praise. I was left quite speechless, wondering how Miles proposed to explain the true cause of Mora's demise. I had not long to wait for an answer.

"Gentlemen," Miles said to the gaggle of men who had begun to gather, some bearing torches that cast our forms into the deep chiaroscuro of a Rembrandt scene, "our work here is far from done."

"How so? I'm ready to claim the *re*-ward!" shouted a local deputy I heard others call Pearl-Handle Pete.

"A culprit is abroad that poses a far greater danger than this dead man to the heir of the Wolverton house—and the public," said Miles, his volume rising to reach the growing audience now assembling beneath the rim of the canyon. "And I have come to see the creature hunted down."

"By creature, I assume you mean the lobo?" cried out a voice from the darkness.

"We done tried every trap we can think of," said another.

"He's a wily one."

A tall, gaunt figure standing beside Deputy Pete cleared his throat, lifted his torch higher, and called out, "I know there's some hereabouts think this wolf is, well, beyond the realm of men."

Another echoed his sentiment. "You tell 'em, Preacher. I ain't goin' out there tonight after any spawn of Satan."

"I've heard stories all my life about the dire wolf," said a grizzled old cowboy.

The tall man spoke again. "I have seen the mark of this beast's foot. It is unearthly, I tell you. We will need unearthly means to capture him." His tone rose to a tremolo as he offered, "Let us go unto the tabernacle of the Lord and repent of our sins, and pray for a mighty revival that shall lift this terror from our land!"

Before the sentiment could take hold from a few muttered "Amens" to become a full-blown camp meeting, Miles boomed out above the assembly, "I have brought with me one whose talents, while not those of the pulpit, come highly recommended by the top stockmen of Texas. Might I propose that we move this gathering to the greater comforts of the Wolverton house, so that you may all make the acquaintance of the famed 'Catch-'em-Alive Jack' Abernathy?"

I was grateful for the ability of Derrick Miles to persuade a mob to his will. But even more grateful was I at the sight, greeting us as we topped the edge of the caprock, of our absent client Trey Wolverton, to all appearances in fine fettle. And glad was he, too, at my own return unharmed.

No sooner had Wolverton identified me among the throng of his neighbors, and welcomed me with an arm on the shoulder, than he caught sight of Miles.

"Good God, I hardly recognized you, Captain! I'd have taken

you for one of the posse any day. But how the hell did you get here?"

"How the hell indeed," said Miles, shaking Wolverton's hand. "We have much to relate about our days undercover in the very shadow of your ranch. And to tell of our encounter with the unfortunate Mora, whose body we have recovered. But first I want to introduce you to my companion on the journey, Jack Abernathy of the Goodnight outfit."

Wolverton extended his hand to the new visitor as well. "Abernathy. I've heard of you. Or maybe that was your pa?"

The youth straightened his shoulders as if to stretch his height even further, and shook Wolverton's hand vigorously. "You got the right Abernathy. I'll be sixteen in January, and that's also the number of lobos I've caught. It's that number sixteen you probably heard about."

"I read the story in the paper. You captured a wolf with your bare hands?" he said, his skepticism barely disguised.

Miles stepped in. "Why don't we all gather round and let young Abernathy tell us the tale himself, Trey, if the men will oblige? Then we can determine if he's able to be of assistance in our current plight."

Wolverton gave orders as though he'd been born to the role. Miles and the preacher, he sent inside to break the news of Mora's death to López and his wife. He dispatched Pearl-Handle Pete the deputy with them, to certify identification of the body, while asking Sheriff Harkey to stay close and assess what Abernathy had to say.

I was sent to fetch water for the posse members, and when I returned from the cistern with a full jug and a bag of dried jerky to share, young Abernathy had already begun relating his tale as men crouched on the ground or tended their horses in the lamplight that streamed from the porch lanterns.

"—caught down in a side canyon away from the other

hunters, on foot. My horse was tied up a few yards away, with my rifle in the saddle holster. All I had with me was a long knife in my boot.

"I had been just about to rejoin the others when, all of a sudden, I heard that growl of a loafer wolf. You know what I mean. Nothing else sounds like it. The lobo was blocking my way out of the canyon. It wasn't a huge one as wolves go, but its fangs were bared and plenty scary.

"My cur dog was there at my side to warn it off, and I thought it might decide to wander on away. But then I noticed something else. It was a she-wolf, and her teats were full. I guessed I was in for worse trouble once I figured out I was standing between her and her cubs back in the canyon.

"All at once she rushed past my dog and was coming at me, and I didn't have the time or sense to think. As she opened that big maw and showed that mouthful of teeth, I just stuck out my forearm like this"—he demonstrated the motion—"and jammed it straight to the back of her jaws."

At this, the cowboys who'd been leaning against a farther post of the porch shuffled in to hear better.

"I got my other hand around her muzzle and grabbed hard," said Abernathy. "Well, she found she couldn't open her mouth, so she couldn't bite me, and she fought like the devil. And I found I couldn't let go without being seriously harmed. But I got on top of her and managed to tie her jaw shut with my bandana. By that time the men heard the barking and commotion and came running, and they helped me tie her up good and fix up a travois to drag her back to camp."

Abernathy paused long enough to take a swig of water, and Harkey said, "I heard that was some sight when you came riding back to the JA with half a dozen wolf carcasses plus a live one!"

"You speak the God's truth, sir," said Abernathy. "None of

'em had ever heard tell of capturing a lobo in full health, in her prime. Went back to get the litter, too. We sold 'em all to a traveling circus act and made a pretty penny."

Miles, who had quietly rejoined the group, now spoke up. "I had heard of Abernathy's exploits myself, and went straightway to the Goodnight camp to talk with the Colonel. Goodnight gladly lent this courageous lad to our mission, with his highest praise and best wishes. If we are to capture this fiend wolf that may have contributed to the deaths of two men, we are fortunate indeed to have the young man's talents at our disposal."

Heads nodded, slowly and sagely, and Trey Wolverton put his two cents in. "I appreciate your assistance, gentlemen, and it is more gratifying than you realize to have the support of a community I have known for only a matter of days. If you feel your homes, or your livestock, or your families are in any way threatened by this animal, you are welcome to join in the search for it, especially now that the human threat has been tracked down and removed from our midst. But if for any reason you are not inclined to take part in a further hunt, please feel free to depart with only my sincerest thanks, no obligation, no questions asked.

"I for one want to assure you," he continued, "I do not hold with any theory of a supernatural beast or dire wolf and am prepared to put our best efforts to capturing this animal, *dead or alive!*"

A collective roar went up at these words, and every man present held his ground.

Had they but seen and heard what we had witnessed hours before, I thought, they might not have been so sure.

At dawn on Saturday, the hunters and horses having rested and the men partaken of a breakfast of cold biscuits (the Lópezes having departed with the deputy, accompanying Mora's body to

Espuela), Sheriff Harkey called participants together beside the stables. Significantly absent from the group was Rufus Griswall, who, it was reported, had begged off as having no interest in the slaughter of wild animals aside from the pursuit of science.

I, for one, had never participated in a hunt of any sort, for sport or blood, much less that for *canis lupus*. I listened especially carefully.

While neither the dark of night nor the heat of midday were ideal for taking wolves, the sheriff explained, the early morning and early evening hours, when these predators were themselves on the prowl, generally proved most successful. So we would make a first go right away, before the sun rose high over the caprock.

The hunters, about two dozen strong, would proceed across the breaks, mounted and armed, in a line spaced apart for a half mile. Several other riders, including Jack Abernathy, would ride ahead as beaters to flush game and sound wolf calls, potentially attracting a predator to show itself. Any man was authorized to shoot any wolf on sight—except that if Abernathy were to experience the good fortune to encounter one near enough to attempt a live capture, he would do so, with his companions approaching close by to assist. Success in a kill would be signaled by two shots in the air in quick succession, a capture by three. By midmorning, if the hunt had yielded nothing, riders were to return to headquarters, rest up, and await dusk for a second attempt.

We ranged ourselves in a line below the rim as instructed, though as a virgin huntsman I stuck pretty close to Miles, who himself rode close behind Abernathy. I checked my pistol as well as the long gun Wolverton had loaned me. We spurred our horses lightly down the uneven terrain, training watchful eyes on every strewn boulder, red stone hoodoo, or clump of sage. In our segment at least, we managed to scare out quite a quantity of jackrabbits and prairie dogs, and a clutch of wild turkeys, but detected no sign of wolf. The occasional single shot from our left or right that was not soon followed by a deliberate signal told us the men were not passing up the opportunity to bag game along the way.

After two hours of similar activity, Miles and I reined in our horses. Abernathy trotted up to our position and pulled the bandana down from his face. "Nothin's afoot this morning, Captain. I recommend we reverse our tracks to the left a few yards and head back up to the ranch."

Miles nodded to concur, and Abernathy rode off to spread the word. I glanced upward at the climbing sun, wiped the sweat from my nose and readjusted my bowler, and wondered whether my aching frame would endure the return journey.

In the event, however, the uphill ride proved less demanding than the downhill, as the cantle of my saddle supported my backside in a way that was more relaxing than the pressure of the horn on my private parts when we'd stumbled down across rocks or my horse sidestepped a thorn bush. I was unequivocally glad when my horse attained flat ground at the top once more. I walked my horse to the water trough, returned him to his stall, and stretched out on a blanket on the porch just like all the cowboys. I did not think I could make the stairs back to my comfortable bed, nor would that have been sporting of me.

"Well, Hooper," said Miles, taking a cross-legged seat beside me and pulling out a pipe and pouch from his shirt pocket, "we may not have got our beast just yet, but we cannot slack off in getting our man in the meantime."

I opened one eye in his direction and wiped sand granules from it. "What did you have in mind?"

He spoke quietly, beyond the hearing of the others. "You may have gathered that the wolf hunt is partly a diversion to allow us to tighten a net around our foeman. I think, while you get your beauty rest here, I have a few matters to attend to."

I was too fatigued to ask what he meant, and when I woke at dinnertime from a sound nap, he was gone.

The hunt resumed at dusk, as planned. Miles had returned to the ranks, saying nothing to me about his midday mission, and the hunting party assembled as before at a location a bit farther west. This also took us, I observed, farther from the site of the Griswall homestead, and I wondered if our chances of spotting the giant animal were consequently reduced, but I asked no questions.

Abernathy stayed some yards ahead of us, according to the original plan. In the fading light, I soon lost sight of his brown jacket among the brush.

We were rounding a striated, conical hill that gave onto a deep draw beside a grassy clearing when I heard it. Above us, on a shelf of the hill, came a howl, muscular and voluminous and easily differentiated from the yips and yahoos of the coyotes. Wolf, no doubt about it.

The sound of hooves approached my position, and Miles arrived by my side at the same time Abernathy stopped and dismounted in front of me. He laid a finger across his lips for silence.

Other men had heard the howling, too, and those nearest us arrived in the clearing, guns drawn. Trey Wolverton quietly reined in next to Abernathy and bent to hear what his expert guide had to say. That message I could only guess, as Abernathy indicated the rock shelf with a wave of his hand and seemed to motion for one of the other men, a beater, to ride around behind and drive the animal downwards. Others, it appeared, were to form a perimeter preventing it from escaping. Abernathy would wait, afoot and armed with knife and pistol, in the center.

In this endeavor I doubted I would be as much a help as

hindrance, and I whispered to Miles that I might be of more use armed with camera than shotgun. He concurred, perhaps too swiftly for my ego. But I slid from my mount as silently as I could manage and pulled the Kodak from my saddlebag, along with the small tripod that could be extended to an appropriate height. I focused to a wide depth of field and aimed the lens at the lightest portion of the grass, hoping for a clear shot.

It was from behind the black box, then, that I saw a series of astonishing events unfold; and thus I cannot fully trust, to this moment, the accuracy of my observations.

I heard, uphill to my right, a systematic, rustling noise I took for attempts to flush the beast from its stronghold, followed by a scrambling of animal claws on sandstone and a terrifying series of growls. The wolf eventually retreated down the steep incline and came into my vision as it rushed the slight figure of Abernathy down on the flat—putting me in mind of an enraged bull charging a matador or a heavyweight prizefighter coming off the ropes for a knockout.

I shifted the camera to capture the action and clicked the shutter, taking no time to refocus and hoping for the best. I advanced the film and shot again.

The other hunters closed ranks—as much out of curiosity and wonder as out of protection for Jack, I surmised—but none fired a weapon. They were going to let him fight this out as long as he could.

Abernathy moved sideways in a crouch, like a wrestler, as the beast lowered its head and crept backward, step by slow step. If the wolf felt cornered, as it surely did, I could imagine it would spring on its adversary in an instant; its foam-laced fangs could sink into the youth's flesh in a second. But if it continued retreating toward the line of hunters behind and around it, a man would be forced to take a lucky shot at close range to disable it without injuring one of his counterparts. I reached into the camera bag for a flash pan and powder, and swiftly set it up the apparatus, as the torches lent only intermittent light to the scene.

Abernathy chose the offense. He leapt toward the wolf, catching it sufficiently by surprise to jam a leather-gloved forearm between its jaws, just behind the molars. What a brilliant maneuver it was!

I had in that same moment—how I managed to time it right I shall never know—opened the camera's shutter and touched a match to the pan. With a puff of smoke the powder burst into a half-second of daylight, and the shutter clicked shut again.

The wolf, not accustomed to such movement as the lad's by any known prey, whimpered and snarled but could not frighten its attacker away. Quickly, the cowboys were on it with ropes. One man held the beast's top jaw while another restrained the lower, and Jack Abernathy was able to step free of its entanglement, victorious.

A whoop went out from the hunters, weary but reenergized by their success. The sheriff fired off three shots in the air, and soon even the farthest rangers had arrived in the clearing, to a ruckus of hollering that I was sure could be heard clear to the next county.

"We got 'im!" I heard Ranger McDonald exclaim, as I examined Jack's arm and found no damage other than a bit of bruising.

"Big'un, ain't it?" Jack said.

"This lobo won't be a problem to you now!" said a rancher neighbor to Wolverton. In the near-complete darkness, Miles helped Wolverton and the rest of the men bind the animal surely to a makeshift sled, and the cowboys lashed it to the strongest horse and dragged it uphill toward headquarters.

I hung back at the end of the line, not wanting my slowness to impede the party's progress, and was slogging my way up the path when Miles trotted back to join me.

Looking back over his shoulder, down toward the ever-mysterious Croton Breaks, he leaned over and whispered, "Good show, wasn't it? But I fear they've got the wrong wolf."

Chapter 15
A Wake for Wolverton

{In which a family resemblance is revealed.}

Trey Wolverton was in an expansive, though serious, mood.

"My gratitude," he was saying to the company gathered in the Wolverton great hall as I entered with Miles and Abernathy, "is hardly sufficient to your sacrifice in risking mortal danger." The ranchers and farmers and yeomen and ministers who'd taken on the mantle of Nimrod for a day and a night were congratulating themselves, beer steins raised high, for prevailing against a terrible foe.

Wolverton paced around the banquet table, thanking individual men, while Jack occupied the piano bench. The newest member of our party was proving a surprise on many fronts: he played pretty well for a kid. As he segued from a meditative minor key into a lively polka, the men seemed to catch the rhythm, relaxing and loosening the kerchiefs from around their necks. Clutches of hunters recounted the day's exploits. No one seemed quite ready to part company, though the hour was quite late.

"I've had an idea," the Wolverton heir cried out suddenly, stopping mid-stride and stepping onto a chair to get everyone's attention. Abernathy lowered the volume and deftly switched tunes to suit the boss's mien. The chat stopped, as eyes turned in Wolverton's direction.

All, that was, except those of Miles, whose gaze systematically ranged the hall like a Pharos light sweeping a harbor. From the doorway, standing, he cast the arc of his view over every face present, every detail of the room and its furnishings, forming, I knew from experience, a mental archive far deeper than most men's surface impressions. I caught one particular instant as the great detective's eye widened, then narrowed on a portion of the far wall, examining the portraits of dead Wolvertons that hung above the heads of the lively men. The harbor lens quickly came back around to Wolverton and fixed its beam there as our host continued with his announcement.

"You know," he said, "I've struggled, these past days, to think of a way to properly honor the memory of my late uncle. You all knew him as fellow stockman, or neighbor, or philanthropist. I, however, knew him hardly at all. To gather in a chapel seemed impractical, as we have no house of worship hereabouts large enough for the purpose. To stand over a plot of earth under an autumn sky and say a few words of eulogy seemed, well, anticlimactic. To simply bury him and omit any ceremony to mark his good works or pray for his soul in the next world would not do. But I believe I have just the right thing."

He paused, looked briefly heavenward, and then, almost in defiance, stared right toward the doorway where Miles and I stood, and said, "We shall have a wake."

A few whispers erupted, then ceased altogether.

"A good old-fashioned send-off with music and merriment, on the eve of All Saints," said he, nodding in agreement with his own emerging concept. "Now that we have rid the Wolverton line of the curse that has dogged it down through the centuries by removing this beast from our line, let us celebrate! Nevermore shall the wolf hound the Wolverton!"

The cowboys took this plan with particular cheer, and reached to refill their steins. Even the man called Preacher appeared to approve when Wolverton tempered his design with the previously decided Sabbath-day funeral service on the first of November. "Let us gather here on Saturday, a week from this night, for a true cowboy's ball, if that invitation suits your fancy. Spread the word across the countryside, and bring your wives and families. It will be an affair worthy of the Wolverton name."

A cowhand, likely in his cups, shouted out, "It's Hallowe'en, y'know. I think I'll come as the Pres-i-*dent!*"

"Woo-hoo—I'll be the First Lady!" yelled another.

Wolverton caught the spirit of the idea. "That's it! A *costume* ball!"

I raised an eyebrow at this and stole a glance at Miles, whose visage remained stoic. In a baritone stage whisper beneath the chatter he uttered words for my ear alone.

"Let us humor our client's grand wishes, my dear Hooper, for I begin to believe the party may play perfectly into our game."

"But aren't you worried—"

"That not only is a fiend-wolf still at large; but that we have not yet ascertained if, or even how, it intersects with the designs of the treacherous Griswall; nor how, or if, either of these factors figured into the death of the Earl?"

I nodded. "Couldn't have said it better myself."

With the prospect of such a gathering only a week hence, the men began to locate their hats and disperse for the stables.

"Mr. Wolverton, my wife, for one, will welcome the invite," said rancher Browning as he bid his host farewell for now. "I'd best be moving on down the trail. But I'll sure rest easier on the ride home."

Pearl-Handle Pete headed for his horse as well. "Have to be honest, Wolverton, I had my doubts about ye. Th'Earl cast a long shadow. But I think you're gonna measure up."

"Your vote of confidence means a great deal," said Wolverton.

The man called Preacher made his exit with the excuse of a sermon still to prepare for the morrow. The sheriff hung back after the others, and Abernathy slid the cover back down over the ivories and strode over to join us.

"Good work tonight," said Harkey to Wolverton. "I have to ask, though, what do you propose to do with that lobo tied up out there?"

"Frankly, I hadn't expected to end up with a live one on my hands. What do *you* suggest?"

"Well, I've been thinking. I got this old calaboose made out of strap iron, bought it down in Parker County and had an idea of setting it up in Espuela for a jail. It's up at the crossroads five miles from here, on a wagon. We might be able to use it for a cage."

"That's a grand idea, Sheriff," said the ranch owner. "Why don't you gather a few men, and Abernathy and I will help bring the animal to the cage? And I suppose you have a chain and lock as well?"

"Thee does not fear any chance of a supernatural disappearance of this beast, then!" chuckled Wesley Barlow.

"I'd fear more the likelihood of bounty hunters spiriting it away for the pelt," said Wolverton, and the sheriff agreed.

Wolverton went with the group to saddle up and depart right away. Abernathy pulled a knot of jerky from his pocket to chew and hung back with Miles and me for a brief spell.

"You don't suppose they realize it ain't the same wolf they were looking for, do you, Captain?" said Abernathy.

Miles glanced slantwise at me, his eyes silver slits in the moonlight, and I could scarcely read him. "Let us say nothing of this to Trey Wolverton for now, Jack. He, too, saw the photographs Dr. Hooper took, and no doubt was witness to the discovery of the footprints themselves, but in the excitement of the capture has not recalled this. Let us not rob him of his glory, as we may yet use these circumstances to our advantage."

Abernathy nodded and was off to claim a horse from the remuda.

"Godspeed and safe return," Miles called after him.

I woke and started downstairs the next morning to find Miles already up and dressed, standing on a chair, hands clasped behind his back and examining a portrait in the great hall more closely. No other soul stirred, as Wolverton and Abernathy had returned well after midnight and remained in their beds. Absent the familiar household activities of the Lópezes going about their chores, the place possessed a graveyard stillness, as though the entire house were holding its breath.

Miles motioned me with a wave of his hand. I padded over soundlessly in my slippers, and he whispered, "I trust you are rested well after our season of adventure, Hooper."

I nodded, and whispered back, "An early hour for a museum tour, is it not?"

"I know you are unlikely to allow that I know a thing about art, but I must say, I found myself quite taken with this collection of canvases last eve."

"However so? Many appear quite primitive, if I do say so."

"Well you might. However, it is not their style that interests me, but their substance. They are all family portraits, I presume?"

"Wolvertons for generations back, as López explained to us, and as I learned from Miss—Mrs. LaBorde, some are copies made by her itinerant-painter husband."

"I assumed as much, since the identifying plaques affixed to the frames differ, as do the, er, techniques. You wouldn't notice the names, necessarily, unless you periodically assumed sufficient height to dust—or knew the lineage by heart, as the Earl must have."

"López knew enough to coach Trey Wolverton in some of the history."

"I suspected as much. So you recognize, over there with the hunting rifle, Colonel William Wolverton, who served with Wellington in India."

"Yes."

"And Sir Grenville Wolverton, there, who by the appurtenances in the portrait distinguished himself with engineering achievements."

I nodded, as I had learned of the bridge-builder by reading the genealogical volume that lay on my own bedside table upstairs.

"And this red-bearded *cavalero* right in front of me, in black velvet and lace?"

I gazed up at the portrait with increased interest as I replied, " 'Tis assumed to be the wicked Basil, the first baronet Wolverton, who brought down upon himself the curse of the wolf."

"I knew it!" said Miles, his voice echoing suddenly through the empty hall. "He seems an ordinary enough figure for his generation, quite the type of the Restoration loyalist, but do you not catch the glint in his eyes? Villainous, I would say. Scheming. Though I had pictured a more brutish and muscular person."

"Everything Trey and I learned came at secondhand, through López's retelling, of course. But there was a family history in the parlor, and I took it up and read the accounts for myself."

"The name and the date, 1647, are on the plaque, which attributes this painting to none other than van Dyck," Miles said, whistling in admiration.

"I was not aware you could tell a van Dyck from a van Gogh," I yawned.

"Hmphf," Miles responded. "I took quite an interest in the latter's paintings while studying the psychotic mind at Saint-

Rémy year before last, must I remind you? But that is hardly the point. Will you light that candle and hand it up?"

I did as bidden, and its weak flame illuminated the fine features of the portrait as Miles moved it over the canvas.

"Do you see anything there?" I looked at the plumed hat, the curling lovelocks, the white lace collar, and the straight, severe face which was framed between them. It was not a brutal countenance, but it was prim, hard, and stern, with a firm-set, thin-lipped mouth and a coldly intolerant eye.

"Is it like anyone you know?"

"There is something of Trey Wolverton about the jaw."

"Just a suggestion, perhaps. But wait an instant!" Switching the light to his left hand, he curved his right arm over the broad hat and around the long auburn ringlets.

"Good heavens!" I cried in amazement. The face of Rufus Griswall had sprung out of the canvas.

"Ha, you see it now. My eyes have been trained to examine faces and not their trimmings. It is the first quality of a criminal investigator that he should see through a disguise."

"But this is incredible. It might be his own portrait."

"Yes, it is an interesting instance of a throwback, which appears to be both physical and spiritual. A study of family portraits is enough to convert a man to the doctrine of reincarnation. The fellow is a Wolverton—that is evident."

"With designs upon an inheritance."

"Exactly. This chance of the picture has supplied us with one of our most obvious motives. We have him, Hooper, we *have* him, and I dare swear that before tomorrow night he will be fluttering in our net as helpless as one of his own butterflies. A pin, a cork, and a card, and we add him to the Houston Street collection!" He burst into one of his rare fits of laughter as he turned away from the picture. I have not heard him laugh often, but when I have it has always boded ill to somebody.

CHAPTER 16
PREPARATIONS LAID

{In which the sheriff reports another death.}

"I'm gettin' good enough at this I just might have to give up cowboyin'," said the fifteen-year-old, with the solemn introspection of a cowpuncher several decades more advanced in the profession. Jack Abernathy held his reins lightly in one hand as he admired the wolf-capture photograph he brandished in the other. "What do you think, Cap'n Miles?"

Young Abernathy's scheme was to sell the captured wolf to a big-city outfit that might be interested in founding a zoological park, as soon as he could figure out a plan for transporting the animal safely to Fort Worth.

Miles and I had taken Sunday to rest up from the week's exploits, clean our guns, refresh our wardrobes, and enjoy an excellent supper of chicken and dumplings, which seemed to restore our souls as much as it did our bellies. I had relaxed in the Earl's comfortable chair and before nodding off in an untroubled nap at last reached the satisfying end of *The Sign of Four*. I had printed my most recent photographs, too, which made for much interest and speculation.

Now, our party of four—plus an extra packhorse to throw off any trackers—made its way south and east in the morning mist, as though to see Miles across the river in the direction of Albany. In reality he would follow the valley to the Putoff Canyon lodge north of Jay Flat, there to inquire a bit more information about the painter LaBorde and his portrait commissions for the Earl. By nightfall, long after Barlow, Abernathy, and I had circled back the way we'd come, he would slip back into his stone-cottage lair, there to lie low for a duration while we all helped Wolverton spread invitations far and wide for the Hallowe'en ball.

"I think the world's a wider place than the haunts of wolves or beeves either one," Miles replied after a moment. "When I was your age, I was about to make my way across the Atlantic to study in London. Never underestimate what a boy may be capable of, Jack."

Abernathy pondered the words. "Well, I surely won't, sir. But in the meantime, I think I might be onto something—like this Hou-deeny fellow!"

"Who?" I responded, not quite following his words.

"Hou-deeny, that's who. That circus ringleader in Wichita Falls was talking about him. Does card tricks and a disappearing act, like nothing anybody's ever seen before. Well, they ain't ever seen the likes of Catch-'em-Alive Jack neither. That Wichita Falls reporter come up with the name."

"Hmm. How long will you stay?" Barlow asked him.

Jack shrugged, keeping mum about the big loafer still at large as Miles had requested, and we plodded on toward the fording spot.

Miles's plan was shrewdly calculated to convince Griswall, or anyone else involved, to let down his guard once he believed the famous detective absent once more. The scheme brought risks, to be sure, though Miles was counting on bringing one surprise trump into play. He now had Lili LaBorde on our side.

It was she to whom Miles had paid a visit on Saturday at the Barlow homestead. "A quick study," Miles had described her to me upon his return, "and no admirer of Rufus Griswall. Her antipathy for him, and her friendship with Maria, as I guessed, make her the perfect ally in our cause. She will work with us to unmask the man, I am certain."

Miles had gone so far as to persuade the young woman to accompany him, along with Mr. Barlow, back to the Wolverton headquarters, where her services would be useful during a frenzied week of party preparations and also provide an occasion to search for the metal box she had seen Griswall bury.

We came at length to the wide ford of Croton Creek, a crossing where we had been assured of finding a reliable bottom, as the region had experienced no adverse weather since the previous week's sudden storm. We bid Miles farewell on the western bank as he led his horse and the pack animal through the shallow water without incident. He walked the horses up the rise and back down again until he seemed confident in creating a convincing misdirection, then rode away. I could only hope for conditions as easy that night, when he would retrace his route under the dark of a waning moon.

As it transpired, we had yet another calamity on our hands before the day was out.

When our band arrived back at the ranch at dinnertime, Sheriff Harkey was waiting, grim-faced. He strode over to us before we could dismount.

"That lobo—I found it dead in the cage this morning. You ought to—"

"How?!" cried Abernathy, as though he'd lost his best friend.

"That's what we need to determine. It was . . . rigid and foaming at the mouth."

"My God!" I interjected. "Hydrophobia."

"I can't be sure, but I think it best to examine the boy and keep him closely quarantined."

Abernathy's expression turned from incredulity to rage. "That wolf didn't look mad to me. Somebody *did* this!"

"We must take a look, Jack. If the skin was broken in even the smallest place you could be in mortal danger," I said.

"Damned if I'll sit by and be nursed while somebody's kilt my capture," he replied, spurring his horse out into the night.

For all the youth's skill, the sheriff and Wolverton quickly cut him off and led him back to the house, where he agreed to submit to a thorough check.

Though I could detect no breaks in the skin, I knew that even minor scratches, already starting to heal, could pose a concern. Had Abernathy come in contact with the animal's saliva, even through a wound caused by thorns in the brush rather than a wolf's bite, the deadly agent could have been transmitted. We could not know for some while whether symptoms might arise.

"I concur with Sheriff Harkey's advice to remain here under observation," I said. "I can make inquiries regarding Pasteur's new vaccination treatment, though that will take some days, and since I have never myself administered it, I heartily recommend that you rest here and await the doctor's reply."

Abernathy rebuttoned his shirt, nonplussed but still angry. "That was my shot, don't you see? My *big* shot."

It was with mixed feelings that I learned the Lópezes had returned to the ranch in the company of the deputy. While Trey Wolverton had seen no reason to refuse the assistance of such able-bodied and knowledgeable help at such a crucial time, I was uneasy about the questions that remained unanswered regarding the Earl's demise. The case on which Miles and I had been summoned from the outset was by no means settled, and with each passing day I saw that this state of affairs bothered the Wolverton heir less and less.

"Felicia López has suffered enough, I imagine," he said when I questioned the wisdom of flinging the ranch doors open to them again. "We have no conclusive reason to doubt that she and her husband acted out of anything but compassion for her desperate brother. I might well do the same. As a doctor, mightn't you?"

"You make a convincing point," I said. "But I want to remind you that *no one* in your uncle's orbit is beyond suspicion, notwithstanding that we have narrowed our focus to one neighbor who appears to have a singularly compelling motive for murder. We have proven *nothing* to date!"

I registered, in Wolverton's hint of a smirk, that derisive disregard in which he had at the outset held all our efforts. I abandoned my line of argument, for I was acutely aware that Miles's methodical approach to the work for which Mr. Barlow had hired us might well test the limits of Wolverton's good graces. It had not been Trey Wolverton's idea to bring us here; we stayed on at his pleasure, and so far the star detective had spent only forty-eight hours under his roof before making scarce again. Such actions surely did not instill the highest level of confidence in a young and impetuous client with plans of his own. I backed down.

"Dr. Hooper," said Wolverton as he sat down in the leather chair and took out the notebook in which he had begun making lists and sketches, "It's admirable that you're looking out for my welfare. But maybe it's better in any case to have los López here under your watchful eye."

How Miles would view this sentiment I knew not, but how eagerly I would welcome a hot meal by now was indisputable. I went down to the kitchen, where Barlow was checking to see how Lili was getting on with her newly arrived supervisors. The young woman seemed to be quite adaptable. In a setting very different from tending to the crotchety old Judge or to the lively Larkin household, either one, she seemed to bring a confident sense of organization and capability. Her independent spirit had metamorphosed, it appeared to me, from insolence to co-operation, while her quirky wit seemed to have been tempered somewhat by the somber demeanor of Mrs. López. Her condition—about twenty-five weeks gone, I had estimated—was masked to all but knowledgeable eyes by a generous apron. All this I observed in the brief span of waiting for her to scramble three eggs, fold them into a tortilla along with a spiced beef mixture, beans, and piquant sauce, and hand the plate to me on a tray with strong coffee to carry up to my quarters. Arrangements in the frontier household did not extend to room service.

I savored every bite of the delicious creation Mrs. López had called a *burrito* while I penned my notes for Miles. Still stinging from Wolverton's rebuff, I laid out my observations and speculations as well as a complete summary of the facts to date, as I saw them. The undertaking took some hours and a hefty stack of the Earl's quality paper. On what occasion I might deliver such a report to Miles I was not sure, since he had deemed it no longer safe for him to use the telegrapher's son as his go-between.

I then documented a medical report of Abernathy's encounter with the wolf and my examinations both in the field and *ex post facto*. I desperately hoped it would never prove necessary to consult it. Hydrophobia was a horrid way for any man or beast to die.

On the morrow Mr. Barlow would ride to Espuela to spread word of Wolverton's invitation and, most vitally, to post a telegram for me to the Pasteur Institute. At the same time he would put out the story, in a few key places, of Miles's abrupt journey back eastward. (There was in fact a shred of truth in the statement, and I hoped the deception did not trouble Barlow's conscience overmuch.) The rest of us would wait here and watch, and assist as we could with women's work, I expected, in preparation for the Saturday night shindig.

Before turning in I doused my candle and opened the window, gazing into the broken blackness beyond and wishing once again that I knew the answer to one burning question: *What would Derrick Miles do?*

Chapter 17
Tools of the Trade

*{In which there is a time to build up,
and a time to tear down.}*

I woke to the grind of saws and the ring of hammers. Flinging on my dressing gown over my long-handles—as it had turned off quite chilly—I stepped over to the window I'd left open and looked around below me. In the front yard of the house were assembled numerous sawhorses; workmen scrambled to nail up scaffolding around the unfinished wing of the structure while others, some of them cowboys I recognized from Saturday's hunt, split cedar shakes or cut lumber to size. One wagon stood nearby, filled with kegs and cartons; another, outfitted with a variation of Goodnight's chuck box, held hogsheads of what I took to be comestibles for a crowd.

"Oh, Doctor," shouted Wolverton jovially when he spied me in the window, "are you quite done with your breakfast tray? We could use an extra hand!"

I combed through the garments in my clothes press for suitable attire—my everyday trousers being nearly worn through at the seams from the strain of daily riding—and double-timed it downstairs.

" 'Zounds," I declared. "Do you plan to build Rome in a day?"

"I wasn't idle while you were away yesterday," said Wolverton, who was dressed sensibly in the sort of riveted waist overalls I now envied. "Pete and Louie gathered the ranch hands from all about, and we're going to raise a roof in record time!" López, he told me, was happy to be back after his brother-in-law's burial and excited to be in charge of such an ambitious project. " 'Happy' and 'excited' in relative terms, for López, of course."

I, for one, was grateful for Wolverton's own improved mood.

Their combined industry was impressive indeed, forming a moving assembly that turned as smoothly as finely meshed rods and gears, rhythmically timed. Already a pair of the nimblest youths had climbed to the second-story level, where they were nailing long rafters into place. Beside me, carpenters were stacking lengths that looked suitable to serve as horizontal members. While I did not consider my skills might add much—having reserved the use of my hands throughout my career for scalpel and suture—I asked how I might help.

"You," said my host, "start counting out twenty-penny nails from this barrel, if you would. Hand each man a fistful and keep passing up more as needed."

I did as compelled, watching as each worker filled his pouch with nails and considering the strictly ceremonial nature of my own mason's apron back home in Fort Worth. There, the freemasons gathered to discuss matters of government and society, lending their moral support at the leveling of the occasional cornerstone. Here on the frontier, each workman was needed to pull his weight in a fully physical sense.

Throughout the morning and afternoon the crew muscled beams and roof into form, pausing only for a bowl of beans and a cup of coffee from the chuck wagon. At the end of the day Wolverton paid their wages and asked them back if they could spare any hours for the rest of the week, when help would be needed in constructing exterior and interior walls, laying floors, and hanging doors. Windowpanes and other factory-made features would have to wait for another day—not to mention such niceties as we had in the city, like flush toilets and gas lights, that might be years in coming to a remote ranch.

I climbed the stairs once more to my quarters, washed up in

the basin, and searched once again through the stack of garments I had set aside. The morning's search for appropriate work clothing reminded me that I had need also to invent a costume for Saturday night's party. What had I been thinking, exactly, back in the comforts of the city, to pack that fancy cravat, pinstriped jacket, and walking cane for the wilds of the Croton Breaks? I looked through the extra clothing Miles had left behind in his room as well, at last coming upon a few items, such as the houndstooth-patterned hunting cap he'd brought, that might prove useful.

Taking my pile of mending and my old traveling cloak, along with the sewing kit from my valise, I sank into the easy chair next to the lamp in my room. There I took needle and thread in hand, along with the large reading-glass from the side table, to repair my torn britches. I inspected my handiwork—a series of square knots like those I'd mastered in surgery—and judged it satisfactory.

I then cut pieces on the bias from the brown tartan cloak and began to stitch together my own inspiration for the coming soirée. We would require disguise, both Miles and I, if we were to carry out his plan. I thought I'd landed on the perfect idea, if I did say so myself.

I had the opportunity, on the following morning, to talk with Mrs. López alone, and to set my mind somewhat at ease. Rising at dawn, I found her alone at the kitchen table, rosary in her brown hands, while Lili slept on in the warm quarters near the chimney.

"I am sorry for the trouble José brought to this house," she said, "but even more the shame. I grieve for his soul and hope we can make atonement for his mortal wrongs."

"For that, I cannot speak, madam," I told her quietly, as she fingered the beads. "Your brother paid with his life, without benefit of witness from his family. Derrick Miles and I have been hired to uncover the truth of Basil Wolverton's death, and when we are successful, facts will surely be more comforting to everyone than rumor and speculation."

She nodded, wiping tears from her eyes. I only hoped our abilities would be equal to my words.

With the rising of the sun arrived more wagonloads of raw lumber; bars and rods of iron for the forge; lengths of tin and tar paper; cartloads of chopped cedar wood; household appurtenances of canvas and oilcloth and braided wool. Ranch hands whose bosses gave them a few hours' leave showed up to swing a hammer or wield a saw for a stint. Rapidly, the house began to take on a handsome unity of material outside and in.

The constant industry put me in mind of the buzz of activity at the Galveston wharves during cotton harvest or the Fort Worth stockyards at the end of a cattle drive, or the oceangoing docks of the Thames, which I had once visited in my youth. It was not so much the hum of commerce itself as the vitality of storing up, nest-lining, log-chinking, laying-by. Of preparations for a coming winter.

Beeves were slaughtered and salted; a hog was butchered. The enormous kettle was scrubbed. Butter was churned. Beans soaked. Apples baked.

In that reflective frame of mind I received a *sub rosa* missive from Miles, delivered by the hand of Billy McDonald. The ranger had reported nothing unusual at the Griswall household. As for Miles, he moved from dark camp to camp by night, searching quietly by day for the site of the metal box Lili LaBorde had reported, while Captain McDonald kept watch.

Wolverton and I rode out at dusk to a predetermined spot where we strung up a cache of food and water, along with my reports, for Miles to collect later. We neither saw nor heard further sign of wolf, though we spotted numerous trails of riders—not surprising, as much activity as there had been to and from all points of the Wolverton Ranch.

"You've determined to stay, it seems," I said, testing the waters of our host's mood as we rode abreast on a wide swath of cattle trail.

"Two weeks ago you couldn't have paid me in bullion to consider it," he said. "But it's funny. The place grows on you."

"Perhaps," I ventured, "there is some*one* who has grown on you as well?"

"Let us say—there is a spark that warrants tending. I believe that, with all this nasty superstition business put to rest, we may at last also discover that my uncle's death was no more than an accident, and that if as a result of that unfortunate occurrence some nervy neighbor is looking to jump my claim, well, I intend to stay and defend it. And very soon to make a claim of my own."

"You—you have reason to believe the lady knows of your intentions?"

"By George, she will, come Saturday night!" he exclaimed. "I won't leave Maria to rot away as handmaid to her father's schemes, to waste her beauty and youth in a dirt dugout when she deserves the finest home in the county!"

He looked up the path toward his ranch and seemed to spur his horse more energetically. Suddenly the true objective of all the building and housekeeping activity came clearly into focus for me. In a flash I perceived the doubtless reason for the increased industry: *Wolverton was preparing a home for his beloved.* How had I not seen this before? Deaf to love's ambition, I suppose, thrown over as I had been so many years earlier in favor of another suitor, I lamented the limitations of my empathy that had prevented me from understanding more clearly my own client's motivations. And by failing to see the obvious, I was

235

putting him in peril. I must not, I determined, allow myself to be so out of tune again.

It was with just such a pledge in mind that I insinuated myself and Mr. Barlow into Trey Wolverton's hopes to ride over to the Griswall place toward the end of the week and personally ensure that his invitation to the ball had been received.

"The work on the house is complete, or at least as complete as it's going to get until the day comes that we have more than a damned wagon road to get supplies in here," said Wolverton as he gathered his spade and froe and lifted them into the cart with the rest of his job tools.

"You have wreaked an impressive transformation," I admitted to him. "I'm sure every soul within a hundred miles will be champing at the bit to see it and meet the one responsible, whether they knew Sir Basil or not."

"I daresay we'll have a bigger crowd than I first envisioned," he admitted, wiping the sweat from his brow with a soiled bandana. "All the more reason to keep Griswall close within our view and Maria safe."

"We should put the ranger, McDonald, in charge of security. He can handpick his men. They can keep a lid on any rowdiness and watch for trouble. With your permission, of course."

"Agreed."

"Now, as for your desire to drop in on the Griswall place . . . I have a counterproposal that might serve a dual purpose."

"Shoot, then. Though I could wash up, ride out there, and be back before nightfall."

"Mr. Barlow and I shall pay a call on your behalf in the morning. I believe such a gesture will prove persuasive without raising any ire."

Wolverton must have been exceedingly weary, as he gave in without much of a fight. His only condition was that Barlow and I were to speak with Maria in person and not be shunted off by her father. I pledged that we would do our best.

We set out at midmorning in the wagon with the sheet raised. Brief fits of rain punctuated the gloomy day, though ashen clouds held mostly to the north, rumbling by against a gunmetal sky like ghostly herds of cattle on the trail. Occasional shouts of thunder boomed out of them, followed by lashes of lightning. It was ghoulish weather for the penultimate day of October, I remarked to Barlow, and I hazarded a worry about whether we would crack our case before winter advanced on the plains.

"I daresay thee and Captain Miles will indeed break through soon," said he. "I hired the best men for the job as we knew it at the outset, and now that Wolverton seems persuaded to take up residence, it is all the more imperative that we protect him—and his household and neighbors—from those who wish him ill. I have faith."

"You do not still hold reservations that our enemy is beyond the realm of men?"

Barlow gave the reins a taut shake to urge the team over a rise, revealing to us the stream bed of Croton Creek and the easy ford. He leaned gently on the brake, with just as much skill, to negotiate the switchback that brought us almost level with the creek bank. At last he spoke again.

"Of mortal activity I find the physical evidence thee has presented to date most compelling. A link between our suspect and a killer wolf, thee has not yet forged."

Barlow cracked the whip to urge the horses and wagon across the creek. In a single dash the team took the last sloping yard down the bluff and crossed the shallow stream with alacrity. In a flash we found ourselves on the sandy bank opposite the hill and moving toward the meadow where we had first made acquaintance of the Griswalls.

I saw no sign of the dowser-naturalist, and well it was, since we had hoped to encounter father and daughter at home in their own dwelling, to make good on our promise to speak with Maria herself. I gauged the dugout to be another mile and a half via this route, and thirty minutes' easy ride brought us to the place.

The rain had ceased, and rays of sun broke through sufficient to cast the humble residence into a golden glow that left me with an entirely different impression from that which registered with me on our first visit. Yellow roses bloomed beside the doorway. Prickly pear cactus presented its purple fruits to a dozen orange monarchs. Nearby, mourning doves cooed from an unseen branch.

One could almost cast aside suspicion, accepting Rufus Griswall as nothing more than an eccentric, bumbling explorer of the wild, a champion of dumb creatures, a rustic but useful mechanic of winches and wells. Almost.

The naturalist opened the door immediately at our knock, as though he had been standing on the other side awaiting us. And then I recalled with a stab of self-recrimination the telescope through which he might have spied on our approach across the meadow.

"A pleasant afternoon to you, gentlemen. What brings you here on the eve of the big celebration? Oh, don't say that our host has canceled!"

"So you *do* already have your calendar marked?" said Barlow. "We have come only to make sure of it. Trey Wolverton is most eager to thank neighbors he has met, and meet those he has not. We drove out to convey his personal wish to see you and your daughter there."

I saw a flicker of light pass across Griswall's visage, and as he lifted his chin I could not help but see the dashing seventeenth-century baronet of the portrait standing before me. I fought the urge to interrogate him then and there. Only the measured voice of Derrick Miles in my head prevented me from pursuing such a rash line of inquiry.

I said to him instead, "You and Maria will certainly not want to miss the treats in store. It promises to be a feast for the senses."

Once again, his eyes sparkled in my direction. "Then I give you my word, Griswall shall be present. Now that the specter of the lupine predator no longer threatens safe journeys."

"And Maria? She is well, I hope?"

"In the kitchen ready to serve lunch. Had we known, we could have prepared for more . . ."

"As it so happens, we brought our own sandwiches, plus extra," said Barlow. "Barbecued brisket wrapped in a tortilla. Thee has enjoyed Señora López's tortillas on previous occasions. May I offer thee one?"

Barlow held out the canvas tuck bag, and Griswall took two of the wrapped delicacies but did not invite us in.

I played my final card. "Before we depart, then, Trey Wolverton has sent a small favor to your daughter. Might I—"

Before I could finish my sentence, I heard quick footsteps behind Griswall, and Maria appeared in the doorway. She appeared tired and anxious, but she smiled at the oilcloth-wrapped package I handed toward her. Griswall intercepted it and slipped the item out of its protective covering.

"*A History of the Wolvertons of Brent*," he read as he turned the book over in his hands with a *hrrumph*. "Well, Maria. Looks as though our new neighbor is taking to his British roots. Maybe he means for us to have a little reading to occupy us in case the weather should keep us home."

Maria glanced around at the volume and up to me but did not reach for it.

"Mademoiselle, Trey Wolverton hopes you will save him a spot on your card," I said, aiming for a levity that might mask my concerns. "As for my own part, I am not adept at reels and waltzes and the like but am very eager to observe how dinner and dancing are done in Dickens."

She nodded agreement, and without speaking so much as a word, retreated into the shadows.

"Well," said I, and bid Griswall good-bye. "We shall see you tomorrow evening." My next words were out before I could hold my tongue. "I hope you won't be cavalier with your costuming, either!"

Barlow and I returned to the wagon and retraced our path homeward, speaking little. My companion, I guessed, found our errand less than successful too.

"What do you expect Griswall's next intentions to be?" I asked Barlow once we had reached the edge of the meadow and started to climb the main trail again. Deep shadows punctuated the remaining shafts of sunlight as the day faded. I had to admit I disliked the sensation of our enemy's eyes on our backs, picturing his long spyglass trained in our direction. I would feel better once we had rounded the canyon edge out of his sight.

Barlow thought on the matter for a second, clicked the reins gently to guide the team toward the leftward path, then replied, "I rather think the question to be, what do we expect Derrick Miles's next intentions to be?"

As we topped the hill I was preparing to offer some observations when suddenly a feminine howl erupted from the back of the wagon.

"There! Stop the wagon! That's the place! *Stop!*"

I had no chance to ask a stowaway Lili LaBorde *what* place before the horses, spooked by the outcry, bolted around the rocks and straight down toward the creek. I held to the side rail of my seat to keep from being thrown headlong into a jumble of mesquite thorns, while Barlow tightened his grip on the reins and struggled to pull the team up. Still they raced for the water.

Even in the darkling canyon I could make out a singular confluence of events that lay before us. The creek whose depth had registered in inches only two hours before now bore down on the draw in a roiling wave, the vanguard of collected rain currents triggered miles upstream from us. The trajectory of the runaway wagon looked to collide, in a matter of seconds, with that of the flash flood.

Barlow set the wagon brake, flung the lines at me wordlessly, and motioned me to rein in hard. I pulled with all my might as I watched the quiet Quaker leap from the wagon seat onto the back of the nearest horse and, reaching behind him, deftly unfasten the traces. The wagon came sliding to a halt on the bank of Croton Creek as the team and its rider plunged into the wave. Barlow gripped his horse around the withers and hung on. The horses, still braced together, swam with the flow for ten yards or so before regaining solid ground, white-eyed and snorting.

Barlow patted his horse under control and led the pair back to where I waited in the wagon with our unexpected passenger.

"God *damn*, woman," he shouted. "Thee almost got all *six* of us killed."

We wasted no attention on Lili's pleas for leniency, nor her white lie of accompanying Barlow to visit her mother's grave in Espuela. Dusk was coming on in earnest, and we now faced the dual challenge of discovering the location of the purported metal box, and resuming our journey quickly in case Griswall had followed us or observed the mishap.

How we would defend ourselves against such a cunning foe, with a crippled wagon and a pregnant passenger, I did not want to contemplate.

"I recognized the place. I know it was the right spot. I had been looking out for it the whole way," said Lili. "But it wasn't until I saw it from the same angle that it stood out. That's why I could never find it again on horseback."

Barlow stayed behind to mend the wagon and rest the horses while I clambered back up the hill with Lili, shovel in hand. When we reached the fork in the trail again, she pointed to a formation of rocks that, viewed from our vantage point, resembled a group of three bears. I could appreciate the strategic location for Griswall's purposes: it could be found without confusion if one knew where to look, and it was situated within the arc of the telescope's view. We kept low and stayed within the shadow of the rocks.

It was dark enough by now to render the telescope ineffective. But Griswall could be anywhere about. I handed my revolver to Lili.

"You know how to shoot if needed?"

She nodded.

"Then it's up to you to keep watch while I dig. Show me where."

Lili indicated a flat stone covering a patch of dirt that turned out to have been disturbed. I slid the spade point down at a shallow angle, and the earth yielded. Lili indicated I should continue.

It did not take long to confirm that her memory had been precise. I marveled at the tin box, about the size of a large Bible, that I lifted from the hole. I brushed off a coating of red mud with a sumac branch and pried back the lid. Wrapped in a gutta-percha bag within were a handful of folded documents—maps, perhaps. Further examination would have to wait. Whatever the papers were, I set aside any reservations about stealing, rewrapped them, and closed the lid of the box. I handed it to Lili and returned the dirt and stone to their previous condition as best I could.

"Deeds," said Barlow, examining the documents by the light of the candle lantern in the smokehouse-darkroom. "Quitclaim deeds and land patents."

Bringing his legal experience to bear, he pointed out that the papers concerned small parcels, generally scattered, quarter-section lots, in the names of dozens of grantees. The grantor, in almost every case, was the State of Texas.

"Maps, too," he added. "See, here: this sketch map corresponds to that grant for a homestead in Young County. It's marked as rangeland; fences are drawn in. But there are markings drawn at several locations along this ridge."

"This one is marked with circles too. What do you think they denote?"

"I would guess sites of wells."

"I understand that water is a valuable commodity. But why take such pains to keep the maps in so unhandy a place?"

"Someone wants to hide the owners' identities, perhaps," Barlow mused as he continued to peruse the documents by candlelight.

"We know that Griswall practices water-witchery. Could these not simply be the records of clients for whom he was worked?"

"We must not rule out that sensible possibility."

I picked up the loupe from the tray of photographic tools, then lifted the top map from the stack and studied it at close range. "Tell me what you think about this," I said to Barlow, indicating a series of circles with dots in the centers and short lines extending from their perimeters. These sites, I pointed out to him, were located neither in valleys nor near spring sources.

"Suppose there is not water to be found here," he said after a moment's thought, "but *oil*?"

"Miles surmised as much. And indicated the finds might be lucrative. Perhaps petroleum is Griswall's game. Even if so, there's nothing criminal in it."

"Unless he would stop at nothing to obtain rights. Do you discern any pattern in the plots?"

I sifted through the stack again, noting only random names and locations. Until suddenly one particular name leapt from the page.

"See here," I said to Barlow. "A patent from 1868 in the names of one Roderick Hugh Graham and his wife, Nancy Griswall Graham. Can that occurrence be coincidental?"

Barlow took the paper from me and examined it closely. "The land is in Wise County, along the west fork of the Trinity. A couple hundred miles from here."

"If these were Rufus Griswall's kin who homesteaded in Texas, we surely have a solid lead to pursue." I told him of Miles's wild hunch regarding a familial connection between Griswall and the Wolverton line, the idea now seeming not so far-fetched.

I knew I must find a way to bring Miles abreast of these developments, posthaste.

The opportunity presented itself only a few hours later.

Mr. Barlow and I had hidden the box in the rafters of the smokehouse and retreated upstairs to our rooms. I had extinguished the lamp and slept fitfully for a few hours when a single *plink* sound, from outside, caught my attention. A night bird colliding with the window shutter? Raindrops on the roof? It came again, from the direction of the window. I tiptoed over and peeked through the small gap between the closed shutters. All was black as soot beneath the thinnest slice of moon.

A third time, the source of the noise was unmistakable. A small pebble struck the shutter near my eye, and before jumping back I distinguished the form of the one who had tossed it.

Derrick Miles, his face almost entirely wrapped in a long scarf so that only his eyes were revealed, peeked from behind a cedar post and motioned to me.

I slipped down the stairs nonchalantly, as though headed to the privy, observing my surroundings with care in case Wolverton had set a watch. I allowed Miles to see me taking that path but at the last moment ducking into the smokehouse, where I lit the ruby lamp. The most recent photographs I had left to dry hung like fiesta flags, eerily pink against the blackened boards.

The dark-hooded figure entered and closed the door behind him.

"I have had an unlooked-for visitor, Hooper," he hissed. "And I'm afraid it's taken every trick I can muster to give him the slip."

I poured water into the beaker for him, and he downed it eagerly.

"You came on foot?"

"After leaving the pony in the paddock, yes."

"Who could have caused you such alarm?" I asked.

"Who indeed?"

He needed not say more. *Morland,* I whispered.

"He brings useful news. But always at a price."

"Always." Among the Texas Rangers of our day there were good and honorable men, to be sure. Gareth Morland was not one of them. Not, at least, from what Miles and others had told me. I had never met the man myself, but the stories were enough.

"I have stayed on the move since you and I parted company on Monday," Miles explained after catching his breath. "Slept in the canyons by day, traveled by night. I was able to keep an eye on our foeman Griswall that way. I spied nothing untoward, even during your brief sojourn yesterday."

"You knew of that?"

"I watched until your group topped the hill, then lost track of you. I can assure you Griswall did not follow."

"You did not witness our discovery, then?"

"A discovery? Hooper, you surprise me at every turn. I shall be most curious to learn of it."

"But the wolf—no sign of it?"

"None. Griswall is biding his time; this is useful. I have discerned his patterns."

"He must have swallowed your ruse."

"He acts with insouciance. So confident was he of my departure, he did not believe himself to be watched; this much seems evident. But I was not the only watcher."

Miles paused, and we listened for any sound outside the shack. Only the wind rustled in the grasses. When he spoke again, he lowered his tone even further. "After you and Mr. Barlow continued on your way homeward, I emerged just before sunset from my most recent place of concealment on a ledge above the Griswall place shielded thickly by cedars. The sun at my back would make it almost impossible for one looking up in my direction to spot me. Just as I raised my spyglass I felt a meaty hand clamp upon my shoulder. Oh, Hooper, I cannot do justice in describing the admixture of fear and revulsion brought on by that gesture, and the unmistakable stench that accompanied it. Had I not been upwind of Morland I surely would have smelled him before he was upon me."

This, from a man who did not use the word "fear" lightly.

"That instant brought back every unsavory scene from my youth, from the time my father abandoned me to the care of his erstwhile Ranger associates—if 'care' it could be called—to the day I slipped their greasy grasp, and I knew I must once again reckon with my enemy, the despicable ringleader of that reprobate band of hornswogglers.

"Morland must have registered my shock at encountering him in the remote reaches of Brazos country, for when we parted ways back in sixty-nine, I swore I would never return to Texas. He had to know I had broken that vow, of course, but in all the time I served in the secret employ of the Wells Fargo Company and the army, never again until this night had I come face to face with the man."

"It must have been an equal shock to him," I said.

"Oh, Morland is as cold-livered as they come. 'Well, Derrick Miles, as I live and breathe,' said he, as though we'd casually passed on the streets of Fort Worth. I regained my equanimity and asked what scent he was trailing. And his answer was equally astonishing."

"What?"

" 'A wolf,' he said. He watched for my reaction; I simply took a seat on a cedar stump and waited for him to say more. Yes, he told me, he'd heard all about the big wolf hunt, and the kid's stunt. But he said he'd instead come to Dickens County in search of a wolf in sheep's clothing. I asked what he meant by that, and he said he'd been contracted by the Pinkertons to trace a land swindler from Travis County by the name of Roderick Graham—who was posing under a false identity."

"Graham, you say?"

"That is correct. And he tossed me a tidbit in trade for any useful information I could tell him. I did not, of course, reveal the true nature of our mission here—though if a rogue like Gareth Morland has been nosing about, he surely is not unaware of Sir Basil Wolverton's mysterious death and our interest in it."

"You will certainly find *this* enlightening, then," I said as I pulled my chair over to the wall and climbed upon it, reaching for the concealed shelf above the rafter.

"Show me quickly, as our situation grows urgent," replied Miles. "For we are going to have to inform our client that the woman living under Rufus Griswall's roof is not his daughter."

"Who, then, is she?" I said at this startling revelation.

"Maria is his wife."

Chapter 18
Unexpected Guests

{In which kings, queens, colonels, captains, and knaves visit the Wolverton estate.}

Dawn was beginning to spread rosy fingertips across a cloud-studded sky as we exited our lair. Afraid that López or one of the visitors might be rising, I spirited Miles up to the house and into my own room to get a few hours of rest.

There being only one narrow bed, I offered this to Miles, but he refused in favor of the upholstered wingback chair in which I had become accustomed to reading. My recent literary diversions lay stacked on the side table alongside the bottle of liniment I employed on my sore muscles each evening. I skipped either of these and gratefully slipped my sore bones beneath the covers, to sleep, perchance to dream.

I woke with a start, choking, many hours later. What time *was* it? And what was the source of the thick smoke? I feared the house was on fire.

I leapt from the mattress, fled to the window, and flung open the shutter, allowing my lungs to fill with damp, clean air. And then I remembered.

Turning, I found Miles seated in the tall chair enveloped in a cloud of cedar vapors. The Indian pipe lay, lit, in a tray on the table. His head wrapped in the black scarf, Miles resembled some dark, meditative mogul. Before I could wish him a good morning and rouse him from his ruminations, however, a pert knock sounded at the door.

"Dr. Hooper," came Lili LaBorde's stage-whisper voice. "Are you well? Lunch is ready—and I'm dying to see what's in the you-know-what!"

"Ah, why, yes," I sputtered. "I have been absorbed in . . . studies. I shall be right down."

I dashed about, getting dressed with little care for my toilette, leaving Miles to his schemes. I descended the stair into a level of frenetic activity. Tables and chairs were being arranged around the perimeter of the main hall; atop a ladder in the center, López was tacking streamers of orange and black cloth intermingled with colorful branches of agarita and soapberry. Enamelware plates and cups had been stacked upon a sideboard, where new, unlit beeswax candles awaited in dozens of pewter lanterns.

Lili grabbed my arm and whisked me to the empty kitchen, handing me a sandwich wrapped in newspaper.

"Do tell!" she said. "I could hardly sleep for wondering!"

I swallowed the first bite nearly whole and lowered my voice. "Your instincts have proved most valuable indeed, young woman," I assured her. "We shall need your help further to distract Maria Griswall tonight, for the documents in that box show her, ah, father to be involved in enterprises central to our investigation. You were right to divine trouble there. I cannot say more at the moment, except that Derrick Miles himself is requesting your further assistance."

Her eyes lit up. "Just name it! Will I be going undercover?"

"Not in the manner you imagine. But do you still have your typewriting machine handy here?"

I left Lili to fetch her apparatus and fresh paper and meet me in the smokehouse. There, I asked her to set up shop on the table I had used as my photographic laboratory. I opened the metal box to reveal the deeds and set her to transcribing each of them as accurately as she could manage. She took eagerly to the task, taking in the documents' content as she went.

"If you believe this information will bring Baz's killer to

justice," she said soberly, "I shall give the job my very best."

"Put it this way: we believe the facts to be incriminating at some level. The gap is closing, and I have complete faith in Captain Miles's ability to soon present an airtight case to the authorities."

"I want to see my friend Maria find the happiness she deserves," said she, her fingers never slowing over the keys.

"As do we all," I sighed. "As do we all."

I left a lamp burning for her and locked her in, tacking a note to the door warning any curious visitors that photographic development was taking place within. That, I hoped, would be a sufficient deterrent, while I sought out our client.

"Confound it, maybe I should just call the whole blasted thing off," Wolverton muttered, one eye on the wind-driven clouds and another on the last-minute reinforcements a lazy cowhand was attempting to execute on the corral. Already the volume and energy of horseflesh was straining the ranch's equine accommodations as guests from all corners arrived. "Maybe I should just go fetch her and elope to New Mexico. Be done with all this party fuss."

"That," I replied as evenly as I could manage, "might not be the wisest plan."

"Give me one good reason I ought to wait on asking Maria to marry me, man," he said, and I was on the verge of doing so when another guest rode up to the gate.

Dismounting expertly, he removed his traveling hat and kerchief to reveal a healthy shock of brown hair and a goatee beard. He strode over to where we stood. He had the comportment of a seasoned cowman, and I tried to place the face though his brow was dusty from the trail. "Either of you gentlemen know where I can find Basil Wolverton the third?"

"Here, sir," said Wolverton. "Welcome to the Wolverton Ranch."

"Well, I'm pleased to be here at your invitation, although Molly wasn't able to make the trip this time," said the man, accepting Wolverton's handshake. "I'm Charlie Goodnight, son. I'm sorry for the loss of your uncle. He was a fine businessman and an honest dealer."

"Thank you for those kind words," said our host. "And you may already know the esteemed Dr. Hooper?"

"Haven't had the pleasure, but I've read your accounts in the papers," said Goodnight.

"And I've seen your likeness there, too," I replied. "It's an honor to meet you."

"Now," said Goodnight, tying his horse to the rail, "if you'll just point me in the direction of a privy, I'll make myself more presentable, and find out what my hand Abernathy has been up to. Hope the kid hasn't worn out his welcome."

Wolverton smiled and shook his head, glancing back in my direction. The earth-shattering news would have to wait. "Come inside while I tell you the whole story, sir," he said to the cattleman. "We'll find you some sarsaparilla and a bite to tide you over before dinner."

I sought out Mr. Barlow and Ranger McDonald to bring them current on the facts as Miles had related them to me. "Give us half an hour, and let us meet upstairs in my quarters. If I know Derrick Miles as well as I think I do, he will have precise instructions for us."

I knocked three times gently and turned the knob of my bedroom door.

Miles stood at the window, his back to me, dressed in his deerstalker cap and the tartan cape I had left on a hook for him. The effect was more convincing than any expectation of my imagination.

"Holmes!" I said, delighted. "Time for you to crack another case and best Scotland Yard."

He turned slightly in my direction. In one hand he held my copy of the most recent *Strand* issue, in the other the magnifying glass from the reading table. Between his teeth he clenched his meerschaum pipe. The profile was perfect, just as in Paget's illustration. "I stayed up all night reading that damned novel, I'll have you know. Don't quite understand what you see in it. But if it aids our cause this evening, well, I'm game, my dear Watson."

I hastened to the washstand to prepare my own getup. While I shaved, Miles began to lay out his strategy. I had just finished cleaning up and changing into my city duds when Barlow and McDonald arrived. The three sat while I used the wardrobe mirror to comb and wax my moustache just so. I had to admit to a twinge of embarrassment, participating in the serious business at hand while attired in such fakery, but as I brushed my collar and turned my full attention to the gathering I set aside my misgivings.

McDonald, in red cravat, black duster, and ten-gallon hat, with quite convincing handlebar moustaches, his badge and pistol readily displayed, looked the very image of the famous Wyatt Earp. Barlow, colonial buttons and oversized cuffs affixed to his everyday coat and a white peruke beneath his wide-awake hat, was unmistakable as William Penn.

Our multifarious assembly got down to business.

"Hooper," said Miles, "stick close to Maria Griswall, and call on McDonald here if you sense any threat to her safety. Watch well, too, for her actions might give away the intentions of her husband."

"Her *husband?*" exclaimed Barlow, and Miles recounted the background that had lately come his way, though with fewer particulars regarding the informant.

"Does Trey Wolverton know?" asked McDonald.

"No," said Miles, "and we might as well keep it that way for now. Our client's reactions are unpredictable as it stands; with such knowledge he might spook Rufus Griswall entirely, allowing him to slip from our grasp. Or he might do something even more rash or regrettable. We do not need another murder on our hands."

McDonald nodded in agreement. "Then at what point do we nab the suspect?"

"Only when we are certain we have sufficient evidence to persuade a jury," said Miles in his most calculated tone. I had known him, over fifteen years' experience, to bide his time with feline patience until the very instant the precise testimony, or damning document, or reliable witness fell into his claws before pouncing upon his target. Not once had he failed to bring a criminal to justice. He would not risk missing the mark now, though we could not predict in what manner—or whether—our man would show his hand this night. We could only do our utmost to place him in the path of revealing his nefarious intentions.

"I stand ready to obtain a warrant from Harkey," replied McDonald. "He'll be here tonight with his wife—as George and Martha, I understand."

"Thank you. Now, Barlow, your job is especially vital," said Miles. "As Griswall's most trusted neighbor, you will be in the best position to shadow him."

"If he does not take our visit yesterday too pointedly," the Quaker said. "Rest assured I shall stick to him like glue. How shall I signal thee, if I should observe anything amiss?"

"Tip thy hat, Friend," replied Miles. "I shall be watching from the gallery. Elizabeth LaBorde has been recruited as extra eyes for us downstairs. As for all of you, make sure your weapons and ammunition remain at the ready—especially you, Sheriff Earp. I do not doubt that others upon this occasion will be armed, despite our host's general request to check guns at the door. Barlow, I trust your piece has been cleaned and concealed?"

The attorney nodded. Not until now in my nearly three weeks' acquaintance with the man had I seen him so fixed in his determination—nor so ashen.

Our orders given and accepted, we departed downstairs one by one, leaving only Miles and myself to make an entrance as a pair. The revelry, it appeared, had already begun, with Jack Abernathy at the center of attention dressed in a Greek costume Lili had sewn for him and a wooden sword and shield he'd fashioned from scrap lumber. Hercules, I gathered. Candles and lanterns flickered. Fiddle music filtered down from the opposite end of the gallery, though dancing had not yet commenced at this early hour.

On the grounds, cowboys and range bosses had set up dozens of tents, now illuminated by campfires against the last faded clouds out of the west. Watches had been set to guard the wagons and corrals. Somewhere in the offing a harmonica breathed a mournful tune.

No moon shone for Hallowe'en, I noted, the age of the lunar crescent crossing zero during this last evening of October 1891. I was no horologist or stargazer myself, but Miles maintained an archaeoastronomist's fascination with phases of the moon and the mythology of the zodiac, intermingled with the native's conceptions of the four worlds, and I suspected that among the rationalist's science there lurked a savage foreboding of what such a night might signify.

Not one guest had commented on the detective duo circulating among their midst and making rounds of the outbuildings, at least until Judge McQuarrie, who had been specially invited and urged to attend, halted us coming back into the main hall.

"What ho, the boarders of Baker Street!" the old codger cried. "Here are characters after my own heart indeed. I had not the expectation of meeting up with the distinguished Sherlock Holmes and Dr. Watson in our midst!"

Miles nodded obsequiously, peering at the Judge through the magnifying glass. "My colleague and I are pleased to have made your evening, sir. Now, we are equally honored to find ourselves in the company of the Bard of Ayrshire."

"Ah, ye put me in fond recollection of the auld country. If only my progeny had found her heritage so attractive. D'ye ken that we are descended, in actuality, from Burns?" he said. "The tale is that Mary Campbell did in truth give birth to his living child. Their issue, the story goes, is our lost Scottish ancestor. I choose to accept it as gospel."

"Then your family history holds true to form," said Miles. "And mayhap you will yet live to see the bairn in due time."

We took our leave of the thunderstruck Judge, as I repressed an unbecoming smirk.

Inside the hall, the feast was being laid. The Lópezes appeared in authentic Mexican garb, while Lili, her condition disguised beneath a high-waisted Empire frock, played the part of a mobcapped French maid. When she spotted Miles, she raised a finger indicating for him to wait, and in a moment brought him a thick envelope of papers.

"Thank you, Madame," said Miles. "Your service shall be rewarded much sooner than heaven. Keep an eye out."

We sought out General Washington to deliver the package, in itself nearly sufficient for a sheriff's warrant and, likely, proof of the older charges the mercenary Morland had been sent to investigate. But there remained the necessity of linking Griswall's wolf to the Earl's death from shock. That, we acceded, would be a tall order. How or whether we might uncover such, we did not yet know.

The fiddlers had struck up a lively reel, and cowboys and their ladies stepped into line with Judge McQuarrie leading the way. A sprightly Mrs. Larkin as Lady Jane Grey served as his partner. In the lineup also appeared a racy Cleopatra and Marc Antony, a quite convincing witch and warlock, and a Hunchback of Notre Dame carrying a handbell he rang every time he wished his cup refilled.

Miles milled about making mental notes, then retreated upstairs for a bird's-eye view of the proceedings, while I mingled and searched for Maria Griswall. She had not, as I could tell, made an appearance, nor had her father. About that moment Barlow and I encountered Trey Wolverton, tall, dashing, and popular in the getup of William Barret Travis with bars on his epaulets and a lone star on his stand-up collar. Our host scanned the room continuously for the one figure he most desired to see.

I asked how I could help. "Go find her, Doc," he said, evidence of spirits on his breath, "or I shall do so myself."

I pledged to assist, to the best of my ability. Wolverton sighed and turned his attention to the crowd he had called together, and when the reel ended, he quieted them with a loud whistle from his lips.

As he had done on the evening of the wolf hunt, when he had so ably coalesced a community's will around him, Wolverton thanked his many guests and reminded them of the obligation they owed to his uncle, Sir Basil, whose memory they would honor on the morrow. He pledged his full participation in county matters and his support of local interests in Austin.

His fine speech completed, however, Wolverton seemed at a loss to draw the party back into a celebratory mood. I thought the occasion might end then and there, its dual purpose unfulfilled and its key figures dispersed into the night, until I glanced upward and saw, out of the corner of my eye, a tartan-clad sleuth slip to the musicians' corner and borrow an instrument.

Derrick Miles set bow to string and began to tease from the violin a haunting lyric, smooth as silk with its occasional minor chords, that drew all eyes to his position. Yet cloaked as he was in shadows, few recognized the player. A hush fell as the mysterious performer finished the first song and shifted tempo seamlessly into somber notes that every Texan present recognized.

"El Degüello" pierced the air above their heads, a string rendition of the bugle call for no mercy. Somewhere in the assembly came a cry of "Remember the Alamo!"

Just as the mood risked turning morose, however, the tempo shifted once again, to the victorious "Santa Anna's Retreat," stirring passions and inciting feet to tapping. Hoots and hollers rose up, and the other musicians fell in. A flag appeared and rose over the floor; quickly the dancers resumed their steps. The popular number reached its end amid the applause of onlookers, and Miles handed the bow back to its owner.

I caught a glimpse of Wolverton outside the kitchen passage, engaged in low but animated argument with Lili LaBorde. An odd melodrama was playing out below us: Lili appeared to be trying to snatch a serving of food from the master's hand. With a clatter the tin plate fell to the floor, spilling beans and beef on William Travis's trousers. Barlow's mongrel appeared from the kitchen and made quick work of the mess before Lili could return with a dishcloth; the sight appeared to agitate her considerably. Wolverton angrily pushed his way past her and strode toward the front door.

"Good heavens," Barlow leaned over and said to me. "We'd

better go see what the ruckus is about. He looks as though he intends to give no quarter himself."

By the time we reached the kitchen, Wolverton was nowhere to be seen.

Lili was absorbed in ministering to the little dog. "Oh, Mr. Barlow, I am so afraid . . . your wife brought the dog to the party with her, and I saw Mr. Griswall . . . I saw him mix something into Trey Wolverton's food! I swear, he followed me into the kitchen—"

"The dog, you mean?" I asked, still puzzled.

"No—Mr. Griswall! He followed me in here when I was carrying the plate I was preparing for Mr. Wolverton, who hadn't had a bite all evening.

"I asked about Maria, whom he said had stayed home, feeling poorly. I set the plate down and went over to take the fresh cornbread from the oven, and when I turned back around, I caught him slipping a bottle back into his pocket. He left out the kitchen door, and in came Mr. Wolverton from the hall to check on his meal. I wouldn't let him have it; it smelled off, and I was afraid—" she threw up her hands in frustration—"oh, it sounds stupid now. I was afraid it had been poisoned!"

"Does Mrs. López keep syrup of ipecac?" I asked.

"I think I know where, if I cannot find her."

"Force the dog to swallow a spoonful, and more if needed to make him vomit. Right now, Barlow, you and I had better see to our client."

Barlow agreed, and added, "Lili, did you say anything else to Trey Wolverton?"

"Yes—he asked me whether I had seen Maria, and I told him what Mr. Griswall had said."

We dashed out the nearest door in search of Wolverton. We turned the corner to hear the sound of hoofbeats fading into the distance, in the ink-black night. The only pools of light came from the great windows at the front and back, but here on the side all was dark as pitch, and we'd taken no time to bring a lantern.

"We must alert Miles," I said, wondering why no watchman had raised an alarm already, if the master had departed alone.

A chilly, vexed voice came from the shadows behind us, as though disembodied.

"You must alert the great Derrick Miles, you say. Of course."

"Mr. Griswall!" I said. "What—are you doing out here, instead of inside enjoying the party?"

"I could ask the same of you two," Griswall demanded of us. Rage seemed to ooze from the very sweat of his brow. "Where is it?"

"Where is what?" I asked evenly.

"You know. The box. You came after it, didn't you?"

"A box?" said Barlow, as dissembling as myself. "I'm sure thee is—"

"Don't play the fool with me, Barlow. I'm onto you. Imagine, Wesley Barlow, friend to all, enemy to none, guest at my own table, being drawn into a despicable conspiracy of thievery and lies. I'll see every one of you on the gallows. Especially the one who covets my daughter."

"Now, there, Mr. Griswall," I said, inching back toward the door. "You've no grounds for these claims. Trey Wolverton invited you freely, as a neighbor. He will be eager to greet you and set your concerns to rest."

Griswall advanced on us. Barlow and I matched every measured step with one of our own, speaking to him calmly, and within five paces we had rounded the corner and nearly attained the doorway. I could see the anger in his eyes now, though the rest of his figure and head were veiled in the guise of a dark Bedouin.

"Pray let me call Wolverton out for thee?" urged Barlow. "I'm sure he will be pleased to speak with thee personally." At that Barlow ducked through the doorway, leaving me alone on the stoop with a crazed villain.

I kept up the ruse. "Tell me, Mr. Griswall, where *is* your lovely daughter this evening?"

"I'll just bet you'd like to know."

"Wo—we were all looking forward to seeing her."

He slid his hand into the pocket of his coat, and a knife flashed. "I'd slit your throat, Hooper, but I need those documents. Get them for me." He brandished the blade closer.

Before I could move away, he had me by the arm, the knife point at my temple.

"Go," he ordered.

I made as though to enter the doorway.

"Not that direction." He steered me swiftly toward the nearest structure, the smokehouse.

I played for time. "What makes you think we have any papers of yours?"

"The box was missing," he hissed.

"If it was yours, then the law is likely on your trail already."

From the house, a commotion rose. Boots clattered and urgent voices rose. Griswall shoved me, hard, toward the smokehouse door, muttering, "In here, if you'll not cooperate."

I moved to knock the knife from his grip, but he was quicker, and for my pains I received a wicked slash across the upper arm. My thick dress coat blunted a deeper cut, fortunately, but my assailant took advantage of the moment to shove me into the darkness and slide the bolt closed behind me.

All I could hear, from within the tightly shut space, were footsteps running toward the corral. More than one set of feet, as best I could discern.

Suddenly there were others, and I heard Miles's voice call out for me.

I could not at first find my voice, and before I could reply, the shouts echoed farther down, toward the canyon.

Derrick Miles was not one to be so easily deceived, however, and as I found the will to call out "In here!" my partner was already at the smokehouse door, flinging it practically off the hinges. I grabbed the unlit red-filtered candle lantern, the only object close at hand.

"Hooper, are you hurt?"

"It can wait. Where is Griswall?"

"Fled across the breaks after Wolverton, I fear. We must go."

Captain McDonald was already waiting by the corral with horses for us. The ranger and Miles mounted more swiftly than I, especially with my arm bleeding and throbbing, and were off down the trail before me. Goodnight, Abernathy, and Sheriff Harkey, also summoned, quickly caught up to them.

I thanked the gods for the return of Barlow, who helped me into the saddle before climbing onto his own horse, and together we brought up the rear.

At the back gate I saw the searchers hold their lanterns aloft to search momentarily for fresh hoofprints heading toward the canyon—then abandon the shortcut route, the one that had been Sir Basil's undoing, for the main road.

McDonald called to the lookout posted at the turnoff. But it was no use. The cowhand was passed out cold, an empty whiskey bottle still clutched in his grasp. That explained a few things, I supposed. I wouldn't have been surprised if Griswall had not arrived with a bribe ready for the offering.

"Head for the Griswall dugout," shouted Miles. "We'll look for tracks at the ford."

"A wise choice," Barlow leaned over and said to me. "Though the canyon trail would be quicker, that crossing will be treacherous after the rain. 'Tis well Wolverton did not risk it."

With no moon and only the candle lantern for light, Barlow and I found ourselves disadvantaged and slow, though our horses seemed confident of the way. Even at less than full gallop, I worried my horse might throw me right over an invisible ledge, into an unseen stream. On we bolted into the night, around curve after curve, around hulking hoodoos, until the ground leveled off and I knew we were somewhere on the margin of the creek, and that wide meadow where the Griswall dugout was located.

The ford lay about a quarter mile ahead of us still, and I wondered how we would manage it, isolated from the others.

We halted our horses and listened. Away to the east—at least, I believed it to be east, by memory—we could make out the sounds of voices and horse hooves.

"Can you see Wolverton?" I asked Barlow. I was nearly winded from the mad dash.

Panting, he replied, "Too much of a head start on us. Can't see a thing."

"God, let us hope we are not too late."

"Let us ride on, then. Look for their lights."

We resumed our dark course, the horses picking their way more slowly around stones and thorns. I thought I could just make out the homestead on the other side of the creek. The other riders could not be far ahead of us now.

I could feel my mare's hooves encounter the sandy berm of the creek. I spurred her on, trusting her to pick out the safest course through the knee-deep water. I did not realize I had been holding my breath until we reached the other side and I exhaled loudly, in relief.

Chapter 19
A Wolf Is Loosed

{In which men track a savage beast in the mist.}

"Listen," said Barlow. Away across the valley there came an unmistakable howl, that voice of the wolf we had not forgotten since the night of the hunt. In the starless black it came, even more disorienting and terrorizing than on previous occasions. Out there, a creature, *some* creature, still lurked. But where?

From the north and west, behind us, I felt a sudden chill on the nape of my neck. I turned to glance over my shoulder and saw, rolling down like an atmospheric tide out of the dark, a phenomenon I had never before beheld. White and ethereal as a phantom, a wall of vapor crept steadily toward us down the canyon, its leading tendrils perhaps half a mile off. Like cold smoke, it conjured up in my mind the sublimation of cardice I had once witnessed in a London laboratory.

"What—what *is* that?" I asked, not expecting an answer.

"A norther can push dense fog ahead of it out here," Barlow said. "The temperature must be dropping rapidly."

The blanket of mist was still advancing. "If that fog bank reaches us, we won't stand a chance of finding Wolverton. Or the others."

Yet we didn't dare shout out; Griswall could be anywhere. Likewise the monster wolf.

Its haunting cry came again, and Barlow led us tentatively toward it, deeper into the dismal breaks.

Suddenly we heard other horses coming full gallop, out of the fog. We raised our lanterns. Miles and McDonald, guns

The Wolf Hunt: A Tale of the Texas Badlands

drawn, broke through the mist, their boots dripping and their horses soaked to the withers.

"Ho there!" I called out. "Where is Wolverton? Is all well?"

"Hooper! Mr. Barlow, if I had a deity to thank, I would kneel in praise this moment for your safety," said Miles. "But as it stands I may well curse our fortune. This mist may be our undoing." The wind from the approaching norther whipped our hair and kerchiefs into our faces.

Other horses rode up. First Sheriff Harkey on his large bay, then Goodnight's white horse and Abernathy's gray seemed to materialize out of nowhere, wraiths out of a tomblike dark.

"We were hoping Wolverton had caught up with you," said the Colonel. "I heard another horse, by itself. Our friend cannot be far."

"Nor can the wolf," Abernathy added.

"Or perhaps the horse you heard was Griswall's," Miles observed. "Damn this night! And damn me, for playing along with Wolverton's folly!"

Through the gloom, just as the first tendrils of fog slid snakelike along the ground toward us, muffled footsteps could be heard in the midst of it, running.

"Something's coming!" shouted Harkey.

We stared into the roiling white ocean and raised our guns, unsure quite from whence the sounds emanated. I pointed the pistol's sight straight ahead of me, blindly.

"Shhh!" said McDonald, drawing his pistol. I raised my little lantern against the gusty wind and turned toward the steps.

Trey Wolverton burst into the diffuse and moving circle of light not ten paces from me. A look of utter fright wrenched his handsome features. He was holding his left arm steady with his right as he stumbled and fell, unable to draw a weapon.

I heard the guttural growl before I saw the nightmarish apparition burst from the mist on his heels. My hand shook and I may—or may not—have let out a scream at the demon that bounded from the cloud of vapor and took the shape of a gigantic wolf.

Never in the delirious dream of a disordered brain could anything more brutal, more appalling, more hellish be conceived than that dark form and savage face which broke upon us out of the wall of fog. Tall as a young steer it appeared, bony and head lowered, its fur spiked with streaks of blue flame. Fire seemed to stream from its pointed ears, its hackles, its brushy tail. Its very saliva appeared to leak flame, leaving a bright trail on the ground. Its luminous yellow eyes intent on its object of prey, the beast closed in for the kill.

Chaos ensued in that instant, as the fiend leapt for Wolverton's throat. Our man, immobilized on the ground, emitted a cry of mortal terror. Jack Abernathy jumped from his horse and lunged in the wolf's direction with a gloved hand. I saw McDonald raise his rifle, then hesitate, daring not take a shot with men at such close range. Instead a single crack of a pistol split the night, as though exploding from the very heart of the enveloping norther.

The wolf roared in agony, snapping and clawing, disoriented. Miles, suddenly finding himself with a clear opportunity, blasted three or four bullets from his revolver—so rapidly he fired, I could not be sure how many—into its ghastly hide. A sickly, glowing blue stained the moist earth along with the creature's steaming, crimson blood. The wolf dropped to the ground with a last hideous snarl in front of Miles's horse, which reared and snorted until its rider managed to slide from the saddle.

Miles rushed to Wolverton's side and cried out his name, but no answer was forthcoming.

"Hooper, get over here!" he ordered. "If we have failed to protect this young man from those who have meant him evil . . ."

I bent over the prone form and was just about to loosen Wolverton's neckerchief and check his pulse when he opened his eyes and raised himself up on one elbow. I drew out a capsule of salts from my vest pocket and broke it open beneath his nose. "I've got to find—Maria," he said, before realizing that his other arm was doing him no good.

Only then did I see, in the shadows, Mr. Barlow standing there, holding his discharged Colt in his quivering hand. "I think . . . I *think* I got him."

"You seem to have fired the fatal shot, Mr. Barlow," said Harkey, who had also pumped a couple of shots into the carcass.

"The dire wolf of legend will surely trouble us no more," Barlow said, staring at his Peacemaker as though the pistol had acted of its own volition.

Abernathy was kneeling, lamp lifted, to study the wolf's paw. "See here, his injured foot. Dollars to doughnuts it matches the print you saw, Dr. Hooper."

"The beast is abnormally large but hardly immortal after all, do you not agree, Barlow?" said Miles, examining it more closely. As the wind picked up, the mist began to fade somewhat, and I could make out the full effect of the monster lying stretched before us. It was the size of a young bison and nearly as shaggy, its fur matted in clumps and emanating a gaseous light. Its lips and dewlaps, drawn back over vicious fangs, glowed as well. "One can only speculate where and how such a freak was spawned."

"And see here, the source of its ghoulish luminosity," I said, turning my attention from our shaken client to the corpse of the wolf. "A phosphorescent mineral paste. Celestite, I presume from the blue color."

Miles reached a finger down into the fluids pooling around the dead creature. "I detect no odor which might have interfered with the wolf's power of scent," he said. "Whoever distilled a solvent with such qualities is cunning indeed. We owe you a deep apology, Trey Wolverton, for allowing you to light out on your own out here."

Our client had dragged himself to his feet but still held his left arm gingerly. "Chains and bars would not have deterred me, I swear," he said. "Now we must find the villain responsible. And his wife, whom I pledge to protect despite their deception."

"You—know of this?" Barlow asked.

"The kitchen maid, Lili, blurted it out when she tried to persuade me that Griswall had attempted to poison me."

"We feared you might dash off unaided like this," I said. "Now let me bind that arm for you. Where is your horse?" I removed my long scarf and began folding it into a sling, the rising wind hampering my efforts.

"Threw me when that hound of hell appeared," said Wolverton. "I had almost made it to the dugout, I think, when this fog blew in. If you believe Griswall to be about, I never saw sign of him."

I considered this. "Griswall pursued you from the ranch and could not have been far behind. I cannot fathom how he could have reached the animal's lair—presuming he must have loosed it and set it upon your scent—ahead of you."

"He has taken the shorter route, then," said Miles, snapping into action. "McDonald, can you see well enough to take two men and search upstream?"

"The fog is clearing. Let Goodnight and Harkey come with me. Harkey, you've reloaded?"

The sheriff nodded.

Miles directed Abernathy and Barlow to remain with the carcass while he and I rode with Wolverton to the dugout. The charge to each team was equally stern: *We must not let Griswall slip from our net, at all costs.* We had to learn his criminal intent and see to it that he faced justice for his deeds. We set out with care, our skittish mounts stepping like sprites through the rapidly evaporating tendrils of mist.

As the air grew colder, it cleared, and we saw that the Griswall dugout lay just ahead. No light burned within. Or it was possible that the one window was draped thoroughly, for all was quiet except for the echo of our hoofbeats off the canyon walls.

We knocked at the Griswall door only once before trying the knob. It was locked fast.

"Rufus Griswall!" Miles called out. "If you are here, let us in. We have news for you."

There was no response. "Surely he's heard the commotion and the gunshots," I said. "Do you think he would barricade himself within?"

"Not likely, but we must proceed with care." Miles drew his pistol and, with one sharp blow of his bootheel, freed the door from its latch and pushed it in slowly. In the dark, the place resembled a crypt carved into the side of a hill more so than the home and study of an educated man.

No sign did we find of our suspect. From the back of the structure, however, behind a heavy drapery, I detected the barest hint of a cry. A moan, more like it; an utterance that could have been mistaken for animal but for its urgent, beseeching tone.

The plea repeated, and we stepped toward it. Miles pushed back the curtain that divided the sleeping area from the kitchen. A lantern, its wick blackened and sputtering, shone suspended from a hook on the low ceiling, casting the cramped room into macabre shadow. I raised my own light to discern a most bizarre assemblage of objects mounted on the rough-timbered walls: a series of exquisite vitrines in which were pinned a collection of butterflies and moths, from the giant luna down to the tiniest, most delicate specimens a quarter inch in wingspan.

So stunned was I by this museum in miniature, I nearly failed to notice the bed, constructed of hewn cedar limbs, in the midst of it. I shifted the lantern to reveal a form face down upon the mattress. I would not have recognized it as human were it not for the bare, outstretched arms each bound at the wrist to a corner bedpost. Flowing garments lay in disarray like the plucked plumage of a flightless bird. Legs extended, contorted, from the tatters of a skirt. I brought my lantern closer and discerned a satin bodice, torn down the back and revealing a series of red wheals.

"Mrs. Griswall!" I cried as Miles leapt to untie her from the silken bindings. "Help is here." Having no success with the knots, he drew his knife and swiftly cut her loose.

A groan of relief emanated from her throat, but she made no attempt to turn over.

"Miles, quick, she's gagged." My hands felt for a knot tangled in the mass of brown curls that had escaped from under a gipsy headscarf, and I held it for him to cut that bond too.

"Maria, can you move?" I asked. She coughed, slowly straightened her legs, and raised her hand to her head, but sank back onto the mattress.

"That brandy bottle there, Hooper!" He pointed toward the kitchen shelf. I stepped around the table where we had sat for refreshments with our hosts and retrieved it. Gently I lifted up the limp figure and urged a sip to her lips.

She came to, pulling the bedsheet up around her neck to hide her disheveled costume, though not before I made out the dark marks on her arms. She had struggled, clearly. "Is he safe?" she asked, as though in a fog. "Has he escaped?"

"He cannot escape us, madam."

"No, no, I mean Trey Wolverton! Is he safe?"

"Yes, and gone in pursuit of your husband. We must find him."

Maria sighed heavily, and Miles took a gentler tone. "Yes, we know the truth. Now, can you help us? How badly are you injured?"

"The bruises will fade. Shame may not. If only I had spoken up sooner . . . if only—" She broke off suddenly, and cried out, "The wolf! What about the wolf?!"

"Quite dead," Miles replied.

"Thank God! The man's lies and deception I have endured, his threats to harm me if I did not keep quiet. But this most recent scheme . . . poor Sir Basil! It was too much. Rufus Roderick Graham—if you did not already know his true name—would not risk killing him outright for the land. No, he tortured his mind instead. Just as he has mine. He suspected that his hold over my soul was slipping, and he rightly guessed that I intended to tell Trey Wolverton the facts." She broke down, sobbing.

"You can tell us how to find him now," I said. "We will protect you."

Maria rose and stood slowly, turned her back to us, and relaced the stays of her bodice. She rearranged the gaudy scarves and skirts of her gipsy costume, pulled a shawl from the pile of bedclothes, and beckoned us to follow her.

"There are many places in the breaks for a man to hide," she said. "But there is one so remote and concealed that it has remained Rod's own secret. I can point you toward it and describe it, though you will have no easy time finding it by night or day. It is a den deep in a cliff, well shielded by stones, already known to him before he rescued the wolf cub from a trap and took it there to raise and train. That, you can be sure, is where he would flee."

I held the door open for Maria and Miles to pass. The night had grown colder, but the wind had not completely dispelled the bank of fog that still blanketed the valley.

The woman, her hair whipping loose across her face and her gold earrings tinkling like bells, suddenly broke into mad, cackling laughter.

"What, madam, what?" I said, as she threw her head back and raised her bangled arms like some ecstatic sorceress.

"No man could find his way across the Croton Breaks tonight!" She cackled and clapped her hands. Her eyes and teeth gleamed with fierce merriment. "He may find his way in, but never out," she cried.

"How can you be sure? Our party found our way here across the ford," said Miles.

"Don't you see? Rod would've left for the Wolverton Ranch at dusk by the main road—after flying into a rage and tying me up when he saw that I meant to attend the party. I daresay once he put his malicious plan into place, he would have taken the shorter but more dangerous trail across the breaks coming back."

"Did he not tell us that he had a marked route across the creek?" I asked.

She laughed again, this time gleefully as a child. "I went there earlier today, while Rod was out fooling with his cursed wolf. I moved the markers myself. I promise you, following them tonight, he would have ridden straightway into the deadliest pit of quicksand."

Chapter 20
Day of the Dead

{In which something is found, something not.}

Past midnight Derrick Miles, who had struck out alone and left me to tend to Maria, returned to the Griswall dugout with the sheriff and Mr. Barlow. Goodnight and Abernathy had insisted on escorting Trey Wolverton home. "The Colonel's powers of persuasion were formidable," Miles related to me as he removed his deerstalker cap and perched on a chair in the small parlor, "Wolverton's own strong will notwithstanding. They very nearly came to blows over the matter. But it would not have done for young Wolverton to encounter the woman in this state."

"Speaking of Maria," I said, "she is resting well under the influence of a dose of laudanum. I found salve in their stores to use on her abrasions, which proved superficial, and on her contusions, which are not serious."

"Her husband did not return?"

"All has been quiet here. Her scheme may, alas, have worked as she intended."

Miles nodded ruefully. "Then we may never have the satisfaction of wringing the full truth from the villain. Harkey, you'll want to question Mrs. Griswall further in the morning?"

"I will indeed. I should take over the case from you at this point, sir, if you're agreeable," said the sheriff. "Why don't I resume the vigil here for the night, and you and your colleague make your way back to Wolverton's place, where you will find more rest?"

"A capital plan," agreed Barlow. "I shall accompany you."

We bid farewell to the courageous Jeff Harkey, urging him to bolt the door upon our departure. I was, at least, settled in my mind that we would encounter no further denizens of the spectral world on our homeward journey this night.

Hardly had I laid my weary head upon the pillow and dispelled an hour's troubled dreams when López fetched me to bring my bag to Trey Wolverton's bedside. Our host had awakened with chills, headache, and fever, which I deduced to be the result of an ague brought on by nerve strain and exposure. Nearly delirious he lay, breaking out in cold sweats one moment, flesh burning hot the next. I sat up with him, applying damp cloths to his blazing forehead and forcing a bit of clear liquid down his throat.

I continued this routine on the quarter hour until, somewhere around daybreak, our client eased into sleep and I lay back in the chair for a nap. Scenes of the previous night formed themselves into fearful tableaux in my mind, which was haunted by a luminous, phantasmagorical figure emerging from the mist. At times the specter would be that of the wolf, at others Trey Wolverton, at others a desperate Maria.

I startled awake just as the shape leaping out of the fog transmogrified from that of the four-legged beast to Derrick Miles, whose paw began shaking my shoulder.

"Hooper!" a voice said. "Come, we have little time before the memorial service."

"Mercy, I had forgotten," I replied in a stupor.

"And little time before all clues will have been erased."

We dressed hastily, saddled up, and rode for the ford, leaving Mrs. López to watch over Wolverton and Mr. Barlow to ready his wagon for our trip to Espuela.

Sheriff Harkey, appearing none the worse for the evening's exertions, and Maria were waiting there for us; Maria, clad in sturdy trousers and a thick Mexican blanket, looked confident and ready to lead us to the wolf-cave. It helped me to realize the disguised misery of this woman's life when we saw the eagerness and joy with which she laid us on her husband's track.

We came presently to the spot where Croton Creek narrowed and bent. Up the rise on our side, a trace through the red rocks was barely discernible. We dismounted and took it on foot. Climbing into a zigzagging box canyon, we ducked behind a tumble of giant stones and emerged at a cleft in the canyon wall that somewhat resembled the small spring where we had first spied the wolf's paw print, except in its astonishing scale. Lush ferns cascaded fifty feet down the steep walls on three sides. Sunlight was blocked directly from our view, but filtered as though through a cathedral's rose window. Trickles of water seeped noiselessly from an unknown source, forming a still pool at our feet.

Miles commented on the numerous species of insect hovering and lighting about us. "The grotto is a botanist's paradise, madam. But where would one keep so large a mammal here?" She turned with a smile. I, too, would have guessed this spot, hardly wider than a man's arm span, to be the terminus of the canyon. But we watched as Maria stepped across the pool, parted the curtain of green, and disappeared. A beckoning arm extended to us, and Miles followed. Not until both assured me they were standing on solid ground did I do the same.

The cave was not large. A narrow shaft of light bore down from far above, illuminating the center of the pit. A stone ledge provided a dry resting spot, and into it had been sunk a sturdy iron post with holes forged for a chain. Desiccated skeletons of small animals in the clefts of the rock lent the place a feeling of some medieval ossuary. Tins of beans and fruit were stored along a higher shelf along with eating utensils and a cup. Clearly the cave had been prepared as a hiding place for human and animal alike.

"See how the vent would serve to amplify the wolf's howls?" said Miles, pointing upward. "Griswall could lock it away but could not keep it quiet."

Maria explained. "Rod—for you may as well call him by his true name—came upon the yearling wolf last winter not far from here. Its back leg had been caught in the jaws of a trap. He released it and brought it here to mend. About the time, the Earl let slip a mention that an agent from St. Louis was inquiring about mineral rights, and Rod latched onto the old family legend of the wolf. He knew Sir Basil was troubled and ill and considering selling out; he felt that at all costs, once he had succeeded in relocating us here, so close to the ranch, he must prevent the prize from slipping out of his grasp.

"It would not have taken much to frighten Sir Basil into leaving, but what Rod feared most was a sale of the property, which he could never have afforded even at a deflated price. No, I could tell how his twisted mind was working. He would rather see the old man dead and seize the ranch by villainous means than to make amends honestly and hope for an inheritance."

Maria paused in her story long enough to guide us back out of the pit into the fern grotto. We emerged into the chilly November air and streaming sunlight as though we had been transported to a different latitude. She gazed off in the direction of the Wolverton place as she spoke again.

"What he did not count on was the appearance of an heir with a stronger claim. When Mr. Barlow told my husband of Trey Wolverton's imminent arrival, he flew into a rage such as I had not seen even in our three years of troubled marriage. He hatched a plan to dissuade his distant cousin right from the start. I tried to warn him off."

"So that was you who created the pasted-up note?" Miles asked.

"Yes. It was all I could think to do, since Rod watched my

every move. I had the newspaper with me on the stagecoach. I'd seen the idea somewhere in a novel."

"But you never considered yourself an aid in the plot? An accomplice?"

"Never!" she said, leading us back down the path toward the creek. She was as surefooted as a goat, and I struggled to catch her expression as I watched my step. "You cannot imagine what these thirty-eight months of cohabitation have been like, or the shame I endured after we had to flee Austin under a cloud of suspicion. He had me under his thumb, scared to speak my own mind. Frightened of inciting his anger. I was forced into submission. And can you picture how demeaning, how insulting it was, to have to pose as his *daughter*?"

We had come, by this point, to the sharp turn in the watercourse where the stream ran deeper and swifter at the far side but shallow and deceptively smooth on the wider, outside arc. There we surveyed up and down wherever compressed earth allowed us to walk, taking care at every step lest a bootheel puncture the surface and snag in the grip of quicksand. Such pits, we surmised, would be found more frequently and treacherously beneath the stream surface, where the force of moving water would make it harder to recover one's balance.

Miles and I left Maria standing on the muddy bank, as close to the edge as she dared go. From there she pointed to a cedar stake driven into the shallow part of the creek, resembling a post such as one might find anchoring a weir for catching fish. Another was situated close to the far bank. I marveled at the poor wife's desperation, that had driven her to risk wading in and placing these guideposts of deadly misdirection.

"See that one, farther along, and the next?"

I nodded. She waved us well away from it while indicating that we should search for footprints in this vicinity.

For a good thirty minutes Miles and I examined the creek

bank, spying a few muddled prints of horse and deer hooves in the layer of silt but none of the two-legged variety. I was climbing the low bank again, ready to sit on a driftwood log and rest, when I chanced to look back over my shoulder and spotted a foreign object half-submerged in the creek.

"There, Miles—what do you make of it?"

"Good eye, Hooper. It could be material. Throw me the rope from your horse, will you?" I complied, and, making a sheet bend to combine it with his own, he tied a loop around his waist while securing the other end of the lengthened rope to the horn of his saddle.

Miles trod warily into the stream, testing every step as he waded deeper, from calf-height to the knee before emerging again on the sandbar where the object was lodged. From my vantage point I directed him toward it. At times he sank into an unseen quagmire only to use the rope to pull himself free again. Maria steadied his horse by its halter.

The dark object came within inches of his grasp when I felt the line go taut and saw Miles stumble into the water. Maria urged the horse back while I applied my full strength to the rope. Miles was pulling hard from his end, too, but I could see that one leg had been sucked down nearly to the top of his thigh, while he knelt on the other and struggled to break free.

"Move to the left!" shouted Miles. "Go with the current!"

Only with the greatest of effort, and Maria's skill in guiding the horse, did Miles at last overcome the grip of the quicksand pit. His legs shot loose with a loud pop and splash, as he wrapped the full length of his arm around the rope and pulled. Finding the shallows once again and covered in red mud from the chest down, he held tight to his lifeline until gaining the solid bank once more. There he collapsed into a seated heap, where he examined his bare right foot, his ruined trousers, and the object he held in his hand.

"Confound it, I believe we've located Trey Wolverton's missing new boot," he said. "But I've lost my own favorite one."

I took the black boot to the stream and rinsed it thoroughly. "M. Goldwater & Sons, Gila City," I confirmed from the stamping inside the upper. "We guessed right, that Griswall must have used it to set the wolf on the track of his intended victim."

"If Griswall lost it there—or flung it on purpose—we can surmise that he made it that far," said Miles. "More, we may never know."

"Nor has his horse reappeared," said Maria coldly. Evil indeed, I mused, is the man who has not one woman to mourn him.

Miles reminded us that we had a further obligation today. "Let us take what object fortune has placed in our path, and return to the Wolverton Ranch to make ourselves presentable again," he suggested. "Though we may have been cheated of the chance to bring in our man in cuffs, we may rest assured he has suffered a much worse end. And we may best honor the deceased Earl by bringing back some evidence of our theory."

We did not, suffice it to say, take the shortcut across the Croton Breaks, where beneath the cold currents of the creek, lost somewhere in the hypogean realm that had claimed him, a cruel and desperate man lay forever buried.

Chapter 21
A Braided Rope

{In which strands of a story come together.}

Toward the middle of November, upon a raw and rainy Thursday, Miles and I sat on either side of a blazing fire in our Houston Street hearth. The gash Griswall had inflicted on my left upper arm, which had required a few sutures and daily replacement of bandages, had healed almost completely, though with a four-inch scar I would carry with me as memory of our adventure for the remainder of my life—but it pained me no longer.

The bootmaker's shop below us bustled with business as cowpunchers and capitalists alike stopped in for new soles and heels. The small bell of the streetcar clanged as it passed, and the large bells of the First Methodist Church answered with the toll of half past twelve. Mrs. Simpson's boy had brought up a covered tray of sandwiches and a pot of coffee.

Miles had pulled a gusseted envelope from the "W" drawer of his extensive case files and laid it on the oval table between us. He undid the string and withdrew a sheaf of papers and the fat leather volume of *The Wolvertons of Brent*.

"Before our guests arrive, I thought a quick refresher on the lineage of Sir Basil might prove useful," said he. When I looked at him with an expression that must have conveyed my perplexity at any intimation his memory might have faded over the course of a fortnight, he quickly set me straight. "For you."

"I must confess," I said, "that for all my perusal of the family ancestry, I cannot make out why their troubles all converged here in America."

"The erstwhile Ranger Morland's intrusion turned out fortuitous for us, for all its unpleasantness. His revelation that Miss Maria Griswall was in truth Mrs. Roderick Graham removed from my eyes the veil of expectancy—the principle that one sees what one is prepared to see. But not even Maria herself knew of the connections revealed between these covers," he said, opening the book. "She had no initial knowledge that her husband and Sir Basil possessed a common ancestor. However, much of what she wrote to me in this letter has been very useful in confirming details of his motives."

"The extent of her husband's perfidy must have shocked her."

"I should say so." He lifted the top page of the typewritten letter, peered down the length of his beaked nose, and read, " 'Dear Captain Miles, Thanks to the balm of friendship and the hospitality of the McQuarrie household, I am recovering well from the strain of mental torment to which I had been subjected. You should be gratified to learn, too, how warmly the old Judge has welcomed Elizabeth back into the fold now that the expectancy of a grandchild is apparent to him. We have all been grateful for the attentions of Trey Wolverton, who has come to call daily despite the sprained arm. He is absorbing a few tricks of the livestock trade from the Judge and Mr. Barlow.'

"Now we are caught up with their news of the present," Miles continued, laying the letter aside and leaning back on the settee, "let us delve more into the past. As you may recall, Trey Wolverton told us that his father, Nigel, held little regard for his older brother, Basil. He hinted at some malfeasance, though in the course of our dealings we never came to know exactly what that was. Yet some perusal of the family history provides a clue. While it was intimated that Sir Basil left his native England under a cloud, the fact is, some ancient disagreements were at work, of which we could understand little until braided threads came together in the end.

"Let us look back to those generations of Wolvertons who distinguished themselves in the service of the monarchy a century and a half ago. We saw their portraits on the wall in the ranch house: the bridge builder, Grenville; and the soldier of the empire, Arthur. Tories and traditionalists these men were, devoted subjects and loyal servants."

"Yes, that is as I understand it from the book," I replied.

"But turn to the entry for Hugh, the seventh baronet. Kindly read me the basic facts of his biography."

"Let's see . . . page four-oh- . . . five. Born April 1776; Devonshire industrialist, made his fortune in mines and metals; four sons and three daughters, of whom five lived to adulthood; died 1814 in the Tower of London."

"Does it not seem curious to you, in this cursory sketch, that a British peer born the same year as the American nation should end his life in the tower?"

"Curious indeed, now that you draw attention to the fact."

"I found it so. Inquiring of an old University of London acquaintance, I learned that Hugh Wolverton quite fully identified with, and allied with, the United States. So much so that, during the War of 1812 he diverted much-needed raw material from the needs of the Napoleonic Wars to American causes, circumventing blockades and inflating prices at home. Once his treachery was discovered, he hanged for it. Of course such detail is absent from the family history, but it was readily tracked down in contemporary newspapers."

I tapped my finger on the arm of my chair and glanced up at the mantel clock. "Still, dear Miles, I do not make any connection to our case."

"You will, Hooper, you will. I realize I must draw together three disparate threads to make a rope that will hold, for you have not the advantage of the additional background which Maria Griswall and her able transcriptionist, Mrs. LaBorde, sent our way only yesterday."

"Additional background, you say?"

"Patience, and all will be revealed. Thus, we left off in England of 1814. Arthur, eldest son of Hugh, was an angry young man of fifteen the year his father was summarily executed, bringing shame upon the family name. He never forgave the crown, instead pledging privately to assist the American cause in any way possible. This he did by investing in mining equipment at home and abroad during the industrial revolution, and in due time trading on the black market during our Civil War. You will see, on page 432, that his wife, Constance, died when sons Basil—yes, *our* Sir Basil—and Nigel were not yet school age, and Sir Arthur raised them in the factory rather than in the classroom, even after he had remarried. Basil remained in the family seat of Brent to inherit his father's business and learn his trade. Nigel sailed for the goldfields of California in '49. By then half-brother Randall and half-sister Susan had grown to majority, and this is where the story takes an interesting twist.

"Greatly influenced by her mother, who had been a minor figure in the court of Victoria, Lady Susan Wolverton staunchly supported the Queen and objected heartily to her father's activities. A strong-minded young woman with a contrary streak, she alienated her father and half-brothers and campaigned especially to undermine Sir Basil's reputation."

I found the puzzle beginning to take shape. "Hmm. This Lady Susan's opinion might have been the cause, I take it, of the low esteem in which Trey Wolverton held his uncle?"

"According to my source, yes." Miles cleared his throat and slipped a thick envelope of papers from the pocket of his dressing gown. "Now, let us close the gap between Lady Susan and another disaffected member of the clan, her distant kinsman Roderick Graham's son Rufus Roderick Graham."

"A.k.a. Rufus Griswall."

"None of this connection would have come to light had it not been for the patient deciphering of letters contained, along with the damning legal documents, in Griswall's metal box that you uncovered in Dickens County," said Miles. "That Rufus Griswall had corresponded for some years with a second cousin in Devonshire was unknown to Maria until Mr. Barlow looked into them and had Mrs. LaBorde type them up. Here"—he tapped the packet on his knee as though to indicate its importance—"are found some of Lady Susan's most vicious screeds, penned late in life when Sir Basil had already shed his title and decamped for Texas. She denounces him for demeaning the Wolverton name and censures him for 'selling out' to the almighty American dollar. Reading between the lines, I might interpret her words as inciting young Rod to seek revenge. See, here, she closes this letter with an account of the wolf legend."

"You believe he planned to make use of it?"

"I believe, from what Maria herself has written to me, that Griswall had no certain scheme in mind when he set his sights on Dickens County, situating himself and his pretty, young wife in such proximity to Sir Basil's valuable estate. But it is evident, from the way in which he posed Maria as his daughter, that he meant mischief from the outset. He was willing to bide his time applying his water-witching skills and lepidopterist hobby while cultivating a friendship with Basil Wolverton and other Dickens neighbors. Not to mention, scouting for petroleum deposits on the q.t."

I pondered all this, marveling at what malevolent mind could contrive, and what crafty countenance could disguise, such a plan. "Griswall—Graham—appears ready to have used any means, or run any risk, to achieve his ends."

"Yet achieve his end he did," remarked Miles mordantly. "And here we weave into the story the third and final thread. For Sir Basil himself told the legend of the family wolf, unwittingly lending weight to this myth as the instrument of his own doom.

"Griswall had learned from Mr. Barlow that the Earl's heart was weak and susceptible to shock or overexertion. He had also observed firsthand the man's particular fears, bordering on superstition. He must have calculated various plots for driving the man to his doom without implicating the true murderer or motive."

I nodded. It all fit so perfectly. "The chance discovery of a trapped wolf played right into his scheme."

"Yes; and further, the use of a phosphorescent mineral paste to lend the creature an otherworldly appearance was truly inspired. No man but one so intimately familiar with the Croton Breaks as he, on his many rambles, would have known such a hiding place as the cave. None but one with keen talent could have set the stage by training the animal to his will, then releasing it on random occasions to stir up rumor among the cowboys. None would have known where to find and extract the celestite, about which you were quite correct, by the way. None but one deranged would have waited so patiently for the right moment.

"Maria describes, in this letter, how her duplicitous husband tried to force her into the scheme. Griswall grew increasingly obsessed with his plan, of which she suspected only the faintest details, and he also grew uneasy as colder weather came on and he feared the Earl would cease his evening rides. He concocted a scheme for her to lure him into a romantic attachment, and threatened her with bodily harm when she refused to cooperate in such a ruse."

"How strange," I commented at this juncture. "Maria seemed, during our brief acquaintance, quite a level-headed and intelligent person. And I am not completely unfamiliar with the workings of the female temperament, Miles, whatever you may believe to the contrary."

"Ah, but it is the *criminal* temperament with which we are more concerned here, Hooper. Do not underestimate the power this scoundrel exercised over one so junior in years, whom he kept under his will and almost constantly under his watchful eye. Only on those brief occasions when Griswall was out tending to his wolf did Maria experience the freedom of movement that allowed her to meet a friend like Elizabeth McQuarrie. She possessed no independent means, not a dime to call her own.

"Even that budding friendship, Griswall found a way to exploit. Maria, in hindsight, confesses that he must have gotten wind of his wife's plan to escape in the company of Elizabeth— Lili. It was *he* who planted the seed of an assignation on that fateful evening. Had Lili McQuarrie LaBorde kept the appointment, the wolf might have claimed a second victim!"

"My God," I said, taking this all in. "And Griswall's schemes must have grown urgent when he learned of Mr. Barlow's recommendation that Sir Basil take a vacation for his health."

"Yes, that revelation provided both a threat to his plan, and a catalyst to its immediate implementation. Let us revisit the night of Sir Basil's death. Having realized that Thursday evening would likely provide his only opportunity, Griswall departed the Wolverton house promptly after supper, riding toward his domicile via the usual main route. But rather than returning straight home, he made all speed for the wolf-cave, loosing the animal and treating it with his infernal paint mixture. He then guided it toward the back trail at the Wolverton ranch and set it upon Sir Basil's scent.

"The wolf, incited by its master, sprang over the fence and pursued the unfortunate victim, who fled screaming down the trail on foot. Imagine what a dreadful sight must have presented itself to the already weakened rancher: there you are standing at the gatepost, eyes trained on the darkness in anticipation of your young visitor, smoking your cigar and every moment growing more anxious at her tardiness. You are just about to give up and mount your horse again when out of the shadows leaps a monstrous, gray, four-legged creature larger than a man, its jaws flaming and eyes blazing. In terror you run, unaware of your direction, *anywhere* to avoid this demon of your dreams."

"One might well succumb to the exertion," I noted. "The heart would bear the strain no longer."

"The wolf had kept to the slightly higher ground above while Sir Basil fled down the open trail, so that no track but the man's was visible. Upon seeing the man fallen and lying still, the animal might have approached to sniff at its quarry, but finding him dead turned away—leaving the lone print which was observed soon afterward by Mr. Barlow. As for Griswall, whether or not he then approached closely enough to ascertain the outcome of his plot we shall never know; but he must have summoned his creature back to its lair in the Croton Breaks before venturing near enough to learn of developments from the household."

I mused, "Griswall must not have expected anyone, especially the meek Barlow, to venture so far in stirring up an investigation into Sir Basil's death."

"On that score I believe you are right. Nor must he have anticipated the obstacle of Trey Wolverton. Griswall had figured the Grahams of East Texas to pose no threat, but it is quite likely he knew nothing of the existence of an heir in Arizona. Thus, when Barlow shared news among his circle regarding his mission to rendezvous with young Wolverton here, and departed promptly for Fort Worth, Griswall had no choice but to follow, bringing his wife along to keep her under his thumb. He'd distrusted her ever since she had refused to help him in laying a trap for the old man, and he dared not leave her long out of his sight for fear he should lose his influence over her, as she explains in her letter. Thus he took her on the long journey eastward with him—traveling to Fort Worth *incognito* on the very same train as Mr. Barlow himself took."

"It is not difficult to surmise that Mr. Barlow's anxious state of mind prevented him from making much observation of his fellow passengers," I commented.

"On this point I believe you are right. And given Griswall's expertise at disguise, I believe him capable of deceiving even a familiar neighbor. His wife's face and form, of course, were readily concealed by veil and mantle.

"Upon reaching our city and ascertaining Barlow's accommodations, then, the Griswalls checked in at the Southern Hotel, where Maria was kept imprisoned in the room while he went abroad in his beard disguise. Whatever suspicion she held regarding his plans, she feared him so greatly that she dare not write in her own hand to warn the man whom she suspected to be in mortal danger. If a letter should fall into her husband's hands more than one life would not be safe. She hit upon the design of cutting out the words which would form the message from the newspaper she'd brought along to read on the trip and the daily *Gazette*. The missive reached Wolverton at the Pickwick—but, craftier than we surmised, she folded the clipped papers and hid them in the lining of her cloak, thwarting our search for evidence. Griswall, meanwhile, had found himself with an even more difficult challenge."

"Yourself, you mean?"

"Precisely. If Griswall's first thought was that this young stranger from the Southwest might possibly meet his doom in Fort Worth before ever casting an eye on his inheritance, well, that scheme faded in light of a consulting detective on the trail. Griswall did his best to throw us off in Fort Worth, but he found it necessary to plan for the long game. It became essential that he lay hands on some article of Trey Wolverton's attire in preparation for employing the wolf again, so he might always have the means of setting him upon his track."

"The boot, yes!"

"Having succeeded in so cleverly obtaining it—no doubt by means of a healthy bribe to a hotel clerk—he must have been sorely chagrined to discover that it was a new one and utterly useless for his purposes. He then returned and filched another, and it was this turn of events that proved to me beyond doubt that we were dealing with a *real* four-legged predator and no specter of the spirit world. No other scenario could explain the desperation of this otherwise bizarre incident. The stranger an incident appears, my dear Hooper, the more carefully it cries out to be considered on its face, and the more a thing appears to complicate a case, the likelier it is, when subjected to rational and scientific inquiry, to bear on a solution.

"Then, as I deduced from our as yet unknown foe's crafty and careful knowledge of our persons and our rooms, he was a man of practiced stealth whose criminal deeds had not been limited to the situation at hand. It was, as they say, *not* his first time at the circus. That conclusion was borne out, of course, as we learned of the extent of his success in bilking landowners of their future mineral rights.

"As soon as our enemy had secured a personal item that might prove of use, and sent us his audacious signal that he was onto us—"

"By sending your own name back via the cabman!" I could not help recalling the moment with some glee.

Miles himself suppressed a wry smile. "From that moment he understood that I had taken over the case in Fort Worth, and, having lost his advantage there, he hastened to Dickens County with his wife and awaited the arrival of the heir."

"One point," said I, "leaves me wondering, in this sequence of events which you have doubtless outlined with uncanny accuracy. What became of the wolf when its master was away in Fort Worth?"

"I have given some attention to this matter and it is surely of importance. There can be no question that Griswall had a confidant, though it is unlikely that he ever placed himself in an ally's power by sharing all his plans with him. Though I cannot know for a certainty, I believe it may well have been the criminal, José Mora. Do you concur with this theory, Hooper?"

I rubbed my chin and nodded agreement, before consulting my watch. Our guests were due in fifteen minutes, and Miles had not yet attended to his public attire. Yet he showed no sign of hurry. He lit his pipe and took a deep draw before joining the disparate threads together in a coherent story for my benefit.

"Yes, where was I, then . . . the Griswalls flew back to Dickens County, not far ahead of Trey Wolverton and you and Mr. Barlow. I arranged a ruse to remain behind, much to your consternation, I know, so that I might move freely about the countryside and in due time employ the element of surprise. You cannot know how greatly it pained me, during those tense days, to absent myself so mysteriously from the direct management of the case. You likely do not know, either, that even before the train pulled out of the Union Station with the three of you aboard—oh, make that four, I've overlooked the pet dog—I had already come to a correct deduction about the perpetrator.

"You may remember that when I examined the paper bearing the pasted words I made a close inspection for the watermark. As I held the sheet close to my face I also caught the faintest scent of bergamot. Now, among the seventy-five perfumes of the world, which any criminal expert must be prepared to distinguish from one another, bergamot is among the most common and by no means costly; thus while providing no specific clue to any exotic identity, it did tell me one thing."

"What was that?" I asked, marveling that this case still had anything of substance remaining to be revealed.

"This type of perfume simply suggested the sender of the note was female. And as Mr. Barlow had told us of only two women in the vicinity of the Wolverton Ranch, my thoughts immediately turned toward the Griswalls. Though some suspicion had fallen on the servant López, it seemed implausible that his wife's frontier ménage might include such fripperies as fragrance. Thus I had made certain of the predator wolf and guessed at the criminal's identity before you ever set foot on the train.

"With such knowledge I understood it would be necessary to watch Griswall from a position of secrecy unattainable if I were to have accompanied you. Through some careful arrangements I achieved my goal of deception with success, much as it pained me to keep you all in the dark. For myself I did not mind the temporary privations of living underneath the stars in the ruined hut—I was accustomed to far worse back in the army—but such sacrifices must never interfere with an investigation in any case. It did take some doing to arrange for the telegrapher's young son to relay messages and bring food. I lucked out there, as the lad proved to be both trustworthy and alert, and he kept me informed of your own comings and goings as well.

"I have already told you that your reports reached me rapidly. They were of great service to me, and especially one tiny clue of wildlife science that persuaded me Griswall would willingly deceive you when it served his purposes to do so."

"What, pray tell?" I asked.

"You wrote that Griswall described a strange animal sound to you as the booming of the prairie chicken—a fascinating bird but one that naturalists know mates only in the spring. Griswall was having you on, and diverting your attention at the same time."

"Hmm, I suppose so. You are right, that bit of biology was quite lost on me, my specialty being the human animal and not the habits of fowl." I hoped the tone of rue in my voice did not come off as chagrin, for it was only myself I chided.

"As for the human animal, Griswall proved a rare specimen, one whose calculated patience tested our own ability to wait him out. By the time that you discovered me down in the breaks I had worked out the whole business, but I had not yet formed a case solid enough to persuade a jury. I would not have our client risk so much only to find his nemesis go free after trial and wreak havoc again, no! In my continued quest to catch Griswall red-handed, there was no alternative but to use Trey Wolverton as bait, leaving him inadequately protected at times, as he was a man of free will and slipped your surveillance at times. Even after Griswall's first attempt on Wolverton's life resulted in the gruesome death of El Puño, the circumstances failed to provide us with evidence sufficient for the sheriff, much less a jury. I was forced to look for another avenue, and Wolverton's celebration provided it.

"I take it as a reproach to my management of the case," he said, "that, even with so perfect an opportunity, I underestimated the shock to which our client was subjected by the horrific figure of the luminous beast. And I should never have underestimated the role the weather might play."

If such an expert as Derrick Miles could express regret over any miscalculation, I supposed my shortcomings were not so great after all, and I allowed my self-chastisement to abate somewhat. I ventured, "What of the lady's role in her husband's black business? Could she not have come forward sooner?"

"Ah, Hooper," began he slowly, "you may believe that in my quest for scientific precision I grasp little of the ways of the heart. But the realm of emotion is one which we must seek to understand with this same precision. There can be no doubt that Griswall exercised an influence over the young Maria that may have sprung from love or from fear, or very possibly both, since these are by no means incompatible emotions. He had persuaded her to elope with him during her final year of study at the Austin Female Collegiate Institute, where he taught classes in biology as a junior lecturer, and she complied readily enough, she says. She also stood by him when he was dismissed from that post, and, the following year, quit his clerk's job at the General Land Office, leaving them with no means of support. Only when compelled to act as a direct accessory to murder did she resist, breaking her husband's complete power over her. In this, her awakening to the appeal of Trey Wolverton's sincere and innocent advances, and possibly to feelings of her own, at last drove Griswall to act out of jealousy that clouded his cool judgment.

"As she reveals in this letter, she confronted her husband with suspicion of his plan for that fatal evening, and he retaliated in fury. In the instant that she threw off the chains of emotional bondage in which he had held her, he saw that she would betray him—and the bonds became very real. He tied her up and prevented any chance of her warning Wolverton. I surmise that he speculated, once the entire county attributed a second death as due to the family curse, any suspicion of crime would have faded away, and she would continue under his power as before."

I thought solemnly of the eventuality we had probably forestalled. "We can be thankful for Maria's safety, then."

"Her decision to commit so much of the matter to writing seems restorative," said Miles as he folded the letter and deposited it into the file, followed by the book, my reports, and other papers.

"I have continued to wonder about another aspect of the case, however," said I. "If Griswall were so sure in his plan to use the wolf as the mechanism of Trey Wolverton's demise, why did he risk discovery by attempting to poison his mark first? And to dispatch Mr. Barlow's poor mongrel in the process . . ."

"Ah, Hooper, do not neglect to recognize how much we know—and our perpetrator knew—*ex post facto*. I surmise that Griswall would not have risked the entire success of his scheme without an alternative. So much depended on the complicated machinations of the wolf attack plan: Suppose Wolverton could not have been lured away from the guests he was entertaining? Suppose others accompanied him? Suppose the scent of the intended victim's boot had faded from the wolf's recognition after so many days? No, too many factors could have gone awry for him to count on a failproof execution."

"It did occur to me that Griswall could not hope to frighten Trey Wolverton to death by means of the doctored wolf, as he had done the old Earl."

"Yes," Miles agreed. "I have no doubt that, as the stakes rose with the appearance of a virile young heir on the scene, so did Griswall's deadly intentions. He was able to play on growing public fears, and the grim demise of the criminal, to incite a frenzy. He allowed the beast to nearly starve, increasing both the chances that it would paralyze any resistance its victim might offer, or do him in by tearing him limb from limb."

I shuddered at the thought of how narrowly we had missed just such an outcome, and Miles returned to flesh out his other hypothesis.

"We can now be reasonably certain it was he who tested the potent toxin of the croton plant, *C. texensis,* on Abernathy's captured wolf," said he. "Once Griswall was sure of its proper extraction and dosage, he could plan to slip in undercover and taint Wolverton's meal with the poison. An amount sufficient to kill a grown man or wolf proved quickly fatal to the small dog, I fear. With the unintended effect that the event galvanized our friend Barlow into determined action."

"Hmm. I believe we are indeed in Mr. Barlow's debt, for having seen his case through from start to finish with the sacrifice of his own valuable time and resources, and the life of his pet. I know few men to have risked as much to serve not only the memory of a friend, but the long-term good of his community," I offered.

"On this observation I heartily agree with you. I believe, at this juncture, we have reviewed the case sufficiently to answer the remaining questions our client Barlow may pose to us." Miles tapped his pipe into the ashtray, returned it to his lips, and settled back, staring into the far distance in the direction of Dickens County.

I sighed and interrupted his reverie. "I must importune you, my dear Miles, to make haste in dressing before our guests arrive. Wolverton has also asked that we help him in securing some home furnishings for a lady's taste, and Mr. Barlow wishes you to investigate some matters with the Railroad Commission on the morrow."

"Hooper," he said, "I can always count on you to bring my multifarious thoughts back around to the quotidian and immediate, and for this I am genuinely appreciative. We have had some weeks of severe work, have we not?—and for one evening, I think, we may turn our thoughts into more pleasant channels. You should be happy to learn that I have reserved a box at Greenwall's for tonight, after our afternoon's chores are done. We shall treat our guests to a bite of dinner at the White Elephant on the way. So, say, have you heard of the Jersey Lilly? I understand her vocal talents are unrivaled in the nation, and it is to be her first appearance in these parts."

I stood, encouraged suddenly at this prospect, and listened

out for footfalls at the bottom of the stair. Miles set the pipe back down in its tray, rose and tightened the sash of his dressing gown, and took a few steps down the hallway to his room.

I laid a troubled finger to my lips and said, almost to myself, "There remains only one difficulty I have not been able to resolve in my mind. If Griswall were to have succeeded in doing away with Trey Wolverton, and had laid claim to the estate, how would he have explained the fact that he—a legitimate heir—had been living *incognito* so close to the property? How could he step up without causing suspicion and inquiry?"

Miles turned and leaned an elbow against the wainscoting. "Though we are patently unable to peer into the thoughts of a murderer who managed to slip the noose of due process," he said, "I have given the matter some thought. I have already proceeded some way ahead of you, Hooper, down that shadowed path of speculation."

"And?"

"We can be sure from what we know of our foe that he would have found some way out of the tangle he had created. Were I to guess, from the pattern of documents discovered in his strongbox, I venture he planned to bribe a third-party agent to stand in, an expedient he appears to have used in filing fraudulent claims on multiple homesteads throughout the Lone Star State. Or he might have adopted an elaborate disguise during the short time that he need be in Fort Worth; of this we know he was capable."

"Or—" I offered yet another possibility—"he might even have pressed Maria to step forward to the authorities, in the guise of his daughter!" I closed the matter in my mind with some satisfaction at having contributed one theory.

"Elementary, my dear Hooper," Miles called out as he strode away down the corridor. "Elementary, when you think about it."

AFTERWORD

Sherlock Holmes, as the *Guinness Book of World Records* notes, is the most adapted human literary character in film and television, having been depicted on screen more than 250 times since his creation in 1887—not to mention scores of Holmes stories, books, comics, video games, and the like that were not authored by Sir Arthur Conan Doyle. So I have no reservations about transporting Holmes and Watson to the Texas frontier, nor about reimagining the plot of Doyle's esteemed short novel *The Hound of the Baskervilles* in the era of "Catch-'em-Alive Jack" Abernathy, the legendary wolf hunter. Any qualms I may have had about lifting occasional brief passages from Conan Doyle's text I set aside, justifying such takings as readily discernible homage to the master, clues for those who require them, and echoes for those who will find delight in them. Shakespeare read Holinshed and ratcheted him up a notch; I could only wish to be nearly so adept at adaptation in this work.

Numerous standard sources of Texas history inform this book and numerous real-life figures populate it, though the main characters are fabrications, and so are certain circumstances I have ascribed to recognizable names and places. If the reader's curiosity about the true past is stirred sufficiently to consult reliable nonfiction works, I am satisfied that I have done my job.

I am grateful to the Ad Hoc Writers of Lubbock, Texas, fine stylists and many of them former students of Professor Walt

Afterword

McDonald of Texas Tech University, for reading this work as it emerged in an earlier draft. Their knowledgeable critiques are always invaluable. I also want to acknowledge the good work of the editorial team at Five Star Publishing, Tiffany Schofield, Gordon K. Aalborg, and Erin Bealmear, and to thank Patrick Dearen for setting me on their scent.

I am grateful, too, to my partner, Kay Ellington, for allowing me to gain practice in the craft of fiction by collaborating with her on an earlier series of West Texas novels. The Paragraph Ranch has proved the best laboratory a writer could want.

ABOUT THE AUTHOR

Will Brandon is a pseudonym for Barbara Brannon of Spur, Texas. In her work in preservation and tourism and throughout her career as writer and editor, Barbara has dug deep into the history of the Lone Star State and traveled many miles of its highways and byways. Her history articles have appeared in the *Journal of the Wild West History Association,* *Authentic Texas* magazine, and *Lubbock Magazine,* and her Western-themed poems in *Weaving the Terrain: 100-Word Southwestern Poems* and *Bearing the Mask: Southwest Persona Poems.* She holds an M.A. and Ph.D. from the University of South Carolina, where she studied with novelist and poet James Dickey, and is coauthor, with Kay Ellington, of the Paragraph Ranch series of contemporary West Texas novels. www.BarbaraBrannon.com

The employees of Five Star Publishing hope you have enjoyed this book.

Our Five Star novels explore little-known chapters from America's history, stories told from unique perspectives that will entertain a broad range of readers.

Other Five Star books are available at your local library, bookstore, all major book distributors, and directly from Five Star/Gale.

Connect with Five Star Publishing

Visit us on Facebook:
 https://www.facebook.com/FiveStarCengage

Email:
 FiveStar@cengage.com

For information about titles and placing orders:
 (800) 223-1244
 gale.orders@cengage.com

To share your comments, write to us:
 Five Star Publishing
 Attn: Publisher
 10 Water St., Suite 310
 Waterville, ME 04901